HOUSE OF BLADES

HOUSE OF BLADES

THE TRAVELER'S GATE TRILOGY | BOOK ONE

WILL WIGHT

HIDDEN
GNOME
PUBLISHING

ISBN 978-0-9896717-0-5
(print edition)

www.WillWight.com
will@willwight.com

For my sister Rebecca, whose nagging skills are the stuff of legend.

CONTENTS

PROLOGUE

350TH YEAR OF THE DAMASCAN CALENDAR
16TH YEAR IN THE REIGN OF KING ZAKARETH VI
10 DAYS UNTIL MIDSUMMER

Simon was huddled under a tree when he saw the ghost.

He could barely make it out through the darkness and the pouring rain, but he knew a ghost when he saw one. A man-shaped cloud of mist drifting through the air in the opposite direction of the wind, glowing softly with its own blue-white light, couldn't be anything but a ghost. It had no face and no features, just a blank doll's body of mist and moonlight.

The ghost raised one hand and pointed straight at Simon.

Terror gripped him, but he clung closer to his mother, who sat beside him at the base of the tree. He looked up to make sure she had seen, and was relieved when he saw her staring straight at the spirit. Now he wouldn't have to waste time trying to convince her that yes, he really *had* seen a ghost.

Simon's father, Kalman, stood only paces away, standing over their wooden cart, trying to rearrange the bags and barrels inside so that they were all covered by one old oilskin tarp. Simon's father was a tall man, and lean, with arms so long that he could reach all the way across the cart without bending. He was too absorbed in his work to notice anything else until his wife called his name.

"Kalman," she said softly. He looked up, startled. "What is that?" she asked. She didn't sound worried, but she stroked Simon's hair like she did when she thought he needed soothing.

Kalman frowned. "I don't know what that is." He walked around the cart, toward the glowing spirit. He probably wanted a better look, but Simon decided to stay curled up, dry and warm, next to his mother underneath their tree. He was as close to the ghost as he wanted to be.

When Simon's father was only a pace away, the ghost vanished. It just blew apart, as though the wind were suddenly too strong for it to hold together, scattering into a thousand drifting particles and dissolving into the rain.

Simon's mother gasped and stood up, and Simon let himself be pulled along with her. She was a tiny woman, only a few inches taller than her son, but she had a grip like a vice. Besides, he felt better with his hand in hers. Simon was eight years old, in his opinion more than old enough to take care of himself, but for some reason he wanted his parents close tonight.

Kalman waved a hand through the space where the ghost had been. "Travelers?" he muttered. "Here? This has to be Traveler work."

"Travelers?" Simon asked, perking up. He had always wanted to see a Traveler.

"It's not always Travelers," Simon's mother said. Her voice sparkled like it did whenever she told a joke, and she grinned at him. "It could have been something worse. Maybe it was a demon. The villagers near here tell stories about a demon in Latari Forest, right where we are, that catches innocent people and cuts them all up." Simon rolled his eyes. Even at eight years old, he had learned not to listen to his mother's stories.

Simon's father gave his wife an amused smile, but he did start tying the tarp down over his cart. "Well, if that was the demon, everyone in the village can relax. You'd think a real demon could do better than a little mist."

Their miserable donkey—still hitched to the cart, despite the weather—snapped at Simon's father when he moved too close. Kalman whispered soothingly and patted the donkey's side, all the while buckling straps and checking the cart for damage.

Simon's mother laughed. "And how many demons have you seen in your life, misty or otherwise?"

Kalman glanced out into the rain, his face serious. "Well," he said, "there's something here that has the locals worried. I was willing to risk it before, but now…well, it might be smarter to ride all the way back to Myria in the rain. That's all."

"Wait," Simon said. "Is there really a demon here?" He had thought his mother was only joking, but if his father took the threat seriously, maybe there really was something out there. The forest suddenly looked much darker than it had before.

Simon's mother squeezed his hand and looked down, her face solemn. "Who knows?" she said. "But we talked to some of the people in the village last night. They were supposed to get visits from three different merchants this year, not just us. We made it, and so did one other man. But the third merchant…"

"What happened to him?" Simon whispered.

"Well, they went looking for him last week. And they found him. His goods were all spoiled, his cart was broken, and he and his donkey were dead. Something cut them all to pieces."

Simon shivered. *She's probably making this up*, he thought. *This is just an-*

other one of her jokes. Right?

"But here's the crazy thing," his mother went on. "Any team of bandits can cut somebody up, there's nothing special about that. But this merchant had on a full suit of chainmail and carried a sword. Whatever killed him cut straight through his chain armor like it was made of cheese. And they found his sword in three pieces, with no blood on it. The Demon cut straight through it."

"No, he didn't," Simon said, sure that he'd caught her in a lie this time. "You can't cut through metal."

"You can't and I can't," his mother said. "But a demon? Who knows? They say he has claws the size of—"

"Stop it, Edina," Simon's father said. "You're going to give him nightmares."

Edina laughed and hugged Simon. "No, he knows better than that. Right, Simon?"

"Right," Simon said shakily. He eyed the dark forest again.

"We're about ready now," his father said. "Let's get moving before that thing comes back."

"How's the tarp?" Edina asked.

Kalman sighed. "Full of holes and far too small. The paper will be ruined by the time we get back, and half the salt will probably be useless. But it's the best I can do."

Edina smiled and reached up to clap her husband on the shoulder. "No need to worry about what you can't change. Let's just get a move on, all right?"

Simon's father agreed, so Simon climbed up and sat on the edge of the cart. Once they started moving, his father would make him crawl under the tarp, but until then Simon preferred to be up high.

That was when he saw a torch in the forest. In the darkness under the trees, all Simon could see was an orange light bobbing in the distance, but he immediately pointed. "Look! There's somebody in there."

Simon's mother and father shared a worried look.

"We could just keep going, hope they go their own way," Edina said quietly.

"Too late now," Kalman responded. "There's only one road out of here. Might as well see what they want." He walked over to stand between the cart and the incoming torch, his arms crossed.

They didn't have long to wait. There were two people, it turned out, the one in front carrying a torch that looked a little too bright to Simon. It burned too steadily, like an orange star instead of a dirty, smoky, regular fire, and it didn't hiss or throw up steam when it passed through the rain.

The one with the strange torch was a big man with scars all over his face, so much that you could barely see any unscarred skin, and he wore a grey cloak the color of the rain. Simon would have expected someone with that many scars to look mean, but he didn't; he looked peaceful. He smiled at Simon as he approached, though he seemed a little sad.

Next to him was a woman with yellow hair in dark red, almost black, robes. She was short—though taller than Simon's mother—and she had blue eyes. Simon had never seen anyone with blue eyes before. When she saw Simon's family, she looked angry, not sad.

"You said this wouldn't happen," the woman said to her companion.

"We had to check it out," the man said. His voice was deep and calm. "This is going to be hard enough when we find a real one. Slow and steady, that's the way."

"Ho there," Simon's father called.

The two strangers did not even acknowledge him. They kept walking, closer and closer.

"Start calling another seeker, then, I suppose," the woman said with a sigh.

"Are you going to take care of this?"

"We have to," she said. Then she turned and looked straight at Simon, and suddenly he found her blue eyes far more frightening than the ghost. "I'm sorry," she said. "This is not justice. But it is necessary."

Edina tugged on her husband's sleeve. "I think it's time to go," she said, her voice low. Simon agreed.

Then the woman in the red robes raised her hands toward them, palm out. She had a design tattooed in the middle of her hand, maybe a letter in some strange language. It glowed bright red.

"We're leaving now," Simon's father said. He held his own hands up to show that he wasn't armed. "We're leaving right now." Edina had already grabbed the donkey's reins and was scrambling up onto his back.

Neither stranger responded. The woman moved her hand in a twisting circle, over and over, the symbol on her palm flaring brighter.

The cart finally started to move forward, and Simon thought that the yellow-haired woman might stop her strange dance now that they were leaving. Instead she ended by thrusting her glowing palm toward them. She grimaced at the same time and raised her free hand to her head, as though she had a sudden headache.

There was a flash of red light from her palm, and a monster appeared, buzzing in the air in front of her. It was like a wasp the size of a small dog, and it glowed with an orange light like dying coals.

They are Travelers! Simon thought. *Real ones!* He had always imagined what it would be like seeing a Traveler in person, but he'd thought it would be exciting. Not terrifying.

The wasp let out a noise like a screaming wood saw, flexed its stinger, and flew straight toward Simon.

Simon shrank backwards, still frozen on the edge of the cart. He couldn't move. He knew he needed to run, that even throwing himself off the edge and onto the ground would be better than letting that huge wasp stab him with its stinger, but his body wouldn't listen.

"No!" his father cried, and ran after the cart. When he got close enough, he lunged at the wasp with his whole body, tackling it to the ground. He drew it into his chest, curling himself around the monster, though Simon could see its wings and glowing legs struggling, trying to escape.

Edina screamed, wrestling the donkey to a stop. She scrambled down, running toward her husband.

Then the wasp flashed brighter, coal-orange, and Simon's father caught flame.

Kalman's agonized screams were too much for Simon. He wanted to help, but he was too scared, and he didn't know what to do. He slid down into the cart, wedging himself between two barrels. The tarp was level with his eyes; he could still see, still hear everything that happened. He covered his ears with both hands, trying to block out the screams, crying helplessly.

His mother ran over to Kalman's side, shouting "Stop, please! Stop this!" The woman in red ignored her. This time her companion stepped forward, the man in the rain-colored cloak, and he rested one huge, scarred hand on her forehead.

At Edina's feet, another shape of glowing mist rose from the ground, just like the ghost. This one wasn't shaped like a man, but like a long tendril, like an earthworm, sticking its head up and questing around in the air. The mist touched Edina's cheek tenderly, feather-light, and then it pulled back a few inches. It hesitated, weaving in front of her face, for just a second or two.

Then it struck like a snake, the mist plunging into Edina's open mouth. She inhaled roughly, like screaming in reverse, but she didn't look in pain. At first she just looked stunned, as if she had seen Simon do something so bad that she was too surprised to punish him for it.

Then she sagged in place, going entirely limp and starting to collapse.

Something caught her. Something invisible, like the strings on a puppet. Then those strings began to pull. Edina twitched violently, arms bending one way, neck stretching back farther than it should have. Her head moved side to side, jerking back and forth. Moon-colored mist swirled around her form, and Simon could have sworn he saw brightly colored flower petals drifting down around her.

The scarred man watched her sadly. Then he shook his head, turned, and walked over to his companion.

Simon choked down a scream. He had to help; he knew he had to help. But all he seemed to be able to do was hide in the cart and cry.

Kalman's screams had stopped.

"I'll get back to searching," the man said calmly. "Will you be okay here?"

The woman turned her head and spat on the ground. "This is wrong," she said. She looked disgusted, like she would rather be anywhere else, but she raised her red-marked hand toward Simon again.

"I'm sorry," she said.

Then a burning hand grabbed her ankle.

His father had been burned so badly that Simon barely recognized him. All his clothes had burned away, his hair was gone, and his skin was a hor-rible reddish-black. Simon couldn't look too closely, because he was afraid he'd throw up. His father was even still on fire in a few places.

But he wasn't dead. He crawled forward, one hand on the robed woman's ankle, pulling his body off the crushed and broken form of the fiery monster wasp. With an inhuman scream, Kalman heaved the red-robed woman off her feet.

She tumbled to the ground, but that seemed to have been the end of his father's strength. He fell to the ground and didn't move any more.

Simon held his breath and stared at his father's body. He couldn't be dead. He was just unconscious. He would sleep for a while and then get better. But Simon had seen people die before.

A new voice, a man's voice, cut through the rain behind Simon. "I've never seen a man go more bravely than that," the voice said.

Terrified, Simon turned to face whatever new horror was coming. He tried to hunch lower in the cart.

There was a third stranger in the forest now, standing on the other side of the cart from the two Travelers. He wore a fine black cloak, with the hood up, so Simon couldn't see what he looked like, but he was sure he had never met this man before. From the depths of the hood, the man flashed Simon a wide smile.

How could he smile at a time like this? Did death make him smile?

The yellow-haired woman scrambled to her feet. "Did you know these people?" she asked.

The hooded man ignored her. "Are you hurt?" he asked Simon.

Simon shook his head, speaking through the tears. "My mother and father are hurt. Please, don't hurt me."

"We found them like this," the scarred man said. He spoke calmly, as though telling a story. "If you could come over here and identify them for us, we would be more than grateful."

The hooded man said nothing. He moved forward, around the cart, toward the other two strangers. As he walked, he extended one hand out into the rain. His long arm was heavy with muscle and bare to the shoulder, as though he had cut the sleeves off his shirt. A tattoo of a chain wrapped around his arm from wrist to shoulder, spiraling up like a snake wrapped around the trunk of a tree.

Suddenly he held a gleaming sword in his outstretched hand, even though he wasn't holding anything just a moment before. Simon didn't know much about swords, but this didn't look like a very good one. It was chipped and pitted, as though he had spent years cutting wood with it.

The blade was long, though. Huge. And when they saw it, the other two strangers looked as frightened as Simon felt.

"Here he is," the man in gray said urgently. He raised his hands in front of him. "This is one of them!"

"Stop him!" The woman cried. Mist spun around the scar-faced man, and the woman began waving her glowing red hand again.

The hooded man stepped forward, and it was as though he moved so fast that he didn't even need to walk. First he was ten paces away, and then he was right in front of the other two strangers.

A bright orange ball of flame flashed into existence only a pace from the hooded man's chest, shrieking with a human voice. The hooded man batted the flame away with the flat of his sword, sending the fireball blasting into the dark forest like a bolt of orange lightning.

His sword flashed again, and the woman's red-marked hand fell away. She gasped. Her other hand followed, and then the sword slid into her chest.

As the yellow-haired woman fell onto her face, she seemed surprised, not as frightened as Simon would have expected.

Not as frightened as he felt in that moment.

The scarred man did not shout or roar, or beg for his life. Instead, he calmly gestured, and the mist wrapped around the swordsman just as it had done to Simon's mother. Not just one tendril stood up from the ground, though, but half a dozen, weaving up and climbing over the hooded man.

But this man just walked through the mist as if it were...well, as if it were mist.

The scarred man's eyes widened, and he turned to run.

"If I had been frightened, that much mist might have killed me," the hooded man said. "Maybe even driven me insane. I hear the Mists of Asphodel have that effect on some people. But guess what?"

Again, the swordsman moved so fast that Simon couldn't see him. Then he was right behind the running man, and his chipped sword stuck into the other man's back and out into the rain.

He was far enough away now that Simon almost didn't hear what he said next. "I'm not afraid," he said. Then he stepped back, pulling his sword with him.

The body of the big, scarred man joined the others on the ground.

Simon tried to be quiet, so the man wouldn't notice and kill him next, but the hooded man didn't even look at the cart. He knelt beside Simon's father, holding two fingers to his neck and staring into his face.

Then the man sighed, shook his head, and walked over to Simon's mother.

At some point the invisible rope holding her up had been cut, and she lay sprawled on the ground. At first, Simon was afraid she was dead, but as he watched she twitched like a dog having a bad dream.

The hooded man bent and scooped Simon's mother up in both arms like she weighed no more than a pillow. He carried her over and tucked her gently into the back of the cart, next to Simon, pulling a corner of the tarp over her to keep her dry.

Simon latched onto his mother, pulling her away from the hooded stranger.

"Are you the Forest Demon?" he whispered through his tears.

The man flashed him another smile from within his dark hood. "Don't worry," he said. "I'm not going to hurt you."

But he hadn't said he *wasn't* the Demon, so Simon kept crying.

"What's your name?" the hooded man asked.

"Simon, son of Kalman."

"Very pleased to meet you," he said. "And this is your mother?"

Simon nodded.

The hooded man shook his head again. "I'm sorry. There's nothing I can do for her. If it was just the body...but Asphodel attacks the mind. The spirit.

It will be years before she recovers, if ever."

A fresh wave of tears overwhelmed Simon, and he sobbed again. "I couldn't do anything," he said. "I just wanted to help, but I couldn't do it. I couldn't move."

The hooded man hesitated, as if trying to find the right words. "It's not your fault, Simon. Not at all. But you can do something now, all right? I need you to take care of your mother for me. Can you do that?"

Simon nodded again.

"All right. Now, where do you live?"

"Myria village," Simon responded, trying to clean his face off with the back of his sleeve.

"Myria village," the man repeated. "That's...a day or two northwest, I think. I can make it." He glanced back at Simon and said, "I'll make it."

He didn't seem to be talking to Simon, so Simon didn't say anything.

Somehow the hooded man got the donkey moving, and Simon clung to his mother's sleeping form as the cart rattled down the road. Simon had pulled the tarp off the goods, laying it over his mother and himself, keeping them as dry and warm as he could.

"Once you get a little older," the hooded man called from the driver's seat, "you should come back to the Forest, if you can. I'll teach you how to make it so that Travelers never bother you again."

"They were Travelers, then," Simon said. He had hoped he was wrong.

"Yes."

"Why did they hurt us?" Simon asked. He could feel a fresh batch of tears leaking out, and he sniffed, trying to hold back. He had to be strong now, to take care of his mother. Strong men didn't cry.

"Nothing you did," the hooded man said, "I promise you that. They were... looking for something. When we reach Myria, I'll do what I can for you, help you take care of your mother as best I can. For a little while. But I can't leave my forest undefended for long. Not now."

Simon clutched his mother tighter. "It's okay. I can take care of her."

"I know you can," the hooded man said.

I will take care of her, he promised himself. He had been useless tonight, he knew that, but next time he wouldn't be.

Next time, he would keep his family safe.

Chapter 1
SACRIFICES

358ᵗʰ Year of the Damascan Calendar
24ᵗʰ Year in the Reign of King Zakareth VI
51 Days Until Midsummer

Eight years later, Simon shoved his sword into the bottom of the cabinet, desperate to keep it hidden. He didn't have much time.

His mother was waking up.

He had secretly bartered for the sword almost five years ago, trading a few old pots and a bottle of wine to a desperate Badari trader. It was a good deal, even for a sword as worn and poorly forged as this one, but his mother could never find out. He couldn't trust her with it.

Edina screamed, thrashing around in her blankets, and he rushed over to keep her shoulders pressed against the ground.

He held her there, keeping his full weight against her body, as she screamed and cursed and spat into his face. It took a good ten minutes for her to settle down and her breathing to return to normal. Finally, after murmuring a few more times, she opened her eyes.

"Good morning," Simon said. "How are you feeling?"

His mother coughed, reaching out to the side. Her hand groped blindly on the ground.

Simon moved the wineskin into her grasping hand. She seized it, raising it to her mouth and drinking thirstily.

After a moment, Simon put a hand on the wineskin. "Go easy," he said.

With her other hand she had grabbed her walking stick, and she swung it now into the side of Simon's head. Pain flared in his head, and he cried out.

"Who are you?" Edina croaked. Beneath her wild, matted hair, her eyes narrowed in suspicion. When she spoke, her voice creaked like a dungeon door. "Are you you? You look like my son, but are you? Are any of you who you are?"

Simon blinked the pain in his head away, gently taking the wine from her mouth. She was worse than usual today, which meant she would drink more, which would make her even worse. He would have to take care of her while she was still conscious and reasonably sane. "Why don't we get you some dinner first?" he said gently.

18

She glared at him. "Breakfast," she said.

"It's almost sunset," Simon pointed out. If she was interested in food at all, though, that was a good sign. Usually she insisted she wasn't hungry right up until she shouted that Simon was trying to starve her.

"I'm not hungry anyway," she whispered. Simon sighed.

His mother burrowed back into her blankets, clutching the wineskin to her chest like a little girl's stuffed doll.

"Good night," Simon said.

He had considered trying to keep her awake, but decided it wasn't worth the effort. She would undoubtedly wake him up in the middle of the night anyway, and he could just as easily feed her then.

He glanced at the cabinet, where his sword waited for him. He debated taking it back out; he had only had a scarce fifteen minutes of practice today before his mother began thrashing and screaming. Not even long enough to break a sweat. He had always meant to return to the Latari Forest someday, to take up the hooded man on his offer of training. If only his mother didn't need him. Well, he worked hard enough on his own; surely that was worth something.

Maybe he could head back out to his spot behind the village woodshed for more practice; out there, it was close enough that he could hear his mother shout, but secluded enough that no one would notice the fact that he had a sword.

Behind him, the door creaked open. He turned to see Leah, daughter of Kelia, standing in his doorway holding a basket. She kept the door propped open with her shoulder as she slid inside.

"Eggs for you," she said, without greeting him or asking permission to enter. "And a head of cabbage. Boez had some extra pins, so those are in there, and my aunt sewed you an extra shirt. There's some bread, too, but I don't know who sent it. You'll have to return the basket, though."

"Leah, I don't need gifts." He rose stiffly to meet her eye to eye. She was an inch or two taller than he, though, which stung his pride. His father had never had to look up to anyone.

"Thank you, but I can earn what we need," Simon said.

Leah arched one eyebrow at him. Though she had the same tan skin and dark hair as everyone else in Myria, her eyes were a bright blue. She was only the second person Simon had seen with blue eyes; everyone else he knew, including Simon himself, had brown. But blue eyes somehow made her look even older, like she was a grown woman and Simon just a little boy who had stepped out of line.

"This is payment for the wood last week," she said. "And an advance payment for fixing her door." Leah walked by him, setting the basket down on top of his cabinet and beginning to unpack.

"I haven't done enough work for this," Simon protested. "This is too much."

Leah shrugged without turning around as she folded his shirt and tucked it away into the cabinet. "I remembered who baked you the bread, by the way. My sister."

"Sister?" He only vaguely remembered that Leah had a sister.

She gave him an amused glance out of the corner of her eye. "Rutha."

"Right, right, Rutha." A plain girl, quiet, Rutha usually followed in Leah's shadow and said little. Simon had trouble picturing her. Leah had gotten all the good looks in that family.

"You can thank her, and everyone, tonight at the fires. Something's happening. The Mayor and most of the men have left, and nobody told us why."

"Really?" Simon felt a surge of irritation that no one had asked him to come along, but he quickly squashed the feeling. He would have refused anyway, to take care of his mother, and everyone knew it.

"Really," Leah said. Task done, she brushed off her hands and picked the basket back up. She smiled at him on her way out and held the door open for him. "Are you coming?"

Simon glanced back at his mother before following Leah out. He couldn't be around all the time. If Edina woke up, she would just have to fend for herself.

Alin's voice, strong and confident, carried across the whole crowd. Simon had heard the story before, but he still found himself listening intently.

"Three doors, each identical, two guarded by ferocious creatures from the depths of Naraka. The Lost Badarin knew that only one would lead to the highest room of the tallest tower, where the princess waited. He had only one chance. So he turned to the owl in the golden cage.

'What will happen if I enter the door on the left?' the Badarin asked.

'Feed me a mouse and I shall tell you,' the owl said. So the Lost Badarin caught a mouse and fed it to the owl.

'I see you enter the door on the left. You are torn, limb from limb, by creatures hungrier and more terrible than lions.'"

A little boy, seated on a log next to his mother, gasped. A few of the adults chuckled. There must have been thirty or forty people there, most seated on logs that encircled a huge bonfire. This had been the tradition as long as Simon could remember: the women and children sat on logs around the bonfire, trading stories, while the men stood in groups outside the firelight and pretended not to listen. Simon would have stood with the men, not sat with the children, had Leah not insisted he join them.

"The Lost Badarin searched and searched, then he finally found another mouse. He fed it to the owl.

'What about the door in the center?' he asked.

'I see you enter the door in the center, and leave scarcely an hour later...in a dustpan,' the owl said.

"Well, knowing what lay beyond two of the doors, the Lost Badarin entered the third. And very soon he knew he was in the right place, for the staircase seemed to never end. For a whole day and a whole night he walked up the stairs, heading for the highest room of the tallest tower of the evil Traveler's entire castle.

"He finally reached the top of the tower, exhausted and out of breath. But he was glad, because he knew that he had finally reached the princess. He threw open the door...and to his horror, came face-to-face with the evil Traveler himself!

"The Lost Badarin had never seen anyone as hideous as this Traveler. He wore dirty robes, covered in mud and blood and other, stranger stains. His eyes were solid black, like rocks, and his hands were old and twisted. His beard reached almost to his knees, and it crawled with spiders and earthworms.

"The Traveler laughed, a cruel and evil laugh, and he began to speak horrible words, summoning unspeakable creatures to swallow the Badarin whole..."

Everyone was silent, even Simon, each of them hanging on Alin's words.

"...but that is a story for tomorrow night," Alin said, and everyone laughed.

Alin smiled and swept a bow, and all the women around the fire burst into applause. Simon shook his head and stirred up the fire with a stick. Alin might not have been the best storyteller in Myria, but he was certainly enthusiastic. Even some of the older men, who were not strictly supposed to listen to fire-ring stories any longer, clapped along with good grace from the edge of the fire's light.

Storytelling had never been Simon's gift, but whenever he watched Alin he wished it were otherwise. Story done, Alin sat down on a log next to Leah, who was one of the only girls present around his age. And, incidentally, the prettiest. Leah's sister—what was her name again? Ruth? Rutha? Ruthie—sat on her other side, and she said something as Alin sat down that made him laugh.

Simon missed it, squatting as he was two logs away. He poked at the coals again.

There were a dozen similar fires all around the village of Myria, each inside—but well away from—the head-high wooden walls that encircled the entire village. The walls were mostly sharp sticks shoved into the ground and tied together, but they kept out most of the wild beasts that wandered down from the desert. They should even do a little to keep out heretics marching from Enosh in the west, but fortunately that theory had never been tested.

A horn-call drifted over from the gate, signaling riders returning. Several people around the fire gave each other relieved smiles, and Simon heard more than a few sighs as tension released.

The Mayor and most of his advisors had ridden out only a few hours before, taking many of the grown men with them, and they hadn't told anyone why. It was enough to keep everyone left behind on edge, but now the trumpet call said they had returned. Everything would be all right.

The horn warbled and cut off before the end of the note, as if whoever was on watch-duty had dropped the horn. A few of the older women looked up in concern, but Simon wasn't worried. It had probably been one of the younger boys on watch, and he would get what he deserved later for dropping the valuable horn in the sand.

"It looks like somebody kept the good wine for watch duty," Alin said lightly, earning him several chuckles. Even Simon would admit he was good-looking: tall, strong, and vibrant, with hair of dark gold instead of the usual brown. More than that, he had an aura of radiant confidence that he carried with him like a torch. He never had to do his chores alone; one or another of the young villagers would always help him get his work done.

On the other side of the coin, Simon preferred working quietly, by himself, with as few others involved as possible. It was easier that way.

"Ladies, it's been a pleasure," Alin said, rising to his feet. "But if the riders are coming in, I should go meet them. Would anyone like to come with me? Leah?" He extended a hand to her. She blushed and took it, leading to some cackling from the rest of the circle.

Alin turned to Simon. "Simon? How about you?" That took Simon off guard. Why would Alin want him along on what could be time alone with Leah? He couldn't think of anything appropriate to say, so he just tossed his stick into the fire and rose to join the other two.

With another wave to the circle in general, Alin set off, keeping Leah's hand in his. Simon trailed awkwardly after.

They wound through the tangled mass of houses that formed the center of Myria, picking their way carefully over casks, tools, and sleeping dogs concealed by the dim light just before moonrise. The houses pushed and jostled together, most made of wood or baked clay bricks, no two alike. In places the homes were so close together that Simon had to turn sideways to squeeze between, but he barely noticed; he had grown up here, and he could find his way through this maze of houses hobbled and blindfolded.

"You had better be careful around my aunt," Leah said to Alin, as soon as they were far enough away from the fire ring. "Soon she'll have you married and settled, whether you like it or not."

Alin laughed. "And what about you? You've got the whole village eating out of your hand."

Great Maker above, Simon thought. *If they're just going to flatter each other all night, I'm leaving.*

Alin was right, as far as it went: Leah really did have the whole village eating out of her hand, or near enough. She had come from Bel Calem only two years before, moving in with her aunt in the village. It was whispered that her mother had gotten herself killed, maybe even murdered by some criminal from the city. The bracelet Leah wore—silver, with a clear white crystal dangling from the chain—was supposed to be a memento of her mother's. Simon didn't know whether that was true, but it was a generally accepted fact that she never took it off, not even to sleep.

Her blue eyes should have been enough to set her apart, but Leah had the same natural charm as Alin; people welcomed her, accepted her, and treated her as warmly as if she had always been one of their own.

The other villagers often treated her better than they treated Simon, actually, though that didn't bother him much. He rarely minded being left alone.

"Oh, how's your mother, Simon?" Alin asked. "I haven't seen her in a while." Alin's tone was polite and open, but Simon flinched. At the moment, his mother was likely lying on the floor of their home, soaked in wine and huddled in filthy blankets, probably murmuring nonsense to herself.

"She's fine. Some days are better than others."

Leah made a sympathetic noise and turned to look at Simon. "That must be hard, taking care of her by yourself," she said. "I don't know if I could do it."

Pride warred with embarrassment inside Simon, and his tongue got caught in the crossfire. He mumbled something about it not being that hard, but he wasn't sure it emerged as anything coherent. Alin opened his mouth to respond, but he was interrupted by a huge noise: a sudden crash and the screams of a crowd of men, accompanied by the pounding of several dozen sets of hooves.

It was coming from the direction of the village gate. Simon pushed past Alin and Leah, rushing to get free of the houses so that he could have a clear view of the gate. After a startled second, he heard Alin and Leah running after him.

Simon cleared the last house in the row just in time to see an arrow land inches from his head, cracking the baked clay bricks of a nearby wall. He tore his eyes from the arrow that had almost killed him.

As he had feared, the gate had been broken down, slammed flat into the ground. Riders on horses poured in through the broken wall, trampling the gate and two wet mounds that had to have been whoever was on watch duty. Some of the soldiers held torches, some swords, and some short composite bows meant to be fired from horseback.

Raiders. And, judging from the brown-and-purple cloths tied around the horses' necks, not Enoshian heretics, but official soldiers of Overlord Malachi.

Simon stumbled backwards, knocking into Alin and Leah and pushing them back into the shadow of the houses. Why had this happened? What had Myria or its people done to anger their Overlord?

Leah stuck her head out from the corner of a house and stared at the soldiers. For a few seconds, she went completely still, like a deer about to bolt. Then she turned and grabbed Alin and Simon by their arms, pulling them deeper into the circle of homes.

"We've got to get as many people as we can out the back gate," she said. "Tell everyone you can to run, not fight. They'll butcher us if we resist." Oddly, she didn't look frightened. Her face had gone harder than Simon had ever seen it, and she burned with anger, as though these soldiers had some-how offended her personally. Well, he supposed that invading your hometown should be enough insult for anyone.

"Let's raise a cry," Alin responded. He was breathing heavily and his eyes moved everywhere at once, but his mouth was set in a firm line. "You two start running from house to house, and I'll warn everyone still at the fires."

"No one uses the north gate. Maybe we can go out there, circle around, and head for Kortan," Leah said. Kortan was the closest village, though Simon had only been there three times. It was most of a day's walk away, and he couldn't abandon his mother.

"Simon, you—"

"My mother!" Simon blurted, and he started to run.

Dogs had begun to bark, and in several of the houses, people were emerging to find out what was going on. Behind Simon, Alin and Leah started yelling as loud as they could, trying to attract attention.

Simon rushed through the tangled knot of homes in a pattern he had memorized when he could barely walk. It would take anyone on a horse some time to penetrate this deeply into the village, and hopefully by then he could take his mother and be gone.

In a matter of minutes he reached his house, which was easily the worst-looking in the village. He had made the door himself when he was twelve, and it barely held together; the roof leaked, and many of the pale bricks in the wall were cracked and could use replacing. He tore open the door and stumbled inside, for once not feeling a surge of shame at the house's appearance. He didn't have time.

He passed the bundle of rags curled up near the door, stepping over them to reach the cabinet. Throwing the doors open, he rummaged around for his sword. He had hidden it here, he knew he had, but where? He finally found the sword wrapped up inside a dusty rug, where he had hidden it from his mother. She would have hurt herself on it by now, or else sold it.

The wooden scabbard was chipped and stained, and it didn't quite fit; the blade rattled slightly when he picked it up. The sword itself wasn't in any better condition, but he worked with what he had.

Eight years ago, he had sworn to protect his family. And now the time had come for him to keep that promise.

He buckled the sword around his waist, then moved over to the rags beside the door. He reached down and shook them vigorously. "Mother," he said. "Mother, you have to get up!"

The rags stirred feebly, and a puddle of sharp-smelling wine rolled out.

Simon shook harder. "On your feet, Mother, now! We have to get out—"
A wooden stick cracked into his skull and white pain blossomed behind his eyes. He fell backwards as his mother crawled out from her blankets.

She clutched her walking stick, though she dropped it immediately to shield her eyes from the light coming in from the door. Her black hair stood up at every angle, and she was covered in grime.

"What's all the noise?" she asked. Her voice whispered through a raspy throat.

"Raiders at the front gate, Mother," Simon said. "We have to go out."

She didn't say anything, but groped around with her walking stick and, once she had found the floor, pushed up to her feet and began hobbling toward the door. She was barely five feet tall even when she was capable of standing upright, and when she leaned on her stick she looked fifty years older than she was.

Sorrow and frustration welled up in Simon's chest, as usual, but today they couldn't compete with urgency. He all but pushed his mother out of the door.

Outside, the air was thick with smoke, screams, and the sounds of combat and furiously barking dogs.

Simon grabbed his mother by the shoulders and guided her between houses. The smoke burned his eyes, and he began to cough. His mother still didn't seem to know where she was; she giggled to herself and swayed on her feet. Obviously this wasn't just the alcohol, then; her disease had returned. Now, of all times.

Through a veil of smoke, Simon saw someone's dark outline running toward them, clutching something in its hand. He thought it was a sword. Simon spun his mother behind him and stood between her and the stranger, determined to keep her out of harm.

The figure pushed through the smoke. It was Leah, holding a bloodstained sword in one hand and coughing into the other. Her crystal bracelet gleamed in the firelight.

"Simon," she said hoarsely, "there are too many of them. We have to go now." She gestured with the sword for him to follow and headed back into the smoke. Simon tried to chase after her, pulling his mother behind him, but she dragged her feet and refused to budge. After a few seconds, she began to scream, a harsh, ear-piercing wail.

Simon clapped a hand over her mouth. No one could likely make out one scream among all the others, but who knew? He wasn't going to take any chances with soldiers. They might want slaves, and a woman's cries from down a dark alley would draw slavers the way screams of pain would draw jackals.

His mother bit down on his hand, hard. Her teeth sank into the flesh of his hand, drawing blood, and he set his jaw against the pain. He had no time for this. Besides, this was hardly the first scar his mother had given him, and it wouldn't be the last.

Letting her chew on his left hand, Simon scooped her up under his right arm and hauled her along after Leah's quickly-vanishing silhouette.

It didn't take long for Simon's arms to begin burning, even under his mother's slight weight. Terror kept him moving forward, and the fact that Leah didn't seem tired at all.

Their run was quick and brutal. Every second Simon had to choke down another mouthful of smoke, and he couldn't help but imagine a huge soldier with a bloody sword in every shifting shadow. His legs began to ache, his arm burned, and the pain in his hand throbbed. He was so focused on forcing one leg in front of the other, over and over, that he almost stumbled over Leah. She had suddenly halted, and was crouched behind the smoldering half of a ruined horse-cart.

Simon's mother had finally—thankfully—gone limp in his arms, and he dumped her on the ground beside Leah as he crouched to join her. Silently, Leah pointed over the cart to Myria's north gate. A huge soldier in dark, gleaming armor trotted his horse in a circle. He kept his own helmeted head constantly twisting, as if he were searching for someone through the smoke.

Leah's whisper was so quiet that Simon barely heard it over the crackling of the burning cart. "We should wait and see if he withdraws."

Simon nodded his agreement, but at that moment, the ground thundered under the pounding of hooves. Simon and Leah spun around together, Simon's breath coming even faster. Three raiders on horseback trotted out of the houses behind them, escorting another walking soldier. The one on foot was pulling one end of a long rope, which was attached to a series of collars. Each of which was wrapped around a child's neck.

Four girls and two boys, the oldest not quite Simon's age, and the youngest almost ten. Simon had grown up with all of them. Their clothes were torn, and most of them were visibly injured or covered in blood. What would a group of Damascan soldiers want with *children?*

While Simon's thoughts were still paralyzed, Leah grabbed his arm and pulled him under the cart. His mother began to thrash and to try and crawl away, but he pulled her along. Only the top half of the cart burned, so embers dropped through the cracks, stinging his face, but they weren't in any immediate danger. Simon turned to face Leah and had to flinch back to avoid cutting his face on her sword. He looked past it, looking into her bright blue eyes. They still blazed with that strange anger.

27

She glanced down at the sword on his hip, which dug painfully into his side. "Do you know how to use that?" she asked quietly.

"I've done what training I could," he said. In truth, his training consisted almost entirely of swinging the sword around alone, in the dark, behind the town woodshed. But she didn't need to know that.

"In other words, no," Leah said. Her voice sounded businesslike, not cruel, but he still flinched at the brutal truth. He spoke out of wounded pride.

"That's more than you've ever had," he said.

Leah arched one eyebrow, and for a moment she looked just like her aunt Nurita faced with a child spouting nonsense. Then she sighed. "I meant no offense, Simon. Forgive me. But you can't do enough to protect us from a squad of professional soldiers."

"So what do we do?" he asked. Leah had a way of taking charge that sometimes irritated him, but now he was grateful.

Leah focused on a point behind his head, flicking her eyes from side to side as though she read from a page. "Give me a moment," she whispered. Behind her, beyond the cart, the soldiers had grouped up and were gesturing wildly at the bound prisoners. One of the girls dropped to her knees and wept; a raider hit her on the back of the head with the flat of his sword, and she fell onto her face.

"All right Simon, listen. If they stay there, none of us are going to be able to leave," Leah said. "Do you understand? If nothing draws them off, we're going to die under here."

"You don't know that" Simon said. Why had she even said anything? The situation looked hopeless enough without her stating the obvious.

Leah's face softened a bit, though she still sounded like she was passing sentence. "Stay with your mother," she said. "When you get a chance, run for the gate. Tell my aunt..." Her voice trailed off, and one side of her mouth quirked up into a smile. "Never mind."

Leah shifted enough to reach over her sword and patted Simon on the cheek. "Be good, Simon," she said, and rolled out from under the wagon.

Stunned, Simon just watched as she jumped to her feet and ran straight for the captive children. One of the raiders noticed her and shouted, but before anyone else could react she was at the rope, hacking and sawing with her sword. The soldier holding the rope reached out to grab her, but one of the boys from Myria knocked him to the ground. The other raiders spun their horses around and headed for Leah, but before they reached her the rope was cut. Its severed ends slid through loops in half a dozen collars, and the children bolted.

At first, Simon expected them to run straight for the gate, but they didn't; they scattered in every other direction. After a second, he realized that most of the nearby raiders were clustered between the captives and the gate itself. The children were just running anywhere they could see that wasn't towards a raider.

Including, unfortunately, directly towards Simon.

A girl of about eleven or twelve dashed past Simon's cart, her bare feet kicking up bursts of sand. A few seconds later, a steel-shod horse followed her.

Simon rested a hand on the hilt of his sword. This was the time. If he was ever going to make a difference, if his time practicing was going to mean anything, he should go out now and make a stand. Maybe he would die fighting, like his father, but at least he could make a difference.

Simon's mother started to squirm in his arms. "Where's my blanket?" she said. Her voice, thankfully, came out as a weak croak.

"Hush, Mother. I'll go back and get your blanket in just a minute. You need to be quiet right now."

"I don't want to be quiet, I want my blanket." She was trying to make her voice louder, but it just came out scratchier.

Simon leaned close to her ear and pleaded, "Mother, please, we need to be quiet. We don't want them to find us. After we get away, I'll come back for your blanket, I promise."

His mother mumbled something in response, but he only understood the word "promise."

No, he couldn't help the other villagers. His mother needed him.

After another minute, the dust cleared enough that he could see the way to the gate. It was clear, except for a few bundles lying on the sandy ground. He started to wonder who those bundles had been, but his mind shied away from the thought and focused on more immediate matters. The raiders were gone, but they could return at any time. And there were surely more of them.

He had to move now.

Simon slid out on his belly, sticking his head warily up to check for danger. Nothing moved. Moving with the quick, jerky motions of fear, he reached back and pulled his mother up and out from under the cart.

Picking her up again, and stumbling under the sudden weight, Simon began to jog towards the gate. He kept his ears sharp and tuned to any close sound. As he hurried past the bodies, he couldn't help but glance down to see if either one had belonged to Leah.

He almost breathed a sigh of relief when he passed them. Almost, except that he had known the two children in the dust for their entire lives. One of them was a nine-year-old boy.

A new feeling rose up through his fear: determination. Since he was a boy, Simon had cared for his mother. He had worked for anyone who would take him, for as long as they would let him, barely earning enough supplies to scrape by. He was driven by a resolution, a stone-solid certainty: he would do whatever it took to keep his mother alive. If he had to crawl through the flames in the blackest pits of Naraka to do it, so be it. But by the Maker, Simon and his mother were going to make it out alive. He owed his father no less.

Simon kept his resolve clutched close to his chest, like a blanket in the dead of winter. It warmed him, gave him the strength to keep running when all he wanted was to collapse and let the wind blow him away like so much sand.

Leah had never run so hard in her life.

She dashed over dirt and hard-packed sand, slipping through the broken remnants of the village gate, which had been shattered when Malachi's soldiers attacked. Two of those soldiers followed her, shouting threats and curses at her back, and part of her wanted to turn and look behind her even though she knew that could only end in disaster. The soldiers were mounted on horses, and she knew that over open ground they would run her down in seconds. The only reason they hadn't so far was because they were inside the village walls, and right now the village was a chaotic field of debris sown with bodies and wreckage. Urging their horses faster than a walk would be risking a broken leg for the mount and a nasty spill for the rider.

But she was headed outside the village. And there, on the flat and sandy plains outside Myria, the picture would be much different.

Leah, daughter of Kelia, felt a tiny spark of terror at the thought of being caught. A poor city girl who had been forced to move, alone, to her mother's village to live with strange relatives, the daughter of Kelia would have no idea how to react to this attack. She would have looked for somewhere to run, or someone to hide her, though if the worst did happen she could face it with strength and honor, on her feet.

Leah sometimes thought she had played that character too long. If she kept reacting as the village girl, she would just get herself killed. Well, if the village girl wouldn't do any longer, she'd have to try something better.

Only a few paces outside the village gates, she strangled her fear and stopped running.

One of Malachi's sergeants, an honest-looking, blocky man perhaps in his fifties, stood, barking orders, maybe a hundred paces away from the village walls. He was surrounded by a hive of soldiers running or riding this way and that, coordinating the chaos of his raid on Myria. Beside him stood a bald man in the leather uniform of an Endross, idly making blue-white sparks appear and disappear at the ends of his fingertips. He might pose some difficulty, but nothing she hadn't dealt with before.

None of the sacrifices had been brought in yet, thank the Maker—no, wait, not the Maker. The Maker was a village superstition. Seven stones, how deep into her role *was* she, that even her thoughts were suspect?

Leah began walking toward the sergeant and his Traveler, letting the daughter of Kelia fall behind her like a shed cloak. She drew herself up, moving with steady confidence, with purpose, the way she had been trained. People responded to body language, to the authority implicit in one's bearing. And she would need every scrap of authority she could get, if she wanted them to take her seriously.

Hoofbeats sounded behind her, but Leah kept walking. She very carefully did not turn around.

One of the two soldiers that had been following her pulled his horse to a stop only a few feet in front of her, so that she would be forced to run another direction. The other rode up to her right and hopped down.

He snarled roughly at her, reaching to grab her arm. "If you think—" he began.

Leah did not respond. She did not look at him. She did not even slow down, though in just a few seconds she was going to collide with a wall of horseflesh.

She twisted her wrist, letting moonlight fall on the crystal she wore on a thin silver bracelet. As she did, she cast her mind out, calling for the power of Lirial.

And her Territory answered.

A jagged spike of milky white crystal erupted from the ground, growing in half a second into a five-foot-high stalagmite that stabbed the air inches from Leah's shoulder. The soldier's hand was in the way, caught in the act of reaching out for Leah. By all logic the crystal should have impaled the man's arm, perhaps taking the hand off at the wrist. But Lirial did not destroy. It revealed. It protected.

And it preserved.

The soldier's hand, from his wrist to the tips of his outstretched fingers, had been frozen inside the jagged mound of crystal as if within ice. Unlike ice, though, this crystal would never thaw or melt. And it was hard as stone.

The soldier tried to pull his arm out of the crystal. For a few futile moments he heaved his body backwards, planted a leg on the crystal and shoved, hammered at the crystal with his fists. Then he started to scream.

Leah gestured again, and another crystal spike burst from the ground in front of the horse barring her way. The horse reared, screamed, and galloped in the other direction. She doubted that the rider minded.

The sergeant and his entire entourage were looking at her now, including the bald Endross Traveler. His eyes, a bright green that she could make out even at this distance, widened when he recognized what she had done. With a shout he raised both palms, calling what looked like a ball of rolling storm-clouds into his hands.

Keeping her face blank, Leah continued walking. She did nothing to let her sudden wariness show. Endross was widely considered one of the most formidable Territories for combat, and Lirial's strengths lay in other areas. If she made a mistake, she could find herself seriously injured before she managed to reveal her identity.

But she had met dozens of Endross Travelers in her childhood, and they had all shared a single trait: they were jackals. Predators. Scavengers, concerned with preserving their own safety above all else. A rare few would seek out their equals for the pleasure of testing themselves against a rival, but none would dare challenge a superior.

So before she dealt with him, she needed to show—beyond all doubt— that she was his superior.

Glittering lights flashed in the Traveler's handheld storm, like half-hidden strikes of lightning, and about a dozen shapes the size of dragonflies burst forth into the air, streaking towards Leah. She recognized the shapes from her education in the ways of Endross: storm-drakes, tiny flying lizards that would latch onto their prey and shock it to death with sparks of lightning. Not something Leah wanted to happen to her.

There were a handful of easy ways she could deal with this summoning, but any one of them would just invite another attack from the Endross. She would have to come up with something more impressive.

Sending a mental call into Lirial, Leah turned her left hand palm-up. A crystal ball slightly bigger than her fist fell out of thin air, landing in her outstretched hand. She stared into it instead of at the oncoming storm-drakes.

In the crystal's depths, a hundred symbols flashed and rolled as the orb performed a thousand arcane calculations in a fraction of the time it would have taken her. To her eyes, the symbols spelled out precise directions.

And with another flash of her crystal bracelet, and another mental call to her Territory, Leah followed those directions.

Fourteen spires of white crystal speared from the ground and into the air. They were made out of the same substance as the jagged crystals she had already summoned, but unlike the rough mounds she had called the first time, these were finger-thin and needle sharp. They grew from the earth and stretched to their full height of six feet in a fraction of a second.

Each crystal needle had speared the exact center of an Endross storm-drake. The lizards' tiny bodies were now trapped in milk-white crystal, but, for the moment, they still lived. Their legs scratched feebly at the pale needles, and their wings beat at the air.

Leah dropped the crystal ball from her hand and kept walking, not slowing by a hair. The orb evaporated before it hit the ground. Each of the white needles had burst from the ground at an angle, leaving her just enough room to walk straight through the forest of crystal needles without cutting herself. She kept her eyes locked on the sergeant, ignoring the Traveler entirely.

She certainly did not let her relief show. There had been precious little opportunity to practice her Traveling over the past two years in Myria, and even with the crystal ball's assistance she had worried about making a mistake. Come to think of it, she was lucky the orb had stayed where she left it all this time; if the crystal ball had rolled off, she would never have been able to summon it. That was a restriction unique to Lirial, one that Travelers of other Territories did not have to put up with. If someone had broken into her Lirial sanctum and taken her orb, even just to move it across the room, her summons would have gone unanswered and she would have been torn to shreds by Endross storm-drakes.

Leah shook that image away. She had succeeded, that was what mattered, and now would come the real test.

She walked the last few paces to Malachi's sergeant, looking neither left nor right, before she stopped. Out of the corner of her eye, she recognized that the Traveler had let his storm dissipate. That was a good sign.

When she stood only a few feet from the sergeant, she released Lirial and called upon her other Territory. This power was wilder, hungrier, more dangerous, but she would only need it for a quick demonstration.

Hopefully.

A hot weight settled on her head as she summoned her crown. A thin circlet of mirror-bright steel that shone an unnatural shade of red, the crown was not particularly impressive on its own. Certainly not compared to her father's. But it represented something that carried far more weight.

The blocky sergeant's eyes went wide, then narrowed in calculation. Leah tensed, preparing for combat, but at last the man went down on his knees. The gesture was awkward, given the man's age and his armor, but he finally managed it. Then he pressed his forehead to the sand.

"How may I serve?" he asked. His voice was both loud and clear, even speaking into the ground.

Immediately all the soldiers around him copied his pose, faces to the sand. They almost certainly would not recognize her, even by reputation, but her demonstration of Lirial and their leader's behavior would have told them all they needed to know. Only the bald Traveler remained standing.

Leah fixed her gaze on the Traveler's acidic green eyes and waited. Either he would give in or she would have to kill him. At this point she had no chance of failure, not with her crown on her head and his Gate closed, but she had no way of knowing which way the soldiers would go. It would make things so much easier if he would just submit.

So she stared him down, projecting absolute certainty and command.

He opened his mouth as if to speak, hesitated, and then reluctantly bent forward in a bow. Just to teach him his place, Leah then pretended he didn't exist. It was more merciful than he deserved.

"Stand, sergeant," she said. "What is your name?"

"Yakir, Your Highness," he said, struggling to his feet.

Leah let some of the cold fury she felt leak into her voice. "Sergeant Yakir. On whose orders are you here, interfering with royal business?"

Yakir's voice went hoarse, and he did not meet her gaze. "My apologies, Highness, but I am here on the orders of Overlord Malachi."

"For what purpose, sergeant?"

"Well...for the midsummer sacrifice, Highness. We're here to collect the nine."

The sacrifice? Leah thought. *Surely not.* The timing was right, but how could something so routine have led to this debacle?

"Do you usually have to burn a town to the ground to collect the sacrifice,

Sergeant Yakir?" That was something of an exaggeration, since the fires burning around Myria would likely be extinguished by morning, but he would not dare to correct her.

Yakir glanced up at the Traveler next to him, who suddenly looked uneasy. "We met a party of village leaders out on the road, Highness. Some among my staff—" Leah felt sure he meant the Endross Traveler—"believed that they were, uh, a little too resistant. We decided that a more forceful hand was needed here."

Reading into what was not said, Leah could put together a picture of what had happened. The sergeant had, as was his right as a representative of Malachi, demanded nine villagers for the King's sacrifice. He would have been vague about their ultimate fate, since very few in the kingdom knew what really happened to the annual sacrifices, but clear that he would need nine people to come with him to the capital. The Mayor and his advisors had balked.

And this Traveler, impatient and offended, had led an attack. The sergeant had probably had no choice but to go along. Still, it was his mission, and therefore ultimately his responsibility.

"That was a foolish decision, Sergeant Yakir," Leah said coldly. "The people of this village have no identity as Damascans, and no idea of the sacrifice. They certainly could have done nothing that would justify such a forceful response."

Yakir paled and bowed again, almost certainly aware that she could take his life with a stray thought. She wouldn't, though, unless she had no other choice.

"I must speak with the Overlord regarding these matters," Leah continued. "But until then, my own orders remain. They come from the King himself."

Yakir cleared his throat. "Your orders, Highness?"

Leah nodded, already planning ahead. These next few weeks would be far more dangerous for her than the past two years, but she could see no other alternative.

"You will take me to Bel Calem," Leah commanded. "As a sacrifice."

Sergeant Yakir turned white.

CHAPTER 2

TRAVELERS

The land north of Myria was not as fertile as to the south, but neither had it yet become the forbidding wasteland of the Badari Desert. It was mostly long stretches of rock and scraggly trees, broken by occasional hills and tiny creeks. Simon hadn't run more than two or three miles when a young man stepped out from behind a stand of rocks and waved him down. Alin's gold hair flashed in the moonlight.

If Simon had had the strength, he would have waved and shouted back. Instead, he fell to his knees, letting his mother spill to the ground. She had lost consciousness at some point, but Simon hadn't even noticed.

Alin ran over and gathered Simon's mother in his arms. His head was half-covered by a dirty cloth bandage, and blood trickled down from his scalp to drip onto his shirt. He still managed to look like a ragged hero, injured in battle but still radiating strength, rather than the helpless victim of a mad Traveler. Simon knew he himself probably looked like a boy exhausted by a day of work. A skinny boy.

"Who's with you?" Simon asked, once he had a moment to catch his breath.

Alin shook his head, looking grim. "Only a few. Mostly old people, and the ones who lived right next to the north gate. We think they were probably looking for slaves, so they didn't care if the old or the weak got away."

"Those looked like Overlord Malachi's men," Simon said. "We're his people. Why would he do this?" Simon had grown up with stories of Malachi, the Overlord who managed their corner of Damasca in the name of the King. His reputation said he was distant but just, not a murderous tyrant.

Alin set his jaw, and his eyes blazed. He held Simon's mother in his arms as if she weighed nothing. "The King will punish Malachi as he deserves," Alin said. "And if he does not...if he doesn't, then we are his people no longer." His voice trembled with rage, but Simon almost rolled his eyes.

What would Overlord Malachi or His Majesty Zakareth care if the people of one small village refused to obey him? He had already demonstrated his willingness to burn their homes to the ground; he would hardly care about some empty threats.

He didn't say any of that to Alin, of course. No need to start a fight.

Alin led Simon to a shallow cave, barely more than a depression in the rocks, less than a hundred paces from where Alin had first appeared. About two dozen people from the village had crammed themselves inside. Simon spotted Chaim, a large man and the only one of the Mayor's advisors who hadn't ridden out of the village. He had his sturdy arms wrapped around his wife and three children. The three of them were all close to Simon's age, but they clung to their father like toddlers.

Leah's aunt Nurita held a cluster of her many nieces and nephews in one protective bundle; her stern face showed no sign of tears or dirt. Other than those two families, Simon and Alin were the only two visible without white in their hair.

Someone passed Simon a skin of water, and he took it gratefully. After a few tries, he was able to get his mother to drink a little, though she didn't wake. After she stopped drinking and turned over on her side, Simon raised the skin to his own lips and set about washing away the coating of dry, stinging dust in his throat.

Alin began to speak as Simon drank, keeping his voice low to avoid bothering the others. "We talked before you got here. The soldiers burned what they could, but the fire wouldn't have spread far. There's just not enough wood. We're going to go back in tomorrow and see what can be saved. We think that, over the next few days, some of the others might come back to us."

Simon thought of Leah's hand on his face and hoped fervently that Alin was right.

"We talked about going to Kortan," Alin continued, "but it's far enough away that we're not sure some of the people here will make it on foot, in the middle of the night with no supplies. And the raiders are probably gone by now." He spat the last sentence like he wished the soldiers had stayed, so that he could kill them himself.

Alin appeared to notice Simon's sword for the first time, and he brightened. "You have a weapon? Did you take it from one of the soldiers?"

Simon opened his mouth to respond, but Nurita stirred and raised her head. "Did you hear that?" she demanded.

Raiders appeared as if summoned to answer her question. They were on foot this time, and their dark armor glistened in the moonlight as they spread out to encircle the cave entrance. Everyone scrambled to their feet and someone began to cry, but no one made any other sound. They simply stood in the silence of shock and despair.

"They must have left the village right after we did," Alin whispered. Anger and frustration tightened his voice. "They had to have followed right on our heels. Why would they do that? *Why?*"

After they had finished surrounding the entrance, the raiders stopped moving. They stood with weapons drawn, in silence, waiting. After a moment or two, a lean man in a hooded cloak stepped forward. He carried a torch in one hand, and by its light Simon could see the man's clothes more clearly: the cloak was brown, the shirt beneath purple. Malachi's colors.

As the man approached, he used his other hand to draw the hood back from his face. His head was entirely hairless, his skin pale, and his eyes a luminous green that shone in the torchlight. He turned his head to survey the situation and grimaced as if displeased.

"I am Cormac, a Traveler of Endross in service to Overlord Malachi." Several people moaned, and Simon felt his chest tighten. Travelers had a thousand powers, most of them gruesome and terrible. He had heard the legends of Endross as a boy from his father: Endross was the place where storms were born, a blasted desert wasteland where only the most twisted and horrible monsters lived.

Of course, Simon's father had never actually seen a Traveler before the one that killed him.

"Your village was given the honor of providing a small sacrifice to the Overlord," Cormac continued. "But you have reacted with blasphemy and sedition. You are too close, no doubt, to the heretics of Enosh who fail to worship the Evening Star. You will all be taken to the Overlord's seat in Bel Calem, where you will face his judgment. And, of course, we have taken the necessary sacrifices in spite of your...lack of cooperation."

He made a gesture with his free hand, and one of the soldiers appeared, hauling a line of collared villagers just like the one Simon had seen earlier. This one was longer, however, and its occupants had their wrists and ankles bound as well as their necks. Rather than children, these slaves were mostly grown men, except for one woman who shuffled along behind them. They were eleven in total.

One of the collared men—a butcher, who had more than once given Simon a meal—shouted and jumped forward, leaping onto a nearby shoulder and grappling at him with bound hands. The other ten captives staggered toward him, jerked along by the rope.

Cormac turned his back to the cave and moved toward the struggling prisoner. The soldier shoved the bound man to the ground, kicking him as he huddled in his bonds.

"Unfortunately for you," Cormac said, "we seem to have a spare." He raised one cupped hand, which filled with a dark and swirling mass of clouds. The tiny mass began to spin, faster and faster, and to fill with flashes of unseen lightning, until he held a thunderstorm in the palm of his hand.

Cormac looked over the villagers huddled in the rest of the cave. "He was disobedient. This is the punishment for the disobedient."

As Cormac stepped toward the butcher and raised his arm, Simon cried out. The light from Cormac's torch had fallen on the woman at the end of the line, revealing her face for the first time.

It was Leah.

CHAPTER 3

HIDDEN TALENTS

Cormac held a hand over his head, and the storm inside it flashed. Thorned purplish vines sprouted from the earth around the captive butcher, crawling up his legs like questing snakes. The man's scream was terrible. Each vine had inch-long thorns that dragged over the man's skin, leaving deep red lines that trickled down his flesh. He clawed desperately at the vines, trying to peel them apart, but all he accomplished was shredding his fingers.

Simon had never seen anyone in that much agony. A twisting sympathetic pain in his own stomach made him think he was going to vomit, but he couldn't look away. Someone should help, he knew that. His hand tightened on the hilt of his sword. But what could an ordinary blade do?

He stood there, frozen.

The dying man continued to produce a whimpering scream until the storm in Cormac's hand flashed again, and blue sparks jumped from all the thorns at once. The man convulsed, spasming like he had lost all control of his muscles. The air filled with the smell of charred meat and hair. The other people in the cave screamed and pushed back into the rock; Simon himself felt paralyzed. The other captives tied to the same rope tried to pull away, but they were held firmly by their Damascan captors. Simon noticed that many of the soldiers looked sickened, and some had turned completely away, but none dared oppose the Traveler.

After a few moments, the sparks stopped and the body slumped to the ground. His skin was red and swollen, and smoke rose gently from his chest. The smell was nauseating, and Simon heard several people behind him empty their stomachs on the cave floor.

The purple-green vines slithered back into the rocky ground and vanished.

Cormac looked vaguely disgusted, as though he had been forced to step on a spider while wearing a silk slipper. He waved at the smoke in front of his face and grimaced. "You take my point," he said. "Follow quietly, and I won't need to make another example."

The Damascan soldiers pulled on the rope of captives, trying to maneuver them into position, but now everyone in the line was panicking, trying desperately to get as far away from Cormac as possible.

"Honestly," Cormac said. He tossed the torch to a nearby soldier. "Struggling solves nothing. We're leaving."

Cormac raised his hand-held thunderstorm over the struggling mass of captured villagers. Simon caught a glimpse of Leah's panicked face as she strained against the chains on her limbs and the collar around her neck. She didn't even look afraid, just angry. And resolved.

Simon himself could never have shown such strength in her position. If he could give her a moment more to live, maybe even a chance to escape, he had to try. No matter what it cost.

Quietly, afraid the Traveler would hear him, Simon eased the sword from its scabbard. As soon as he had the weapon free he kicked forward, screaming, and slashed at Cormac's legs.

The Traveler didn't even look back, but a gust of wind smacked into Simon's chest like a giant's kick. The wind felt heavy and wet, far more so than the night air surrounding them, and it smelled like iron and rotting vegetation. It shoved Simon back, tumbling him over backwards until he landed very near where he had started, staring up at the cave roof. He could just see a wedge of stars outside.

Simon tried to stand, to catch a breath, but it seemed like his body had died below the neck. He couldn't make his legs move, his lungs inflate. He tried to close his fingers around his sword, but felt nothing. Had he dropped it? He lay on the sand, wheezing and looking up at the stars as footsteps crunched over closer to his head.

Cormac's head gleamed as it blocked out the handful of stars, but his poisonous green eyes flashed brighter.

"Did that make you feel better?" the Traveler asked. Then Simon's view was obscured by an up-close vision of lightning flashes and dark, swirling clouds.

Simon closed his eyes, but opened them again instantly. His father had died facing his killer; so would he. Kalman's son would watch the storm that killed him. His lungs remembered their job as he stared, and he drew in a deep, ragged breath.

"Don't worry, Simon," someone said. Not Cormac. A younger, firmer voice. Alin? The storm shivered, as though the hand holding it had trembled. Heat lightning flared inches from Simon's nose.

"I'll take care of this," Alin said. It was Alin's confidence, but far more serious in tone than Simon had ever heard from him before. He wanted to look, to see what Alin had planned that could stand against a Traveler, but his vision was filled with clouds of rolling black.

"What are y—" Cormac began, but there was a flash of golden light so bright that it caused a blast of pain in Simon's eyes. Simon flinched, and when he could see clearly again the storm in front of his face had vanished. He blinked hurriedly, trying to clear his eyes. Something like a bundled-up cloak arched through the air and landed heavily in the distance, far behind the ring of Damascan soldiers.

Was that Cormac's body?

Simon sat up, ribs aching in protest, and turned around.

Alin stood, radiating sunlight. His hair gleamed like polished gold, his clothes drifted on an otherworldly breeze, and wisps of light rose like smoke from his right hand.

Chaim, the Mayor's advisor, spoke from the corner of the cave, his voice full of awe. "Alin," he said. "What have you done?"

Alin's response was hesitant. "I'm...not sure."

Cormac slammed into the rocky ground. He heard his body crack, and lost all feeling in a blast of white-hot pain. His consciousness fuzzed, but he knew that without the protection of Endross worked into his armor, he would be dead. As it was, the wind cushioned his fall enough so that he only cracked a rib.

He levered himself into a sitting position and nearly blacked out from the fire that exploded in his head. Perhaps he had cracked more than a rib after all.

He would have to finish this quickly. Patrols from Enosh sometimes extended this far south, and he didn't want to find a pair of hostile Grandmasters stepping out of nowhere to drag him back for interrogation. In fact, prudence suggested he should just take the royal girl and as many prisoners as he could grab and retreat, rather than face this unknown Traveler and possible Enosh reinforcements.

But he couldn't. Not now. He had been challenged.

Shame and rage rose up inside him, forcing him to his feet despite the blinding pain. He focused his fury on a spot a few inches from his palm, tearing open a rift between worlds with vicious effort.

Cormac was a Traveler of Endross, the most brutal of all known Territories. Endross was a vast desert wasteland, broken only by the occasional oasis of lush jungle. The jungles were arguably even more deadly than the harsh wastes, as they were home to a thousand species of predator. And every day without fail, unpredictable thunderstorms blasted the land with lightning and flogged it with harsh wind.

There was no weakness in Cormac's Territory. The weak died. To claim power from Endross, a Traveler had to conquer. And that meant responding to every challenge with swift, lethal force.

Never back down from a predator, Cormac thought. *He will only attack.* That was one of the first lessons any Endross Traveler learned.

A Gate to Endross opened in his palm: an angry, flashing thunderstorm the size of a marble. Endross Gates were unique among all the Territories in that they grew larger and more powerful the longer they stood open. The storm in his hand would grow and grow, granting him access to more and more power. That is, until he lost control. If the Gate became too powerful it could easily go wild, all the power of Endross unleashed without Cormac's will to restrain it. That was how many Endross Travelers died, consumed by the powers they had conjured.

But Cormac never lost control.

He passed a free hand over his smooth scalp, trying to regain himself, drowning his pain in Endross power.

The storm in his hand now filled his entire palm.

The time was here. Before Enosh discovered their presence, and before Sergeant Yakir did something he would regret, Cormac would attack.

It was the only way he knew.

Simon picked up his sword, which—as it turned out—had lain on the ground only inches from his body. Not that it had done any good. Absently he sheathed the weapon and looked over at Alin.

He was beginning to get tired of world-changing revelations. The Overlord sent soldiers to destroy his village, then a girl he barely knew sacrificed herself to save him, then a Traveler showed up and proved himself a horrifying monster. To top it off, apparently a boy Simon had known all his life turned out to have some sort of powers himself.

He'd think it was a bad dream, but Simon's nightmares had never been this strange.

"Alin," Simon said, "are you a Traveler?"

Alin's gaze wavered, and he looked down at his hand as though he had just noticed it shining. The sunlight glow around him flickered, dimmed, and quit completely.

"I think I just killed someone," Alin said. His voice was shaken. So he really didn't know what was happening.

Even as stunned and frightened as he was, Simon felt a spark of pity. If Alin didn't have any more idea what was going on than Simon did, he must be incredibly confused.

The Damascan soldiers had frozen in the face of an unknown Traveler, but now that Alin had stopped glowing, one of them walked to the mouth of the cave and stopped.

"My name is Sergeant Yakir," the soldier said. "In the absence of Traveler Cormac, I have command of this unit, and I'd like to speak with the Traveler of Myria." He nodded to Alin. "Step forward, Traveler, and identify yourself." Yakir's face was indistinct behind his helmet, but his eyes were hard.

Alin cleared his throat. "My name is Alin, and my father is Torin. But I'm not a Traveler." He hesitated for a moment, then added, "At least, I don't think I am."

The Damascan soldiers tensed almost imperceptibly, and turned their heads to see Yakir's reaction. A shiver crawled down Simon's spine as he realized each one had their hands on a weapon. If they decided Alin wasn't really a Traveler, things could get even more dangerous. Or maybe if they decided he was; Simon wasn't sure which would be worse.

Sergeant Yakir snorted and waved a hand, and his men relaxed. "Yeah, I throw shooting stars every time somebody pisses me off, too." A few of his men chuckled nervously. "Make this easier on everyone, son, and come with me. If you come peaceful, we'll pretend like none of this ever happened."

Simon watched the thoughts on Alin's face. Fear gave way to uncertainty, which hardened into determination and anger.

"If I come with you," Alin said, "you release the captives. Everybody here goes free." His anger had bled through into his voice, and in that moment he looked ten years older.

Yakir let out a breath and shook his head. "I can let everybody not in chains go, but anyone on a rope is a prisoner of war. They have to come with us. If you want to buy them from the Overlord in exchange for your loyalty, I think he'll go for it. Travelers get whatever they want, in my experience. But until such time as that happens, they're my prisoners."

Alin matched stares with Sergeant Yakir for a long moment. The older man's eyes never wavered. Some of the soldiers' hands flexed on their swords.

Leah looked like she was on the verge of calling out to Alin, but she said nothing. Simon wondered what she had meant to say.

"I agree," Alin told the soldiers. "Move your men back."

Sergeant Yakir nodded and opened his mouth to respond.

Then his head exploded. A lightning bolt blasted into the cave from outside, blowing Yakir's head into a thousand pieces.

Blood and gore splattered villagers and soldiers alike, and Simon shouted as he felt warm drops splash on his skin. More shouts and screams, from both the Damascans and the Myrians, joined his.

Sergeant Yakir's body fell much more slowly than Simon would have expected. It slumped to its knees, as though Yakir had just heard terrible news, then flopped over to one side. The air where his head used to be crackled and sparked visibly, and steam rose from his neck.

One of the soldiers yelled "He'll kill us all!" and loosed an arrow in Alin's direction. The lightning bolt had come from outside the cave, not from Alin, but the soldier must have panicked.

Alin didn't so much dodge as collapse to one side, and the arrow shattered against rock. Some of the others took up bows or spears and advanced on Alin, faces cold. They formed a human wall, pushing into the cave side-by-side. Simon would have had no chance of slipping through the soldiers, and neither did Alin.

Cormac shouldered them aside.

He was covered in dirt and sand. His scalp had split open, leaking blood that sealed one eye shut, and he moved with a noticeable limp. His one open eye blazed with green fury, and the thunderstorm swirling in his right hand was twice the size of the one he had held earlier. The storm's flashes did not come from hidden heat lightning this time, but from a roiling nest of lightning unleashed among its dark clouds.

Simon backed up until he stood over his mother's unconscious form. He huddled over her, behind Alin. If Alin had a Traveler's powers, then he should handle this. Besides, there was nothing Simon could do.

"There will be no deals," Cormac hissed. "No agreements. I will scatter your ashes from here to Bel Calem."

He thrust the storm forward, and lightning flared. An enormous serpent's head, eyes glowing and fangs gleaming, pushed its way out of the center of the storm as if hatching from an egg. As it emerged, the snake hissed and bared its six-inch fangs. The inside of its mouth glowed blue, as though lit by lightning from within.

The serpent oozed from the thunderstorm, sliding out in foot after foot of deep green scales. It seemed to move slowly, but in only a handful of seconds it sat coiled on the cave floor. If it stretched out to its full length it might be five or six paces long, and it looked as big around as Simon's waist.

Simon clutched his mother to his chest and looked at Alin. If he was going to do something with his newfound Traveler powers, now was the time. Every eye in and around the cave was locked on Alin, waiting for him to summon light and blast the snake into steaming pieces.

Alin raised his hand and pointed it at the serpent. Nothing happened. A panicked look crossed his face, and he shouted, gesturing as though throwing an invisible ball. Nothing.

Simon's stomach dropped.

Cormac snarled a word, and the snake struck forward like a bolt of lightning.

It drove its head towards Orlina, Chaim's daughter, who had been leaning against the wall between her parents. The creature snatched her up like a bird grabbing a mouse, driving its fangs deep into her torso.

Her scream was weak and wet, and the snake lifted her up in its jaws and shook her. There came a flash of blue light from the snake's mouth and the girl's body convulsed. One of her legs kicked wildly, flinging her sandal off and sending it sailing over Simon's head.

Chaim yelled and slammed his fists down on the serpent's head, again and again, but it didn't seem to be particularly bothered. After a few seconds it flicked its tail, knocking Chaim onto his back.

The blood leaking from Orlina's body steamed, and the cave once again filled with the smell of seared meat.

The Traveler growled and snapped another word, gesturing at Alin. The serpent's head jerked back like it had reached the end of an invisible leash, and it dropped Orlina's body from limp jaws. It slithered over to Alin and levered its shining blue eyes up to a level even with his.

To Alin's credit, he only flinched once. Then he visibly steeled himself and stared back at the monstrous snake.

The serpent hissed, its eyes flared brighter, and its jaws cracked. Simon almost looked away to avoid seeing Alin's head torn off, but he forced himself to look. Alin was man enough to look the serpent in the face, so Simon should at least have the courage to watch his friend die.

Instead, his blood froze as the serpent turned and looked straight at Simon.

Alin yelled and tried to grab the snake, but its head was already in Simon's face. Cormac cursed, and Simon stumbled backwards, trying instinctively to put as much distance as possible between himself and the snake from another world.

"Get the Traveler!" Cormac yelled. His face was red and strained, like he was lifting a load too heavy for him. "Ignore the rest!"

The serpent yawned, displaying its blue-lit teeth inches from Simon's mouth.

Then it shot towards Simon's feet. He jerked his legs back before he realized the truth: it was going for his mother.

Simon screamed as the snake's fangs stabbed into his mother's body, crackling with lightning.

His mother convulsed like the others, but she remained silent. Simon drew his sword at last, knowing it was hopeless, slamming its edge against the scales again and again. It accomplished nothing except to dull his blade. He had to do something; every second brought his mother closer to death. Desperate, he stabbed at the snake's eyes. Surely it had to be vulnerable there.

The blade skittered off the serpent's head. It didn't even notice. Another pulse of lightning flashed down its fangs, and Simon's mother shook again.

A gold light poured forth from the center of the cave.

"Call it off," Alin said, his voice once more grim and resonant. Simon didn't turn, still hammering his blade against the creature. He had to protect her this time. He had to.

Cormac shouted and thrust both hands at the serpent, the storm boiling in his palm. His serpent turned and hissed at him, its mouth sticky and dark with blood.

"Fine," Alin said. His hands were shrouded in misty white-gold light. "If you won't do it, I will."

He hurled golden light at the snake, not in a ball this time, but in a tight circle. The loop of light wrapped itself around the snake's neck, just beneath the skull, in a shining golden collar. The serpent writhed and flapped below Simon, trying to escape the binding. Its heavy head smacked into Simon's gut, knocking the breath from him and driving him to his knees. He barely managed to hang on to his sword.

Alin raised a glowing hand and clenched his fist. The collar tightened, and the snake had time to let out one inhuman shriek before the collar did what Simon's blade couldn't: it sliced the monster in half.

Two smoking pieces of snake fell to the cave floor and dissolved into rolling black clouds, which vanished instantly. Nothing was left of the serpent but corpses and wounds.

Cormac screamed, a sound of pure frustration, and thrust his hands in front of him as if he were trying to push down a tree. Lightning blasted forth from Cormac's storm cloud, lighting the sandy cave like a newborn star. Thunder rocked Simon's ears.

Halfway through the shallow cave, only a few feet in front of Cormac, the lightning slammed into a golden blast from Alin.

The lightning bolt shattered into pieces that turned back upon its summoner, scourging Cormac's flesh and singeing the edges of his cloak. Some of the Damascan soldiers ran, and those remaining looked ready to flee at any time. Among them, the captives cowered helplessly, hoping to avoid the deadly bolts.

Cormac, breathing heavily, said something that Simon didn't catch through the ringing in his ears.

Alin evidently did, though, because as Simon's hearing returned he heard the young Traveler say, "...so it seems judgment is mine to pass." Alin extended his right hand, and light gathered in it, resolving into the shining shape of a translucent sword. It looked like the golden ghost of a magnificent blade, and Alin swung it twice through the air as if it had no weight.

Cormac moved the storm toward the ground, and thorned vines spun up from it, crackling with blue sparks. Alin's sword flashed down one, two, three, four times, rhythmically, as though he were chopping wood. The vines fell to the ground in pieces, and Alin advanced.

They had moved out of the cave entirely now, standing on the sandy earth beneath the stars. Cormac retreated into his soldiers and Alin steadily moved forward, driving the other man backwards. The Damascan soldiers clutched their weapons uncertainly, clearly not sure whether to interfere.

"Loose!" Cormac screamed, moving back and bringing the storm up. "Shoot him! Shoot him!"

One of the archers had his bow ready, and an arrow blurred towards Alin. His sword flashed out of existence, a ball of gold light blasted the arrow from the air. Cormac summoned up more vines around Alin's feet as more arrows whizzed around him.

Simon saw the dilemma instantly. If Alin summoned the sword to destroy Cormac's vines, he would be filled with arrows. If he continued to defend himself from the arrows, the vines would turn him into another burned-out corpse on the cave floor.

Alin struck arrows from the air with one glowing hand and moved the other down to point at the vines. His muscles tightened, as though he were gathering his strength.

Then the vines burst into flames.

At first Simon thought Alin had set the vines on fire himself, but he and Cormac both started and looked around at the interruption. Not in time.

A swirling white hole in the world, the size of a barn door, floated in the air outside of the cave. Two figures stepped out, both wearing heavy coats: a young man, barely older than Simon, and an older woman who looked as though she could chew nails and spit horseshoes. They were both covered in snowflakes, and Simon realized with a start that the portal led straight into a blizzard.

Two more Travelers had arrived.

Simon set his mother to one side and scrambled to his feet, snatching up his sword. His heart hammered in his chest, and his hands grew slick on the sword's grip. He knew, with a sick feeling in his gut, that they were all about to die.

The young man stepped from the portal, his eyes squeezed shut. His hand had been moving the whole time, a red symbol on his palm leaving streaks of light in the air as it passed. It had been eight years since Simon had seen a mark like that, but the sight of it made his hands shake. This was how his father had died.

At least I won't go out alone, Simon thought. The thought shouldn't have comforted him, but it did. His hands steadied. He moved forward.

Then the new Traveler thrust out his red-marked hand, and fire poured from the night sky down onto Cormac. Cormac threw up the storm in his hand as a shield, and wind met fire. The heat scorched Simon's face, and savage air tore at his eyes.

A pair of Damascan soldiers charged at the new Travelers from behind, drawn steel in their hands. The woman flicked something small and silver into her hand—maybe a key?—and held it in front of her, twisting it as though unlocking a door.

A spinning silver disc the size of a cartwheel blasted out of thin air, rushing forward and slicing the two soldiers in two like an enormous razor. A splatter of red sprayed off into the night. The spinning razor blinked away a second later, vanishing as suddenly as it had appeared.

Her partner, the young man with the red palm, didn't open his eyes or stop moving his right hand. He simply gestured with his left hand, as though shooing away a fly, and spoke a word Simon couldn't hear.

Nothing happened for a second, and then a clump of snow leaped out of the blizzard and through the portal. To Simon, it looked like a poorly formed snowball the size of a barrel. The snow stuck to the ground, quivering and snarling like a horde of badgers. Simon was still trying to decide whether there was some living creature inside the snow or whether the snow itself was alive when the mound of snow jumped into the air and latched onto the next Damascan soldier in line.

The snow clung to the man, shaking back and forth as it worried at the soldier's breastplate like a dog shaking a rabbit. Blood sprayed up from his chest, and he screamed wordlessly. Was the snow...eating him?

Simon shivered and lowered his sword, backing up a step. Maybe these two Travelers would take care of the Damascans on their own, and maybe they would decide that the villagers deserved the same treatment. Simon would wait to act until they had taken care of Cormac.

Not that he could really make a difference, anyway. He couldn't shake the image of a spinning razor slicing two armored men in half in a blink, their bodies falling to the ground as just so many pieces of meat. How was his sword supposed to protect anyone?

One of the other soldiers had a bow prepared, and they loosed an arrow at the carnivorous snow. The arrow landed in the snow bank and stuck there, to no apparent effect. Black fletching stuck out at an angle from the pristine white. The soldier stopped screaming and fell over, a gurgle escaping his mouth as he died. The snow growled again and leaped at another soldier. The rest of them finally got the hint and fled, some throwing down weapons as they ran.

The young Traveler kept his eyes shut and his right arm moving, palm flaring with red light. The fire from heaven, raining down from nowhere onto Cormac, never slowed. Cormac shouted, straining to keep the fire off of him.

Seeing his enemy distracted, Alin brought both hands up. A golden, shining tear in reality appeared before him, and it spewed forth a ragged wave of solid light that slammed into Cormac like a hammer. Blue light flared from his back, blending with the red light from above and gold from behind in a confusing rainbow that left Simon blinded.

When his eyes cleared, Cormac lay on his back. The thunderstorm hung in the air underneath the stream of falling fire, still keeping the fire off of him. It was almost the size of a pony now, and it floated five feet off the ground. Lightning crackled and black clouds swirled, silently consuming the torrent of fire from above.

Cormac stirred, groaning. When he saw the thunderstorm above him, his eyes widened, and he reached out as if to pluck the storm from midair. For a moment, nothing else happened. The cave fell into an eerie silence.

Then the floating storm, out of Cormac's control, exploded into a thousand screaming bolts of lightning. The fire, with nothing left to stop it, poured in a waterfall down on Cormac's head. Lightning and fire crashed into him.

Simon expected to hear him shriek, or scream, or call for help, but the thunderous detonation of power swallowed anything the Traveler might have said. A sound like trapped thunder rocked the cave, and a searing wind blew Simon off his feet, along with most of his fellow villagers. Only Alin and the two strange Travelers remained standing, and only barely.

When the smoke, dust, and light cleared, no sign of Cormac remained. The ground outside the cavern was littered with abandoned spears, swords, and body parts belonging to the soldiers. Simon saw a few in the distance, still running.

Fire still fell in an endless torrent, blackening the ground. The younger Traveler made a slashing gesture with his red-branded right hand, and the fire vanished. Then he clenched his left fist and spoke a word, and the living snow died—releasing one still-breathing Damascan soldier who stumbled uncertainly away. The snow crawled away from the cavern and back into the snowy portal, purring contentedly. One black arrow still stuck up from its otherwise-pristine back. Once it crossed the threshold of the blizzard, the portal vanished.

When both ice and fire vanished, the new Traveler opened his eyes and blinked.

"Uh...is everybody okay?" he asked. Orlina's mother began to weep. Simon looked down at the corpse of his mother, bundled at his feet, and had to choke back a sob himself.

The older woman sighed loudly and patted him on the shoulder. "You did well, Gilad. Now let me take it from here."

The young Traveler—Gilad—nodded, and sat down against a rock. His face showed exhaustion, but he also just looked relieved to be done with the fighting.

The woman faced Alin, who still glowed like a sunrise. He had an arm half-raised, and light drifted up from it like luminescent smoke. "My name is Miram, and I speak for myself and my companion Gilad. We are Travelers, from the free city of Enosh. Who are you?"

Alin's eyes held steady on her for a moment before he spoke. "The last time I gave someone my name," he said, "his head burst like a dropped fruit.

I'm not sure you want me to answer."

Miram had her small silver key up in an instant. "Is that a threat?" she asked.

Sheepishly Alin smiled, but he didn't lower his arm. Wisps of light drifted up from his hand. "No, I'm sorry, it was a poor joke. I am Alin, son of Torin, born in Myria village inside the realm of Overlord Malachi. If you are truly from Enosh, we are not enemies."

Oh sweet Maker, Alin was trying to make a speech. Nurita was the only one in the village who would talk like that, and everyone knew she was too pompous by half. Alin sounded ridiculous trying it, as though his new powers made him the equal of some lord or lady from the stories. Then again, he was a Traveler now. Maybe that was how he was supposed to talk.

Simon knelt down, adjusting his mother so she looked more comfortable. She was beyond caring, of course, but he couldn't stand to see her like that, with her neck twisted at almost a right angle.

He almost wept, but he had to pay attention. This was likely one of the most important exchanges he would ever witness. His mother—the one he remembered from her few lucid periods when she was both sober and sane—would have wanted him to pay attention.

"I am Miram, Master Traveler of Tartarus," the woman said. "This is my companion, Gilad." Gilad looked up at the sound of his name, blinked, and gave a startled wave.

"We will give you whatever help you need," Miram continued, "and we are willing to transport the surviving people of Myria to Enosh for medical care and supplies. But first"—and here her voice sharpened— "I must know, Alin son of Torin, what Territory have you summoned?"

Alin hesitated. "Territory?"

"The power you're using right now," Miram said impatiently. "It comes from somewhere. Where?"

"I...I don't know."

"Could you show us?" Gilad asked. "Just do whatever you did before."

Alin took a deep breath. "Okay. I think I can..." his voice trailed off. His hand moved uncertainly in front of him, questing, until his fingers seemed to find something in empty air.

His eyes blazed, the glow around him intensified, and a golden sword appeared in his hand. Translucent and softly golden, it looked like the shining ghost of a real weapon.

"And a little more," Alin murmured. Light poured up from his left hand again, and he released it to hang in midair. It hung in a golden globe, lighting the cave and the surrounding area up like midday.

The battle with Cormac had made it clear, but somehow it only really sank in now. Alin was a Traveler. Alin was a Traveler, and Simon wasn't.

His mother's sightless eyes were bloodshot. Simon slid them closed with a gentle hand.

Miram dropped to her knees in front of Alin, and her face softened. "I greet you, Eliadel, the Rising Sun, and I bid you welcome to the gates of Enosh." She bowed until her head rested against the stone floor, and when she next spoke, her voice sounded of unshed tears. "You have not come too soon."

Gilad joined her, mirroring her position more awkwardly.

The other villagers stared at Alin with open mouths. Some of them bowed, though Simon was sure they had no more idea what was going on than he did. One woman wept with joy and relief, reaching out as though to touch him.

Simon glanced over to see how Leah was taking it, and fear jolted through him. He slid away from his mother's body, rose unsteadily to his feet, and walked over to tug on Alin's sleeve.

"Alin," Simon said. "Where's Leah?"

Since they had been tied together, of course, all of the prisoners had vanished.

The golden glow had faded from Alin seconds after he had realized Leah was missing, but the Travelers all obeyed him when he ordered a search. For that matter, so did the villagers. But after two hours of exhaustive searching, aided by the powers of three Travelers, no one had found a trace.

"Enough," Miram finally called. "Gilad, signal everyone to return."

Gilad raised a hand and launched three orange sparks into the air. Three flares: the signal for all those searching to return.

"We just need to spread out farther," Simon insisted. "They could still be out here."

Alin looked troubled, but he didn't say anything to agree.

Miram walked over and put a hand on Simon's shoulder. "I'm sorry about your friends. Or perhaps your family?" When Simon glanced over at his mother's body instead of responding, Miram went on. Her voice sounded a touch more sympathetic. "It looks like Cormac stowed the prisoners away in a Gate when no one was paying attention. He probably didn't want to keep watching them. Or maybe there was a second Traveler among the soldiers; who knows? But there are no tracks. I assure you, we would have found them. Your friends are on their way to Malachi by now."

"Alin, we shouldn't—" Simon began, but his friend cut him off by shaking his head. Simon was too startled to be offended. At first.

"She's right, Simon," Alin said. "They're with Malachi. The only way we're going to get them back is by force."

How would you know that? Simon wondered.

"But first we must return to Enosh," Miram said, "and gather our forces. Alin, you should come with us, along with any wounded. Everyone else should return to your village and wait for word and supplies."

"But why do you need me?" Alin asked. "My people are in need, and I would not abandon them lightly." Again, he spoke as if he had real authority. Or a swollen head.

Miram smiled a bitter smile. "There is a bigger picture here than just your family and friends, Alin. Even if we bring them back from Malachi, they will never be safe. Not until King Zakareth is no longer in control."

"We have a prophecy, Alin, uh, I mean, Eliadel," Gilad said. "It is prophesied that a Traveler of Elysium, the City of Light, will return and lead the free city of Enosh against the King of Damasca and bring him down."

"And that's me?" Alin asked. He sounded a little excited.

Gilad shrugged. "It seems like it."

Miram nodded. "Please come with us, Alin. We will treat you as royalty, and teach you. You will become powerful, so that you will be able to protect your friends, your home...and ours."

Alin straightened his shoulders and met Miram's eyes. "I will join you for now," he said. "So that I can see if you are telling the truth." Alin sounded serious, but Simon thought he still looked childishly eager.

Miram almost smiled. "Good enough. Gilad, open a Gate. Take us through Helgard to the nearest Naraka waypoint; we need the fast route home."

Simon hesitated to speak, but he felt like he had to say something. "Do you think I have time to bury my mother?" he said. "I want to make sure she's taken care of before we leave."

Alin and Miram exchanged glances, and Simon got the impression that his friend was years older instead of only a few months.

Alin took him by both shoulders and looked at him compassionately. "Simon, I think you should stay with the village. They will need your help in rebuilding."

Simon had to crush the thought of punching Alin right in his condescending face. Alin could probably set Simon on fire with his thoughts or something, but he had no right to speak like that. Besides, after Simon buried his mother, what was he supposed to do? Go back to the smoldering ruins of an empty house?

"There are lots of our people missing," Simon said, making his voice reasonable. "Not just Leah and the others. A bunch of people ran off. Malachi may have caught dozens of villagers. And I want to help." Even to his ears, it sounded like a child's plea.

"Simon, you'll be helping build something they can come home to. Besides, I will bring back as many as I can. I promise." Alin's voice was earnest, but it left Simon feeling hollow.

Simon agreed, though he felt sick. All he had done to prepare, all those hours practicing, and he had been useless against a real Traveler. Again.

"Thanks Simon," Alin said, and there was real relief in his eyes. "Tell my sisters not to worry, all right? I'll be back for them."

Simon nodded and trudged back to the cave where his mother lay, silent and motionless. She was not near the other corpses but separate, alone, wrapped in the same filthy rags she wore for clothing.

And so she died as she had lived.

Simon gathered her in his arms and turned to watch the Travelers depart. They stood under the moonlight, leading the wounded villagers one by one through a Gate and into another swirling blizzard. Each villager hesitated when he or she first looked into the portal, but no one bolted. One at a time, they forced themselves through.

At last, only Alin and Gilad were left. Alin turned, saw Simon, and smiled a little. Then he waved good-bye and passed through the portal. Gilad glanced around nervously and followed, and with his passing, the Gate vanished.

Simon hefted his mother's corpse in his arms and followed the few other weary villagers, heading for what remained of their home.

Leah stood on the gray plains of Lirial, still leashed to the nine other prisoners.

Above her, in a sky locked in perpetual night, a dozen moons whirled and shifted. One orange harvest moon drifted slowly overhead, full tonight, while a smaller silver-blue moon whirled from new moon to crescent to half moon to full in the space of five seconds, then back again. A red moon and a purple crossed each other, then switched positions.

There was a pattern to each of the Lirial moons, and understanding their interactions was vitally important to any Lirial Traveler. To Leah, they spoke of a steadily shifting interaction of subtle forces.

But, of course, Leah the daughter of Kelia—as the uneducated child of a Myrian villager—would know none of that. So...

"Where are we?" Leah asked, as if panicked.

One of the soldiers, a young man barely older than herself, stared at her in shock. He would have no more idea what was going on than one of the villagers, except he knew that she had done it. She had, of course—as soon as she had realized Cormac was going to lose his confrontation with Alin, she had opened a Gate and brought the sacrifices through. Along with a handful of soldiers, just to help her out.

Leah gestured quickly to the soldier, trying to signal him to catch on. At last, understanding lit his face.

"Um, yes," he said. "This is a...Territory. For Travelers."

"You're still taking us to Bel Calem?" Leah asked, in a fearful tone.

The soldier cleared his throat. "That's exactly what I'm doing, yes. Well? Let's get moving."

Leah shot him another covert gesture, pointing to her left, where a cliff of pure crystal glinted in the distance.

"This way!" the young soldier called, pointing in the direction Leah had indicated. With another glance at her—really, he was going to have to be more subtle than that—he started off in the right direction.

The sacrifices followed, most of them still hushed by the idea that they were actually in one of the mythical Territories. Rutha, who still believed she was Leah's half-sister, clung to Leah's shirt like a child to her mother's apron. Leah patted her hand soothingly.

Though she was actually not supposed to form any real attachments to the Myrians, she still hoped she could find a way to spare Rutha. They may not be true blood relatives, but Leah had spent the past two years living with the girl as a sister. She couldn't help but feel protective. Rutha was certainly a long sight better than Leah's real sisters.

More importantly, how was she going to explain to her father about Alin? The Elysian Traveler *had* been in Myria after all, when Leah had spent most of the past two years insisting that the story was just a myth. And he wasn't just anyone in Myria, but a boy who had nursed a painfully obvious crush on her almost since she had walked into the village.

She would have to find a way to get Alin back in hand, or else make a formal apology to her father. A particularly long and painful apology.

At all costs, she had to avoid that. Which meant that she would have to bring Alin back and get him under control.

Somehow.

CHAPTER 4
A STEP FORWARD

Over the next three days, almost a hundred villagers trickled back to the scorched ruins of Myria.

They scooped out a shallow pit just outside the village borders and dumped into it the fourteen bodies they could find. Chaim said, as Simon helped him heave his daughter's limp corpse into the mass grave, that they had gotten lucky. He said the words bitterly, and spat to one side afterwards.

The body count was too low for a real attack. In Chaim's reckoning, it had only been a raid for slaves, or to keep the people in line. His daughter stared up at Simon, never blinking as he pushed a pile of dirt onto her face.

Simon buried his mother himself, separate from the rest. He buried her by starlight, on a hill next to a wizened fig tree. He didn't own a shovel, so he used a board that had once been part of a window shutter. By the time he finished, fingers cracked and bleeding, the sun had begun to peek over the horizon.

He didn't feel the pain in his fingers. The wind was chill, and he was a little cold. It felt as if his tears had frozen on his face.

But there was still work to be done.

His house stank after years of his mother's illness, so he brought in fresh sand for the floor, scooping out the old grit. He even found a carpet in the house of a family he had buried. They were beyond using it now, so he rolled it up and dragged it back home.

New boards were plentiful, lying about the streets in the form of broken crates or feeding troughs, so he brought a few home and tried fixing his door. He gave up after only an hour; the frame was fine, but the original door was too warped and cracked to be worth fixing. He built himself a new one.

Scrubbing the wax from old candlesticks, sifting the flour, replacing the wineskins, and laundering his few remaining rags took another day. As the moon rose for the fourth time since his return to Myria, Simon found himself wondering:

What now?

He sat on a log with his back to the communal bonfire. Villagers huddled around it—men, women, young, old—with no regard for social standing. They muttered to each other about grief and anger and revenge, but here and there a soft laugh would break the night. They were beginning to get used to the smaller size of the village, and some had begun to say that most of those missing would return, too, in time.

"But what about the ones that were captured?" Chaim said. His voice was scraped raw from crying over his slain daughter. "That Traveler got ten of them, and they're probably slaves in the capital by now. What if they got more? What are we going to do about it?"

A woman humphed dismissively. "That's not a concern of ours," she said. By her voice, Simon identified Nurita, Leah's aunt. She had no children of her own, and spent most of her time bullying the town leaders into one decision or another. "Torin's son Alin will take care of the ones at the capital, and you can count on that."

There was a chorus of murmured agreements from around the fire.

Simon's chest tightened. Alin would take care of it, sure. While Simon and the rest sat at home, scraping together ashes.

"Besides," Nurita continued. "We're not Travelers. We can't stand up to the Overlord."

That was true. There was no way any of them could face the powers Simon had seen the night Myria burned. Alin was the only one who stood a chance. The only thing Simon could do against a Traveler was die. Even now, with nothing left to live for, he still didn't want to die.

"We'll just do what we can," Nurita said. "We'll stay here and pull our homes back together. No matter what happens to us, we'll keep on living like we always have."

Like they always had. Simon remembered a stone-marked grave next to a fig tree, and Leah's face before she rolled out of hiding and was taken by enemy soldiers.

Everyone voiced their agreement to Nurita's words. Even Chaim, though he sounded like he was going to cry again. When Simon turned around to face the fire, they were all still nodding along.

"That's not good enough," Simon said.

Everyone stopped to look at him. They looked mildly surprised at his presence, as though they had forgotten he was even there.

"We have to do something," Simon said. "We have to do better."

Chaim laughed bitterly, and Nurita arched one eyebrow. "If you think you know a better way," she said, "then by all means show us."

Simon rose to his feet.

"Okay," he said.

He kept his sword buckled to his waist at all times, now. There was nothing else he owned that he needed, or cared enough about to gather. He thought briefly about bringing some food, but he just couldn't summon up the energy.

Alone, Simon walked out of the south gate without looking back.

He hadn't been back to the Latari Forest since he was eight years old. In fact, no one from the village had. Kalman vanishing and his wife Edira turning up insane had apparently been enough warning for all of Myria to stay away. Simon had certainly never intended to return.

Except that he wanted to fight Travelers, and he had only ever met one man who could do that.

Simon reached the wall of trees after two full days of walking. The sun weighed down upon him, and sand swirled in his path, but the wind coming out of Latari was cool and wet.

Simon had imagined this moment as dire and significant. He had pictured himself facing down the dark forest, building his courage until he could force himself to walk into the trees.

But he was about to collapse, and all he could think about was how nice that cool air would feel after two days exposed to the heat. His eyes were caked with grit, and his throat felt like he had been chugging sand. His stomach growled, reminding him that he hadn't had a bite to eat since he had left the village.

In the end, he rushed eagerly into the forest's shadows.

He collapsed in the sparse grass near the border, letting the cool air wash over him, and he swore he was just going to sleep there on the ground. But it took only a few seconds for thirst to drive him back to his feet.

Simon stumbled around for almost an hour looking for water before he realized he had been hearing the bubbling voice of a creek almost since the moment he crossed the border. He cursed his own lack of attention and forced his body to stagger nearer to the sound of water.

When he finally found the creek, a small but steady flow between loose banks of pebbles, clothed in reeds and thin grasses, he fell into it facedown. Once his thirst was satisfied, he made a bed of leaves and grass and curled up next to the trunk of a tall tree. By the position of the sun it was still early afternoon, and the Demon might come after him as he slept. But surely he could sleep for a few hours and wake up before dark.

Simon relaxed on the soft grass and let his mind drift. He had begun to wonder if maybe he shouldn't go to sleep after all when darkness took him.

He woke to a man looming over him in the darkness, dagger drawn. Night had truly fallen, and the moon gleamed along the man's drawn blade.

Simon had heard rumors that bandits were moving in and out of the Latari forest, but he had secretly laughed at the idea. The forest's Demon would not allow such a thing.

Except apparently, he would.

Simon panicked. He grabbed at the arm holding the knife and kicked as hard as he could in the direction of the man's knees.

The man yelled and staggered, but he put more pressure on the dagger. It lowered to within two inches of Simon's eye, shining from a finger's length in front of him. Simon grabbed the other man's wrist with both arms and pushed, but he was fighting against a grown man's entire weight.

With the strength of panic, Simon kicked up again and again, trying to land a hit between the man's legs, but he was running out of time. He couldn't hold the dagger off of him forever, and he couldn't reach down to his own sword. If he got a little space, maybe he could put up a fight.

Someone nearby chuckled. "You can't handle him, huh? You think maybe I should take over for you?" Another shadow appeared at the corner of Simon's vision, and his fear surged up again. There were two of them.

Simon pushed the man's arm to the side, and the dagger plunged down, slicing a burning line into his left cheek. The knife bit into the soil, and Simon tried to scramble out from under his attacker.

The second man grunted and planted a boot on Simon's forehead, shoving him back.

Simon continued to struggle, shouting for help whenever he could, but in his head he had given up. He couldn't escape from two of them. He would fight until the end, but it was over.

At least he would die in the same place as his father.

A sing-song voice drifted through the forest, barely louder than the sounds of rustling leaves.

"Hush, little one. It's loud, I fear. Three little mice have come to play. No, don't fret; I know just what to do. I will send them all away."

The second man spun to the side, and a bush in front of him rustled. He drew a short sword. Simon tried to cry out, to encourage whoever or whatever was hiding in the bush, but the man in front of him covered his mouth with a foul-smelling hand. The point of a dagger pressed into his ribs, and he fell as still as possible.

"Not a word," the man whispered, and Simon gave a tiny nod. "We're all on the same road now. You're quiet, and we might all live."

Simon smiled, though neither of the men could see it, scanning the bushes as they were. As much as he had a plan, this was it. The Demon of the forest had let him live once, so why not twice?

"Oh no, my dear, the first little mouse has a sword. What is he going to do with that, I wonder?"

"We're here on order of the King himself," called the man with the drawn sword. "We're his property, see. So get on out of here and leave us to our business!"

A shadow detached itself from the darkness, and moonlight flashed on steel. The bandit's sword hand vanished, and it tumbled to the ground still clutching the weapon. But the sword's owner did not scream; blood sprayed from his sliced throat.

As he watched the man clutch at his throat, Simon noticed something that he had missed in the darkness: the man he had taken for a bandit wore an iron collar around his neck.

Not a bandit, then. A slave, like the nobles of Damasca supposedly kept. But who left their slaves to wander around the Latari Forest in the middle of the night? Were they runaways?

The slave man holding Simon made a sound like a sob and pulled the dagger away from Simon to point into the darkness.

That sing-song whisper cut through the forest again. "One little mouse is bleeding, my dear. What will the other ones do?"

"Stay back!" The slave yelled. He pushed Simon aside and rose to his feet. "I'm not afraid of demons. I eat 'em before breakfast, just to wake up my appetite!"

Only a breeze responded, rustling the leaves overhead.

"I'll show you what I do to demons!" the man called. He stepped forward to challenge the invisible Demon, sword raised in front of him.

Then he bolted. He ran as hard as he could away from Simon, leaping over low-rising bushes, trying desperately to get away.

He made it maybe fifteen paces before a sword drove through his heart. The blade was long and curved, sharp on one edge. Simon got a good look as the shadow slowly pulled the sword from the dying man's chest.

The sword had a ridiculously long blade, maybe six or seven feet, though it was slender and slightly curved along its whole length. The shadowed Demon held it lightly in one hand, angled out and to the side so that the blade did not scrape along the dirt. How much did a sword like that weigh? No one could hold it so easily. And how did anyone sheathe a blade that long?

The Demon of the forest spoke to something he held in his left hand, though Simon couldn't see it clearly through the underbrush. "What do you think, little one? Will the third mouse run for its hole? Or will it stay for cheese?"

"I'm not with them!" Simon said. He had to fight the impulse to edge backwards, to get further away from that huge sword. "They found me sleeping and tried to kill me."

The shadow cocked his head in Simon's direction, like a bird confronted by a worm. Then he stepped forward into the moonlight and began unwrapping a dark cloth from around his head. It had hidden his hair and mouth, leaving only his eyes uncovered. Simon assumed it was meant to keep the man as covered in darkness as possible, to make him harder to spot in the woods at night. So the fact that he was taking it off should be a good sign, right? Or it could mean that he wasn't planning to leave any witnesses.

When he pulled away the cloth, one of Simon's hopes was confirmed: he was just a man, if an odd-looking one. Judging by the smooth skin of his face, he was only twice Simon's age, but his tangled, wiry hair was pure white. Clumps of it hung down into his face, obscuring his eyes.

But this wasn't the man who had saved him when he was a child. Who was he, then? Or did this forest have more than one demon with a sword?

"You speak as if to a blind man," he said. "I may not have the sharpest eyes, but when one man holds his knife to another, I begin to think that perhaps they are not the closest friends." He was using a more normal speaking voice, now, but it still had something of a lilt to it. The white-haired man raised his left hand to his ear, and Simon saw that he held a doll: a little girl with long black hair, wearing a dress patterned in red flowers.

"What's that, my dear? Oh-ho, it could be so." He returned his attention to Simon. "She thinks that because you cannot see my eyes, perhaps you think I have none." He lifted the doll to his face and used her wooden arm to pull aside the veil of his hair. He blinked out at Simon.

"You see?" he said. "Not so blind as you thought." The swordsman let his hair drop and raised the sword to point at Simon. They stood perhaps ten feet apart, but the sword was so long it came within a foot of touching Simon's chest. "Now, maybe the little mouse wants to tell us why it's sleeping in *my* burrow."

Simon tried to speak, cleared his throat, and tried again. "I was looking for you."

The man gave a mocking half-bow, somehow without moving his sword a hair. "Congratulations on your success."

"I need your help. Overlord Malachi has taken some people from my village. I want to take them back." He tried to sound as firm as possible, determined, as though he knew what he was doing.

"Then you have risked so much for so little," the other man said. "I don't leave my forest." He pulled his sword back and turned as if to walk away.

"You don't need to leave!" Simon cried. He was desperate now, and he wanted this man to see it, to see that it was important for him to listen. "I don't want you to leave the forest. I've been here before; I've seen you kill Travelers. If you don't help me...I mean, the first Damascan Traveler I meet is going to eat me alive."

The man cocked his head again. "You have a sword," he said. "Draw it." Simon did, warily. The old leather of the hilt felt rough and heavy in his hand.

"Can you defend yourself?" the white-haired man asked. He flicked his long sword, and Simon's blade rang with a shock that shook his whole upper body. It felt like someone had rung a tuning fork and shoved it against his bones. His wounded hands jerked back instinctively, and the sword fell to the ground.

"Pick it up again." This time his voice was light, as if it were a suggestion. Simon did so.

"Now, can you attack?" The man spread his hands wide—one holding a hilt, the other a doll—leaving his chest bare in invitation.

After a moment's hesitation, Simon rushed forward, stabbing his sword at the man's heart. At the last second, the white-haired man vanished, sliding to one side and out of Simon's view so fast that it looked like he had ceased to exist. Simon's ankle snagged on the man's foot, and he spilled to the ground, barely managing to toss his sword aside before he fell on it. He crashed into some roots and lay groaning on the forest floor.

He ached all over, his sliced cheek burned, and the ghost of his fear made him shake like his mother on one of her worst days. This was not working out as he had hoped.

The white-haired man leaned down beside Simon and held the doll in front of his face. Her painted eyes looked startled.

"Otoku is laughing at you, little mouse. Can you hear her?"

Shame and desperation drove Simon back to his feet, reaching for his dropped sword. "Let me try again."

"If you like the taste of dirt so much, there are easier ways."

"Please. One more time."

The man sighed and stepped back, putting some distance between himself and Simon. He spoke to the doll again. "I'm sorry, my dear, but fools must learn every lesson thrice."

He drove his blade into the ground at an angle, because only a giant could have driven it straight down, and set the doll gently on the ground beside it. "Don't worry, dear one. This will only take a moment."

He stepped out in front of Simon and beckoned with one hand. "Come, little mouse."

Simon ran up and tried to sweep his sword at the other man's stomach, but the man was too fast. He grabbed Simon's wrist and twisted. The sudden pain and pressure were too much for Simon to resist, and he dropped his sword to the ground.

"Again," Simon said, as soon as the older man released him. If this was what it took to get the Myrian prisoners back, he would do it every night for a thousand nights.

The man shook his white, shaggy head. "No," he said. "It's my turn to play."

He kicked Simon's short sword up off the ground and snagged it out of the air, then turned it on Simon in a blur of steel. The point of the sword pricked him in the shoulder, in the chest, on each arm. Simon tried to move away, but he couldn't escape. The swordsman was just so *fast*; he kept Simon on his heels until his back pressed against a tree. Then the man put the blade's point against Simon's throat.

"I win again. Such an easy game."

The man dropped the sword at Simon's feet and walked away. He picked up his doll and brushed off her dress.

"One more time," Simon said. He had already retrieved the sword.

With one hand, the other man extracted his huge blade from the ground. He shook his head. "You're just too flimsy. You would break."

"No, I won't! Please!" But Simon could see he was getting nowhere. He tried a different tactic. "Is there someone else I could talk to? One of you who helped me before. He wore a cloak, and had a damaged sword. Please, could I speak with him?"

The swordsman froze on the brink of turning away. Simon actually caught a glimpse of one eye through the veil of white hair as he cocked his head back toward Simon. "Before?"

"When I was a child," Simon said. "I was with my mother and father on the edge of the forest. We took shelter from a storm, and Travelers attacked. He saved us. Well, my mother and me."

The man continued to stare. Finally, he said, "Hmmm. And your mother? You would leave her behind?"

Simon's voice went hoarse, suddenly. "She's dead. Another Traveler, from Overlord Malachi. I'm alone now."

The other man sighed in a strangely musical fashion. "No, I'm sorry, it would be too cruel. Trust me when I say that you would not survive."

"No, I will! I'll do whatever I have to!"

"Go back to your burrow, little mouse." The man's last words drifted on the wind as he stepped into the shadows and vanished.

Simon rushed after him. He searched all night, but found no trace of anyone else in the woods. No footprints, no shred of cloth, no lingering bloodstain. By the time the sun came up, he had begun searching for trap doors or camouflaged tents.

As the rosy light of dawn filtered through the forest, Simon sank to his knees.

What was he supposed to do now?

CHAPTER 5

WELCOME TO VALINHALL

Simon went hungry for almost two more days before he found a patch of berries. A rust-colored squirrel munched on a few, so he figured they probably weren't poisonous, but he was almost too hungry to care.

He took the edge off his appetite, wrapped an extra handful of berries in a little pouch made of leaves, and marked the spot with a patch of cloth he had cut from one of the dead slaves. He wanted to be able to find his way back to the berries when he needed to. He stopped by the creek for a quick drink, then made his way to his "hut": a nest of dried leaves and dead branches that he had built against the thick trunk of an old tree. He had curled up inside it for the past two nights, trying to get some rest as he figured out a course of action.

Unfortunately, his only plan was to stay here and wait to see if the swordsman showed up again. He didn't know where else to go to learn how to fight Travelers, and he refused to return to Myria. That mostly left staying here and waiting. At first Simon had tried to practice on his own; he had swung his sword until his hands bled, and now they were wrapped in bandages made from the clothing of dead men. The practice may or may not have done him any good, but his arms ached, and Simon took that as a sign of progress.

Now Simon slumped inside his hut, bandaged hands on the ground, sword resting beside him. The wood was peaceful, filled with birdsong and green-tinted light. A squirrel rummaged through the bushes beside him, and the wind flowed gently through the trees. If something didn't happen soon, he was going to go crazy.

He popped a leftover berry in his mouth and shouted: "Hey! I'm still here! I'm not leaving!"

The volume of his voice surprised even him. He could barely remember ever yelling at someone out of anger or frustration.

"Do you hear me?" he called. "I'm staying here! I'm staying here until you help me!"

The squirrel ran off. Otherwise, nothing happened.

Simon clutched his limbs around him and leaned his head back against the tree. It was already cool in the forest, and night would fall in a few hours. Maybe he should catch some sleep now and move around in the dark, for the sake of warmth.

A doll's painted face peeked around the edges of his hut. It wasn't the same one as before; this one had short, curly blond hair, with a sky blue bonnet and matching dress. She had a peaceful smile on her painted face.

"What do you see, my dear? Is it a big squirrel, making nests and noise in my forest?"

Simon scrambled out of his nest of branches to see the white-haired man kneeling down, holding his doll at arm's length. He had no sword with him this time.

Simon bowed in the man's direction. "Please. I'm not going to leave until you teach me."

The man cocked his head, like a curious sparrow. Simon still couldn't see his eyes through his bangs, but he seemed puzzled. "Who is this, my dear?"

"I've been waiting for you to come back for almost three days," Simon said.

"Aaahh, the little mouse. Three days, you say? One does lose track."

"Oh," Simon said. "Well, I—"

"What do you want to learn?"

"I told you. I want to be able to fight Travelers. I need to, to bring the people of my village back."

The white-haired man held up a hand for silence, and with the other, raised the blue-dressed doll up to his ear. "Oh-ho, do you think so? I suppose. But—" he cut off as if interrupted, and his mouth twisted in distaste. "I do think that would be fair. But...No, of course not. Wise as the Maker, bright as the heavens, you are." He began to stroke the doll's blond hair.

It was probably Simon's imagination, but he thought the doll's painted face suddenly looked sick.

The man looked at Simon again, though his eyes were still hidden. "My conscience tells me I must ask you one more thing. Did the kingdom take many slaves from among you?"

Simon sensed an opportunity to win the man's sympathy, so he hurried to answer. "Ten, that we know of."

"Ten," the man sighed. "They brought a spare. Time, it presses on and on. And we can never run from history."

Simon's heart clenched suddenly. "Do you know something?"

The white-haired man shook his head again. "This is not about me, little mouse, but about you. Is there not someone else who can teach you?"

Simon stared firmly at the place on the man's face where he imagined his eyes must be. He tried to keep his gaze steady, to impress on the man the depth of his resolution and dedication. "I don't have any talent. My friend ended up being a Traveler, and I guess he was born to it. I'm not like that. I came to you because I thought…I thought that, since you're not a Traveler, you could teach anyone. But if you think I should study Traveling, I'll do that."

A tiny quirk appeared at the corner of the man's mouth, and he walked into a clearing between several trees.

"You've got one thing right, little mouse, and one thing wrong. Yes, I can teach anyone. Not everyone learns it well, but I can teach them. But what makes you think—" he put a hand out to the side of his body, as if holding an invisible rod— "that I'm not a Traveler?"

The air shimmered in his hand and stretched in a line across the forest, like a seven-foot strip of heat haze. Starting at the far end, the haze stripped away, revealing inch after inch of blade, until finally the man held his absurdly long, slightly curved sword in one hand.

"This is my graceful beauty, Azura." He held the flat of the blade up to his eyes and smiled fondly. "She's got a cruel sense of humor and a nasty temper, but she cares for me like no one else."

He turned his head to Simon. "She's also the key to my Territory. If we wanted, we could take you there. Tell me why we would do that, little mouse."

Hope bubbled up in Simon's chest, but he knew he had to speak swiftly and well or lose his chance. The problem was, he didn't know what would persuade this man. "Overlord Malachi captured people, innocent people, from my home. If you teach me, I'll do what I can to bring them back."

Kai studied him for a moment, bird-like. "But why you? Surely someone else is taking care of this. You are without power, little mouse. Why do you have to do anything at all?"

Simon swallowed and thought carefully before answering. "Everyone believes my friend, the Traveler, will bring them back. But I don't know if he will. And one of the captives is a girl I know. She…saved my life, and she didn't have to. I don't want to just sit back and trust somebody else to help her."

The man did not react for a moment, then he held the blond doll up to his ear. "Mm-hmm? Yes. That's a good point, Caela. What do you think, Azura?" He held his sword up to the other ear. "Oh, of course. Such language."

When he was finished with his bizarre conversation he lowered his arms and shook his head. "We all agree: that was not a good answer."

Simon's heart sank, and he opened his mouth.

"We'll have to help you think of a better one," the man said. He swept his sword in an arc and the air parted, as if he had sliced a hole in the world. Wind poured into the ragged floating gateway, and beyond it, Simon glimpsed the dim interior of a huge, lavish house.

"This," he said, "is called a Gate. It is an opening between our world and a Territory. In this case, mine."

The opening was wider than it was tall, but easily high enough for Simon to walk through. He hesitated, though the white-haired man ducked through without a care.

"Follow us, little mouse," he said. "We'll see if we can give you some teeth."

Simon practically ran through the portal, half eager and half trying to get it over with. "Thank you, sir. You won't regret this."

"You will regret it if you leave your sword," he said. He hadn't even looked to see if Simon was carrying it.

Simon dashed back to his nest, snatched up his sword in its wooden scabbard, and ran back to join the white-haired man.

"My name is Simon, sir."

"The lady in blue is Caela, and you've already met Azura. You can call me Kai."

"Yes, sir."

Together, Simon and Kai walked into the Gate.

The air beyond the Gate was warm and dry, and filled with scents that Simon barely recognized: wood varnish, aged paper, and the dust of years. He and Kai stepped into a richly appointed, luxurious room. Simon had heard about the huge houses of the rich, though he'd never seen anything remotely like this. The room was bigger than four of his houses put together, and filled with furniture carved from a delicately polished red-gold wood. There were three red-cushioned couches, each of which looked big enough to hold three or four people, all arranged around a polished table in the center. The table held a huge book, yellowed pages fluttering in the wind from the Gate behind them, and a collection of crumbling scrolls.

Wooden racks on the walls held a small collection of lightly curved long swords, like Kai's Azura, though each one seemed unique. There were spaces for twelve swords, but only four were occupied.

A series of mirrors stood around the room, and none of them had a single bubble or blemish. Unlike most of the warped or hazy mirrors Simon had seen in his life, these showed Simon perfect reflections of everything in the room. A single tall, gilded lamp in the corner cast a warm light over everything.

"Welcome to Valinhall," Kai said. The Gate closed behind him, and his sword had somehow vanished as he stepped through. Simon was startled to find that it now rested on a wooden rack on the left side of the room.

"How much did this all cost?" Simon asked.

"Everything in this house is part of the Territory. Most of what you see we found right where it is."

Simon set his short sword down so he could pick up one of the scrolls. He squinted at it, trying to read in the dim light. "Are there other houses like this in the Territory?"

Kai chuckled. "My, you are in for a fun time, aren't you? This house isn't *part* of a Territory, this house *is* the Territory. Beginning, middle, end. All of a world is contained within these walls. You will find no doors or windows to the outside here."

Simon glanced around and saw that it was true: the walls held only wood-framed mirrors, reflecting his grimy face. There was only one door, on the opposite wall, and it was halfway open. Beyond it was only a candle-lit hallway surrounded by more doors. Simon had the uneasy sensation that he had been trapped. Kai was the only one who could let him out, by opening another one of those Gates.

Simon shook himself and firmed up his courage. He had come this far. So he couldn't leave by himself; what did that matter? He didn't intend to leave before he was ready, anyway.

"First, little Simon, you smell like mouse droppings and sweat. Let's get you a bath, and then we'll have some rest."

Kai beckoned with one hand and, cradling Caela carefully, walked into the hallway. Simon followed.

"I'm sorry, sir," he said, "but do we have time for that?"

"The little mouse rushes forward to meet the cat. If you want to be a Traveler, it is not the study of an afternoon. It will take you years."

"Years? I don't know how long my friends will live. They might not let them live out the week!"

"I may have some insight into that, and I will share with you on a later day. But don't fret, little mouse. Time is on our side."

Kai's tone made it sound like he had answered the question, though

71

Simon wasn't sure he had. He resolved to bring this question up again soon, when Kai was more willing to talk.

The hallway was longer than Simon had expected, with intricately carved wooden doors every few feet. The doors had odd symbols carved into their centers: large circles, half-circles, and small dots. The door to his left had only one small dot, the door to his right two small dots. As he progressed down the hall, large circles and half-circles appeared in the sequence. Some way to tell the rooms apart? Maybe the phases of the moon?

Finally they reached another open room. It looked much like the entry hall, but this had many doors, each unique. Kai gestured to a circular door made of stone and lined with gold.

A door, lined in gold. What was the point? Why waste the money putting gold on a door, of all things?

"The bath awaits you," Kai said. "I'll go settle Caela among her sisters, and then I will return." Kai gave a cheery wave and then headed back into the hallway. He stopped before he left and added, in a casual voice: "By the way, here's a piece of advice: don't let your guard down."

Then he left. Simon looked around hesitantly for a moment before he stepped through the door to the bath.

The interior resembled a rough, naturally formed cave more than anything built by man. The floor was smooth enough to look lightly polished, but not so slick that Simon thought he might slip. The room was much more brightly lit than the rest of the house, almost as though the noon sun shone directly into the room, although Simon saw no obvious light source. A single mirror took up one wall, large enough to reflect the entire room, and the floor was dominated by a pool in the center of the floor.

The pool was big enough to allow an entire family to swim comfortably, and steam rose lightly from its surface. Soapy lather rested on the water, drifting gently on shallow ripples. He smelled flower-scented soap, the sort his mother always wanted but hadn't been able to afford in years, and the bath looked so inviting that he peeled off his filthy clothes and slid in.

The heat of the water seeped into his exhausted muscles, loosening tightness he hadn't felt. It was like sinking into a soft, warm cushion, and Simon slumped against the edge of the bath. He relaxed as he hadn't for over a week. Had it only been that long? It seemed impossible, but nine days ago he had spent every hour delivering messages, cleaning the tavern, chopping wood, organizing herbs; anything he could use to take care of his mother. It hadn't been a happy life, but it had been comfortable, and it had held memories of brighter times. No one paid Simon any attention, Alin had just been the boy everyone liked instead of their promised savior, and the village had been whole. No one taken away to work as a slave in a far-off city.

Simon had no experience with slaves, but he had heard the stories. Old men forced to work until their hearts gave out, children mauled while caring for dangerous animals, women held captive by lecherous lords and subjected to unnamed horrors. Unbidden, an image rose in Simon's mind: Leah, wearing a steel collar and a shapeless brown sack, back bent under a pack far too heavy for her. She stumbled to her knees, unable to bear the burden, and a huge man in a Damascan uniform was on her immediately. He yelled and raised a whip, making her flinch defensively. But instead of striking her, he seized her by the arm and pulled her into a nearby building, away from the eyes of witnesses. She struggled and screamed for help, but the other slaves kept about their work, afraid to lift their eyes. No one would help her. They had their own worries.

Simon jerked back from the edge of sleep, no longer comfortable enough to relax. How could he? He was here so that he could fight, not to start a new life. It was for that that he had worked his hands until they bled. He scratched absently at one palm. Where blisters had been he felt only calluses, and the wound was barely tender. He probably wouldn't even feel it tomorrow.

Wait. That couldn't be right. He had just injured his hand yesterday; how could it have healed by now? He looked down at his palm and nearly choked: he could actually see the redness and swelling in his hand fading. Dried blood flaked off and dissolved into the water, leaving flesh that visibly softened from angry red to soft pink. At this rate, the wound would be gone without a scar in a matter of minutes.

Simon pressed fingers to his ribs, where bruises had formed after Kai's lesson. They were barely even tender. His feet, cut and sore from all the walking he had endured, felt clean and whole. On an impulse, he ducked his head under the water. The slice along his cheek felt cold, then cool, then the same as any other stretch of skin. He raised a hand to it and felt nothing.

He paddled over to the mirror outside the pool and tilted his head. The cut on his cheek was gone. On top of that, he could never remember being this clean in his life.

Simon's doubts about following a Traveler into his lair began to fade with his wounds. He imagined the fabled Damascan lords might live in a house like this, but he was sure even they didn't have self-heating baths whose waters magically healed wounds. Maybe, if he proved a skilled enough student,

Kai would give him a key to this Territory, and he could enter whenever he wanted. After he rescued the villagers, he could live here, and then do...anything. Anything at all.

If only his mother could see him now.

Simon decided he should get a little closer to the mirror, to take a look at the places where his many small wounds had been healed. He planted his hands on the edge of the pool and pushed, levering his body out of the water.

A claw seized his ankle and jerked him back.

He lost his balance and fell onto his chest, smacking his chin on the marble basin. On instinct Simon kicked backwards, striking something rough and spiny. It felt like kicking a pinecone wrapped in thin leather. The clawed hand yanked on his ankle again, and his chin scraped on the stone as he was pulled deep into the water.

He spun around to get a glimpse of whatever was holding his leg. When he saw it through the murky water, he nearly lost what air he had left. It was an impish creature, about the size of a four- or five-year-old child, but with ridged greenish skin and thorny spikes on the top of its head. Its eyes were red and reflective, its teeth needle-sharp. It gave him a wicked smirk and tugged him down and dragged him farther under the pool.

Simon kicked and strained, trying to reach the glimmering surface, but the imp's arms were stronger than they should have been. He couldn't reach the surface if he tried to swim against the creature's strength.

So he reached toward it instead. The tiny monster's eyes widened in apparent surprise just before his fingers closed around its ridged throat.

Close up, Simon saw the creature in more detail. Its knobby green skin looked to be made out of twisted moss-covered bark. Its sharp fingernails and the spikes on its head looked like rusty nails. It snarled into the water, and Simon saw a mouthful of steel needles instead of teeth.

The water-imp clawed at him, drawing burning slashes down the skin of his wrist, and it twisted until it could sink its fangs into his arms. The pain burned enough that he almost released it, but the water continued to work its magic. Every wound the imp opened sealed itself immediately. Simon was healing faster than the imp could damage him, but his lungs were beginning to burn, and his chest started to convulse as if his body was going to take a breath without asking his consent.

Finally, the imp swam off for the far, unlit corners of the pool. Simon kicked once for the surface, desperately, and sucked in a huge breath of air before he started scrambling for the edge. The suds that covered the surface of the water now seemed like an ominous veil, hiding monsters beneath its surface. He imagined dozens of those things down there, maybe hundreds, and the one he had just driven off was just going for reinforcements.

He had almost reached the edge of the pool when his imagination was proven right. Four pairs of clawed hands pulled him back under.

Simon barely managed to get a breath before he plunged once again under the surface of the water. The four imps, all identical, crawled all over him, inflicting dozens of tiny wounds that healed instantly but burned his skin like a web of thorns.

They were working together to drown him. As panicked as he was, he couldn't shake the image of the four hideous creatures gnawing at his blue, floating corpse. He refused to let that happen. If he drowned, so be it, but he wouldn't let these water-demons get a meal out of it.

He fought desperately, with more savagery than skill, knocking the creatures into the depths, cracking their heads against the side, breaking their spines. Anything he could do to get away.

Simon had barely dealt with those four when something else, not an imp, stirred at the far edge of the pool. Much bigger than the tiny wooden creatures he had seen so far, this shadow wriggled and writhed like a water serpent. But it was at least as thick as his leg.

It squirmed toward him.

Simon leaped out of the pool and ran from the room so fast he barely had time to scoop up his clothes with one hand. He pushed the marble door shut and looked around for a lock. Nothing. He ran out of the room, through the hallway, and didn't stop until he was back in the room with the scrolls, mirrors, and soft furniture. The entry hall, where he and Kai had first entered through the Gate. Nothing had tried to kill him in here last time.

This door did have a lock, so Simon took advantage of it. What was that? Why were there demons in the bathtub? Did Kai know about them? Of course he did, he lived here. Then why were they there? Was it a trap? Were they Kai's pets? Maybe he shouldn't have killed them.

No, that was a stupid thought. Even if it was just a misunderstanding and they had belonged to Kai, Simon had done the man a favor by killing those things. And they weren't the only monsters in the pool; whatever that snake-thing had been, he was glad he hadn't gotten a chance to see it any closer.

He caught a glimpse of himself in the mirror. Shaking, tan skin a shade too pale, covered in rivulets of water and dozens of quickly healing cuts. And also completely naked. He lifted the bundle of clothes in his hand, and for a moment he didn't recognize them.

His outfit had been laundered, pressed, and carefully folded. The shirt and pants were still a plain brown, but they seemed a completely different color now that all the grime had been washed out. The whole outfit smelled of soap and flowers. Someone had even sewn up the rips and tears in his shirt.

Who had done it? And when? Had someone else been in the bathtub? Maybe in this house, clothes magically cleaned and folded themselves. He wouldn't be surprised if they came to life and tried to strangle him.

A shadow flickered in one of the mirrors on the wall, and Simon jerked his head up. Nothing. The mirrors showed an undisturbed room. He glanced all around, but saw nothing out of the ordinary.

A shiver ran over his skin. All the stories he had ever heard about ghosts lurking in old abandoned houses came back to him in full force.

Well, if he was trapped in a haunted house, he might as well be dressed for it. He slipped into his pants, then pulled the shirt over his head. Through the rough fabric, he saw another dark shape flitting through the room. He pulled his shirt down to see it more clearly, but once again nothing.

Maybe, just maybe, he might need to get out of this house.

At that thought, the cold links of a chain pressed against his throat, jerking him backwards.

He barely managed to get a hand between his neck and the chain to allow him enough space to breathe. Someone was pressed up against his back, holding a loop of chain around his neck like a noose.

Simon kicked backwards and pushed his attacker against the wall. It felt like a man—the impact was soft, as if the man was wearing five shirts—but the attacker made no noise. The mirror on the other wall showed a man shrouded in black clothing, hooded, his face totally lost in shadows. He clung to Simon, strangling him with a chain painted black.

Simon's throat felt like it was about to crumple like a bent reed, his vision had begun to blur, and he couldn't get enough leverage to actually hurt the man in black. He needed a weapon, or he was about to die.

His sword. Where had he left his sword?

It had been in his hand when he came with Kai through the Gate, and after that...it hadn't been in the bath with him, had it? If not, the sword must still be in this room.

He shot his eyes from mirror to mirror, trying to keep his goal in mind and not give in to panic. The sword had to be around there somewhere. It had no sheath, so it would gleam...there, in the corner of the mirror in the far side, he saw a silver shine on top of one of the tables. His sword rested on a half-open scroll on a wooden table against the far wall.

Now he had to reach it.

He struggled around for a moment, pulling with both hands and all his weight against the chain. It loosened for a moment as the man of shadows adjusted his balance, and Simon was able to plant one foot against the wall. He pushed, and the two of them stumbled towards the table and the sword. Any other living being would have made some kind of noise, but the man in black remained absolutely silent.

The side of Simon's head smacked against the heavy table leg. Pain bloomed in his skull, and he lost his grip on the chain. It tightened, burning his neck and cutting off his air almost completely.

The world was going gray around him, but he reached for what he thought was the top of the table and fumbled blindly on top of it. Only when something sliced into his fingertips did he realize he had found his sword.

He pulled the weapon off the table and, holding it by the blade in a bleeding hand, thrust the point backwards into the shoulder of the man in black. The attacker flinched and his chain slackened, letting Simon grab the hilt in his other hand and twist around, plunging the sword all the way through the other man's chest.

The man in black shuddered and dropped the chain, falling limp to the ground. Simon's breath wheezed, and his throat felt ruined. Now that he wasn't fighting, his hand burned. It was bleeding so much. He knew that should be alarming, but he couldn't muster up the courage to go back into the bathtub and heal.

The black robes deflated, as though no one had been inside them all along. Simon stared. The inside of the hood began to glow a soft blue-white, the color of moonlight. A ball of that wispy light gathered inside the empty hood and froze for just a second, the dark outfit hanging from the floating ball of light as if from a peg. Then the light swept off, squeezing under the door, dragging the black clothes with it.

"What?" Simon said. He couldn't think of anything better to say, so he said it again. "What? Sweet Maker, what is happening to me?"

Two more dark shapes, identical to the first, appeared from nowhere and closed on Simon. He jumped to his feet, clutching his sword in a hand increasingly slick with blood. Making no sound, the two men brandished black chains.

Simon turned and ran. It seemed the right thing to do.

In the hallway he shouted for Kai, but no one answered. The men in black pursued him, seeming to stroll but steadily eating into his lead. He turned to one of the doors on the side of the hallway, one with a large circle, and tried to open it. Locked. He continued to run, into the room with the gold-edged stone doorway. He hadn't paid much attention to them before, but there were other doors in the walls of this room; he picked one, made of pale wood with a pair of crossed axes carved into its surface, and levered it open.

He had enough time to glimpse a bright room filled with racks of bladed weapons: spears collected in a barrel, swords mounted on the walls, daggers in baskets. Opening the door triggered an odd sound: a soft *snick,* like a pair of scissors cutting through a cloth.

Simon stepped back on instinct, and something whizzed through the air in front of his eyes. A dart buried itself in the wall opposite the door.

Traps. The doors were trapped.

Simon was too scared to weep, but everything was so hopeless he was torn between tears and bitter laughter. He tried the next door, which was trimmed in silver and pressed with the image of a standing knight. It opened onto a dark staircase.

He waited for a moment to see if anything came flying out at him. Nothing did, but he heard a sound like jangling chains at the bottom of the stairs. A hollow wind whispered up from the darkness.

"I wouldn't travel down that stair just yet," Kai said from the hallway. "That door's not quite meant for you."

Simon shut the door and leaned against it, relief draining strength from his muscles. His arms shook, and his sword dropped from bleeding fingers.

"This house is trying to kill me," he said. "It's trying to kill me."

"And failing, so far. That's a good sign." Kai walked into the room, Azura in one hand and a gentle almost-smile on his face. His blade was so long it came close to scraping the far wall. The white-haired swordsman let the sword shimmer and evaporate, leaving Simon to wonder why he had it out in the first place. That was a minor concern, though, compared to what was really on Simon's mind.

"Why is this happening?" Simon asked.

"We should get that hand taken care of."

Simon clenched his bloody fist. "I asked you *why.*"

"You wanted me to teach you what I know. This is how I learned."

Kai gestured around him, at the house in general. "Valinhall tests you. It attacks you. Sometimes it tries to kill you. It teaches you to be on your guard at all times, awake and asleep, and to always keep a weapon close."

"Do you ever get to rest?"

"You learn to sleep with one eye open. After a few years here, you'll react to danger even if you're fast asleep in the heart of an enemy Territory. Assuming you live that long, of course."

"That sounds great. Really. But I told you before, I don't have a few years. I don't even have one year. I might be able to spare a few weeks, but after that—"

"After that?" Kai cut in. "You, a single amateur swordsman, run off to challenge an Overlord of Damasca?"

Simon clutched his bleeding hand to his chest. He didn't respond. There wasn't much he could say.

"Don't worry, little mouse. I told you, didn't I? Time is on our side. How long has it been, do you think, since you entered this house?"

"I don't know. An hour or two?"

"Less than half of one."

Kai must have noticed Simon's look of disbelief, because he smiled and said, "That's time back in our world, of course. Time flows differently in each Territory. A day inside some is two outside; fortunately, Valinhall is the reverse. I will have the time I need to teach you."

It finally struck Simon what he was asking for. How much of his life had he signed away for this project?

"Oh," Simon said. "I see."

Kai's eyes were still hidden, but his face softened into something resembling sympathy. "Last chance, Simon. I can take you back."

It would be easier, certainly. But any other Traveler he found to teach him would be the same; it would take years. If he left, it would be better to give up, to leave everything to Alin and the Travelers from Enosh.

"No. I'm ready." Simon stood as tall as he could and let his firm resolve sound in his voice.

"In that case, let's begin." Kai faced Simon squarely, and Simon tensed his body as he prepared to defend himself. "Today," Kai continued, "we will begin with...lunch."

At that, Kai turned to one of the doors Simon hadn't tried. It bore the image of a flowering tree.

"You must be hungry," Kai said. A breeze flowed through the door, and it smelled sweet and clean. "After you."

Kai could say what he wanted about the whole Territory being inside one house, but this door opened onto a beautiful meadow. The entire room was carpeted in grass, except for a cool, clear stream that cut the field in two. The sky above was a cloudless blue, the sun shone directly overhead, and Simon could probably fit his entire village just into what he could see of the field. A small herd of what looked like oxen ran in the distance, and there were a few different kinds of bushes scattered through the grass, just a little too regular to seem natural. The field was dominated by an enormous tree, the size of an ancient oak, whose limbs were heavy with a dozen different kinds of brightly colored fruits. *Different* fruits, all on one tree.

"I thought you said we couldn't go outside the House," Simon said.

"We're not outside," Kai responded. "Technically." He raised a hand and pointed into the distance, beyond the tree. "What do you see there?"

Simon squinted until he saw something black on the horizon, a rectangular silhouette against the bright blue of the sky. "Is that an outhouse?"

"Not quite. It's a door, leading deeper into the House. We call this room the garden, and it provides most of our food and water while we stay here."

"We?" Simon asked. "Where are the other Valinhall Travelers?"

Kai walked past him instead of answering, and Simon saw that he held Azura casually against one shoulder. Why was he bringing his sword with him to eat?

Kai was obviously focused on something at the base of the tree, and when Simon looked closer he saw what seemed to be a man wrapped in straps of leather.

Simon followed Kai, and as they closed the distance he saw that the man was wrapped in mismatched pieces of leather so that not a patch of skin showed. He was criss-crossed with belts, straps, buckles, and scavenged bits of leather armor. His head was covered in a leather cap, his mouth hidden by a half-mask of dark leather. Most bizarre of all, blades jutted out from his leather sleeves, as though he had lost his hands and had swords grafted onto the stumps.

All in all, he was a disturbing sight.

Two tiny folds of leather over his face flapped up like eyelids, revealing two gleaming yellow gemstones in the place of his eyes. Actual cut gems, where his eyes should be.

Simon began to suspect that this man wasn't human.

A slit opened across the man's face, like the mouth of a leather sack. It took Simon a moment to realize the man was yawning.

"Bloody Maker, that was a good sleep. How long has it been since I seen you, eh? Could be years. That's my time, I suppose, not yours. You spend too much time at the grave, I'd say."

Kai bowed towards the leather man. "It has been too long, Chaka. I'd like you to meet my student."

Chaka cast a quick glance in Simon's direction. Simon felt that he should say something, but nothing appropriate came to mind, so he stayed silent.

"He's a real charmer, isn't he?" Chaka said. Simon winced; he should have spoken up after all.

"He's not here to learn conversation skills," Kai responded.

Chaka snorted, a sound like a leather strap flapping in the wind. "Not from you, right? You lot were all about six hairs short of the bughouse. Speakin' of that, no one's taken a student here before. What's that about?"

Kai angled Azura in front of him. "We're here for lunch, Chaka. Will you let us pass?"

"You know better than that, Kai." Chaka stood, his movements more graceful than Simon would have thought, and crossed his bladed arms in some kind of salute. "You got to earn it, same as always. I don't expect you'll have much trouble, but I can't speak for the boy there. He has a soft look about him."

And what was Simon supposed to say to that?

Kai and Chaka bowed to each other, and then they moved at once. Blades flashed, and the room rang with the sound of steel on steel, but Simon could barely follow the fight.

Kai hardly moved his feet at all, whipping his long sword in great arcs faster than seemed possible for such a heavy length of metal. Chaka dashed and leaped everywhere, his sword-arms blurring, but Azura was always there just in time to deflect a direct hit.

"It's about time," Simon muttered. His heart lifted. This was what he was here for, what he wanted. He had, after all, come to the right place.

The two fighters stopped moving at the same time, facing each other in almost the exact places they had started. A slice of leather drifted to the ground.

"Sweet Maker, you're good. I think you're better now than you were as a boy, and I don't say that often. Good on ya, Kai."

Azura vanished, and Kai bowed to Chaka once again. "You honor me," he said.

"Bleedin' right, I do," Chaka said. Then he sighed and turned to face Simon. "All right, let's see what you got."

"Wait. Me?"

"You gotta fight if you want to eat, kid. Don't worry, I'll make it quick." Chaka crossed his arms and bowed over the blades, like he had done with Kai.

Simon glanced down at his bleeding hand. "I can't hold a sword like this."

"Then stand there and die," Chaka said. His voice was oddly cheery. Simon opened his mouth to protest, but Chaka leaped forward until he was standing inches from Simon's face.

"Ready or not," Chaka said, "here I am." He thrust his right blade forward, and Simon snatched up his own sword in his left hand and knocked Chaka's away. The impact rang up his arm, and almost caused him to drop the weapon.

Chaka's left arm swung in and Simon stumbled backwards, flailing around with his sword and trying to put a little distance between them.

"Grip that sword, you bleedin' moron. You lose hold of it, you're dead."

Simon tightened his grip. He tried a swing at Chaka's head, but the other man caught it casually on one arm. A leather lip twisted into a sneer. "That's not a glass unicorn, princess. Swing it like you mean it."

Chaka raised a boot and kicked. Simon twisted and caught it on his hip, but staggered back a few feet. He moved forward and swung his sword again, but once again Chaka swept it aside with no more effort than Simon would use to dust a shelf. Simon managed to block another strike, but he couldn't keep his balance; he lurched a few feet to his left and almost fell over.

A sword pressed into Simon's neck, and he fell very still. "Pathetic," Chaka said. "Bleedin' *disgusting*. I oughta bleed you right here and save me some time."

Kai's sing-song voice interrupted. "He's mine, not yours, so keep your hands off."

Chaka snorted, but he removed his blade and turned his back to Simon. "I won't kill him, but I'm not passing him either. No food or water for you till you can stand on your own feet."

Chaka walked back to the base of the fruit tree and sat cross-legged on the grass, jeweled eyes locked on Simon.

Kai had plucked a juicy blue fruit, like a blueberry the size of his fist, and was munching on it. Every once in a while he would scoop a bowlful of water from the stream with a wooden bowl and wash down a bite of fruit. He licked his fingers clean with every evidence of enjoyment.

For the first time, Simon really felt like stabbing the man.

His throat burned with thirst, and the only thing he had eaten in over three days was a handful of berries. He tried one last tactic. "How am I supposed to get better if I don't have the strength to move?"

"Are you hungry?" Kai said soothingly. "Here, have some of mine. There, that's good, isn't it?"

Simon stepped forward for a moment before he realized Kai was talking to one of his dolls. He mimed feeding her a piece of fruit, and washed the juice off with a "drink" of water.

Chaka raised a sword in warning. "Take another step there, kid, and I'll be feeding you your own legs."

In the end, Simon went without food again.

Kai accompanied Simon back to the monster-infested pool, where Simon was able to dip his injured hand and heal his wounds without attracting the creatures.

"They only attack," Kai explained, "when you stay long enough and then try to leave. The pool can reverse any kind of injury or illness, even age, to one degree or another. It's the reason why my hair has aged, though my body remains the excellent example of prime manhood that you see before you. But the longer you stay in the pool, the more dangerous it gets."

"You could have told me that before I went in," Simon said.

"That's true, isn't it? How interesting."

Before they left, Simon managed to sneak a drink of the bathwater. It tasted like soap.

CHAPTER 6
SHARP LESSONS

Alin trembled with effort, both hands extended to push against the air as if he were trying to shove over an invisible wagon. He had originally worried about looking ridiculous in front of the crowd—practically every Traveler in Enosh had wanted to come witness his training—but now the strain on his mind left him little room to worry about anything.

Between his outstretched palms, a few gold lights spun in a wide circle. He could dimly sense something beyond, like a fire's heat sensed through the fabric of a tent, but he couldn't quite pierce through.

Grandmaster Naraka cackled with laughter. "Almost there," she said. The Grandmaster had been in charge of teaching Alin since he had first arrived in Enosh, and she was easily the oldest woman he had ever seen. Over one hundred, if the rumors could be believed, and showing every year of it. She was wrinkled, shriveled, and hunched, like a hag out of a children's tale. And he suspected she was blind; he couldn't prove it, but she always wore thick lenses over her eyes, colored a dark red. She called them her "glasses," but they didn't look to be made out of any glass that Alin had ever seen.

"Concentrate!" Grandmaster Naraka barked, all traces of laughter gone from her voice.

Alin focused, reaching his mind out to the warm power he could feel like a tiny sun, burning just out of reach. If only he could stretch, he felt like he could brush the edge...just a little more...

Every other time he had tried to open a Gate to Elysia, it had fallen apart at this point. The golden lights would drift off, he would fall over in exhaustion, and his Territory would remain as distant as ever.

This time, Alin threw all of his focus into one final push against the invisible barrier.

The spinning sparks of light flared and sliced through the world, leaving a shining gold-lined oval doorway hanging in midair. Wind that smelled like flowers, grass, and rain drifted through, clearing out the stuffy air in the hall where Alin stood. And beyond the Gate itself, clearly visible as Alin stared, rested Elysia.

It was a city.

A grassy plain waited close to the Gate, spotted with flowers of white and gold. The field stretched perhaps two hundred paces before it ran against city walls, but like none that Alin had ever seen. The walls of Myria village had been essentially sharpened sticks, bound together by ropes. The walls of Enosh were rough-cut sandstone mortared with clay. But the walls of Elysia...

A vast, curving expanse of pale white stone and pure gold, carved with swirling shapes and patterns that reminded Alin of a rushing river. The wall was broken only by two huge gates, each an intricate work of gold, silver, and a rainbow of precious jewels the size of Alin's head.

While the wall took up most of Alin's vision, it was spectacular enough to blind him to everything else for a moment. Then he looked up.

Over the walls, he could just see the tops of buildings. Most were domed, in gold or copper or silver, but here and there he saw towers and spires in a thousand colors. One tower looked to be made entirely of emerald, though it was crowned in deep purple amethyst.

And the sky behind the city, instead of a comforting blue, was a bright, rich shade of gold, like dawn somehow stretched to last all day.

"Saints above," somebody whispered. Alin could understand the feeling.

Then the gathered Travelers of Enosh burst into applause. That in itself wasn't unusual, since Alin could barely do anything within the walls of Enosh without someone cheering or clapping, but this sounded heartfelt, spontaneous. They had been treated to a vision of rare beauty, and Alin had given it to them.

Alin felt himself grin. On an impulse, he turned and swept a bow to the assembled crowd.

Grandmaster Naraka laughed again, and hobbled over to clap Alin on the shoulder. She had to reach up to do it. "Boy, I never thought I'd live till this day. Well done."

Alin stood, staring into the Elysian Gate. "Is it going to be that hard every time?" Alin asked. Tearing the Gate open had felt like carrying an ox to market on his back.

Adjusting her red glasses, Grandmaster Naraka shook her head. "Not after the first. Now it's just a matter of practice."

Reaching out a hand to the Gate, Alin stretched out the power of Elysia in his mind, intending to close it. "So I just need to close it and try again?"

Naraka snatched his arm in one of her withered claws. "Stop!"

Alin froze, hardly daring to think.

"If we believe the ancient books," Grandmaster Naraka went on, "then you may only open the Gate to Elysia once a day, and only while the sun is in the sky."

"Really? When other Travelers can open their Gates however many times they want to? That doesn't seem fair."

Grandmaster Naraka tilted her red lenses toward him, the corners of her mouth drawn down. "Fair? Each Territory has its own rules and restrictions, and yours are much less burdensome than others. In my own Territory, Naraka, each of our summons costs us in pain. And Endross Travelers must live with the knowledge that a single mistake will destroy them utterly. Do I need to speak to you once again of Elysia's place and purpose?"

"No, Grandmaster," Alin said hurriedly. Naraka could lecture for hours, once she got the bit in her teeth. "I apologize. I only meant—"

"We once only had the Nine Territories, Eliadel," Naraka went on. "But Elysia is the tenth. Why? Why did we need more, when the Territories were already complete?"

"Because—"

"Because men are imperfect!" Naraka finished for him. "They exploit the Territories, compete between them. Elysia exists, *you* exist, to keep the other Territories in line."

"I am honored by the—"

"As a result, you must be stronger than they! You must be more virtuous! You must have a mind and a spirit beyond corruption!"

Alin sighed and gave up. Once again, Grandmaster Naraka explained the philosophy of Elysia, how the Gate would only open once a day so that he could not enter too often and grow too powerful. In all honesty, he didn't really care about the theory behind it, but it would just be easier to wait for Naraka to run out of wind than to stop her.

"...so you should not complain, but rather be thankful for your privilege," Grandmaster Naraka finished.

"I am amazed by your wisdom," Alin said, "as always. But since I can't open another Gate, how do I use this one? I mean, what do I do with it?"

Naraka froze for a moment and then coughed discreetly into one hand, as though he had asked a stupid question and she didn't want to be the one to embarrass him by pointing it out.

"You walk through it, Eliadel." She spoke as if to a child.

"Really? That's it?"

"Why do you think we are called Travelers? Some people believe it is because we can travel from one place to another quickly, but not all Territories are suited for such transport. So why are we all Travelers?"

She paused long enough that Alin began trying to come up with an answer, but she spared him the need by answering her own question. "Because we must Travel through our own Territories, of course. It is the only way for us to grow."

Instead of replying, Alin just nodded and stepped through the Gate.

The air on the other side was pleasantly cool, like a perfect spring day. Alin took a moment to enjoy the weather before he realized that, behind him, the Gate was growing smaller by the second.

Alin cried out in fear and lunged for the portal, but from the other side, Grandmaster Naraka laughed. "Do not worry, Eliadel. You will be able to open a way back."

"I will?" Alin asked, pulling himself up short. The Gate back was now scarcely bigger than his fist.

"Eventually," Naraka responded. "Good luck."

The Gate blinked out, leaving Alin alone in Elysia.

Kai's bedroom matched the rest of the House: huge, expensive, and dimly lit. Most of the room was dominated by a four-poster bed wider than Simon's whole house back in the village, but this wasn't the feature that occupied Simon's attention.

One entire wall was covered in dolls.

Dolls rested on a row of shelves stacked from floor to ceiling. Dozens of dolls, made of carved and polished wood and painted with delicate care. Dolls in green silk, or purple-striped cotton, or brown sackcloth; blond dolls, dark-haired dolls, even dolls with hair the color of flame. Perhaps fifty dolls in total, all carefully arranged on delicately carved wooden shelves, and all staring at the center of the room with their empty eyes.

Simon had wondered if Kai was crazy before, but now he found himself considering that question very carefully.

Kai followed Simon into the room, crooning and caressing a doll in a red dress. His eyes were hidden by his hair, but he had his mouth cocked into a half-crazy smile.

"Sleep now. The day was long, yes? Yes, it was. You'll feel better tucked in with your sisters. All of your sisters."

Simon spoke just to remind the man that he was still there. "These dolls are..." words failed him, but he continued on. "Did you make them yourself?"

"Oh no, no." Kai delicately positioned the doll on the shelf with all the care of a new father placing an infant into a cradle. "They were all over the house when we arrived. Scattered and lonely. But I brought them together, didn't I? What a nice family."

Kai paused as if for a reply, and Simon could have sworn he heard a whisper from the dolls. It was faint enough that, if he were anywhere else, Simon would have thought it was the sound of wind from outside. But this House didn't have an outside, did it?

Kai chuckled and shook his head. "We'll see. He's young yet."

Simon took one careful step back from the shelves.

"Well then, Simon, let's get some sleep. Eventually you'll be able to earn your own bedroom, but you'd have to earn a key. And I don't think the housekeepers would like it too much if you slept in the hall."

"Housekeepers?"

"Right. I think they would kill you. Anyway, I have you a blanket on the floor. Sleep well."

Kai tossed a fluffy red blanket down onto the wooden floor. Simon lay obediently down on the blanket, wrapping it around him like a cocoon. His normal bed at home was nothing more than a mat of reeds and straw—it smelled worse and kept him no warmer than this soft blanket on the floor.

He was all but asleep in seconds. Then he heard a voice whispering next to his ear.

Sweet dreams, said the voice. It sounded like the wind.

Simon's eyes snapped open, but Kai was all the way across the room putting Azura onto a rack above the door. Anyway, it hadn't sounded like his voice. The rest of the room seemed normal, only...

Maybe it was his imagination, but a few of the dolls seemed like they had turned in his direction. Staring with painted eyes.

Suddenly, sleep seemed impossible.

Simon's mother had been haunted by nightmares for years. Sometimes he would wake to her screams; on one memorable occasion, he had woken to find her wielding a knife, thinking he was a stranger who had broken into her hut.

And he couldn't remember the last time he had slept this badly.

Every time he was on the verge of falling asleep, a drifting whisper or a half-heard giggle would bring him back to consciousness. Each time, more of the dolls would be turned to look in his direction.

He tried to trick them, to pretend to sleep and lure them into moving, but he never caught them in motion. Every time he snapped his eyes open, they remained lifeless.

Frightening as it was, that alone wouldn't be so bad. Sometimes he would catch a glimpse of moving shadows out of the corner of his eye, or hear the clink of a chain. He became certain that the room was filled with shadowy creatures like the one that had tried to strangle him earlier. He thought about warning Kai, but the man was sleeping so deeply that he obviously didn't feel himself in any danger. Besides, this was his house. He should be able to handle anything that happened here, right?

Over the bed rose the head and shoulders of a hooded man made of shadows and black cloth. He drew a black chain between two gloved hands and leaned down over Kai's sleeping face.

Simon cried out, but Kai was already moving. He straightened immediately and, in one smooth movement, pulled a dagger from underneath a pillow and plunged it straight into the shadow's heart.

The man dispersed into a cloud of darkness, and Kai fell back onto the bed.

"Wow," Simon said. "That was incredible. Do you—"

He stopped at the sound of light snores. Kai was asleep. He had killed the shadow man in his *sleep*.

So you needed to be at least that alert to survive in this House. Simon felt doomed. He spent the rest of the night huddled against the wall, clutching his sword.

There were no windows, so Simon only knew it was morning when Kai rose from his bed.

He was dressed in only a cloth wrapped around his waist, and his body was covered in long, thin scars. It took Simon a moment to realize that, if the pool in this House could heal, most of Kai's wounds would have left no trace. Only the smallest fraction of his injuries would have left marks, the ones that Kai had been unable or unwilling to heal.

He had hundreds of scars.

"Good morning, little ones," Kai said. "Good morning, Kojina. You look lovely this morning. Good morning, Angeline, and may I compliment your beautiful hair. Good morning, Otoku. Ha! I could say the same to you. Good morning..."

Kai continued to speak, but Simon stopped listening as soon as he realized he was going to address each doll by name. He wondered if Kai had always been like this, or if he had been driven crazy by years of isolation.

Or maybe it was the training that had strained his sanity. That was an uncomfortable thought, but it didn't matter, did it? Even if the training left him old and alone with a creepy obsession over dolls, Simon had no choice but to put up with it. It was that, or wait—helpless and alone—for Alin to do something.

Simon refused to accept that. He wouldn't stand aside this time; win or lose, he was going to make a difference.

"...of course I dreamed of you, Lilia. And now, little mouse, good morning to you."

"Good morning, Kai." His throat was dry and raspy. He hoped that Kai would hear it and offered him something to drink.

"I'm in the mood for some breakfast," Kai said. "How about you?"

When Simon scrambled to stand up, Kai held up a hand. "Don't forget your sword," he said.

Chaka glared at Simon with gleaming yellow eyes as he walked into the garden. "Oh, you're back, boy. I see nothin' ate you in the night."

Simon didn't know what to say, so he laughed nervously. Kai levered Azura off of his shoulder and maneuvered it into place.

"I'll be going first today, Chaka," he said.

Chaka moved forward to face him, and the two met in a clash of steel.

Simon fully intended to watch, but the nights without sleep were catching up to him. He found his eyes drifting to the room around them. The artificial sky spread above them, and Simon even felt a breeze pass over his skin. The huge fruit tree ruffled lightly.

The House may have been deadly, but at least one room was peaceful.

"Good on ya, Kai," Chaka said. "Sharp as ever. Now, boy, think you can keep from shamin' yourself this morning?"

Simon held his sword awkwardly and tried a respectful bow, but had to straighten instantly to avoid Chaka's stab toward his eye.

"Eyes on me, you sod." Chaka's blade came again, and once again Simon felt his hand sting as the sword flew away from him.

"One more time," Simon said, moving to retrieve his sword. But Chaka had other plans; he snarled viciously and lunged forward, pressing a blade against Simon's forehead.

Simon froze. Liquid trickled down his face, and he almost panicked before recognizing it as sweat.

"You think this is a *game*, do ya? You're insultin' me with this garbage. Get out of here before I kill ya." Simon was inches from Chaka's face, and from this distance he could see the blazing light that glowed from within the leather man's yellow eyes.

Simon spoke slowly and carefully, the better to avoid a sword into the brain. "Please, let me try one more time."

Chaka kicked him in the chest and he fell over backwards, choking on air.

"Get out," Chaka said. Then he turned and walked away.

He turned his back on Simon. And Kai just stood there and watched, saying nothing. It was too much. All of the frustration and exhaustion boiled up and over.

Simon gripped his sword so tightly his knuckles burned, and he launched himself at Chaka's back. He swung with his entire body, bringing the sword down at Chaka's neck like an axe at a log.

The leather man didn't turn around. He just raised a hand and caught Simon's blade on his own.

The impact rang up Simon's arms, but he didn't let go. Instead, he screamed wordlessly, pulled his blade back, and stabbed at Chaka's back.

Chaka spun and swiped at Simon's sword. Simon attacked again, pouring all of his frustration into an overhand attack. Chaka blocked it with both his hands crossed into an X.

From behind Chaka, Kai clapped three times. "Tight grip, good stance, strong swing. Looks like he listened after all, leather man."

Chaka snorted and moved out from under Simon's strike. "Barely good enough, if you ask me. Go on, then. Catch a bite."

Simon almost wept in relief. The fruit was delicious, but even more than that was the water. Sweet, cool, refreshing. He drank so much that he almost choked.

Simple as it was, he could never remember such a satisfying meal.

When he was finished, he sprawled on the soft grass and closed his eyes. Maybe he could finally get some sleep.

The toe of a boot nudged his side. "What are you doing, little mouse? We have a long day ahead of us."

Simon groaned, but he didn't want to appear ungrateful this early in his training. Obediently, he sat up.

"Good, good," Kai said. "Now that you're worthy to eat, it's time to begin your training."

"...begin?"

After a few days, Simon had settled in to life in Valinhall.

He was earning meals almost two out of three times now, and had mastered bathing. The imps, it seemed, were easy to slip; it was all about being faster to leave the water than they were in catching you. That, and not staying a long time. Still, he had the habit now of keeping a small dagger tied to his ankle at all times.

His nights were still interrupted halfway through by the shadow-folk, which Kai called the Nye. Nye were exactly as they appeared: humanoids made up of cloth and shadow who tried to strangle outsiders with their chains. They were, also, it turned out, the House's keepers: just as good at laundry and sweeping as they were at choking strangers.

They kept out of sight and left generous hospitality in their wake. They folded clothes, dusted shelves, polished swords; except for the periodic murder attempts, they were perfect hosts. Now that he knew to look for them, Simon was always catching a glimpse of a shadow napping under a table or a cluster of child-sized black robes peering down at him from their perch on a chandelier.

"They don't really mean it, do they?" Simon asked Kai, after a Nye attack interrupted their midday training.

Kai pulled Azura's gleaming length out of one Nye man, who deflated into shadows and blue light, slithering away under the door. "If they wanted to kill you, little mouse, you would not have woken up this morning."

"If they're not going to kill me, then why do they keep trying?"

"You misunderstand me. They *will* kill you. They just don't want to. They think they're helping you by keeping you alert. If you are so defenseless that you can't survive them, well, they've saved you from a worse death."

"How did you find that out?"

Kai shrugged. "Best guess. They're not the most talkative sorts. Now, from the top, and if you keep overextending I might take off a finger!" He sang the last few words, which made them doubly disturbing.

They trained mostly in the huge garden room, whose open skies and grassy fields left plenty of room for swinging a blade as long as Azura. Sometimes Kai showed up with shorter weapons—daggers or a standard infantry sword like Simon's—and they would take the fights into the more cramped corners of the hallway or the bedroom. There were many other rooms into which Kai occasionally vanished, but Simon was never allowed even a glance into a new room. Not that he tried very hard to catch a glimpse; he had a strong suspicion that if Kai considered the other rooms too dangerous, he was probably right.

Sometimes they would train slowly, working on forms for hours at a time. Other days they would only fight for a few minutes and work on building muscles for most of the day. Either way, Simon soon learned that despite the danger it was no worse than a usual day of hard work. After about a week, he even started to enjoy it.

With no sun, he had at first been afraid that he would be unable to tell the time, but once he got used to it he had little trouble figuring out how much time they had spent awake. His body's rhythms adjusted accordingly, and soon his stomach would let him know when mealtime approached.

Kai claimed he could tell time by use of a device called a "clock," but Simon didn't fully trust his master's words or the machine itself. He half-suspected that Kai had been driven insane by the device's non-stop ticking. Besides, he would probably have to fight something to use it.

On the eleventh day since Simon's arrival, Kai cut off training early for the first time.

"Something's bothering you," he said. "Let it out of your mind."

As he caught his breath, Simon rummaged around in his thoughts, trying to figure out what Kai was talking about. "I'm sorry, sir. I was focused on the training."

Kai held Lilia, a doll with a white dress and huge purple eyes, up to his ear. Simon almost thought he heard a whisper, but he shook that idea away. He hoped Kai's madness was not contagious.

"Mmmm. Yes. Lilia thinks that you are unsatisfied."

"I guess, if I had to say something, it's...well, we're Travelers now. And I haven't seen you do anything Traveler-like. You don't throw lightning or anything."

"Oh-ho. Hmmm, hmmm. I think I see what you're getting at." Kai let his sword shimmer and evaporate, then pointed to the door that led to the hallway. "Go back into the hallway and walk into the door marked with a knight. Go inside. When you're finished, come back up and tell me what you've learned."

With that, he sat down on the grass and began to converse more closely with his doll.

Somewhat confused, Simon hesitated a few moments before walking out of the garden, his sword still in his hand.

Last time, Kai had told him to stay away from that door. Maybe he was ready for it now? But as he stood in the doorway gazing down into the shadow-shrouded staircase, he felt a sense of unease. He heard mutters, as of lowered voices and rhythmic clanking, like pots jumbled together in a sack.

He would almost certainly have to fight once he reached the bottom of the stairs. Most likely he would be risking his life. But what choice did he have? An image of Leah in chains rose up in his mind, and he swallowed his fear. If he was going to do anything useful to save his people, he had to move forward. There was no other option.

Simon left the door open for the light and moved slowly down the stairs, sword lifted in front of him. He was halfway down when the sounds from below ceased, as though whoever or whatever waited below had sensed him coming.

"Hello?" Simon called out. "Who's down there?"

There were a few wooden chuckles, and a relaxed voice called up: "Don't worry, kid. We don't bite. Most of us don't have the equipment for it, to tell you the truth."

The casual tone eased Simon's tension somewhat, though he didn't lower his sword. He had learned never to let his guard down too much in this house.

When he finally set his foot down on the floor at the bottom of the stairs, unnatural blue flames ignited all around the room, revealing the basement in a wavy light that made Simon think of being underwater. The flames were cupped by tall black torches, which lined the walls every few feet. The room was a long rectangle that stretched away from him, and the torches were interspersed with bulky black shadows that crouched next to the lights. After a moment, Simon recognized them as suits of armor on pedestals.

At the far end of the room, an obsidian chair gleamed in the blue half-light. No, not a chair; a throne. It was plain and undecorated, but it had a huge sense of weight. On it, with one leg draped casually over one arm, sat a skeleton.

At least, Simon thought it was a skeleton at first. But it shone as if it had been covered in, or made entirely out of, metal. It wore a wide-brimmed hat tilted to cover one eye socket, and the other blazed blue, as if one of the torches that lit the room had been placed within its skull.

The skeleton jumped up from the throne—Simon drew in a breath and took a quick step back—and then it swept a jaunty bow. "Lovely to meet you, kid. The honorable Benson, at your service."

"Uh, my name is Simon. Kai told me to come down here and then come back up, so..."

"Right, then!" Benson clapped his metal hands together with a sound like a handful of knives clashing. "Of course, you'll have to have a go at the boys, first. Just to see if you can handle it, you understand."

"What? Have a go?"

"Sure, yeah. You know. Fighting, and all that. Unless you'd rather dance a turn or two instead."

Benson cackled a laugh. Simon began to dream of a day that Kai would explain something *before* sending him headfirst into it.

From the side, a deep voice, like a bear awakening from hibernation, rumbled forth. "I'd rather dance a turn or two. If you were wondering."

Simon cast his eyes everywhere to try and figure out who was speaking. He spotted a helmet twisting on metal shoulders before he realized that the speaker was one of the suits of armor.

Somehow, it didn't come as much of a surprise.

Benson made a dismissive gesture towards the armor that had moved. "Ah, shut it, Borus. Nobody asked you."

"Who am I fighting, then?" Simon asked. Benson cackled again and waved his arms. With an enormous creak and a jangle of metal, all of the suits of armor stepped forward as one and turned to face him. As if controlled by one mind, they raised enormous weapons—maces, axes, broad cleaver-like swords—up to a ready position.

Simon's hands were moist on his sword, and the temptation to dash back up the stairs was almost too much to take. But he took the fear and shoved it to the back of his mind. His master obviously thought he was ready for this. Kai must have passed this training himself.

Therefore, he would move forward.

He crouched on the balls of his feet, assuming a low ready stance with his sword angled in front of him. The air between him and the iron giants trembled with tension.

"All right," Simon said. "Let's go."

"Dancing?" said Borus.

In the first few moments of the fight, Simon was almost overwhelmed by his own instincts. His mind screamed at him that he was facing two dozen opponents, all much bigger and stronger than he was, and the panic nearly got him killed.

But after the initial fright, as well as a few near misses from shovel-sized axes, he realized that this actually might be easier than winning his supper from Chaka.

The suits of armor and their weapons were too large for the narrow room, and there were so many of them that they crowded each other. He would only face, at most, two at a time, and even those would get in each other's way. One tried an overhand swing with a sword that caught on the decorative spikes covering another's shoulder; the gap that created was more than wide enough to allow Simon to slip under the armor's elbow and thrust his blade into where one of the armor's kidneys would have been.

Or at least, he tried to. The sword screeched and scraped against the armor, but failed to make a dent.

Another swung a mace at his head, and Simon stepped back to avoid it. He would be seriously injured if one of the attacks connected, but they were almost comically slow. As long as he kept moving, he would be in no real danger.

He tried an overhand slash at the helmet, but of course the blow just rebounded off.

"Interesting strategy," Benson said, "attacking the opponent's strong points. I never would have thought of it."

Simon dodged another couple of attacks, then tried what he probably should have done from the beginning. He slipped his sword up under the shoulder of one suit of armor, stabbing it into the weak point under the shoulder joint, where the armor was thin.

The suit shuddered and crashed to the ground, as if the energy animating it had failed.

Benson cackled and crashed his bony hands together again. "Bravo. Twenty-three more to go."

Simon fell into a rhythm, avoiding the slow, heavy attacks and waiting for an opening until he could slide in a single strike. Two more armors went down.

Then he made a mistake.

He stepped in too close as he aimed for underneath an arm, and a heavy iron fist came down on his shoulder. Once. Twice. It felt like his shoulder had shattered like a dropped glass. He took up his sword in his left hand and raised it, but the armor's next blow snapped it in half. A shard from the broken blade flew towards his eye; he flinched, and it slashed across his temple.

He looked up with blurring eyes and saw the fist coming down on his face.

"Stop it, Borus," Benson called out.

The iron gauntlet froze not quite two inches from Simon's forehead.

"I'm glad," Borus rumbled. He pulled his fist back and stood up straighter; all the other suits followed. "Your two-step is good, but your waltz could use a little work."

Simon looked up at him, dazed.

"Honestly," Benson said, "I never know what he's talking about either."

After a quick visit to the imp-infested healing tub, Simon walked back into the garden to see Kai. He rolled his shoulder, trying to work out the stiffness in the newly restored joint.

Kai sat in the grass next to Chaka. His legs were crossed, hands on his knees, head bowed, with Azura resting against his shoulder. His doll Lilia lay in his lap. Next to him, Chaka sat in the exact same pose.

Simon had seen this before. Apparently it was Kai's "meditation position," whatever that meant. Simon supposed he would find out at some point in his training.

"Kai, sir. I've come back."

"And how did it go?" Kai asked. He didn't open his eyes. Or maybe he did; the white hair in his face made it hard to tell.

"I managed to defeat three of the iron armors before I was taken down," Simon said. He supposed that wasn't bad, but of course Kai would have been able to do better.

"I see."

"What was I supposed to learn?"

"If you had learned it," Kai said, "you would know. Try again tomorrow."

Simon held forward the shattered remnants of the weapon he had bought, secondhand, from a desperate merchant's guard. It felt strange, letting the weapon go. "In that case, I'm going to need another sword."

"Then you'll have to go get a spare." He hesitated a moment, then added, "Good luck."

CHAPTER 7
RISKS AND REWARDS

As it turned out, the armory was filled with traps.

Simon recalled his first visit to the armory after opening the door and dodging a dart launched from the opposite wall. This time, another dart followed just as he relaxed and stood up, forcing him to dodge again.

That hadn't happened last time. Someone had to have changed the trap... unless the trap changed itself. That was a depressing thought.

The room was lit by a bright, white light, though Simon could see no source. The light gleamed off weapons of every size, shape, and description, filling the room wall-to-wall and stretching back so that Simon could barely see the far wall. A rack of spears a hundred paces long stood against one wall, arranged from shortest—a spear that was scarcely longer than Simon's forearm—to the longest, which had to be fifteen feet tall and looked as wide around as his neck. Axes of a thousand different shapes stood on individual wooden stands all around the room. Bow staves, some made of horn, some of a dozen different types of wood, and one that looked to be forged entirely of metal, sat in barrels near the door, with coils of bowstring on pegs nearby. Suits of armor—chain, plate, leather, snake scales, animal hides with shaggy fur still attached—were arranged on pedestals against the wall to the right, and Simon made sure not to step too close. They might come to life.

Every step deeper into the armory sprung some new trap. A tripwire he hadn't noticed caused a giant axe to come swinging down for his head. One innocent-looking tile was actually a switch that opened up a chasm in front of him; if he had taken one more step, he would have fallen in. He thought he heard growling from the bottom.

It wasn't nearly as hard as it should have been to build up his courage and keep going. Simon realized some part of him was growing used to constant, unpredictable, mortal danger. He wondered if that was a good thing.

Of course, the rack of swords rested against the back wall, as far as could be from the entrance. It stood right next to the rich wooden door leading into another room, deeper in the House. Simon hesitated, his hand hovering between the hilt of a new sword and the door handle. He had conquered the armory, hadn't he? Surely a peek inside this room wouldn't hurt anything.

He grabbed the door handle and tugged on it, just a little. Nothing happened. The door stayed firmly shut. He pushed, and again the door didn't budge. Maybe he could ask Kai for the key.

Then again, there could be a thousand fiery snakes coiled up just beyond the door, waiting for a single crack so they could spring out and sink their burning fangs into his flesh. In this place it very well could be that, or even something worse. He shook his head to clear it. He really was getting over-confident, if he was trying to recklessly march ahead into an unknown danger. To keep himself distracted, he seized a sword from the rack. This new room could wait until he had conquered all the rooms before it, including the skeleton's basement.

Armed with a new sword, he marched back down to Benson. This time he suffered two fractured shins after defeating only a pair of the black armors. His trip up the stairs and back to the healing bathtub was one of the most agonizing experiences of his life, and he came close to asking Kai to take him back to the real world.

But he didn't.

He settled into a new routine: wake up, challenge Chaka for breakfast, train with Kai all afternoon, then back to the basement before dinner. In time, he grew stronger. Faster. He could swing a sword all day, now, and barely feel it, and he shrugged off minor injuries as unworthy of his attention. Sometimes he could challenge the walking suits of armor twice a day, taking down seven or eight each time before he was defeated.

He was making progress, certainly, but not enough. Not nearly enough. After a month of repeating the same pattern, he cornered Kai after dinner and demanded to know what he was doing wrong.

Kai chuckled. "The little mouse is getting hungry, so he asks why he cannot swallow a tree whole. Like anything else worth doing, it takes time."

He held Otoku in his left hand, and he bent his head closer, listening. He cradled her carefully to avoid wrinkling her red dress.

Otoku whispered in his ear, just on the edge of Simon's hearing, but Simon barely gave it any thought. Amazing what he could get used to, with time.

Kai nodded along with the whispers. "Yes. Good point. Otoku says that there is one rule in this house, above all others: what you want, you must earn."

"But what am I going to earn?" Simon knew his voice was too angry, but he went on. "If I can beat all of the suits of armor, and that skeleton besides, what have I earned? I've just proved that I'm better than they are."

Kai nodded slowly, head tilted like a bird's, and then he rose to his feet.

"You have my apology, little mouse. I have failed you. I have been leading you around by the hand, instead of leaving you to find your own way. And for that I am sorry."

And then he began to walk. Not back, through the bathroom and towards the hallway and the exit, but forward. Into the far door that Simon had never seen open.

"I have earned my way through fourteen rooms of this house," Kai said. "I will make my way through, room by room, at a pace I feel you should be able to manage. If you can find me, then we will travel together. If you do not find me in two weeks, I will consider you dead or a coward. In either case, I will remove you from Valinhall."

"What are you saying?" Simon cried. "You can't just leave me here!"

Kai continued as if he had not spoken, his long-legged strides eating up the grassy plains as Simon hurried to follow. "The door to the library will unlock once you have mastered the skeleton in the basement. I will wait in the library for a time. If you do not catch me there, I will move on."

At the edge of the plains, which dropped off into endless sky, Kai stopped. A door hung at the edge of the grassy plain. It was dark wood, marked with a candle and an open book, but the doorframe stood in emptiness. Surely it just opened up on air.

"You must try harder, Simon," Kai said. "You wanted the fast way? You have it." Then he drew Azura from empty air and swung at Simon's chest.

It wasn't the fastest blow Simon had seen his master deliver, but he was still forced to stumble several steps backward. By the time he caught himself and moved forward, Kai had already vanished through the doorway.

Desperately Simon grabbed the handle and twisted. Nothing. He pulled, pushed, straining against it despite the vertigo that insisted he was about to fall over an endless cliff.

The door was sealed shut. There really would be no appeal to Kai from now on.

He made his way back to the bed in the bedroom even more carefully than usual. He had feared for his life here in the Valinhall House; in fact, hardly a day went by when he wasn't convinced he was going to die. But Kai had always been there, a silent support even when he abandoned Simon to one danger or another. Simon had always had the comforting idea that Kai would only push him into danger that he felt his student could handle.

And now Kai had left him alone. With the traps, the imps, the Nye, and who knew what else? With Kai gone, if Simon failed to beat Chaka too many times in a row, he might really starve to death. He supposed thirst would get him first, actually, unless he could drink his fill from the soapy water of the bathtub, but it hardly mattered. Something was going to kill him.

When Simon reached Kai's sleeping quarters, he curled up on the floor next to the bed and turned his gaze to the wall.

He could stay here. As long as he could beat Chaka two out of three times, he would have all the food and water he needed. The entry room, bedroom, bathroom, and garden were relatively safe, and Simon could just live in this wing until Kai returned. But then he would fail.

He would have let his people down, and he would have left Alin to save their village on his own. But he would also have let Kai down, failed to meet his master's expectation, and that mattered more to Simon than he would have thought.

But how? He wondered. *How am I supposed to just get better all of a sudden?* He supposed that he could just redouble his training, sparring against Chaka and against the black armors in the basement, and steadily learn through effort. But to improve even a little would take time, and somehow Simon doubted that Kai would sit in the library, even assuming it was safe and comfortable, for six months waiting for Simon to improve. Besides, six months here would be three on the outside, and he might not have that long.

"Try harder," Simon muttered. From his position on the floor, he kicked the post of the bed. His toes exploded with pain; he might as well have slammed his bare foot into a tree. The shoes he wore were only thin leather, crafted by the Nye while he slept. He decided not to care about the pain. He didn't care either that kicking a bed was the action of a child.

Anger and frustration boiled up in him, seething underneath his thoughts. He had asked for the training, true, but his abuse had been ridiculous. And now his master abandoned him without even telling him what to do next.

He wanted to vent his emotions somewhere, so he stood up and lifted the mattress with both hands. He tried to flip it, but it was too heavy, and it ended up sliding pathetically to the ground.

That was both unsatisfying and somewhat embarrassing, though no one else was around to see. Fortunately.

He heard the faintest whisper of laughter coming from his left, but he ignored the dolls. Whispering all the time, driving people crazy. What gave them the right? Pulling a knife from a desk next to the bed—Kai always liked to have a weapon close to hand—he threw it at the wall.

Instead of sticking, as he intended, it hit hilt-first and clattered to the floor, doing no damage. The hints laughter from the dolls grew louder.

He grabbed a mirror from the wall and let out a yell of frustration as he slammed it to the ground.

The glass didn't break. He flipped it over and stomped on his reflection a few times. Nothing.

Simon really could hear laughter now, though it sounded distant and somewhat warped, as though coming down a long hallway. His furious anger, matched now by embarrassment, made him want to grab the dolls and smash *them* next. He considered it for a moment, but discarded the idea. Even if the dolls themselves couldn't hurt him—and he wasn't entirely sure that was true—Kai might actually murder him if he found his beloved dolls broken.

Besides, he told himself, they couldn't *really* be laughing at him. Right? He still couldn't make up his mind whether the dolls were somehow magically animated or if his contact with Kai was somehow making him insane.

He sighed and slumped forward, head pressing against the bedpost. His frustration had only grown, but he felt so ridiculous trying to break things that his anger had faded. Still, what was he supposed to do?

He was staring down at his feet, one of which still rested on the unbroken mirror, so he caught a glimpse of a dark hood just an instant before the black chain went around his throat.

Simon's anger flared back to life. He seized the Nye man's wrists, which felt like squeezing a tightly packed bundle of laundry, and heaved it up and over his head. The Nye, lighter than a man of flesh, spun over Simon's head and landed on his feet, though it twisted his arms badly.

Simon kicked the Nye down onto the spilled mattress and picked up his sword, which he had left resting next to his cot. According to Kai, the Nye couldn't really be killed by a sword, and in fact they sought such injuries as badges of honor.

Finally, Simon had an outlet for his frustrations.

The Nye parried Simon's first strike with its chain, and dodged his second. He tried again and again, pouring his frustration into every strike, until he had backed the hooded figure into a corner.

The Nye flipped the short chain like a whip and it crashed into Simon's face, bringing a flair of pain like a hammer blow. But pain was just fuel for Simon's anger now; he grabbed the chain in his left hand. With his right, he skewered the Nye against the wall.

The sword parted flesh that was just layers of black cloth, and pale moonlight flowed like blood. Before Simon's eyes, the Nye began to dissolve into shadow and light, running out the cracks in the bedroom door.

Simon pulled his sword back without surprise; he had seen Nye defeated before. But this time he wasn't satisfied with a shallow victory.

This time he followed the shadow.

The Nye flowed down the hall at the speed of a man running, passing through the hallway and into the round room with all the doors. The basement door, marked with a standing knight, stood to Simon's left, the armory and the garden to the right, and the bathroom in front of him. He tensed, trying to guess which door the Nye would enter.

It spilled into the center of the room and stopped, a pool of silver-blue light and black cloth. Then it began to leak through a rug on the floor.

Simon ran over and pulled away the rug, revealing a trap door. Some people in the village had trap doors built into their roof, but Simon had never seen one go down into the ground. Maybe there was no ground here.

He grabbed a brass ring set into the trap door and pulled, revealing a ladder down into darkness. The Nye immediately braided itself into a rope of light and shadow, swirling down one leg of the ladder like a snake sliding down a tree branch.

Simon hesitated for a moment, fearing to step deeper into an unknown room, but his anger made him stubborn. Someone was going to give him some answers, and if he had his way, it was going to be the Nye.

He slid his sword into his belt, careful not to cut himself, and climbed down the ladder.

The ladder was short, or at least it didn't take him long to reach the floor. The bottom was dimly lit, barely enough for Simon to see, though the floor sounded like wood. This gave him one advantage: he could easily make out the glowing form of the Nye, steadily snaking his way back into the darkness.

Before he could think too much about it, Simon followed.

As his eyes adjusted to the gloom, Simon began to make out his surroundings: he was in a long room that appeared to be filled with junk and furniture, though he could barely see any details in the darkness. Everything had been covered with sheets of black cloth. Some of it drifted slightly as he passed, even pieces that were too far away to be disturbed by the wind of his passage. Simon's fear grew, and he shot a glance back to make sure he could see the glow of the open trap door high in the back of the room. Just in case.

Finally the Nye turned a corner, and Simon found himself facing the one well-lit location in this entire black dungeon: four free-standing paper screens, arranged in a box, standing out from the walls. As though someone had built a room out of paper inside the room. The paper screens were painted with pictures of plants and birds, and they were lit from within by the cheery glow of real candles. After Simon's march through darkness, it looked like sunlight.

There was one door in the paper walls, a sliding door on a wooden frame. It was guarded by two Nye, both with black chains a foot longer than any Simon had ever seen. Both guards were a head taller than Simon, identical except that one had a heavy weight on the end of his chain and the other had his tied into a noose.

Simon attacked immediately, cutting at the neck of the guard on the right. With impressive speed the Nye dropped to a crouch, whipping his chain at Simon's ankles, and his partner flung the noose at Simon's neck. They moved in unison, their empty hoods tracking Simon. Like all the Nye, their movements were both graceful and eerily silent, cloth and shadow brought to life.

Simon's sword, single-edged and curved like Azura but less than half the length, batted the noose away, even as he leaped and twisted to avoid the chain at his ankles. The end of the heavy black chain clipped his foot. It bruised like a hammer through Simon's thin shoes, and he landed awkwardly.

The noose fell next to his shoulder, completely harmless, but the guard holding it flicked his wrist, pulling back and readying another strike. Simon tried to stab at him while he withdrew, but his partner whipped the chain in a defensive circle, forcing Simon to pull his blade back just an inch, buying the Nye with the noose enough time to cast again.

Simon realized then that he would not be able to fight his way past. They were too fast, too skilled, and impossibly coordinated. They fought together like they had done so all their lives, and Simon wasn't good enough to break their formation.

With that knowledge came a cold fear. In his frustration and anger he had almost forgotten his own meager abilities. How long had he been here, after all? A month? More? With no day or night it was hard to tell, but either way, his paltry training counted for nothing in this fight.

His surroundings closed in on him: here he was, deep in a room that Kai had never shown him, about to confront the Nye in their own lair. The Nye could kill him, and if he died here, no one would know it until they found his body. Perhaps they would never know; maybe the Nye would treat his rotting corpse as so much refuse and dispose of it as they cleaned.

The fear made his breath come even faster. He began to fight defensively, backing off instead of testing his opponents. He missed a block, moved a hair too slow to intercept one strike. A chain lash burned his ribs, and pain blossomed inside. Terror had him in his grip now, and he wondered if something inside him had ruptured.

They had steadily pushed him away from the paper screens, so that they had a little room to use their chains. The one with the noose paced in the background, spinning his chain in lazy loops, while his partner stood poised in front, chain held as if ready to throw. Simon felt bile rise in his throat, and his steady grip began to shake.

A harsh, grating whisper came from behind Simon. "So that is all you have? I hoped for more."

Simon spun, spinning his blade in a neck-high arc as he did so. Briefly it occurred to him that the speaker might not be hostile, but that was laughable. Everything in Valinhall was hostile.

The sword whistled through the air, cutting nothing, but Simon completed the turn to face the other two again. He was sure they would have lunged to attack as soon as his attention was directed elsewhere, and his blade came up to deflect a chain. But they had not taken a step forward. In fact, they had each gone down on one knee, black hoods lowered and chains pressed against the hardwood floor.

Simon didn't relax. It could be a trick, or—more disturbing—whoever was behind him could be so deadly that the two Nye had surrendered on sight. He twisted to keep both the Nye in sight and still see the room behind him.

He glanced behind him, just for an instant, and saw nothing in the darkness.

The harsh whisper came again, from so close behind him that Simon imagined he could feel cool breath on his neck. "Where do you look?"

Simon spun around again, sword clutched tightly in shaking hands, and this time he saw the speaker.

It was another of the Nye. But where most of them were identical, distinguishable only by size, this one gave the impression of great age. His outer robe was worn and faded almost to gray, frayed at the edges into tatters of cloth that fluttered when he moved. His sleeves were longer than most, and wide; it looked like there was enough fabric hanging over each of the Nye's hands to sew Simon a new shirt. He kept each hand hidden in the opposite sleeve, and he was hunched over. Simon first thought that he was bowing over his arms and briefly considered a bow in return, but after a moment Simon recognized the look of an old man without a cane. Bent with age, then.

The black hood raised to study Simon, facing him more directly than any of his kind had faced him before, but the deep shadows hiding its face remained solid.

The old Nye drifted forward slowly, as though he had no feet under his robes. "Your master has left you, and you stand alone in a house of shadows." His speech was odd, as if he had learned to speak far away or long ago. "Yet you seek us in the darkness."

"You came to me first," Simon said. He tried to rekindle the spark of his earlier anger, but fear was a cold wind that kept anger from catching.

The old Nye shrugged with one shoulder, and the rustle of cloth was louder than it should have been, as though many layers of clothes had shifted beneath that black cloak. He did not stop moving forward, though his progress was slow. Simon took a hesitant step back.

"We simply test you," the Nye said. "You seek us with rage in your heart, try to find us in our homes." Abruptly the light from the paper screens dimmed, as though a candle within had flickered on the verge of going out. In seconds the room was darker than a moonless night. Terror took control of Simon's limbs, moving him like a puppet, swinging the sword in random defensive arcs. His blow stopped suddenly as his wrist hit something soft but unyielding, like a steel bar wrapped in thick wool. And then total darkness swallowed his vision.

For a wild instant he thought the light had failed entirely, but the truth was almost worse: the old Nye stood a fraction of an inch in front of Simon's face, one hand locking Simon's wrist in place as if it had been rooted in stone. Standing straight, the man of shadows was almost Simon's height, and Simon could smell dust and ash on the cool wind that flowed from its hood. If the Nye had a face, Simon couldn't tell. Perhaps the darkness was his face.

Simon stood frozen, afraid to fight, afraid to back away. The Nye spoke again, and once again it sounded as if his grating whisper came from behind Simon instead of just in front.

"We do not leave our home undefended," he said. "Do not mistake our tests for true attempts on your life. If we should want your life, Simon son of Kalman, it would be ours."

The Nye released him then, but did not move. He stood as if waiting for some response. Simon took a step back, and then, just to be safe, another. A thought struck him.

"My father's name. How did you know my father's name? I never told Kai that."

The old Nye's chuckle sounded like sheets snapping in the wind. "There is little I cannot find out, son of Kalman, if I have a mind to know it. And a reason."

The old Nye hunched over again, folding his arms as if collapsing in on himself. Simon sensed that it was his turn to speak.

"What reason did you have to learn about me?" he asked.

The Nye paused, eyeing Simon, then nodded.

"Come with me," he whispered. "You will learn."

The two Nye guards—Simon had almost forgotten they were there, as the old one spoke—unfolded themselves from the floor at their elder's words and began walking. The elder followed them down one of the hallways.

Confused, not sure what to expect, Simon hurried after.

Facing the shining walls of Elysia, which stretched at least fifteen paces over his head, Alin decided that he should probably try and find his way inside.

He had just begun to walk forward, through the grassy field outside Elysia's walls, when he heard an echoing, powerful noise, like a dog's bark mixed with the ring of a huge bell. He froze in place, trying to look everywhere at once for the source of the noise.

It didn't take him long to find the culprit: a huge white-furred dog, bound in armor that looked like it was made of gold, leaped and bounded to him over the grass. It barked again, with the ear-splitting sound of a pealing bell, and rushed toward him. Even from ten paces away, Alin could see that its eyes were a bright, almost disturbing shade of blue.

Alin backed up, hoping the dog would stop, but it just kept running toward him. He turned to run, but as he did, the dog leaped forward and slammed him to the ground.

After spending several seconds struggling and crying for help, Alin realized that the dog wasn't trying to eat him. It was quite friendly, actually, licking him all over the face and wagging its tail furiously.

He was suddenly very glad that no one had followed him through the Gate.

"You're not dangerous at all, are you?" Alin said, in that voice people always got when they were speaking to dogs. He rubbed the animal's white fur in between its armored plates.

The dog barked in response, and from that distance, the sound nearly burst Alin's ear.

"Okay, let's try and keep you quiet," Alin said. He used a low voice, hoping that would inspire the dog. "What's your name?" Alin asked.

"Keanos," a woman's voice responded. Involuntarily, Alin's head jerked back in surprise. He glanced around from his position lying on the grass, but saw no one else.

"Are you talking?" Alin said to the dog.

"Yes," the voice responded.

How was that possible? Sure, this was a Territory, where all sorts of magical things were supposed to happen, but the dog's lips weren't even moving.

"Huh." Alin took a discreet glance between the dog's legs. "I, uh, thought you were a male."

A woman leaned over him, above the dog standing on his chest. Bright yellow hair fell to brush his face.

She wore a huge grin. "Did you think the dog was talking?" she asked.

Alin scrambled out from under the gold-armored animal so fast he almost burned himself on the grass. "I'm sorry," he said hurriedly, trying to brush off his clothes. "I didn't know anyone else was here."

She laughed, and Alin got a better look at her. She was maybe a few years older than he, pretty in an innocent sort of way. She wore a long white dress, belted in the middle with a gold-colored sash, and her eyes were gold. Gold. Not hazel or a shade of brown or any color he'd ever seen before, but a metallic gold that seemed to shine in the light.

That shocked Alin more than it probably should have. *Remember where you are,* he reminded himself.

"I am Alin, son of Torin," he said politely. "And your name was...Keanos?"

The woman chuckled again, and—to Alin's brief shock—levitated a few inches above the ground. "No, the dog's name is Keanos."

Keanos let out another deafening bark.

"My name is Rhalia." She floated up until she stood on the air five feet above the ground, and swept him an elegant bow.

Alin glanced away, worried that he might accidentally see up her dress. More honestly, he worried that she might *think* he was trying to see up her dress. "Uh, nice to meet you, Rhalia."

"You're a Traveler, right?" Rhalia asked, settling herself down to a more reasonable level. "Great! Then let's Travel. Do you know how Traveling works?"

"Not...exactly," Alin admitted.

"Okay, no problem. Here it is: you explore your Territory. The closer your bond to something, the easier you'll be able to summon it. But thinking people need to give you their consent, and animals need to obey you, either out of fear or loyalty. Isn't that right, Keanos?"

Keanos barked again, the sound echoing like bells off of Elysia's walls.

"And that's it!" Rhalia said, flourishing one arm. "That's Traveling. I like your hair. It looks like mine, only darker."

"Thank you," Alin said. He got the feeling she was vastly oversimplifying Traveling. For one thing, she made it sound safe.

"Now, let's go!" Rhalia said. She flew toward the city gates, her feet barely skimming the tips of the grass. Alin found that a little disorienting, but he hurried after her anyway.

If she was going to teach him to Travel, he'd do whatever he needed. And she sure wouldn't tell him anything more if he just stood around and watched her fly off.

Rhalia stopped in front of the shining gates, hovering next to a silver-set emerald the size of her head. "After you!" she said happily.

Surely there was supposed to be more to it than this. Wasn't she going to prepare him, teach him what to expect?

But, as Grandmaster Naraka had already told him, the only way to become a Traveler was to Travel. And he had a beautiful, shining city just waiting for him, ready to be explored.

Steadying his shaky nerves, Alin placed both hands against the gates of Elysia. His right hand rested on gold, his left hand on silver. Part of him realized that if he could come away with only a fraction of the wealth he saw here, he could buy the whole city of Enosh, with enough left over for Myria.

Alin stored that thought for later and pushed on the gates of Elysia.

The gates opened much easier than the Gate had earlier, swinging open on silent, well-oiled hinges.

Inside was a short tunnel of white stone, most likely leading all the way through the thick walls. He could be sure, because it twisted at enough of an angle to keep him from seeing the end, but the walls and floor were solid white, polished to a mirror finish. The hallway was lit by what seemed to be gold-framed torches, but instead of the rough orange of a natural fire, these blazed like golden stars. As a result of the unnatural light, the hallway sparkled as if it had been piled with gold coins.

Now *this* was Traveling. He could never have seen a sight like this back in the real world.

Alin started to walk forward, almost blinded by the sparkling lights of the hallway, before he noticed a small box of pure gold lying on the floor. The box was large enough to make a fine doghouse for Keanos, and carved all over with whirling symbols and decorations that made no sense to Alin. It sat on the ground just inside of the gates.

Alin looked at it curiously for a moment, trying to figure out what the box was doing there. Was it some kind of treasure chest? Should he open it?

"Duck!" Rhalia called.

The lid of the golden box popped open, and Alin threw himself to one side.

Just in time.

A thousand glowing golden arrows burst from the box, shooting through the open gates as if fired from a legion of bowmen. If Alin had remained standing, they would have certainly shredded him like knives through cheesecloth.

Alin hugged the ground for almost a full minute after the flood of arrows had stopped, shaking against the cold stone floor between the gates. Was Rhalia trying to get him killed?

"I thought you said it was safe!" Alin said. Fear made his voice several shades higher than normal.

Rhalia floated over to the open box and did a little pirouette on top of it. "Safe? I don't think I said that. It's pretty dangerous here."

Alin nearly choked. "Then why didn't you *tell* me?"

"I've got some bad news for you, Alin," Rhalia said. "None of the Territories are safe. You want to Travel, you're going to have to risk it."

He stayed on the floor, thinking. He wasn't exactly thrilled by the prospect of danger, but then again, he had seen what Travelers could do. If he only had to take a few risks for that kind of power, that was a cheap price.

Still, he would either have to get Rhalia talking or else find a more reliable guide. He couldn't risk running into a wall of arrows one more time.

Climbing to his feet, Alin brushed his clothes off again. They were gaining quite a collection of stains. "So what do I do with that?" he asked, gesturing to the box.

Rhalia smiled innocently. "Who knows? You might try and learn to summon it."

"Really?" Alin perked up at the thought. The ability to call up a volley of golden arrows out of nowhere sounded like the kind of thing Travelers were supposed to be able to do. "How do I do that?"

The golden-haired woman waved his question away. "I'll teach you eventually, but there are more important things to see to. The box is just one little thing, just something to help you out if you need it. There are far more impressive powers in Elysia. Like Keanos, here."

The dog let out another ringing bark.

"And you?" Alin asked. "What if I summoned you?"

"Oh yeah, that could be fun!" Rhalia spun a lazy backflip in the air over Alin's head. "I haven't been to the outside world in ages and *ages!*" Then she drifted around to face Alin and shrugged. "But I can't help you much, I don't think. I can't fight. I'm just supposed to be your guide around the city. Test you and see if you're ready, that sort of thing."

"Test me?" Alin asked. He didn't much like the sound of that, especially not after he had just been attacked by a deadly arrow-trap. He edged a little farther from the open box.

"Yeah!" Rhalia responded cheerily. She twirled in place, letting her white dress spin out. All of her motion was starting to make Alin dizzy. "Every Territory does that, in one way or another. You've got to prove you're worth it."

"So what do you test?" Alin asked.

"Your virtues," Rhalia responded. She held out her hand, and a golden orb—like the one Alin had thrown at Cormac—appeared in her palm. She tossed it up into the sky, where it streaked away like a shooting star.

"Here, try one of those."

Alin called a ball of golden light and threw it into the sky. His power felt easier to call here, somehow closer. Well, he supposed it made sense; he was calling power from Elysia, after all. It stood to reason that it would be easier to do while standing in Elysia itself.

"Well done!" Rhalia said. "That gold light is the reward for valor. You have to be really courageous to call *that* from the City. Did you risk your life to defend somebody else?"

Alin stood a little straighter, pride filling him, and nodded. He had stood up against the Damascan Traveler because no one else would or could, but he had been terrified. It was nice to hear someone tell him he had been courageous.

"Then you're well on your way!" Rhalia said cheerily. "Selflessness is the key to most Elysian virtues. It'll take you far."

"Most?" Alin asked, suddenly eager. "There are others?"

Suddenly Rhalia's golden eyes were inches from Alin's own. He stepped back, but she just drifted after him. "How patient are you?" she asked.

"What?" Alin responded.

She didn't say anything, just floated in his face.

Seconds passed. She said nothing. Was she waiting on him?

"I guess I'm—"

"Not very patient," Rhalia said with a sigh. Then she poked him in the ribs. Hard.

"Ouch," Alin said, rubbing his ribs. "What was that—"

She poked him again, harder.

"Stop it!"

Rhalia poked him again, and Alin pushed her hand away.

"Will you stop that!" Alin demanded.

Rhalia sighed and drifted away as if carried off by a gentle wind. "You should keep a lid on that temper, you know. It'll give you wrinkles."

"Wait...are you testing me? Right now? Are these the tests?"

Rhalia held up both hands and moved them up and down, as though weighing something. "They could be. It's more like...if you prove yourself worthy anywhere, you've been tested. But let's talk about that later!"

She floated over and grabbed his hand, pulling him toward the gates of Elysia. "For now, since you've earned the gold, you're allowed inside the gold section of the city. It's amazing! You're going to love it!"

Alin followed along, letting her pull him inside the shining gates. "Are there going to be more traps in here?"

Rhalia laughed. "Who knows? But I promise, this will be good for you."

He walked forward, taking in the wonders of Elysia with half a mind. But the other half was already imagining how he could put his powers to work, and what wonders still awaited him inside. More than anything he'd ever dreamed of before, that was for sure.

What would Leah say if she could see him now?

CHAPTER 8
DEALS AND DARKNESS

After a few moments of walking in silence, Simon decided to risk a question. "You know me, but I don't know you. What is your name?" He almost added "sir," but he still wasn't quite sure the Nye had males and females. He wasn't sure he wanted to find out, either.

"I am the Eldest of my kind," the hunched Nye said, in a voice like a death rattle. "That is my title, and now my name. Eldest I am, and Eldest I am called, until my life leaves me and another takes up the title." The Eldest flowed forward as he spoke, speaking as if in meditation but setting a pace that Simon had to jog to match. The other two Nye took strides just as if there were actually men inside those black wrappings.

Simon pulled himself up the ladder as soon as he reached it, the light at the top giving him more relief than he would have expected. The Nye stood at the bottom of the ladder, and Simon assumed they would climb up after him.

Then he passed through the trap door at the top and into the circular room above. The Eldest and his two attendants stood above, staring down at him.

Simon glanced into the hole, then back up.

"That's just frightening," he said.

The Eldest ignored him, but began walking into the hallway. "What has Kai told you of our history?"

Simon scurried after the Nye. "You mean the history of the House? Not much. Nothing, really."

"For generations beyond remembering, Valinhall has been as it is: separate. Alone. Its own world. Legends say that, in a time before, we were more than we are. We had cities, trees, a sun. Like your own world. But that world was broken, this House one of the shards. The shard drifted into the nothing beyond all worlds, and as it drifted, faded. Became weaker. This I myself watched happen, but we could do nothing. For many long years, we did nothing but watch."

The Eldest stared into the distance as though staring back into an age long past. Simon got the impression that when the Eldest said "many long years," he meant many years indeed. Centuries may have passed as the Territory fell into decline.

"Then the Wanderer came," the Nye Eldest said. His scratchy voice held a note of awe. "I was in my prime then, and I was there to witness his arrival. He fell in the entry hall with a flash of light and a great roar; not as if he came willingly, but as if he was cast here from another place. He stayed long with us. Over time, he mastered many of the first rooms and ventured deep into the House, where even we of the Nye do not go. Valinhall's powers are too strange and unshaped in its far reaches, and not even the boldest of the Nye dare to venture too deep. But the Wanderer did.

"He gathered much power and knowledge, and gained the respect of many of the House's inhabitants. It would not be wrong to say that he ruled the House during that time. He brought to us a life that we had long lacked, and just as important, he gave us a name."

The Eldest stopped as they stepped into the entry hall, with its mirrors and couches. And the wooden sword racks on the wall, three of them holding long, slightly curved blades. "Among men, the Wanderer was known as Valin. When he claimed this House as his own, he gave it a name: Valin's Hall. Valinhall. But he was not satisfied. Using the books collected here, along with his own knowledge, he fashioned a key to open a Gate between his world—your world—and this one."

The Eldest sighed. "We tried to stop him from leaving. I tried, and many others tried with more power and skill than I, but nothing worked. He talked or dodged or cut his way through and returned to his own world. We thought we were doomed to fade once more.

Then, only a few short years later, he returned. This time, he brought twelve young humans with him. He would train them in the powers of this Territory, he said. He wanted to make them into a true force. An army of dragons, he called them. And to each Dragon he gave a Fang."

The Eldest sighed in remembrance, and he lifted a shrouded hand up to the swords on the wall. That was why they were in the entry hall, Simon realized: because the unused swords were stored here.

"So these swords..." Simon began, but he trailed off, not sure how to continue.

"They are keys to the House, forged by the Wanderer himself and presented to the twelve original soldiers of the Dragon Army. Kai was one of them."

In their wooden racks—two rows of six, hung on each wall—the blades almost looked lonely. Of the twelve racks, only three were filled. With Azura, that meant only four of the swords remained in Valinhall. Simon wasn't sure why that was significant, but he sensed that the missing swords struck near the core of the Eldest's story.

And this gave Simon the answer to another question he had buried since

Kai agreed to train him. Twelve, plus this Wanderer. That meant that of the twelve other Valinhall Travelers besides Kai, one of them had saved his life on a rainy day over ten years earlier.

Simon tucked that information away for future use.

"So what did this...'Dragon Army' do?" Simon asked.

"That is Kai's story to tell you, if he wishes," the Nye responded. "I can only tell you mine." He let his shrouded hand rest on the back of a cloth-wrapped hilt. "And I tell you, we thought we were restored when the Wanderer arrived. But it was *nothing* compared to what we gained when twelve young, healthy humans stayed and trained here. Called this place their home. The whole Territory sang with life, as it had not in my whole memory or the memories of my fathers."

The Nye Eldest's black hood swiveled to fix Simon with a stare. "Now, the Dragon Army is broken and scattered. Only four of the thirteen swords remain in use. The others are lost in your world, or are deliberately sealed to keep them from returning here."

He returned his hands to each resting in the opposite sleeve, and he remained hunched over. But when he spoke, it sounded like a vicious threat. "We will not fade once again, Simon son of Kalman. We will not. Our power is declining, but now that we have had a taste of life, we will not give it up."

Out of the corner of his eye, Simon noticed the two Nye guards slipping up behind him to take a stance at either shoulder. The Eldest stood in front of him, the only exit behind. Simon's hand tightened on the hilt of his sword, in the sheath at his belt. If they meant to force something from him, he might have to fight his way clear.

From behind him, cloth rustled and chains clinked softly. He knew he did not have much chance. For the second time that day, Simon grew certain that he was going to die.

He was almost used to the feeling by now.

"I would make a pact with you, son of Kalman," the Eldest said. "You seek the powers of this house. Well, I say to you that the House of Valinhall has many gifts, some of which are mine to pass on."

Hope rose in Simon's chest, though sweat condensed on the grip of his sword. It was possible, just barely, that he might be able to walk away from this with the very thing he wanted.

"I will give you some of the gifts you seek. More, I will give you the chance to earn one of the Dragon's Fangs, that you may call upon Valinhall's power in the outside world."

"You know, my father had a saying," Simon said. "The most beautiful gift is the one that hides a trap. What do you want from me, Eldest?" Defying the leader of the Nye terrified him, but he thought it was better to appear strong. Even if it was just a front.

The Eldest's voice scraped like flint on gravel, but it was firm. "I ask for you to restore the power of my home. The lost keys—the eight missing Dragon's Fangs—must be returned, but that is not the last of it. This House needs students. Perhaps even objects of power collected from other Territories." The Eldest waved a black-sleeved arm dismissively, as if to say that was a matter for another time.

"I will not tell you lies: this task will last for the rest of your life. But what does that concern you? I will lead you to power, and you may use it however you wish, so long as I gain what I want. We would gain power for our people, son of Kalman. And once you are a Traveler of Valinhall, our power is your own."

Think it through, Simon told himself. The Nye didn't care what happened to Simon, he was sure, so long as the Territory ended up the richer. The deal looked good on the surface, but what were the hazards? There was no such thing as a free deal; Simon had learned that early on when trying to trade for his mother's drink and herbs. There had to be some hook to go with the bait.

The problem was that he had no way to see it. He simply didn't know enough. If Kai were around, he would have asked, but his mentor had left him to fend for himself. Speaking of Kai, though...

"Have you offered Kai this deal?" Simon asked.

"Of course," the Eldest rasped. "As one of the last loyal members of the Dragon Army, he was our best hope for restoration. But Kai does not seek power. He fears it, as the candle's wick fears the flame."

So Kai had turned the Eldest down. And Kai had lived in this Territory practically his whole life. If he had not accepted the deal, then Simon probably shouldn't either.

The Eldest appeared to have seen the decision in Simon's face, because he casually said, "One more thing, of course. If you refuse me now, you will have rejected the friendship of the Nye. You are still a guest of this House, so we will not kill you outright, but you will have no friends among us."

Simon considered that, but it didn't seem too bad. Not much worse than what he had lived through already. Still, he could always accept and then break his agreement. The Nye surely had little or no power in the world outside Valinhall.

"Then again, if you accept my deal and then betray us..." The Eldest spread his sleeves out in a shrug. "You will wish for a merciful death. So, son of Kalman, do you want me for a friend?"

Simon heard the rattle of chains again behind him, and did not need to turn around to know that the two taller Nye were readying their weapons. Without thought, he pulled his sword an inch out of its scabbard. His head whirled with ideas, but his thoughts were clouded by fear. Any moment he expected to feel a cold length of black chain around his neck once more.

He was sure there was some danger he couldn't see, and perhaps Kai would tell him not to do this. But he was determined to do whatever it took to personally bring the people of Myria home.

Leah. What would she say, when she saw him free her with the power of a Traveler?

"Give me your power, Eldest," Simon said. "I accept your deal."

The two guards behind him went down to one knee again, like they had when the Eldest had first appeared. Simon heard a rush through the House, as if Valinhall itself had let out a great breath.

The Nye Eldest's face remained shrouded, of course, but Simon got the impression that he smiled. "I am gladdened. Since you have made the right choice, I will give you the gift I promised."

The Eldest unfolded his arms and held one out toward Simon. From the end of the sleeve stuck out a black wooden box. Simon took it—it was about the size of his two hands together, but suspiciously light—and opened it. It was empty.

"The Nye are not now what we once were," the Eldest said, "but we have some powers. The grace to move swiftly, to walk unseen, to run lightly. Let us show you the power of Valinhall."

And a blue-white cloud, like a swirl of moonlit smoke, poured from the Eldest's hood and pooled in the center of the wooden box. Simon started and almost dropped the box in his shock, but he managed to keep his grip. The dark wood of the box was now lit by a cloud of dim blue-white light that darted around like a fish trying to escape a pond.

From either side of him, two other flows of light joined the first, startling Simon as they drifted into view. The other two Nye had joined their power with the Eldest's, and now it was though he held a box full of bright, vivid moonlight.

"Breathe it in, son of Kalman," the Nye Eldest said softly. "This is the core of what makes the Nye. Our essence." He sounded out of breath, as though producing the light had taken something from him.

Before he could think too much about it, Simon inhaled. The pale light rose from the box and shot toward his face. He flinched backward instinctively, but the light followed, pouring into his mouth and nostrils, filling his head with icy cold, expanding as it flowed down his throat, into his lungs. His lungs felt like they were filled to bursting with fresh, cold air. Then the feeling dissipated into his flesh, until everything from the depths of his chest to the tips of his fingers felt chilled from the inside out.

He didn't feel any more powerful, but the cold...surely something was different. The Eldest said something in his soft, rustling language. He said it very slowly for some reason, drawing each hissing word out. Maybe that was just how the language was spoken. Simon was about to ask him to translate when the two Nye guards behind him jumped to their feet and attacked. Slowly. Very slowly.

Simon slipped to one side and his body moved as if it weighed nothing, as if it moved at the speed of his thought without bothering with muscles and bone. A chain whipped through the air where his head had been, but he was already gone. The other Nye sent a punch at Simon's face, and he moved his head a fraction to the right. Again, his body responded almost before he thought about it, and the fist barely scraped his ear on the way past.

Almost playfully, Simon slipped a foot behind one of the Nye's and kicked. The cloth man fell on his back, but his partner whipped a noose at Simon's face. It looked as if the chain was being hurled through deep water instead of empty air.

Simon ducked under the chain and launched himself forward. Before he reached the Nye his sword was out, flowing, flashing with liquid speed. The Nye fell to pieces, then dissolved into shadow. The second scrambled to his feet, but Simon planted a sword straight through his chest and into the floorboards. He, too, fell apart.

It was as though Simon's body weighed nothing. He swung his sword in a complex pattern that Kai had taught him, and executed it in a fraction of a second. The maneuver was so smooth it was like watching Kai himself.

"Incredible," Simon breathed. He couldn't hide his excitement as he turned to the Nye Eldest. "This is incredible. With this, I could have saved my village all by myself. Is this why people are so afraid of Travelers?"

The Eldest chuckled. "This is not the tenth part of what a real Traveler is capable of. Not the hundredth part. But you have begun to discover what separates Valinhall from the other Territories."

Simon was still wrestling with the scope of a Traveler's powers—*Not the hundredth part?*—but he wasn't sure he had grasped what the Eldest was telling him. "And what is that?" he asked.

"A Traveler of Helgard or Ornheim, or any of the other Territories you humans use, summons things that will help him destroy his enemies. He will call up a vicious beast, or a weapon, or some blast of ice or flame. For the most part, a Valinhall Traveler does not do those things.

You will not summon powers outside of yourself, so that they may defeat your opponents. No. You will summon into yourself the power to win your own battles. That is what separates Valinhall from the other Territories, and the Dragon Army from other Travelers."

The cold had begun to bleed from Simon's flesh, and it was as though his bones were suddenly made out of stone. He felt heavy and slow. "It's fading," he said. The Eldest nodded.

"All powers here are temporary. You can call our speed into yourself, but not permanently. Everything lasts for its time, and then fades. With practice it will last longer, but never forever."

"So what now?" Simon asked.

"Now? Unless I am wrong, I think you have an appointment with a skeleton."

Simon smiled and headed for the basement. He kept his sword bared. At last, he was moving forward.

CHAPTER 9
ANOTHER TEST

The Nye's essence didn't make him any more skillful, Simon soon learned: any of the moves he had failed before were still beyond him now. And it didn't make him stronger. But when its chill seeped into his flesh, he was filled with a speed and grace that more than made up for his other deficiencies. Behind him, in the long blue-lit basement of Valinhall, crumpled heaps of armor and shattered metal marked where twenty-three suits of black armor had fallen before him in a matter of moments.

In one smooth movement, he pulled his sword out of the twenty-fourth armor's shoulder joint. As the armor collapsed to its knees, it mumbled, "Such a lively dancer..." Then it clattered to the floor. To Simon's enhanced senses, it looked as if he were sinking through invisible jelly.

Lounging on his dark throne, Benson cackled and clapped his silver hands together with the ring of steel on steel. "Very good, Borus, very good. Don't worry about them, kid; they'll pull themselves together later. Now," the skeleton leaped to his feet, "I think it's my turn." He snatched the hat off his head and swept into an elegant bow. "May I have this dance?"

"If you think you can handle it," Simon said. He found himself grinning. For the first time since he entered the House, he actually looked forward to a fight for its own sake.

Without another word, Benson grabbed one of the huge double-bladed axes from the floor and dashed at Simon. The seven-foot-tall suits of armor had wielded the battle-axe in both hands, but Benson held it easily in one, as if it did not weigh as much as two grown men. He flicked the axe lightly at Simon's side, but Simon was sure it had enough force to cleave stone.

But it would have to be faster to catch Simon, fueled as he was by the Nye's essence. He ducked under the strike with a speed and ease that felt impossible, then launched an attack of his own at the skeleton's ribs.

As he struck, the chill leeched from his flesh. The speed of the Nye left him.

Exhilaration died, replaced by panic. His strike slipped through Benson's ribcage and bit only air.

"Almost tickled me there," the skeleton said, and planted a bare steel-boned foot on Simon's chest. Before Simon could react, Benson kicked, pushing Simon backwards.

No, not pushed. Launched. The kick had such strength behind it that Simon was taken off his feet, hurled backwards halfway across the room. He cleared several piles of now-lifeless black armor and felt his back smack into something cold, smooth, and only slightly more yielding than the stone floor. His skull cracked against a solid surface, and for a moment his world was only darkness and flashing pain.

When his vision cleared he lurched drunkenly to his feet, trying to hold his sword steady. Benson was advancing across the chamber, walking as if in no great hurry towards where Simon stood.

"The one you landed on is a friend of mine," Benson said. He held his battle-axe lightly against his shoulder, like a woman holding a parasol. He even gave it a little twirl. "He's always real cranky when he has to pull himself together. When you try again tomorrow, he'll do his best to give you a good thrashing."

"Not...tomorrow," Simon said, trying to pull words from somewhere in his throbbing head. "This is the last time."

"Maybe when you were zipping around like one of them black robes, sure, you had a shot. But it looks like you've run short."

The essence, Simon thought. He reached out for the power, trying to call it back, but suddenly Benson was right in front of him, axe descending like the final judgment of an executioner.

Simon threw himself out of the way a half-second away from being split apart.

"You think I'm going to let you call some more, boy?" Benson tried to lever his axe up off of the floor, but it got caught on something, delaying him an instant. In desperation, Simon called the Nye's essence, straining to pull just a little more speed. His power was far from recovered, but a wisp of essence rose up inside him, like a tiny shard of cloud. It lent him a tiny pulse of speed, maybe enough for a few seconds. Cold infused him, and his step now felt less like stumbling and more like stalking.

"I guess you will," Simon said, and then he swung his blade.

It was all over but the details. The axe raced through the air in arcs that Simon would have barely been able to follow before, but now stood out like they were written in the air. Each strike was dodged or redirected. Benson couldn't hit him, he was sure, but his own attacks struck sparks when they made contact with Benson's metal bones. Simon could hit, but he couldn't inflict any real damage. And his time was running out.

So he slipped aside from one overhand strike and put his open palm over

Benson's face, tucking his own foot behind the skeleton's. Then he pushed. Benson only stumbled, and would have caught himself, but the great weight of the axe pulled him to the ground.

His fall was deafening, like a rack of spears clashing to a stone floor. His hat rolled across the floor as Simon stood over him, pointing a sword at the skeleton's steel skull. The Nye essence leeched away, and he scrambled to hold just a little inside.

Benson showed his palms in surrender. "Easy, boy, easy. That's my loss."

Simon relaxed, letting the power go. He turned and scanned the basement. The armors he had dismantled were already pulling themselves back together and shambling over to their stands. He had tried for weeks to clear the basement, and now that he had done it, he found it satisfying. But not enough.

Not nearly enough.

"Will the door to the library be open now?" Simon asked. He had already begun to walk towards the entrance.

"I'd be very much surprised if it wasn't," Benson's voice said from behind him. "But here, now. You've forgotten the most important part."

Simon turned, wary of a trick, and was almost hit in the head by something the skeleton had tossed at him. He snatched it out of the air and glanced at it: a tiny stoppered glass vial, filled with what looked like quicksilver.

"What's this?" he asked.

"Strength," Benson said. He had left his hat and axe on the ground, but he lounged on his throne as arrogantly as ever. Both of his eyes glowed with sapphire flame, even in the light of the blue torches. "You think that Nye stuff is fun? That's the best drink you'll ever put in your mouth, and you have my word on that. Remember, though: like everything else, it don't last forever."

Strength? Would he be able to use a sword with the same kind of power Benson had? That would explain something of how Kai was able to swing around a seven-foot piece of steel like it was a willow switch. At the thought, he felt himself smile. For what seemed like the first time, he had taken a step forward.

"Thanks," Simon said, and he walked out of the basement. Heading for the library.

He had to find Kai, and as soon as possible. He was wasting time.

The library was a round, towering room, filled with books and scrolls of all description. Most of them seemed to deal with other Territories: their essential natures, their strengths and weaknesses, and theories on their purposes and origins. It would be good information to know when he was fighting the Travelers of the kingdom, if he could have taken the time to examine it.

The guardians of the library were made of melted wax, their features soft and half-melted. Roughly man-shaped, the librarians fashioned themselves robes from scraps of paper and stuck them directly to their wax skin. They looked like statues of monks created by a madman out of trash and old candles, except that they lurched about their work with a single-minded intensity. They never spoke above a whisper, and they were constantly shuffling and re-ordering the books in a system that made no sense to Simon.

Of course, they had tried to kill him.

They fought with hands and feet, no weapons, and their strength was almost a match for Benson's, but the Nye essence and the skeleton's quicksilver put Simon beyond them. He had looked forward to receiving some other reward for conquering them, only to find out that "Knowledge is the library's truest reward." He had sighed and moved on to the forge.

So far, he had yet to recognize any kind of logic in Valinhall's layout. The garden was nothing but a sky and open plains, but it seemed to be surrounded by indoor rooms. And now the forge was only one door away from the library. Simon wondered briefly how they prevented the books from catching fire, but normal rules obviously didn't apply here.

Simon was locked in a battle with the guardian of the Valinhall forge—a giant serpent of ash and glowing coals, with orbs of white-hot iron for eyes—when someone else walked in. This was the fifteenth day in a row he had challenged the giant burning snake, and the first time anything had changed.

Cold breath suffused his flesh, and steel ran along his veins, but Simon could barely push the massive snake back. The forge was long and intricate, with obsidian walls and anvils of various sizes stacked next to forge equipment and vats of molten metal. The heat in the room was already enough to singe the skin, and with a fiery snake inches from his skin...his sword glowed cherry red in the middle and was beginning to bend. Wisps of smoke curled up as the oil burned off the blade, and the serpent pressed harder, sensing weakness. His forearms felt like they were being pressed against a cook-stove, and the hairs on his arms had almost entirely burned away. Keeping the snake back was agony itself, but he knew that letting it through would be far worse.

"I'm sorry," a polite voice said from behind Simon. "I didn't realize you would be so busy. I can come back later, if you like."

Simon was so startled he almost let the snake past his guard. It lunged, but Simon reacted with the speed of the Nye Eldest, sidestepping and thrusting his warped blade through the serpent's skull.

Simon hopped backwards as the snake writhed in its death throes, orange flames leaping up instead of blood. He leaned his back against the cool obsidian walls and held desperately to the powers inside his body. Only the chill energy flowing through his blood and bones kept him from screaming at the burns.

A stranger stood leaning against one side of the open doorway, arms crossed. He was a tall man in brown and green traveling clothes, with a brown dirt-spattered cloak tossed over his shoulders. On his left side a sword hung sheathed, its hilt wrapped in red cloth and bearing a golden tassel. Under his arm he held an enormous old book, also bound in red and gold. He hadn't shaved for a few days and he looked like he could use some rest, but he wore a kind smile.

"Impressive," the stranger said. "When I was your age, the guardian of the forge was a little old lady who asked me a riddle. They must have traded up. But now we'll need a new one, I suppose."

"Ahem," a second voice said. "That's not entirely accurate." Simon glanced over, still more absorbed in his pain than in anything the stranger might say, but he could only see one man standing in the doorway. And his lips weren't moving. "In point of fact, the forge is one of the few places where the guardian is destroyed upon death. Assignments to this Room have traditionally been decided by a council of the most powerful parties in Valinhall, usually as a sort of prison sentence—"

"Thank you, that's enough," the man said. He sounded weary, as well he might; the other voice spoke with the sort of fussy accuracy Simon associated with irritating old men obsessed with history.

"Who's that talking?" Simon asked. He knew he should ask the man's name, but his power was fading, and the pain was quickly becoming more than he could bear. It was getting harder and harder to focus.

The man let out a long-suffering sigh. "His name is Hariman; he's my advisor. Don't pay attention to a word he says."

"And, uh, where is he?"

The stranger's eyebrows rose for a moment, then he laughed and patted his book. There was a face painted in gold on the cover, and Simon watched as it came to life and slid over to the right, eyeing Simon carefully. "You must need medical attention if your eyesight is failing you that bad," the book said in that fussy voice. "Not to mention the burns."

Simon leaned his head back against the wall. "A talking book," he said. "Of course."

The man's shrug was an audible shuffling of cloth. "At this point, I'm not sure why that surprises you. I'm Denner, by the way. Denner Weeks."

"Simon, son of Kalman." Simon cracked an eye. "Are you Dragon Army?"

Denner smiled easily. "Would I be in here if I wasn't?"

"I am."

Denner waved that away. "Kai took you in. That makes you one of us, and I'm sure you'll choose a sword soon enough. There's plenty available, I'm afraid."

"Really? I didn't think..." his cold power faded further, and he was forced to grit his teeth against the rising pain.

Hariman began to speak, but Denner swatted his binding and he sank into a grumbling silence. "Of the thirteen Dragon's Fangs, only four are active right now. And some are lost. But a few others are just waiting for someone to pick them up."

Simon nodded vaguely. His burns were beginning to feel more distant, as though he was drifting away from his body.

"You could continue educating the boy, which I applaud, or you could keep him alive," Hariman's voice said. "It's up to you, really."

Denner sighed and Simon felt a hand on his shoulder. Then he didn't remember anything for a long time.

When Simon's consciousness returned, he was standing in the open fields of the Valinhall garden, staring blankly at the huge fruit tree in the center. Waking felt like clawing his way up out of a dark void; he hadn't been sleeping, precisely, but he had not been conscious either. It felt as though he had simply left his body behind for a few hours.

Then sound faded back into focus. Not as if he were suddenly able to hear, but as if sounds that he had been hearing all along suddenly gained meaning.

"...must have been some kind of venom," Denner said. "Maybe it bit him."

"Good riddance if it has." Chaka's voice. "I still think it's just shock from the burns. He wasn't man enough to handle them, is all. Wouldn't surprise me."

As Simon absently rubbed at the fresh skin on his forearms—newly healed and hairless; somebody had taken him to the bathroom pool—it finally occurred to him to turn around.

Chaka stood with bladed arms crossed, his yellow eyes focused on Simon and his leather-flap lips set in a disapproving scowl. Denner had had a chance to clean up, it seemed, because his outfit was no longer quite so travel-stained, and he was missing a layer of dirt on his skin. He still carried Hariman, in its red-and-gold binding, under one arm.

"Well," Chaka said, "looks like he decided to stick with us after all."

Denner looked up, surprised, and Simon gave him a sheepish smile. "How long was I out?" he asked.

"Only a few hours," Denner responded. "We got you in the pool fairly quickly."

"Shouldn't have bothered," Chaka put in. "He's gotta be tougher than that if he wants to make it here."

Simon deliberately ignored Chaka, instead turning to Denner. "Thanks. I must have been in trouble if I passed out like that."

"You were badly burned. It took quite a while even for the pool to heal you. The imps were very excited."

Simon shuddered, imagining being at the mercy of the water-imps while unconscious. "Thank you," he said again. "Hopefully I won't need your help for the next room."

Denner frowned and turned a bit to Chaka. "Is Makko still the guardian of the courtyard?"

"How should I know? I'm stuck here, right? Not a lot of social time." Chaka glared rigidly at Denner, who continued waiting for a response. After a moment, Chaka relaxed. "I can't imagine she's gone anywhere else, though. She's a tough one."

"Then you'll need at least a good night's rest, Simon. She may not be as dangerous as some of the others around here, but you don't want to face her when you're not sharp."

Simon hesitated. He hated the idea of wasting any more time when Kai could be moving forward, but even the Nye essence and the liquid steel strength could only go so far. His fingers were trembling slightly and his arms felt like he had been pulling stumps all day. "First thing tomorrow, then. I don't want to waste any time."

For some reason, Denner looked suddenly uncomfortable. "Yes," he said. "About that. If you don't mind me asking, how far along are you?"

Simon stared at him blankly. "With what?"

"What have you earned so far? In the House, I mean."

With a little hesitation—Denner was a stranger, after all, but on the other hand he was Dragon Army—Simon told him about the black box and the vial. Denner frowned at him.

"A wooden box? I don't...hold on. That wasn't from the Nye, was it?"

Feeling like he was stepping into a trap, Simon nodded slowly. Denner gave a low whistle; Chaka let out a choking sound.

"What is it?" Simon asked. "Didn't the Eldest give you one, too?"

Denner shook his head. "One of the silver vials, sure. We all have to face the skeleton if we want to move forward. But the Nye choose who receives their gift. Perhaps two or three of us, at most, have earned that privilege. Only one that I know of for sure."

For a moment Simon's heart swelled with pride that he had been chosen. Just for a moment. Then a thought struck him: if the Eldest had given him something so valuable, that made his bargain more serious. Not for the first time, he wondered if he had made a mistake. But he shook that thought aside; without the Eldest's help, it would have taken him weeks to clear Benson's basement. Weeks, at least.

"It's been a great help to me so far," Simon said, tucking the objects back into his pockets. "Now that I have what I need, I'd hoped Kai would give me my own sword."

Denner sighed and shook his head. "It's not enough, I'm afraid. I have some news for you. Kai made me promise to let you know as soon as I could."

"What news? Wait. You've spoken with Kai? Where is he?"

"I've been scouting in Bel Calem for almost six months now. The Overlord Malachi didn't raid your village for slaves; he's responsible for this year's sacrifice."

A sick feeling began to grow in Simon's gut. "Sacrifice?" he asked.

Denner looked blankly at him, as though Simon were speaking nonsense. "The sacrifice. It's Malachi's year."

"But what does that *mean*?"

The book spoke up from underneath Denner's arm. "I, for one, would be delighted to explain."

"I'm sure you would," Denner said, "but let me—"

"Almost three hundred years ago," Hariman went on, completely ignoring the man carrying him, "the first King of Damasca sealed away a destructive force in order to preserve the security of his realm. He was a Traveler of Ragnarus, however, and you know what that means."

"No," Simon said. "No, I have no idea what that means."

"Kai didn't tell you?" Denner asked. He sounded surprised.

"Kai doesn't tell me anything," Simon said. He sounded more bitter than he intended.

"Ah!" Hariman exclaimed. "You really don't know? Well, the Enosh Grandmasters call Ragnarus the Crimson Vault. It's a Territory exclusive to the Kings of Damasca—that is to say, only those of the royal bloodline can open its Gates. It holds powerful weapons, but each comes at a cost. In this case, of course, the seal placed by the first King of Damasca requires a blood sacrifice every year."

Simon's mind raced down the possibilities. Obviously the sacrifice hadn't taken place yet, or Denner wouldn't need to warn him about it. But if the King had sealed something away...

"What is King Zakareth trying to keep sealed?" Simon asked.

Hariman responded eagerly. "Ah, now that's a matter of much debate. The true identity of the destructive force was only a subject of myth until almost fifty years ago, but now I can say with certainty—"

Denner cleared his throat. "Hariman," he said.

"Oh. Yes," the book responded. "I can say with certainty that we have no way of knowing. Maybe the Overlords know, but who can say for sure?"

They were leaving something out, but time weighed heavily on Simon. Maybe he'd have time to ask more questions later.

"When?" he asked. "When are they going to be...sacrificed?"

Denner looked distinctly uncomfortable. "The sacrifice ends at midsummer each year, but it begins eight days ahead of time. Nine days, nine sacrifices. And midsummer is in only two weeks."

Numbers had never been Simon's greatest friends, but he could do these sums easily enough. Five days until the sacrifices began. And fourteen until they ended.

Not nearly enough time.

He had tried to hurry, but there was only so much he could do. He needed more time. Was Alin ready? Maybe Alin could do it. Maybe Simon wouldn't have to lift a hand.

No. This time, Simon would do more than just sit back and cry. If Alin wanted to save the people of Myria, he would just have to catch up.

"I'm going to need one of the Dragon's Fangs," Simon said, heading for the door. "How do I use it? Can I take one of the ones from the entry hall?"

"I s'pose you could," Chaka called, "and I won't stop you. So long as all you want is a hunk of sharp metal."

Denner hurried over to Simon's side. "He's got a point. It's like anything else in this House; if you don't earn it, you don't get it. You won't be able to summon the sword if you haven't earned its respect, and it won't let you open a Gate."

Simon kicked open the door to the bathroom harder than was absolutely necessary, but he didn't slow his pace. Ripples marred the surface of the healing pool as something writhed underneath. "Then how do I do that?"

"You can't. Not yet. You're not good enough, and you haven't spent enough time in the House. If you try, you'll likely die."

"Try what, Denner?"

Denner sighed. He did that a lot, Simon noticed. "There's a graduation ritual. It's a survival test; if you're alive at the end of seven nights, you graduate. One of the Fangs is yours. It's even more brutal than the House; I almost died, during mine. Several of us did."

Simon threw open the door to the main hallway and strode through, past the rows of bedroom doors, trying to project outward confidence, but inside he hesitated. If it was the final challenge for the Dragon Army, each more qualified than he was, how could he hope to survive?

But he had made his decision when he had walked away from Myria.

"What do I do?" Simon asked. His voice, to his own ears, sounded firm.

Denner hesitated. "Orgrith Cave," he said at last. "Seven nights in Orgrith Cave."

CHAPTER 10

ORGRITH CAVE

Orgrith Cave crouched like a burrowed tick at the southeastern corner of the Latari Forest, corrupting all the nearby land. Simon and Denner were still a good mile out, traveling on foot, when the trees began looking smaller and more shriveled. The grasses blackened and dried up, and the dirt that crunched underneath their feet was more sand than soil.

The land didn't open up much, though; it was as hard to see here as it had been in the thickest of the Latari forest. Jagged spikes of rock dozens of feet tall stabbed into the ground, like the spears of giants. It looked as though someone had stripped the leaves and branches from thousands of trees, leaving only the trunks, and then turned the whole lot to stone.

Denner stopped at the first of the stone spikes, leaning with one hand on its rough surface. Under his other arm he held the red-and-gold book that was Hariman. "I must leave you here. I'm sorry, but it gets dangerous from here on out, and you should face the dangers of the Cave alone."

Simon eyed the stone forest warily. "This doesn't look like a cave."

"The battle that gave birth to Orgrith Cave was long and terrible. The Cave was where it ended; here is where it began. You're much safer out here than you will be inside, but there is still danger."

Denner pointed directly into the rocks. "Keep walking as straight as you can and you should not get lost. In only an hour or two, you will reach the cave entrance. Trust me, you won't miss it."

"So I just have to survive for one week's time?"

"More specifically," Hariman corrected from underneath Denner's arm, "you must survive inside the cave itself for a week. This is an important distinction. You can't stay outside longer than the time it takes you to walk there, and then, after seven nights, to walk back."

"How will you know?" Simon asked. "If I actually go in or not. I could just wait out here until seven nights have passed, and then come back out."

Denner gave him a sad smile. "Trust me, you're not the first to think of that. It would be worse for you if you tried, and there are those in Valinhall who have ways of knowing." Simon shuddered. "I will meet you here seven dawns from now," Denner continued.

Simon glanced at the sun setting over the older man's shoulder. Seven nights. Almost unconsciously, he loosened his sword in its sheath. Another undersized replica of a Dragon's Fang, this sword had come from the Valin-hall armory and was the only weapon he was allowed to bring besides a belt knife. Aside from his knife and sword, he carried nothing. He would have to forage for food and water inside the Cave itself.

Denner and Hariman had given him some tips, of course. He would not head in completely blind. But they had spent less time preparing him and more time reminding him of his own weakness and inexperience. Which did nothing for his confidence.

"Strictly speaking," Denner said, frowning, "Kai should be the one to meet you here after you're done. If I can find him, that is. He's more elusive than usual, lately."

"He went deeper into the House," Simon said. "He said he was trying to force me to clear rooms faster." He still felt a flash of anger at that, even if he had to admit it had worked.

"Strange. I checked up to the attic and saw no sign of him." Denner shrugged. "Still, I suppose I could have missed him. Some of those rooms are quite large, after all. And he could have wandered out of the House for a while. At times, Kai can be...well, you know."

"Yes, I do." Simon glanced at the sun again. He had perhaps an hour and a half until full dark. "Denner, I have a question for you."

Denner seemed startled, but he nodded.

"Ten years ago, around this time of year. It was raining at the edge of a forest. Did you save a boy from Travelers?"

Simon hadn't realized how much he cared about the answer until he felt his heart speed up. It probably wasn't Denner. There were eleven other people it could be, after all. But Denner did seem to wear brown a lot, and the swordsman who had saved Simon's life wore a dark cloak that might have been brown...

"Not me," Denner said slowly. "But I can ask around, if you like. I'm sure one of us will know."

Simon shook his head immediately. "No, it wasn't important. I should probably get going. Thank you for everything you've done."

Denner opened his mouth to reply, but Hariman interrupted him. "Well, of course. It was our pleasure. Do try to survive."

Simon walked all the way to the Orgrith Cave entrance with his sword out and a sharp eye on his surroundings.

The sun had fallen below the horizon but had not entirely left its light behind when the forest of rock spikes began to thin, revealing the entrance.

It was a tall, irregular dome of rock jutting out of the otherwise flat ground around it. The entrance gaped so wide Simon thought half the people of Myria could fit inside, but the dome itself barely seemed broad enough to cover the grassland in the garden of Valinhall. If that was the extent of Orgrith Cave, then it couldn't be so bad.

It was a nice thought, though he was forced to admit that it almost certainly extended deep underground. There might still be hope, though; maybe Denner had exaggerated.

He certainly hadn't mentioned this: the mouth of Orgrith Cave blazed with light, revealing a half-circle of carts and covered wagons almost completely blocking the entrance. Pairs of oxen grazed on the sparse grass outside the wagons. At a distance, Simon could make out a few people running around inside the circle, apparently excited about something. Not enough people to justify that many wagons, it seemed.

He hesitated for a moment, then walked forward, sheathing his sword. He didn't know what their business was, and they would probably be friendly to one young man alone, especially with so many of them together. If they weren't...well, he kept his mind on the brink of calling steel. As long as none of the strangers were Travelers, he was sure he could handle them.

As he approached the circle of carts and wagons, Simon saw only three people. A woman, perhaps ten years younger than Simon's mother, ran frantically from wagon to wagon, peering inside and shouting. Her eyes were wide, her long chestnut hair mussed, and her simple gray dress disheveled. "Andra?" she called. "Lycus? Come out here this instant! Andra!"

She dashed over to the nearest wagon like it held a fortune in gold. "This isn't funny, Andra! Please...please stop..." Her shoulders shook silently, and Simon realized she was crying.

His stomach sank.

The other two people in the camp, both men, rolled on the ground by their bonfire, apparently wrestling. One was younger, though judging by the touches of gray in his hair still old enough to be Simon's father, and the other even older. At least, his hair was entirely silver. The older man sat on the other, holding his arm pinned behind his back. The younger man screamed, and it was a moment before Simon could make out the words.

"LET ME GO! LET ME GO, PLEASE! THEY'RE IN THERE... THEY HAVE TO BE IN THERE! YOU CAN'T DO THIS TO ME!"

The picture resolved itself in Simon's mind: the younger man was trying to crawl to the mouth of the cave, but the older was holding him back.

The older man's reply was firm, but Simon barely heard it over the other's screams. "You'll die, Caius. You'll only die."

Simon stepped into the firelight and intentionally scuffed his feet against the dirt. Hopefully the noise would keep them from thinking he was trying to sneak up. He could have spoken, but he didn't have the words for this situation.

The older man whirled around immediately, pinning Simon with hard gray eyes. He wore a short sword on his left hip, and though he didn't stand up or release his hold on the other man, there was something in his posture of being ready to draw.

"I'm sorry," Simon said. "Is there someone in the cave?"

The screaming man stopped shouting and began to weep, sobbing from deep in his chest, but the other paid him no attention.

Gray-hair spoke, voice like flat iron. "Who are you? What is your purpose here?" He sounded like Nurita, giving an order and expecting to be obeyed. Simon's words caught in his throat, and he suddenly wasn't sure what to say.

"They're my babies," the woman said from behind him. He turned to face her. Her eyes were bright and feverish, and her face was a mask of tears. "My babies are in there."

"What are you doing here, boy?" The gray-haired man demanded again. He had risen to his feet, keeping one boot firmly planted on the grieving father's back. One hand rested on the hilt of the sword at his hip. "Speak or be gone."

Simon looked around, at the weeping mother and the distraught father, at the demanding man with a sword. He never did know what to say at times like this. So he turned and walked straight into the mouth of Orgrith Cave.

As the shadows of the cave swallowed him, he drew his sword.

Kai crouched on top of the stone dome that marked the outer barrier of Orgrith Cave, watching the Damascans down below. They scurried around their bonfire like so many moths fluttering over a candle. So much fuss over missing children. But what would he do if one of his precious little ones managed to run off? The thought almost brought him to tears.

He reached down to Otoku, cradled carefully in his left arm. He ran his right fingers down her dark hair, and along the silky red of her dress.

"I would never leave you," he whispered.

Sometimes I wish you would, she responded, an acid edge to her hazy mental voice.

Kai felt himself smile. She had said something this time; sometimes she would stay silent for days at a time. That was much worse. "I love your spirit and your fire. That is how I know you care."

Maybe I'll get lucky, and you'll get eaten.

"You wound me," he said, but he knew she didn't mean it.

No, I mean it, Otoku said.

He pretended not to hear her.

A few minutes passed before Simon arrived. He spoke with the parents—Kai had known he would—and then walked into the cave. Now there was a student Kai could be proud of. Only a handful of days after Kai left him on his own, and he had already earned Benson's steel and made his way to the Cave. All he had needed was the proper motivation.

Now, if he passed this one more test, he would have fully given himself to Valinhall. And he would be ready to die a man's death.

Why can't you be more like him? Otoku asked. Kai blinked and raised the doll, staring her in the face. For the first time that night, she truly startled him.

"What do you mean?" he asked.

Look how far he's willing to go, the doll said. *Look at how hard he's working to save people from the sacrifice. And what have you done about it?*

"I'm giving him a chance," Kai said, still off-balance. Otoku had never questioned him about this decision before. Why now? "I could have left him in the forest. It would have been safer."

Human sacrifice is a horrible practice, and you should have put a stop to it years ago. You know that's what Valin wanted, before he...changed his mind.

Kai shuddered. Now, why had she brought up *that* topic?

"Nine people a year," Kai whispered. "It could be much worse."

And how many people have died anyway? Not just the sacrifices, but all the others they killed to keep it all running. Is it only hundreds?

"Simon has a chance. He's in this for the right reasons, and I won't stop him."

But you're not going to help him either. The drifting wind behind Otoku's voice sounded harsh, cold.

"I can't help him," Kai pleaded. He couldn't go on with her so disapproving. She almost sounded as if she preferred Simon over him! "Please. I'm doing what I can."

A man sighed heavily from behind Kai. "And you know Indirial would kill us both," he said in a familiar voice.

Kai rose and turned to meet Denner, who was still as rough-looking as ever. He hadn't shaven, and his clothes looked slept-in. Hariman was tucked underneath Denner's arm, but he remained uncharacteristically silent.

"I did what you asked," Denner went on. "He's a good kid, but he's not ready for this. We can still pull him out."

For a moment, Kai considered just waiting on the results of the test. Orgrith Cave had been formed in a chaotic battle between Tartarus, Naraka, and Ornheim Travelers, and the caverns shifted form almost constantly. But the Cave was always deadly. Kai didn't know exactly what Simon would face within, and he could always just let the test run its course. Simon might survive, after all.

Not that Kai would place any heavy bets on it.

"He needs this," Kai said softly.

Denner sighed again and shook his head.

If you leave him in there, Otoku said, *I will tell my sisters. We will never let you sleep again.*

Absently, Kai patted the doll's head. "Don't worry, little one," he said. "I will not leave him alone. But he must never know I'm there, or it will cripple him."

Kai sensed Otoku smile, and it felt like sunlight.

Denner spoke up. "And what about the sacrifice? He's going to stop it, if he can."

Kai stared at his old friend from behind his usual veil of hair, whitened years before its time by the powers of the House. "If you wanted him to fail," Kai said, in close to his usual sing-song tones, "you would have never brought him here."

Glancing around as if for an answer, Denner finally nodded. And sighed.

Simon was almost disappointed. For the first few minutes inside the cave, he kept every sense tuned and his sword in his hand. At every real or imagined scuff of dirt, he swung in one direction or another and froze, waiting for an attack. But inevitably nothing came of it, and he moved on.

The cave led directly into a tunnel, circular and rough-edged, that sloped down into deeper shadows. Once he moved beyond even the faintest light from the cave entrance, Simon began to notice patches of fungus on the walls, glowing softly blue. The deeper he walked, the brighter the fungus grew. Or perhaps he had simply grown used to the light. Either way, it became easier to see.

For perhaps an hour he walked along the tunnel, occasionally following the tunnel's gentle shifts and turns. He found nothing. No branches, no side passages, no monsters, no missing children. Wearily he sheathed his sword. So far, Orgrith Cave had been somewhat disappointing.

If I can just find some water, he thought, *I can just sit in this tunnel until time runs out.* They had never said anything about doing anything in the cave, and there was no reason he should risk his life if he didn't have to.

But what about the kids? He didn't know the family outside the cave, but of course he wanted to find children that had become lost. He wasn't a monster. He had to at least make a decent effort to find them. However many there were. And if they were in the cave at all.

He probably should have asked.

Simon had just decided to continue when he noticed a ripple in the tunnel's stone floor. It was accompanied by a sound like a rock falling into a still pond.

It was difficult to see anything in the blue half-light of the fungus, but he reasoned that there must have been a puddle of water collecting on the floor. If a puddle, though, what had disturbed it? He crossed the distance in two strides and knelt, running his hand over the stone floor. It was completely dry. Somewhat smooth and bare of dust compared to the rest of the ground, but there was certainly no water.

He rose to his feet, a quiet alarm sounding in his head, and caught a glimpse of another ripple, farther down the tunnel. He started toward it, but immediately there came another, this one a whole pace closer to where he stood. Then another, even closer.

His sword came out of his sheath just as the stone rippled inches from his toes. He had a good viewpoint this time: the stone of the tunnel had actually shook like the surface of a pond disturbed by a pebble. He felt no shaking under his feet, so it wasn't some strange earthquake, and the stone seemed solid once the ripples passed. What, then?

A few months ago he would have had no idea. It would have frightened him enough that he would have run from the cave, seeking help. Well, running sounded like a good idea now anyway, but his time in the House had at least taught him one thing: if it's out of the ordinary, it probably means to kill you.

So it was that when the ripples grew quiet, Simon had his sword reversed point-down above the stone. And when a slimy glowing blue creature with fangs longer than his middle finger sprang from the stone, aiming at his face, it swallowed three feet of steel.

The creature was shaped like a cross between a river fish and an eel, with diamond patterns glowing with the same blue phosphorescence as the moss overhead. Its own momentum carried it up the slightly curved sword, until its teeth almost scraped the hilt and the point split its tail nearly in half.

The shock of the impact carried Simon backwards, and he fell onto his tailbone. For a moment he froze, looking into the dying eyes of the eel-fish, which thrashed for only a moment in the throes of death. His heart slammed in his chest for a few minutes, but his first coherent thought was: *Oh, good. Dinner.*

His second thought was that he should ready himself in case of another attack. So he did, springing to his feet and whipping his sword through the air to clear it of its burden. The corpse slid off easily, releasing a tangy smell halfway between fish guts and copper. Simon scanned the area but, seeing nothing, continued.

He remembered to scoop up the corpse of the creature before continuing.

Evidently he had almost reached the end of the tunnel, because moments later the ground began to flatten out. A few minutes after that, the tunnel opened, and he began to see the true face of Orgrith Cave.

It was, as he had feared, enormous. The cavern roof was so far above him that he would almost believe it scraped the sky. It was as though someone had hollowed out a mountain and dropped him inside it. It was far bigger, in fact, than the dome above the Cave entrance, and that confused him for a moment before he realized that he had to be far below and away from that structure.

The open space stretched farther than he could see; infinitely, as far as he could tell, in any direction but behind him. The tunnel through which he came was the only opening in a miles-long wall, flat and massive.

The cavern roof was supported by hundreds if not thousands of stone columns, seemingly formed naturally rather than carved, and so thick around the base that he didn't think he and five others his height could encircle them with their arms. At least he could see; the pillars were ringed with spirals of glowing green mushrooms that shed an acid-green light over everything in the cave, in most places much brighter than the light in the tunnel.

Patches of the glowing blue moss were splashed across the ceiling and walls, and in places mushrooms grew big enough to shelter an entire family under their caps. The underbellies of these huge caps, as well, shed an eerie green radiance. From the ceiling and some of the pillars hung chunks of crystal that shone with a violet light. The overall effect of the clashing lights—blue, green, and purple—was eerie and otherworldly. For some reason, it made him feel cold.

There was plenty of light, but some of the things that light revealed churned his stomach. A worm as fat as a cow, seemingly made of strung-together chunks of boulder, slid across the ground, dipping into the floor inside what was presumably a hidden tunnel. A four-armed crab with a shell that reflected the light like a mirror piled some stones up into an irregular pile, at least until it was suddenly seized and eaten by another eel-fish leaping up from the floor. It let out a piercing cry as the fanged creature bit into its soft underbelly.

Something he could barely see scuttled along the far wall, and he heard motion on the wall behind him. He saw nothing, but something sounded like a dog's claws scrabbling on rock.

This isn't any worse than the House. It can't be. Not everything here wants to kill me. Not that everything there did either, now that I think about it. And at least I know how things work there. And at least I could have a clean bed, and regular meals, as long as—

He shook off those thoughts. They wouldn't be helpful here. Taking a deep breath like he was about to leap into an icy pool, he stepped into the huge cavern.

And none too soon. Just as he cleared the tunnel, he heard a monstrous scraping behind him, like rock sliding across stone. He flattened himself against the wall to the side of the tunnel wall, waiting. Had the cave itself collapsed? Maybe some kind of rock slide?

Foolish hopes, he knew, but he clung to them anyway before he saw the huge rock worm slide out of the tunnel like a maggot through a rotting fruit. It paused for a moment, eerily silent, lifting its boulder-head and waving it into the air, before it continued sliding forward and was lost in the forest of giant columns.

He let out a breath and loosened a white-knuckled grip on his sword. Maybe he should summon the skeleton's power now, just in case. And maybe the Nye essence too, for good measure. Except he didn't want to be in the middle of trouble when they ran out. He touched the cold silver power in his mind, resolving to reach for it as soon as he noticed anything else out of the ordinary.

Out of the ordinary like the high-pitched scream that sliced through the sounds of the cave. His first thought was that it must be some kind of death-scream from one of the cave's monsters, but his mind refused to interpret the sound as anything other than what it was: the terrified cry of a human girl.

Liquid steel surged through his veins before he realized he had decided to check it out. He repeated the process with a deep breath of essence from Valinhall. Then, with icy energy filling him till he felt his skin was ready to burst, he took off. The columns blurred around him as he left them behind, passing the clawed silhouettes of things that probably belonged in nightmares.

He had begun to wonder if he had run too fast and should double back when a scream came again, this time mixed with a terrified sob. It was coming from his left.

He turned to the side as soon as he recognized the direction, but he had never before tried to turn so quickly while moving at his enhanced speed. His own momentum flung him into the air, and he barely twisted to get his feet under him before he was dashed against a stone pillar. He landed with his feet against the pillar and immediately kicked off, shooting in the direction of the cries. The air tore against the corners of his eyes till he could barely see through the tears, and he couldn't get a full breath of air.

At this speed he couldn't see details, and he didn't have time to think. As soon as he saw a splash of color—a yellow light, he thought, next to something red—pressed back against the wall by a monstrous gray shape, he simply reacted. He swept his blade down in an arc, felt it bite something and pass through, then he was past, hurtling towards the floor.

It was even harder getting his feet under him this time, but he barely managed to do so, slamming to the floor in a hard crouch. Only the steel running through him, strengthening his muscles, his bones, kept him from crushing himself on the rocks. Only the spirit of the Nye gave him the reaction to land, the grace to keep from rolling head-over-heels into the wall.

As it was, his landing used up the last of Benson's steel, though his essence lingered. Weakness gripped his muscles, and his sword suddenly felt ten pounds heavier. He looked up from his crouch, hoping desperately that he had not been too late.

Two children—a boy and a girl—cowered against the wall, holding a flickering lantern between them. The splotches of red he had seen were the girl's skirt and the boy's jacket; not blood, he was relieved to see. A skeletal monstrosity loomed over them, something like a praying mantis but covered in rock-plated armor.

It stood there for a moment as though it was about to crash down on them, impaling them on its forearms. Then its head slid slowly off its body and drifted to the floor.

Simon released the Nye essence, letting it flow back into his Territory. The world resumed normal speed, and the head slammed to the floor as if it weighed five hundred pounds. The rest of the body crumbled after.

A trembling ran through Simon's body after the power left him. He shook with relief and with delayed fear, as if he had run blindfolded along the edge of a cliff and only afterwards realized the danger. His breath came in shallow gasps, and he shuddered. One lapse in judgment and he might have crushed himself against the cave wall.

The children's screams faded uncertainly to whimpers. As one, their heads turned to take in Simon, crouched a handful of paces away with his sword still bare. He must have scared them. They looked like they were trying to decide whether or not to run.

"Don't worry, I'm here to help you." Now that he got a closer look at them, they were clearly brother and sister. They each had the same dark skin and light hair, a combination that until now he had only seen on Alin.

"That was amazing," the girl said. She was perhaps twelve years old and over a foot taller than her brother, so Simon took her for the older, even though the boy stood protectively in front of her. His jaw still sat half-open, and Simon wasn't sure if he looked more awed or terrified.

Something else skittered in the darkness, and the girl held the lantern out. A segmented insect claw pulled back from the light into the shadows.

"Could you light that lantern again, if you had to?" Simon asked. She nodded. "Then put it out. Follow me; both of you hang on to my shirt."

Obediently, the girl blew out the light in the lantern and grabbed onto his right sleeve. Her presence would be a nuisance if he had to fight, but any move he made with the sword would shake her off anyway, so he decided to say nothing.

Experimentally, he reached out with his mind to the Nye essence. Nothing yet. He knew from experience that it would take a minute or two for the moonlit mist to begin replacing itself, and a little longer for the steel. He would be completely vulnerable for the next few minutes, and wouldn't be back to full power for almost half an hour afterwards.

He set off at first for the entrance tunnel, hushing the children if either of them tried to say anything. Not that they did speak very often. The dim lighting and the scuttling shapes in the shadows tended to strangle conversation.

As soon as the entrance tunnel came into view, Simon realized he was going to have to re-think his plan. One of the huge boulder-worms lay coiled up around the entrance, plates of its rocky armor shattered and cracked, exposing pale flesh. Dozens of the luminescent eel-fish he had seen earlier leapt from ripples in the stone, crawling all over the gargantuan corpse, tearing away chunks of meat.

Most of the body was piled up at the entrance of the tunnel, but the tip of the tail was out of view. As Simon watched, something tugged the giant worm back up the tunnel. He couldn't get a glimpse of whatever was pulling on the boulder-worm's tail, but it had to have been huge to shift the monster's massive bulk. The fanged eels barely noticed, but continued to feed.

One of the children made a sort of gasping sound behind him, as though they wanted to cry but were afraid to make more noise. Simon could relate; terror hovered around him, not touching him yet, but making its presence known. He was trapped in this cave. Trapped.

Simon turned and looked into the faces of the two children. No matter what happened to him, he needed to get them out.

They walked in silence until they had left the noises of feeding monsters far behind, returning to the spot where he had killed the huge mantis creature. There was a crack in the wall nearby, highlighted by glowing blue moss, that might be big enough to shelter all of them. Maybe. They needed a place to rest and talk, and they wouldn't get it out here in the dark.

Simon eyed the entrance to the shelter for a moment. From here shadows shrouded the entrance; there was no way to tell how deep it was, or what waited inside. He summoned strength from Valinhall and ventured sword-first inside, hoping he could fight well enough in a crouch to keep him alive.

Fortunately, it was empty. Though not nearly high enough for him to stand upright, at least the space was a pace or two deep, and more than wide enough for the three of them to squeeze in and seal the entrance.

The last of the silver flowing through his veins was enough to let him fell one of the giant mushrooms in a single swipe. He severed the cap and pulled it over to the wall, sealing all three of them inside and providing light at the same time. It was like a giant glowing door.

When they were seated, the girl pulled a tinderbox from her pocket to light her lantern. The mushroom door was more than bright enough, but there was something eerie about the spectral blue cave-light. Still, practical considerations had to come first.

"Hold on," Simon said. "We should save the lamp oil. Let's not light the lantern until we really need it."

"No problem," the girl said. Then she looked at him expectantly, as if waiting for his next order. Simon shifted, uncomfortable. He had rarely spent time with children back in the village. Alin, he knew, would have said something comforting and taken care of the problem himself.

"My name is Simon," he said. He used the soothing voice he had used on his mother when she might take off running or attack him with a frying pan. "Don't worry; I'm here to help."

"I know," the girl declared. "I bet Mother and Father sent you down here. I'm right, aren't I?" Her eyes twinkled as if she were ready to tell a joke, or hear one.

Her younger brother breathed, "I've never seen anybody move so fast. Are you an Overlord?"

The girl hit him. "The Overlords wouldn't come down here looking for us. They're too busy."

The boy glared at her. "They could. You don't know."

Simon raised his hands to quiet them. He felt a flash of irritation at being taken for one of the Overlords, but it was quickly suppressed. They were just children, after all. "I'm not an Overlord." He couldn't quite keep a sneer out of that last word. "What are your names?"

The girl rose up to her knees and mimicked a curtsy, smirking like she was playing a prank. "I am the Lady Andra Agnos, at your service. Thirteen years old. This is my younger brother, Lycus. He has a mere ten years."

"Are you really a lady?" Simon asked uncertainly. He had heard stories of the nobility, but he had no idea how he was supposed to behave around them. Did Damasca even have lords and ladies?

"Don't you think I look the part?" She swirled her red wool skirt the way women back in the village would show off holiday dresses. The effect was marred somewhat by the fact that she was kneeling on the floor of a cave.

Lycus glared at his sister. "We are not noble. Our father is a free merchant for Malachi."

Andra giggled. "But you believed it, didn't you?"

Simon looked from one to the other, trying to figure out something that had been bothering him for a while. "You two don't seem very frightened, trapped down here by yourselves. Your parents were convinced you were dead."

A shadow passed over the faces of both siblings. Andra's smile twisted so that she looked like she might cry, and Lycus stared at the stone wall as if at his own corpse.

"It's almost been a whole day," Andra whispered. "Mother and Father were gone. I thought they would never know. Lycus came to bring me out... one of those fish would have gotten me, if not for him."

"We got lost. I thought we were going to be in here forever," Lycus said. But he brightened and turned a wide-eyed gaze on Simon. "Then you came! That monster was nothing for you."

Andra nodded agreement, her smile back in place. Simon's stomach twisted. Denner had been very clear that he wasn't ready for this trial, but Simon had insisted anyway. What if he really wasn't ready?

That's a coward's thought, he reminded himself. *I have to do something. I'm the only one here who can do anything.* But he had to be honest.

"I can't leave the cave for six nights after this one. But I can bring you to the entrance, if we can make it past all the monsters. I'm not sure I can kill them all."

Andra grinned, as if at a joke. "Just do what you did before. It worked well enough for that big bug out there." She slapped a hand against their mushroom-cap door.

"But what if it doesn't work?" As soon as the words were out of his mouth he realized what he sounded like. *Fool. You're asking a thirteen-year-old girl what to do?*

He coughed to cover his embarrassment and continued on. "I mean, it might not be good enough. That's what I meant to say. I just thought you should know. But I'll do everything I can, I promise you that."

They beamed at him, and he had to repress a surge of doubt. What if these kids got killed? It would be his fault. His only consolation was that if they died, he probably wouldn't live to see it.

Not surprisingly, the thought didn't comfort him much.

CHAPTER 11

ESCAPE

After a few more minutes of rest, Simon led the Agnos children out of their little cave. Unaided, he could never have pushed aside the giant mushroom cap, but after a draft of steel strength he pushed it back with one hand.

They almost didn't get any farther.

The carnivorous eels had been drawn to the fresh corpse of the mantis-monster outside, leaping up out of ripples in the stone to tear its rocky plates off and feast on the flesh beneath. When Simon stepped outside, he disturbed their feeding, sending all the fanged creatures into a frenzy. They dove at him, scales rippling with spectral blue light, flashing teeth the size of his fingers.

If he hadn't already summoned steel, they would have torn him to shreds in seconds. Lacking the reflexes from the Nye essence, the only thing he could rely on was raw strength. So that was what he did.

The first fanged horror was inches from his face before he managed to swat it from the air with his palm, but the impact launched it into the distance as if it had been hurled by a catapult. He kicked another just as it left the ripples in the stone, snapping its spine in half, and caught a third by the tail. Then he swung that fish like a flexible club, smacking the rest out of the air before they became a danger.

He was just falling into a rhythm when he heard the beginnings of a scream behind him, and he whirled without conscious thought. A ripple headed straight towards Lycus' feet. He had pushed his sister behind him and now stood between her and the still-submerged creature. His eyes were wide with terror.

Simon had no time to think of a better plan, so he did the first thing that came to mind: he brought his arm back, then swept the fish in his hand down like a hammer. It was stunned but still alive, thrashing weakly in his hand, but he ignored it.

The fish in the stone, expecting to take its prey by surprise, jumped from the ripple in front of Lycus. Its fanged face had barely cleared the rock when Simon's weapon crashed into it.

The scales of both fish cracked, sending dark blood splattering across Simon's face. One of the squirming creatures even let out a weak scream, eerie and shrill. But in seconds both fish were dead, one of them still half-sunk in solid stone.

Simon dropped the eel-thing and wiped his face with a trembling hand. He had not been nearly careful enough. What if these fish had sensed them before he had moved the door? He shuddered; the three of them had sat on the ground. All three humans would have been shredded to pieces before they could react.

The kids were entirely unharmed and, if anything, looked even more impressed with Simon than before. He kept all expression off his face, but inwardly he trembled. That had been entirely too close. He tried to tell himself to relax, but he was only too aware how near his mistake had come to costing lives.

As they walked to the entrance tunnel, Simon kept his sword sheathed. Instead, he kept himself on the brink of summoning his powers. If he so much as sensed a motion in the shadows, he was going to down both of them before he even looked twice. That should have been his policy before he ever set foot in Orgrith Cave, but he had been too shortsighted to plan ahead.

That was one mistake he wouldn't make again.

Finally, they approached a spot Simon recognized as near the entrance. He signaled Lycus and Andra to remain quiet and stay against the wall, then drew on a draught of both the Nye essence and metallic strength. Cool power rushed through his veins, ran along his bones. Everything around him slowed, until it seemed that everyone else moved through thick honey.

He was as ready as he could be. Simon crept forward hesitantly; though, in his accelerated state, he was probably moving at almost his normal running speed. He immediately spotted the tail end of the giant worm they had earlier seen devoured. Though messy—its shell was torn open at several points, its blood splattered on the rocks all around—it appeared to have been abandoned. At least, he saw none of the fish that swam through rock.

That was a relief; maybe the tunnel would be unguarded as well. He pulled his sword out and looked into the tunnel entrance.

It was twice as wide as it had been, and a totally different shape: a horizontal oval where it once had been circular.

Did something make it wider, Simon thought, *or does the entrance change shape?* If so, the tunnel out may be more dangerous now than it had been when he entered. This may not even be the tunnel out any longer; the passage could now lead to a stone wall. Or a nest of unspeakable monsters.

Simon shook himself. This was no Territory, where normal physical laws barely held sway. Tunnels through rock did not simply shift for no reason. Obviously something had happened here to widen the entrance. Maybe this was more evidence of whatever hidden monster had tugged the rock worm's corpse. That was a disturbing enough idea; anything that could drag that enormous corpse and take huge gouges out of stone would probably tear through him like a flimsy cloth.

With that cheery thought in his head, Simon called as loud as he dared, "Lycus. Andra. Come on out."

They peeked their heads around the softly glowing trunk of a giant mushroom, saw he was alone, and hurried over to him.

"Is this the way out?" Lycus whispered.

I hope so, Simon thought, but all he said was, "Yes. Follow me."

"Can't be worse than in here," Andra said with a soft laugh, as she fell in line behind him. Simon wished he agreed.

The tunnel out this time was rougher than Simon remembered, gouges seemingly carved in the floor and tunnel. It was darker, too, since much of the glowing blue moss had been scraped away, so they had to step carefully to avoid putting a foot in shadowed gorges.

Simon's unease grew with every step they took. Whatever had happened in this tunnel during the few hours since he had come in, it was violent and recent. Instincts born in Valinhall screamed at him that something was about to jump out from the dark. He kept his sword in one hand, holding the Nye mist inside him for as long as possible. Even aside from the edge it would give him if they were suddenly attacked, he found that he liked feeling quick and powerful. It helped counteract the all-too-reasonable fear of something lurking in the shadows.

After perhaps half an hour of creeping along, stopping every few paces to listen, Simon whirled around at a scream from Andra. He angled his sword to stab, reaching out to Valinhall for Nye essence.

Andra doubled over laughing. True, she kept her voice down so it didn't quite echo in the stone corridor, but Simon still didn't think it was appropriate. Lycus looked as Simon himself must: shocked, disbelieving, still half-ready to respond to a threat. To the boy's credit, he had lunged forward to try and help his sister at the first sign of danger.

"Your faces," Andra managed to get out, at little above a whisper. "Oh, seven stones." She dissolved into giggles.

"You think this is funny?" Simon said. He hoped it was too dark for them to see his face flushing. Lycus just growled and turned away from her, evidently in disgust.

Andra folded her hands in front of her. "I'm sorry. I'll be good." Her apology was spoiled somewhat by a few lingering giggles.

A sharp grinding noise, like rock scraping across rock, echoed down the tunnel. It seemed to be coming from just ahead of them.

"Is that the wagons?" Lycus asked. He sounded more hopeful than convinced.

"I don't think so," Simon said. He just wished he had a little more light. As it was, if—well, *when*—he had to fight something else, he would have very little warning. "We should be getting close to the entrance by now, though," he said.

Neither of the children said anything, but the longing looks on their faces made him hope desperately that he was right.

As they continued to walk, the grinding noise repeated itself periodically, growing steadily louder as they approached the source of the noise. A feeling gnawed at Simon, telling him that something was different now than when he had come down the tunnel the first time. At first he thought it was the lack of light—surely they would see the light from the entrance soon—but after a while it dawned on him. The tunnel was sloping down.

He took a glance back down the tunnel. The light was too dim for him to see far, but he hadn't been mistaken. It was obviously a downward slope, not a way out. Had he made some kind of mistake? No, there were no other side passages he could have accidentally taken. This was really the only way out. Maybe the tunnel had changed after all. But did it still lead outside?

The Agnos siblings were pushing one another as they walked, Andra with a smirk on her face, Lycus with a serious scowl. He couldn't tell them; they would just worry. Besides, what would they do when they found themselves in the same main chamber as before? He hadn't seen any other ways out. So forward was as good a direction as any.

Simon tightened his grip on his sword until his fingers ached. He would get these children out of here if it killed him. He *would*.

Then the tunnel opened up to another chamber, and he found out what had been making that grinding noise.

This chamber, as much as he could make it out in the shadows, was shaped like an enormous ball. They stood in an entrance about halfway up one wall. In the bowl beneath them, huge rock-worms lay tangled like mating snakes. Thousands of them, twisting and twining together. The pile was mostly still, though occasionally one shifted slowly, producing the grinding noise Simon had heard earlier. Asleep? Or did these things just naturally move that slowly?

The bottom of the chamber was so intimidating that Simon almost didn't notice something else: the chamber held none of that luminous moss. It was bathed in a soft blue-white light, but a paler shade than he had seen so far.

It took him a few seconds to recognize moonlight, pouring in from a crack high in the opposite wall.

Simon's breath caught. It was a way out. Maybe for all of them; the crack looked big enough that they might be able to pass. Of course, it was across the room from those rock-worms. And even if it hadn't been, he wasn't at all sure he could make it up the sides.

Then again...he stuck his head out of the corridor and took a closer look at the walls around him. The stone was rough and knobby, not perfect for climbing, but similar to the rocky bluffs around Myria. Those weren't too hard to climb. And the wall underneath the moonlit crack seemed a bit flatter than the rest of the cavern. It could be an illusion of shadows and soft light, true, but he had his prizes from the House. Maybe, with enhanced strength and reflexes, he could make it.

If the hole was big enough to let him through. If he could get through the rock-worms without waking them. If the land outside was any safer than what they found in here. Far too many ifs.

The children, understandably, kept shooting anxious glances at him. He put a finger to his lips and gestured for them to back up into the tunnel. If enough of those rock-worms woke, they were dead for sure. It just wasn't worth the risk. There had to be another way out of here.

With one eye on the brother and sister and one on the writhing mass of giant worms, Simon almost didn't hear the distant call, drifting to them on the gentle air of the cave. A woman's voice.

"Lycus! Andra! Andra, please..." It was so faint, he almost couldn't understand. Almost.

The way the children stiffened showed Simon they had heard just as well as he had. They stared at him with wide eyes and gestured frantically, as though he didn't understand what they wanted.

Silently, Simon cursed whatever twisted fate had brought them their mother's voice. No hope of safely turning back now; they would balk at every step. How had the woman's voice reached this far, anyway? He would have called it impossible.

Still, it proved one thing: that hole up in the wall did lead to the outside after all. And probably to safety, if they could make it soon.

Simon leaned his face down between the brother and sister. He spoke in a voice that should have been barely audible even from inches away. "We're going to try and climb out through that hole, but that means we have to cross the floor." He pointed with his sword.

Andra choked back a nervous laugh, holding a hand to her mouth. Lycus trembled as if he had asked the boy to stack his own funeral pyre, but his face was as hard as a child could make it. He nodded, as if granting permission.

"I can only take you one at a time," Simon continued. He wasn't sure he had it in him to finish two trips, but then again he wasn't sure he could finish one. "You have to be quiet. If those things wake up..." They nodded vigorously. At least he wouldn't have to explain that.

The trouble began when he asked who wanted to go first.

"Take him," Andra whispered. "He's younger." Lycus shook his head firmly, face fit for a magistrate passing sentence. Silently, he nudged his sister forward, but she stepped back. They gestured silently to each other, clearly arguing.

Simon sighed. Quietly. "Whoever goes first has the best chance. And whoever's second has to wait here alone until I get back."

Andra nodded. "Right. So it should be Lycus." Lycus shook his head and gestured toward his sister.

"I'll be fine," he said.

Simon hoped the shadows hid his surprise. He had been sure they were holding back because of fear, but...were they each trying to give the other a better chance? That was impressive and admirable, but he still had to decide who to take.

Simon's father would have taken the girl first. Kalman had been a chivalrous man, and he would expect any son of his to do whatever it took to bring a woman out of danger. But Simon's mother had been of a more practical bent, at least when sane. She would say to leave the one who could hold their head best alone, male or female. In this case, Simon thought his mother had a better point.

Simon locked eyes with Andra. "Will you be all right alone?"

Her answering smirk had a bit of the gallows in it, but her firm gaze made her look five years older than Simon, not three younger. "I was doing fine before you got here, wasn't I?" That wasn't how Simon recalled it, but he shrugged and scooped up Lycus, tossing him over his left shoulder.

The boy struggled, of course, whispering his protests, but at least he didn't scream.

"Stay low," Simon told Andra. "Don't make any noise. I'll come back for you." *If I can,* he added silently.

Simon peered over the ledge. A patch of bare rock rested between a pair of giant worms, twenty feet below. Icy silver crept into his veins as he called on the vial of steel; his lungs filled with the cool rush of Nye essence.

And he stepped off the ledge.

Filled with essence, Simon felt time slow to cool honey. It seemed to take ten seconds to reach the cavern floor, not less than one. When his feet touched rock, he kept his knees bent, absorbing the impact. It hit him with shivering force, like he was being pressed with a great weight. But the liquid steel hardened his muscles, supported his bones. His legs held.

His slowed vision registered a ring of dust blasted away from him by his impact. In his view, it drifted away on a gentle breeze.

So far so good. Simon kicked forward, leaping over prone figures, sliding past, keeping one hand on his shoulder to lock Lycus in place. It must be incredibly uncomfortable for him, tossed and jostled about like a sack on a galloping horse, but Simon tried to move as smoothly as possible. Slowing too much might kill them both.

Once Simon had to squeeze between two rock-worms, edging along sideways, inches from one of the worm's giant face. It was sleeping; he knew that now. Its broad face held a wide, craggy mouth, like a horizontal canyon, and its eyelids were rounded plates of granite. It looked as though someone had hewn a rough frog's face out of solid rock.

As Simon slid past, silent and quick as a breath of wind, Lycus let out a grunt. That was all. As uncomfortable as it surely was on Simon's shoulder, it was a wonder he hadn't made more noise than that, but one grunt was all it took.

The worm's granite eyes slid open, revealing eyes of burning blue.

Simon was out of the rock-worm's vision immediately, vaulting over another sleeping figure with legs powered by Benson's liquid steel. Still, as he kept running, Simon caught a glimpse of the awakened worm raising its head, twisting it this way and that as it searched for whatever had startled it awake.

The far wall loomed over Simon, that one blessed hole leaking moonlight. The wall was smoother than most of the rest of the chamber, though what little curve it did have actually made the climb easier. He threw himself at the side, both feet and one hand clutching at handholds, one keeping Lycus firmly attached.

Without his Traveler's gifts from Valinhall, he would never have made it. He would have needed both hands and both feet to climb a face like this even without a boy on his shoulder, and with Lycus there he would never be able to bear the weight. As it was, it almost felt like flying.

Simon hurled himself upwards, feet and hand touching the wall only to seize protrusions and push up again and again. Every time he kicked off, he threw himself another five or six feet up the wall, the grace of the Nye keeping him from overbalancing and tipping over backwards. Or else cracking his forehead open on the wall.

It had been hard to tell from across the chamber, but the hole itself could hardly have been in a worse position. Instead of in front of him, moonlight spilled from almost above him, as the wall began to curve into the ceiling. Simon stopped on a ledge, gathering his strength, coiling his legs and arms, building the strength of the steel vial inside his blood.

"Hold on," Simon said. He didn't bother to keep his voice low. Lycus murmured something back, but Simon didn't listen; he launched himself upward, straight at the hole.

Though time moved slowly to him, the roof of the cavern approached with terrible speed. The hole rushed forward to meet him, but he had miscalculated. He was going to miss the center of the hole by two or three feet, slamming into the side of the hole like a melon dropped from a tall tree. At this speed he would crush both himself and Lycus to death on the roof of the cavern, leaving only their lifeless corpses to feed the worms.

Panic and terror surged through him, and his limbs acted almost without his permission. With a speed that blurred even the edges of his Nye-enhanced vision, his hands shot out and seized the edge of the hole. In the bare, shaved second before he smashed into the rock, his arms flexed. Liquid steel and Nye's breath blazed in him, a thousand pinpricks of cold that burned his flesh like winter's own dagger. And with a mighty heave powered by everything he could draw from Valinhall, he pulled himself toward the hole and through. With an inch to spare, they emerged into the night instead of crashing into the ceiling.

The moonlight was so bright compared to the dim moss-lit cave that it almost burned his eyes, but he slid on his belly onto a surface of dusty rock. From Simon's back, Lycus leaned forward and vomited back into the hole. Some of it struck the rock and splattered onto Simon's trousers, but at the moment he wouldn't have cared if the boy had spewed all over his face. They were alive. And they were outside. The wind on Simon's face felt like a mother's embrace.

Simon let out a breath that flared briefly with light as the Nye's essence leaked out of him. His body felt almost uncomfortably warm and heavy as his twin powers faded, leaving him panting. And trembling. Another fraction of a second...

Lycus wiped his mouth with the back of his hand. "I'm sorry," he said. Shame made his voice very small.

It took Simon a moment to figure out what the boy was apologizing for. If he could have spoken, he would have told Lycus not to worry about it; no sensible person should have been able to control their stomach in that situation. But Simon was trembling too much to say anything.

Part of it was the reaction from losing both strength and reflexes at the same time, and so suddenly. Part of it was. But the rest...he had come close to dying tonight. Perhaps as close as he ever had, though his first few nights in the House had surely come near.

He told himself to get up, but his body just lay there and trembled. Long seconds passed before he could pull himself to his feet and look around.

They were standing on a dome of smooth, featureless rock, bare and gray under the light of the moon.

It seemed that they were standing on top of the dome that Simon had seen over the entrance. The positioning didn't seem right—he had expected to break out at ground level—but he pushed that thought aside. The layout of the cave clearly shifted, so this much shouldn't be too surprising. The hole from which they had emerged was the only break in the stone he could see. The dome rose higher and out of sight on one side, on the other sloping gently down until it met the ground.

And there, around the curving corner of the stone, firelight played on the rocky ground. Simon distrusted it immediately. The fires could indicate another trap as easily as safety. Or maybe—Simon's stomach twisted as he considered it, but life in the House had trained him to doubt everything— maybe the Andros family wagons were burning. They would have to approach carefully, that was certain. They couldn't take any foolish actions until they were sure.

Then Simon caught sight of Lycus picking his way down the rocks, towards the fire. He lurched forward with a cry, intending to grab the boy back before he exposed himself to danger.

"It's mother!" Lycus exclaimed, just before Simon could snatch his arm. With a glad shout, Lycus rushed down the side of the slope. And a person stepped half into view, a figure in skirts with long, flowing hair. With the fire behind her, all other detail was washed out into a black silhouette, and for a moment Simon had the panicked thought that she was just a creature of shadows imitating Lycus' mother.

Then she let out a shriek of pure emotion and ran, stumbling and tripping on her skirts, as desperate to reach Lycus as he was to reach her. They collided and collapsed into one another, each seemingly trying to out-weep the other.

Huh. So maybe it wasn't a shadow-beast pretending to be their mother in order to lure them into danger.

Simon could remember a time, not so long ago, when that wouldn't have been his first explanation.

Simon couldn't hear the conversation over the wind and distance, but a female voice said something that sounded like a question, and Lycus gestured up the slope, where Simon surely stood out against the backdrop of the night sky. Lycus' mother looked up.

Though he could barely make out the woman's face in the shadows, Simon dodged her glance, ducking back toward the hole. He couldn't face questions about her daughter; not until he got Andra out of there.

But when he stared down into the cave entrance again, he froze. Wind whistled over the lips of rock, not quite drowning out the grinding of living rock far below. The darkness looked infinite.

Remembered terror shook his limbs. The power of the steel skeleton fortified him some, but it would only go so far. What if he couldn't catch himself in time, and smashed into rock? Worse, what if more of those worms were awake? He had an uncomfortably clear vision of being pulled apart by stone jaws, blood and raw meat splashing on the cave walls...

Simon's time ran out. A young girl's scream echoed up from the cave, cutting over the shrieks of the wind. Cool breath and liquid steel flowed into Simon, flooding him with the power of a Territory. His gifts were weaker than usual, barely returned and not at full strength. But it didn't matter; he was going back in.

Hesitation gone, Simon dropped into the hole.

Maybe he would die, but Andra wouldn't. Not if he could help it.

CHAPTER 12

THE CHAINS OF VALINHALL

Once again, only Simon's enhanced reflexes kept him from dashing himself against rock with lethal speed, but he managed to weave his way through the nest of rock-worms without any of them waking.

When he got closer, he saw Andra. She was curled up on the promontory of rock above the worms, arms wrapped around herself to protect her vitals. A deafening clash of noise sounded from the passage behind her: a wave of snarling, slashing, screaming that meant two creatures were fighting. Like dogs, fighting over a scrap of meat.

Simon leaped up, landing next to the yellow-haired girl in an all-but-soundless crouch. Her lantern lay in shards next to her right hand, pieces of glass scattered over a spreading pool of oil and blood. Simon's breath caught as he saw the blood, but it didn't look serious; her arm was sliced open almost halfway to the elbow, but the cuts looked shallow. It seemed that she had swung the lantern to defend herself.

Simon reached out to check her pulse, but she flinched and made a choking sound, curling tighter. He exhaled in relief; at least she was alive and conscious.

An inhuman scream sounded from the tunnel and Simon looked up. He could only see the bare hint of movement in the blue-tinged shadows, but it was clear that some monstrous thing was locked in combat. As he watched, a claw spun lazily through the air towards them, trailing blood. It landed on the rock outcropping and spun to a halt next to Simon. The creature screamed again. Simon thought he saw something flash in the tunnel.

It was past time to be gone.

"Okay, Andra. Get up." She curled tighter; Simon shook her. "Andra, it's me. Your mother's just outside. Lycus is with her."

That roused her. She shook herself and stared at Simon as if trying to decide whether he was really there.

Something stumbled out of the tunnel. It looked like a cousin to the mantis-thing Simon had killed earlier, all insectile grace and overlapping stony plates. One of its claws was missing, and it oozed ichor.

Andra screamed, and Simon decided it was time to go. He scooped her up and jumped off the ledge, down into the bowl below.

The Nye essence and liquid strength were fading away, but there was enough of each left that he had no trouble landing on the rough, sloped stone surface. He would just have to make it out before his powers left him entirely.

Still carrying Andra, Simon leaped over the body of the nearest worm, clearing it in a single bound. No problem so far, and if he hurried, he should be able to get Andra through the hole in the roof before his powers faded again.

Simon landed on the other side of the sleeping worm. And stared straight into burning eyes.

Somehow the rock-worm's stony face registered surprise. The granite eyelids widened, and its flap of a mouth opened and closed soundlessly. For a second, Simon was too stunned to move. Some part of him wondered whether, if he kept his gaze still enough, the worm might stay where it was.

Trying to maintain eye contact, Simon edged slowly to one side. Maybe he could sneak around the thing, get far enough away to escape while it was confused. He slid another step.

In his arms, Andra let out a shuddering little squeak of fear.

The worm's searing blue eyes, each the size of Simon's two hands together, flicked down to Andra, then back up to Simon. They flared bright, and the rock-worm tossed its head back, letting out a cry halfway between a lion's roar and a trumpet call.

The nest of giant, tangled worms began to writhe. Glowing eyes lifted above the mass as dozens of other rock-worms woke. From the distant corners of the cave, more deafening cries answered the first.

Simon tried very hard not to scream and run.

The closest rock-worm plunged its head at Simon, mouth gaping wide. It was filled with teeth like sharp chips of obsidian. Simon barely had time to duck out of the way, shifting Andra under his left arm as he did so. He should have been faster than that; with the Nye essence in him, it should have looked like the worm was striking through cool honey. He scrambled to hold the glowing essence in him, but it was like trying to hold steam in his fingertips. It was sliding away from him, no matter what he did. And he thought he could feel Andra growing heavier by the second; the quicksilver strength must be draining as well.

Simon turned and ran for the exit. Andra screamed something from under his arm, but the noise of the worms around him was far too loud. He ignored her; if he didn't make it out of the cave before his powers faded, they were both dead. But running through a room full of giant sleeping rock-worms was one thing, and doing it when they were all awake and thirsty for blood was something else entirely.

A flick of a boulder-sized tail clipped his shoulder, and he stumbled forward in between three enormous heads. They snapped at him with mouths big enough to consume his ribs in a single bite. He managed to stab one in the eye and dodge the second, but the third got a mouthful of Andra's hair. She screamed as the worm pulled her by the hair, dragging her out of Simon's grip. Simon lunged for her, but the worm he'd wounded went into a frenzy. Maddened with pain and anger, it flailed about, slamming into Simon with its body and bringing its teeth down on Simon's leg.

It was like someone had wrapped his leg in a blanket of rusty nails and then squeezed tight. Pain flashed, white and hot, and he screamed. The worm shook its head like a dog shaking a rabbit, and the rusty blades sliced through skin and muscle.

Somewhere inside, Simon realized that he was about to die. He and Andra were both about to be eaten. He had never experienced the sheer surge of primal, instinctive terror that thought inspired in him. When he had thought Kai or Chaka was about to kill him, at least he would have died clean; one thrust through the heart, followed by whatever came next. This would be neither clean nor merciful, torn apart by monsters under the earth.

And Simon refused to allow it to happen. He reached for strength, reached deeper than he ever had before. He stretched his mind out to Valin-hall, to the steel skeleton in the depths of the blue-lit basement.

Time slowed. The ring of steel on steel drowned out all other sounds: the sound of Benson clapping.

"Not bad, boy," the skeleton said. "I'm game. Now let's see what you can do."

Icy cold flowed into Simon's veins, not in a smooth trickle, but in a raging torrent that seemed to freeze him from the inside out. It did nothing to soothe the pain, but Simon found that almost didn't matter.

He let his sword fall, grabbing the rock-worm's jaws in both hands. Then he pried his leg out with raw strength.

The worm tried to fight, but it felt like a temperamental dog instead of a rampaging monster. Simon hopped away from its head—careful to avoid landing on his injured leg—and scooped up his sword. One of the other rock-worms struck at him, but he drove his sword so deeply that it must have pierced the brain; the creature simply shuddered and went limp down its whole length, the light in its remaining eye fading. Glowing blue fluid leaked down Simon's blade. The injured worm struck again, and Simon drove his sword up, under the thing's chin, in between its head and body where the armor was weak.

Simon felt the blade shatter, even as gallons of stinking blood poured down from the wound. He let the sword go and glanced around for Andra. The Nye essence had faded, but it barely mattered to Simon. With this much power rolling through him, he felt invincible.

He was almost surprised to see Andra alive, struggling at the worm that still held her hair. It had curled around her lightly, eyeing others of its kind who got too close. Apparently it didn't want to share its meal.

Simon tore the sheath off his belt with his left hand and used it as a cane, hobbling closer to the worm.

Andra spotted him and screamed for help. The rockworm holding her saw him at the same time and roared, lunging. Simon felt a surge of relief; at least he wouldn't have to walk all the way over there.

Simon felt the power of the cold steel flowing through him, and he grabbed the striking worm in both hands.

Even with more strength than he had ever imagined, Simon could feel the weight and power of the monstrous worm. It bore down on him, inexorable, and nothing he could do could directly oppose its weight or break its rocky armored plates.

But with a surge of cold power and a heave of his shoulders, Simon tossed it to one side.

The crash as the monster hit the cave floor was deafening, and a cloud of dust rolled up where the body struck. Andra hurried over to him through the dust, looking stunned.

Simon tried to smile at her. She shoved him towards the opening above. "Go!" she shouted. "Let's go!"

It was an excruciating exercise in torture just walking over to the wall, and the periodic strikes from the rock-worms didn't help. Without the Nye essence, he opposed the creatures with only main strength and his bare hands. His leg felt as if it had been dipped in oil and set aflame.

The climb up the wall was actually easier than walking. He only needed three limbs for the climb, and with the extra strength he thought he made the trip in less time than he had with Lycus.

Andra's whole family was waiting when they emerged from the cave.

Simon popped up from the hole, pushing Andra ahead of him and then sliding up after her onto solid rock. The children's father had to scramble out of the way to make room, but Simon didn't much care.

The Agnos family fell into one another, weeping and clutching each other desperately. The children cried, but they were almost drowned out by their father's sobs. Their mother kept up a stream of soothing whispers, and tears glistened on her cheeks.

It wasn't the kind of scene Simon wanted to watch. This was a private moment; he had no wish to intrude. Andra and Lycus' mother shot him a glowing look over her daughter's head and mouthed 'thank you.' He gave her a sort of jerky nod and looked away, cheeks heating.

A hand extended into his view. He followed it up to the iron-haired man he had seen earlier. His face was largely covered in shadows, but Simon thought it looked softer than before. Simon took his hand, and the older man pulled him to his feet. Well, to his foot. His left leg blazed when he tested his weight on it, so he was forced to lean entirely on his right.

As soon as he stood, the world spun around him. His head felt light, and he eyed his own leg. The cuts were shallow, but they burned, and he suspected he may have lost too much blood.

The other man's eyes widened. "Caius! Olissa!" Lycus and Andra's parents looked up. "He needs help. We should carry him to the wagons."

"I," Simon said, "I'll...have to...back."

Simon tried to tell them he would be fine, that he had to go back, but his head spun again, and he flopped into their waiting arms. If he missed his first night in the cave, Kai would never let him pass the trial. Simon kept up his protests until Olissa cut his pants leg away and started wrapping his wounds. White pain shot up his body, running along his bones, and on top of the blood loss and exhaustion it was too much.

A comfortable warmth surrounded him as he sunk down into sleep.

Distant whispers slid into Simon, banishing dreams. It almost felt like he could make out the words, but recognition slipped away.

Another voice joined the whispers. "He's been a good boy," it sang. "We should give him what he needs."

More whispers, softer this time.

"I could not agree more." The quality of the second voice changed, becoming more amused. "Wake up, little mouse. I know you can hear me. Wake up."

Abruptly Simon recognized Kai's voice, and it acted on him like a spark in a pile of dried leaves. He burst awake, springing up and clawing desperately for a sword. He found none, so he clenched his hands into fists, determined to die with blood on his hands. His eyes never stopped moving, seeking for the threat.

He found nothing.

Simon stood inside what was seemingly a canvas-covered wagon, probably one of those with the Agnos family caravan. The wagon rumbled beneath him, and he heard oxen lowing outside—the wagon was moving. Wooden crates took up most of the wagon's interior, blocking much of the wagon from his view. An oil lantern sat inside one of the crates, cushioned in sawdust, but it was unlit; the only light came from moonlight filtered through the canvas roof.

Someone had spread blankets across three crates and laid him on top. He stood on them now in a fighting crouch.

He faced Kai, who sat at his ease on another stack of crates. His smile was amused, though as usual Simon couldn't see the swordsman's eyes behind white bangs. Azura apparently remained in the House, but Kai cradled a blond doll in a powder-blue dress under his left arm.

"What a jumpy little mouse he is," Kai murmured. "Almost like he had a reason to fear."

"What are you doing here?" Simon asked. He couldn't seem to get his heart to slow down, like his body expected danger and wanted to be ready.

Kai held up a clay jug and shook it. It made no noise. "The leg was quite nicely minced. Much longer and you would have never danced another reel."

Come to think of it, Simon's leg hadn't collapsed when he jumped to his feet. Experimentally, he flexed his left knee. Someone had untied the bandages, but there was no pain. The leg ached a little, maybe felt a little tight, but it didn't hurt. It felt clean.

"From the pool?" Simon asked. He was still having trouble coming to terms with Kai actually being there.

"The water weakens every second it's away from the House. By the time I got here, it was barely enough. Now you can get back to work."

Simon hopped down from the blanket-covered crates, hope surging. Maybe Kai would let him try again after all. "I lost my sword in the Cave. Should I go back in unarmed?"

Kai's head tilted slightly, curiously. "Call steel, little one."

"What?"

"The liquid steel the skeleton brews. Call it to you."

"Oh, right." Simon focused on an image of the liquid metal in the glass vial, locking it in his mind. As usual, he reached into Valinhall for more.

The power flooded into him, far greater than the usual trickle. His muscles tightened until they felt banded with cold iron, and his bones seemed replaced with solid ice. It had only come this strongly once before, when he pulled Andra from the cavern.

The soft light in the wagon wasn't much, but he could see well enough to make out details that had been invisible to him in the cave: a light gray design wrapped around his forearms from wrist to elbow, twisting into a clearly recognizable image. Chains. Like chains had been tied around both his arms and then removed, leaving only their shadows behind.

He stared at his chain-marked arm in horror. What had happened to him? He had never seen the chains before, but he could feel them, cold and hard against his skin, as if he wore actual bonds of steel. Though they looked like harmless gray tattoos, he could see them moving, crawling up his arms. They were past his elbows now. Maybe Kai had done this to him while he was asleep?

Kai nodded slowly. "The marks on your skin show that you have drawn deeply enough," he said. "They prove your bond to the House."

Hesitation crept out through Simon's voice. "So...I passed?"

A sound blew on the wind, like whispered laughter. Kai chuckled along with it. "Oh no, you failed. I don't think anyone has failed any faster. But success was not the point of this exercise. It was only a test to force you into a position in which you had no choice but to rely fully on your new powers."

"What are you saying?" Simon asked.

Instead of answering, Kai reached into the air, never taking his eyes—or his face, at least, since his eyes were still covered by white hair—from Simon. Space shimmered in a long line, and Azura stretched out from Kai's fist, gleaming. It stretched almost half the length of the wagon.

Kai pushed Azura's hilt toward Simon. "Take it."

Hesitantly, Simon did so. The hilt was wrapped in black cloth, but tightly enough that he knew it would never slip. As he had suspected, its length made it awkward; even the slightest shift in his grip made the end swerve toward the wagon's canvas.

"Too heavy?" Kai asked.

It wasn't. The cool power running through his veins mocked weight so trivial; he might as well have been carrying a stalk of wheat. Simon hefted it up and down experimentally, careful not to cut anything.

This is amazing, Simon thought. How had his life changed so much in just a few weeks? His chest tightened abruptly with the realization, the overwhelming feeling, that his world wasn't ever going to be the same.

Plus, now he had a huge sword. His eight-year-old self would have been delighted.

"That's one of the purposes of this trial," Kai continued. "To make sure you're physically strong enough for one of the Dragon's Fangs. But there's one more purpose, too."

Simon's eyes snapped up from the end of the sword to Kai. He didn't want to look too eager, but it sounded like Kai was about to hand him another miracle.

"Reach deeply," Kai said, "as you did before. Only this time, picture the entry hall. Call out to it, like you did to Benson for steel."

Simon reached, stretching out, straining, drawing on the power of Valinhall. Nothing happened.

He opened his mouth to say so, but his master cut him off. "Now move the tip of the sword down, through the air. As if you are tearing a curtain hanging from the wagon's roof, but much slower."

Simon did so slowly, carefully, feeling a little foolish. He held the vision of the entry—with its mirrors, wooden sword racks, and soft red couches—tightly in his mind.

The tip of the sword moved through the air about an inch before Simon felt the faintest resistance, as if the sword had reached the edge of an invisible sheet of parchment. Simon drew the sword down a little at a time, slicing through...something, as he did.

Following Azura's descent, the world tore open, revealing wood-paneled walls, empty sword racks, and gilt-framed mirrors. As though the image of the wagon had just been printed on a curtain, and Valinhall rested behind.

When Simon brought the tip of the sword down to rest on the wooden planks of the wagon bed, wood-scented wind blew from the ragged oval Gate in the air. On an impulse, Simon stuck his arm through, into the entry hall. The air on the other side felt noticeably cooler.

He pulled his arm back out and grinned over at Kai, thrilled with the sense of power. But Kai wasn't smiling anymore. Kai drew the backs of his fingertips slowly down the doll's blond hair. With a look as though he were watching his sister die, Kai set the doll down on the crate next to him.

Then he stood up and walked over to Simon, clapping a hand on his shoulder. Kai never made any sort of friendly gesture, so this one caught Simon off guard. For a moment, he wondered if it meant he had done something wrong.

"Azura is yours," Kai said. "Treat her well."

Simon blinked at him as though he were speaking another language. "There are a bunch of swords without an owner, right? I thought I was going to get one of those."

Kai shook his head. "If we could just hand them out as we wished, much of my life would have been simpler. But if we do, they will be no more than steel for you. The House has chosen, and we must respect its choice. If you tried to use a different blade, you'd never be able to open a Gate, nor would you enjoy its...other benefits."

Simon waited for a moment, but Kai said no more. After a handful of awkward seconds, Simon ventured, "So you want me to ask about the other benefits?"

Kai muttered to himself, then sighed. "You know, little mouse, you... never mind. You've seen already that members of the Army have their own bedroom with its own number. Mine is number seven. Azura is the seventh Demon Fang forged by the Wanderer, so only Azura's bond can open that room. The seventh bedroom is yours now, along with everything in it."

If Simon's jaw wasn't hanging open, it was only because he was too stunned to do more than freeze. The sword he had just received was probably worth more than everything in his house in the village had been, and ordinarily he would have been too shocked to even accept. But he had expected to earn one of the thirteen Fangs, if not Azura, so that hadn't come as much of a surprise. The bedroom was something else entirely. It was twice as big as his house, and a thousand times better appointed. Even sleeping on the floor next to the bed for a few months had been more comfort than Simon had ever expected. To have the whole room to himself was beyond imagining.

Weakly, Simon said, "But it's bigger than my whole house." It was the closest he could come to a protest.

One corner of Kai's mouth twitched up, and it looked like he was about to laugh. "Not anymore." He nodded towards the open Gate. "Now your House is much bigger."

To his shame, Simon almost choked up. Somehow the otherworldly powers of a Traveler didn't seem as great a gift as somewhere to stay.

"I've got other business to see to," Kai said, "and so do you. So listen close, little mouse, and perhaps you won't get eaten up."

"Yes, sir."

"First, each of the swords comes with an advisor. Someone to guide you, to teach you, to help you in battle. You met Hariman, didn't you?"

It took Simon a second to recognize the name of Denner's talking book. He nodded.

"And, of course, you've seen mine." He gestured to the doll lying on the crate, and sadness passed over his face again. "My lovely little ones. I will miss them so. They're so much better than..."

His voice trailed off. Simon glanced back at the doll, remembering all those haunting whispers at odd times. Maybe those had been, as he had once suspected, the dolls communicating with Kai. Giving him advice?

Of course, Kai still might be insane. He had to keep reminding himself of that.

"Now," Kai said, "a warning." He held up the back of his hand, and it took Simon a second to recognize the mark on the back of Kai's hand: a single link of chain, written in shadow.

"I keep my chains under control," Kai said. "The more you use your powers—and the deeper you draw on Valinhall—the more the chains will grow. The longer you resist, the more the chains shrink. Right now they will grow quickly, and they will vanish quickly. This will not always be the case."

Kai's voice got quiet, and he stared at the back of his hand. "Do not let the chains cover your body," he said.

"What? Why?" Simon asked, shaken. The chains were already up past his elbows; how much longer did he have? "What will happen if they do?"

"Incarnation," Kai responded. "Later you should ask the dolls—we are running out of time."

Simon glanced nervously down at his arms.

"One final thing," Kai said, and his voice was strong again. "The children you saved. You know they are Damascan?"

Simon shrugged, uncomfortable. "It's not so rare. Back home, we all thought Leah's father must be Damascan, because her eyes were blue. And Alin's family was supposed to have a touch of it, way back."

"I do not accuse you, little mouse. You did a good thing. But this family has at least one soldier with them."

Simon thought of the man with the iron-gray hair. He nodded.

"One soldier, and enough wagons to supply many more," Kai said. "Why do five people need four wagons? And since you fell asleep, the wagons have been moving. Back toward Myria. Why would they be doing that, I wonder?"

Simon could think of no response. He had felt safe sleeping here, but now he wondered if he was in hostile country after all.

Kai walked through the Gate, still talking. "Troubling questions. I suggest you leave as soon as you can. Nothing good can come of staying here."

"I'll be going to Bel Calem," Simon said. "I've got to get everyone out."

"You've slept a long time, boy," Kai responded. "Nine days left until midsummer. Tomorrow, the sacrifices will begin."

The Gate was closing now, reversing the direction in which Simon had carved it. The hole slid over Kai's feet, his shins, steadily closing him inside the House.

"Master, you won't have your sword anymore. Won't you need one?"

Kai cocked his head. "Azura has always belonged to another. I was only borrowing her for a pleasant while. But now," his face turned grim, "now I have to get *my* sword back."

The opening was only about as big as a window now, and through it Simon saw the older man turn on his heel and walk deeper into Valinhall. Without looking back, Kai waved one hand in the air, a gesture of farewell.

And the Gate winked shut.

The old man's name was Boez, and he screamed her name as Malachi's soldiers dragged him away. He reached out a hand, at the last instant, as though he expected her to save him.

Leah turned her face away, tasting bile.

"Don't tell me you've developed a tender stomach now, of all times," Malachi said. He himself sat across from her, the folding table between them covered in a neat white tablecloth. Breakfast sat before them: sliced bread, tea, a selection of local fruits. Malachi speared a fig on a small two-tined fork, lifting it to his mouth and chewing with obvious pleasure.

Boez's scream, muffled by the wall between them, made her stomach twist again.

"I find that the wails of the damned make a poor appetizer," Leah replied. Her plate was clean, and as far as she was concerned it would remain that way.

Malachi smoothed a lock of silver-streaked hair over his ear, examining the effect in the back of a spoon. He was a vain man, of the sort Leah had never been able to stand. He always wore one or another of his colors, though rarely both at the same time, since 'Purple and brown go together worse than fire and salt.' Those were his exact words, and Naraka take her if she had any idea what they meant. He was wearing brown today, though she more often saw him in purple.

"I had thought you would be accustomed to such accompaniment," he said. He never took his eyes off his own reflection. "After all, you have lived your life in the presence of the King himself. And we have both tasted the fruits of Ragnarus, have we not?"

Leah fixed him with her coolest stare and arched one eyebrow. "You presume to know the nature of my experience?"

Malachi grunted a laugh and took a sip of tea. A sound like weeping drifted through the walls. "Hardly. But I can't help but wonder if your recent experience has softened you, even after a lifetime of training."

She kept her eyes fixed and expressionless, but inside she winced. He was right, as far as it went; she found it almost impossible to retain the necessary distance from the sacrifices when they had fed her and treated her as family for the past year. And she knew they still thought of her as one of them, despite everything.

Deliberately Leah reached for a piece of bread and tore off a corner. "If you are so concerned about my breakfast habits," she said, "then I will put you at ease."

She stared at him in challenge as she ate, and caught a flash of irritation that he was too slow to hide. He obviously considered her presence here a burden, as though the King was directly interfering in his affairs. Well, that was just too bad.

Her latest orders from the capital, passed through her Territory of Ragnarus, had been explicit: stay where you are and wait. The Elysian will come to you.

He hadn't done so thus far, but her father seemed not to care.

"So tell me again about this Elysian Traveler," Malachi said. "Your age, is he? A villager?"

Rather than speak through a mouthful of breakfast, Leah nodded.

"And why do you expect him to come here?"

Leah swallowed and took a sip of tea before answering. The tea was actually quite good. "Based on what I know of him, and what I've heard from Enosh, he has an inflated opinion of his own abilities. And he blames you, personally, for what happened in Myria."

Malachi made a sound like "tsk" and rolled his eyes. "That again. Collecting the sacrifice is usually such a simple affair. Easier than collecting taxes, to tell you the truth. I was hoping Yakir would be able to keep Cormac in line. I'm almost glad he's dead, but he was my only Endross."

"Regardless," Leah went on, "he blames you, not Cormac."

"So he's going to challenge me on his own," Malachi said. Unexpectedly, he smiled. "I like it. Shows spirit. Charge right in and fight, face to face. None of this dancing around and maneuvering business."

"He's a fool," Leah said. The sad thing was, Alin would probably see matters in much the same way. By all accounts, he had taken this hero business far too closely to heart.

Malachi relaxed and popped a fruit in his mouth, leaning back in his chair as he did so. "I don't mind fools," he said. "We should all have a little bit more foolishness in our lives. Don't you agree?"

Leah stared at him a moment before collecting herself. She couldn't help it. For a moment there, as he relaxed, he had seemed almost...competent. Even dangerous. Like a real Overlord. She had always heard rumors that Malachi's wife was the one who kept his realm running smoothly, and in the few weeks she had spent in Bel Calem, she had seen Adrienne prove her worth far more often than her husband. But perhaps there was something in Malachi beneath the surface, after all.

Boez screamed again.

"The sacrifices I have witnessed were not usually so...vocal," Leah said. It was a lie, of course; she had never been allowed to witness a sacrifice. But she had always pictured them as quick, like a clean decapitation or an efficient hanging.

Malachi's eyebrows shot up. "Really? This is only my second round of sacrifices, but they're all drawn-out affairs. Then again, perhaps the others are different."

"Perhaps they are," Leah said. Best to keep her statements as neutral as possible, so Malachi would assume she knew more than she did.

"Or maybe the Tree is hungry today," Malachi said idly.

And, while Leah's thoughts were elsewhere, her mouth betrayed her. "Tree?" she asked.

Malachi froze for a moment, studying her. She realized her mistake immediately, and responded with the speed of a well-trained liar. "Oh, of course," she said, as though she had just realized something. "The Tree. That must be what you call it. In Ragnarus, we use different terms."

Whatever this Tree was, it obviously had something to do with the sacrifice, and the sacrifice was a function of Ragnarus. She just wasn't sure how. In any case, Malachi should now assume that she had misunderstood him for some secret and mystical reason known only to the royal family. He would likely drop the topic immediately.

"Maybe we should inspect it together, then," Malachi suggested. His voice was altogether too light; he suspected something.

Leah laid her fork down calmly across her plate. "Whatever for?"

He shrugged. "If the sacrifice is taking too long, perhaps there is something wrong with the Tree itself. I'm no expert, but it has seemed...restless, for quite some years now. I would certainly not wish to risk the sacrifice on my own ignorance, and a Ragnarus Traveler such as yourself may be able to give me some expert advice."

Leah made a show of brushing her hands and mouth off with a towel while the servants took breakfast away. What could she say? He was obviously just trying to prod her, get her to reveal some weakness. She couldn't back out now. And anyway, all she would have to do is take a quick look and say that everything seemed in order. He would never be able to tell.

"Very well," Leah said. "Lead on."

After all, what could go wrong?

CHAPTER 13
THE WRONG PLACE

Simon stared into the space where Kai's portal had been for a long minute. Excitement warred with fear and nerves inside him, and his stomach churned. The only thing he wanted to do was bring the captive Myrians home, but he wasn't such a fool that he thought there wouldn't be some resistance. But how could he challenge Malachi? An Overlord had years of experience as a Traveler behind him, not Simon's few weeks. And that didn't even count his legions of soldiers, throngs of loyal supporters, and resources Simon likely couldn't even understand.

On the other hand, in about eight more days, people he had known all his life would be dead. He hadn't especially liked any of them except Leah, but they were his own people. Practically family. And you didn't have to like your family to protect them.

At that moment, the steel in his blood ran out. Azura suddenly felt as if it weighed as much as a blacksmith's anvil, and the hilt wrenched itself out of his hand. As soon as the sword left his fingertips, it vanished.

Kai had been able to let the sword go whenever he wanted without it vanishing; there must be some trick. Hopefully he would learn that with time. More importantly, his head swam, and his vision was so blurry he could barely make out anything besides a moonlight-colored smear. He dropped back onto one of the crates.

The chains on his arms didn't vanish, but they started to retreat. He could feel them crawling down his shoulders like steel-scaled serpents.

Was the light-headedness related to the chains in some way? Or was this what happened when he released the liquid metal power too quickly? He had always felt less when he lost his enhanced abilities, but he had assumed that was just what it felt like when you went from being a superhuman Traveler to a young man with too-thin arms. Maybe there was some kind of aftereffect, like with his mother's stronger powders? Or maybe he was just tired.

"Kai could tell me," Simon mumbled thickly. It was a measure of his disorientation that he spoke to himself; he had always hated it when others did that. "If he was here."

Well, he's not, came a woman's voice. *And good riddance.* The voice was soft, as though coming down a long tunnel, and overlaid with a sound like wind whispering through trees.

168

Simon's first thought was to turn to see who had spoken, but he wasn't being honest with himself. He knew who it was.

He met the painted wooden eyes of the doll across from him. "Are you speaking to me?"

No answer.

The dizziness had mostly passed, so he hauled himself over to the doll's crate and picked her up in one hand. She was even lighter than she looked, her light blue dress woven of finer and softer material than anything his mother had ever owned.

"If you're talking to me, talk," Simon said to the doll. She gazed at him out of a wooden face. "What's your name?" Nothing. "Aren't you my advisor? Advise me!"

He had gotten more conversation out of tree roots.

Roughly he shook the doll in his hand. "Answer me!"

Of course, Olissa picked that moment to check on him. She froze halfway inside the wagon, holding the canvas flap over her head with one hand. There he was, holding a little girl's doll in one hand, standing over it, screaming. A rush of heat set his face aflame. He stammered something, trying to come up with a reasonable-sounding explanation, but evidently the fact that he was standing up outweighed his obvious insanity in Olissa's mind. She moved the rest of the way into the wagon, her face firm.

Her voice, however, remained gentle. "You shouldn't be up on your leg so soon," she said. "It needs a chance to heal."

"Um, no ma'am, thank you," Simon responded. "It's better now. See?" He stepped from behind one of the crates so that she would have a clear view of his previously-injured leg.

Her brow furrowed as she looked. The rock-worm's teeth had shredded his pants leg into tatters, most of which had to be removed before they could put bandages on him in the first place. As a result, his left pants leg ended above the knee.

From her distance, Olissa should have been able to make out the lack of blood, even in the dim light. But she frowned and moved closer.

"Put the leg up," she said, motioning to one side. Simon did as he was told and put his right foot on a crate. As though she couldn't believe her eyes, Olissa reached out and poked his leg with a finger. Nothing happened, and she gasped, sharply raising her head to look him in the face.

It occurred to Simon for the first time that Andra and Lycus' mother was a more-than-pretty woman. Her honey-colored hair—a shade lighter than any he'd ever seen, except on her daughter—spilled in waves down her back, and she stared at him with wide eyes of pale green.

If it was possible, the realization made him even less comfortable. She was old enough to be his mother, after all—if she had looked older, maybe put on a few dozen more pounds, he would have had no problem. But as it was, all he saw was a pretty woman, and that weighed down his tongue.

"Uh," he said. "I healed it. It was...I mean, it's healed."

Awkwardly he pulled his leg from the crate and, just to give his hands something to do, began brushing off his pants.

"Amazing," Olissa breathed. "The children told me, but I wasn't sure...You must be a Traveler. Asphodel?"

Simon just stared at her for a moment, trying to figure out the word. Asphodel had to be the name of another Territory. One connected with healing, maybe?

"No," he said. He should say something else, but nothing came to mind.

She leaned forward. "Did you come here for us? Do you work for the Overlord?"

Simon let out a short laugh before he could stop himself. "I mean, no, I don't work for Malachi. I'm just—"

Something she had said jumped out at him, and he stopped mid-sentence. "What do you mean, did I come here for you? Why would the Overlord be sending you a Traveler?"

Olissa shifted her eyes uneasily and opened her mouth as if about to respond, but she was interrupted by the sound of hooves on hard-packed dirt. It sounded like many horses, not just one.

For the first time, Simon realized the wagon wasn't moving. "We're stopped," he said. "Where are we?"

She smiled and gave him a reassuring pat on the arm. "You slept a long time. We've stopped at the northwestern edge of the Latari Forest. Don't worry, we've put that...Cave..." she shuddered, "far behind us."

Northwest of Latari? That would put them close to Myria. Simon opened his mouth to ask what they were doing there, but a voice from outside called Olissa's name. She apologized quickly and hurried out of the wagon, pulling the flap shut behind her.

He should probably leave. Whoever was riding into camp, odds were good that they were Damascan, and there wasn't anything good that could come of mixing with a crowd of strange Damascans. He couldn't escape by Traveling through Valinhall, he knew that; the Gate opened wherever you had last made it. But he could be out the back of the wagon and into the night before anyone knew he was missing. It would probably be the smart thing, in case the Damascans somehow learned he was from Myria.

On the other hand, how would they know him? His skin and hair were too dark for a real Damascan, but they would only think of him as the strange villager boy who had saved two children. Now that he thought of it, the fact that he had rescued Andra and Lycus would probably weigh the scales heavily in his favor. And there was nothing that marked him out as from Myria rather than from a hundred other towns and villages in the realm. He should be safe.

Besides, what if these riders weren't friendly to the Agnos family? His presence could mean the difference between repelling the attackers and the four of them being robbed, captured, or killed.

His stomach rumbled, and that decided the matter. He wasn't going to get any food in here.

He started toward the flap, but something made him hesitate. He turned his gaze back, staring at the doll in the powder-blue dress.

Black painted eyes stared him straight in the face. He was sure that when he sat her down, she had faced a different direction.

With a reluctant sigh, he walked back and picked up the doll. He didn't want to walk out in front of a bunch of strangers carrying a girl's wooden doll, but he couldn't risk leaving her behind. No matter how much the idea appealed to him.

As he crept outside, he thought the doll's face now looked just a bit smug.

Caius and Olissa, their children gathered before them, stood at the very edge of a ring of firelight. Someone, apparently, had built a bonfire as soon as the wagons had stopped, and it was just beginning to really blaze up. In the darkness beyond the fire's reach, Simon caught glimpses of a column of men on horseback. Only one had moved close enough for Simon to make out details: an old man, maybe sixty or seventy, with a wrinkled face that looked like it had dried into an eternal frown.

The man with the iron-gray hair stepped into Simon's view, standing between the Agnos family and the riders. To Simon's surprise, the lead rider saluted, hand to chest.

"Captain Erastes, sir," said the old man on the horse.

"Ansher," Erastes responded. "Come on down. You can make your report after we eat."

So the man with the iron-gray hair—Erastes—was a captain in the Damascan army. He had always looked like a soldier, but knowing his identity for certain somehow made him twice as frightening. Sure, a human soldier wasn't anything compared to a carnivorous serpent of living rock, but in Myria, Damascan soldiers had been the stuff of legend. They were the unending, faceless extensions of Zakareth's will. If Erastes decided Simon looked suspicious, he could have the full might of the Damascan nation behind him.

Ansher shook his head and stayed on his horse. "I'd advise against it, sir. There's something in the trees." He gestured to the edge of the forest, about fifty paces away, where shadows flickered back and forth. "Nobody's seen anything clear, but...I get reports. We're all on edge. Even the captives."

Erastes nodded and cast a glance into the shadows. Even though Simon could only see the back of his head, he got a sense that the man was suddenly alert, ready for action.

"Then we had best get moving," Erastes said. "Bring in the captives; we'll load them up on the wagons and leave this place. Once we're on the road, I'd like to speak with you, Ansher. We've had an eventful evening." His voice turned dry at the last sentence, and Simon was sure the captain was talking about him. It was an uncomfortable feeling. If a Damascan captain had taken a closer interest in Simon, then he should have left long since.

Simon slipped into the shadows between wagons and drew lightly on the Nye's essence. Not enough to slow his perception of time, he breathed in just enough for an extra edge of reflex and coordination that let him move both quickly and silently. His footfalls fell so lightly on the sandy dirt that he doubted anyone would have heard him ten feet away.

Sneaking away, in total silence and under cover of darkness, would be easy as picking fruit. He had even begun when a shout from out beyond the wagons snapped him short. It was a man's voice, strangled and desperate. Simon couldn't quite make out the words, if words there were, but it sounded like he was pleading.

Simon knew that voice.

Without really thinking about it, Simon called steel. Cold ice in his veins joined the cool breath of the Nye, and in one smooth motion he leapt onto the top of a wagon. He was careful to land on one of the broad wooden supports, not on the canvas; no matter how strong or swift he was, he didn't want to risk dropping his full weight on a loose stretch of fabric.

From this vantage point he could make out the Damascan soldiers much more clearly. There were maybe seventy-five of them, about fifteen of whom were on horseback. The rest walked behind in neat ranks. And behind them, stretching off in a line easily as long as the rest of the column, stumbled the captives.

They were all held on one long rope, with both their hands bound and tied on to the main line. They wore loose clothes of brown and tan, desert colors, with worn shoes or sandals and little more than a stretch of rope for belts. The same clothes Simon wore, that he had worn all his life. One of the men, larger than most in the line, crouched on his knees, holding his arms above his head defensively. A soldier standing over him beat him with a long stick, yelling something Simon couldn't catch.

The man on the ground yelled again, pathetically. Simon recognized that voice: Chaim, son of Moseth, as far as Simon knew the only one of the Mayor's advisors to survive the Damascan attack. His daughter, Orlina, had been one of Cormac's victims.

Simon almost lost his balance, and had to steady himself before he fell off the wagon. Now that he was looking for them, he recognized other faces from the village. Why? What were the people of Myria doing all the way out here?

Olissa had told him that the wagons were moving toward Myria, but Simon hadn't thought much about it. Had Kai known something of this?

Was Damasca attacking the village again?

Chaim, in the middle of taking a beating from a Damascan soldier, had already lost his daughter. He didn't deserve this. It was up to Simon to do something, but what was he supposed to do? If the Damascans had another Traveler with them, Simon wasn't sure what he could do about it. If they just summoned a monster, sure, he could fight it. But what would happen if someone hurled lightning at him? Or called fire down on his head? He would just burn and die, he supposed. And even if they had no Traveler, the thought of slicing up seventy-five people—even Damascans—made him a little sick.

Simon felt chains pressing against the backs of his hands, and he glanced down. Between the sinking moon and the nearby fire, he had just enough light to make out the chain-shaped shadows slowly growing on his hands, one link at a time, as the Nye essence drifted through him. How dangerous were these chains, anyway? He needed to ask Kai before he got himself killed. Or maybe...

He looked at the blond doll in his left hand. She still had that peaceful, self-satisfied smile on her face. What was he thinking? Of course she did. She had been painted that way. He wasn't as crazy as Kai, so until one of these dolls proved otherwise he would treat them like ordinary toys.

Still. Maybe she could answer his questions. She might be able to help him decide what to do.

Simon shook his head, disgusted with himself, and pulled his mind back to the task at hand. His anger, buried but never smothered since the attack on his village, demanded that he make an example of these Damascans. If they had no Traveler, he could most likely destroy them singlehandedly. He spun a rage-fueled fantasy of killing them all, piling their heads into one of these wagons, and sending the wagon back to Bel Calem. Let Malachi see what happened when he attacked an innocent village.

Simon's queasiness grew worse when he realized what he was considering; and worse, when he realized that he could actually carry it out. Back home, he had occasionally nursed angry fantasies, mostly about beating an older boy until he gave up. But Simon had never had the power to do anything. Now, though, everything was different.

If he wanted the Damascans dead, he could have it. Right now.

The thought terrified him. And yet, if he did nothing, the people of Myria would continue to suffer.

Finally it occurred to him that he was going about this the wrong way. From his perspective, he could see only two options: attack the Damascans or leave the villagers in captivity. But that was based on only what he knew, which wasn't much. He didn't have the whole picture, and something still didn't make sense. It was three or four days' hard travel to Myria, even for one man alone. He didn't know how much longer it would take a column of soldiers with captives, but certainly at least a day or two longer.

So what were they doing all the way out here? It was a long way for the soldiers to go just to round up some more captives, and the Myrians shouldn't have come so far from their newly rebuilt homes. What was going on?

He had to know before he did something foolish. And there was only one way to get that information.

Ask.

On the far side of the camp, Ansher sat on his horse, barking orders to foot soldiers who hurried to and from various wagons, hauling crates from one to another. The Agnos family rushed along in their preparations to leave: checking wagons, seeing to horses, rubbing down oxen, asking questions of the soldiers and examining the captives.

Lycus glimpsed Simon once and brightened, starting to run over to him, but his mother grabbed him by one arm and spoke to him sternly. Sulkily he levered a bag of some kind of vegetable onto one shoulder and walked off to a wagon in the back of the camp. Olissa gave Simon a hurried smile and a wave, then ran off to complete her work.

Erastes was sitting on the edge of a wagon, pulling on his armored boots, when Simon walked up to him.

"Feeling better?" Erastes asked when he saw Simon. His eyes were as hard as his voice. They flicked down to Simon's bandage-free leg. "I see you are." He didn't seem much surprised at Simon's accelerated healing.

"I came to ask you about the captives," Simon said. "Who are they?"

Erastes looked at him sharply. "Not your concern. Though if you'd like to know, you should travel with us a while longer. I suspect Overlord Malachi would like to meet you himself."

Simon nodded, not in agreement, but because the captain had confirmed something Simon already suspected. "You're heading for Bel Calem, then?" Simon asked.

"We're going in that direction, yes," Erastes said. He seemed determined to give away as little as possible.

"The captives as well?"

Erastes stared at Simon a little too long, clearly trying to come up with an answer that would put him off. Fortunately, at that moment Caius walked by, huffing and hauling a huge crate.

"Captives?" Caius asked. "Rebels and insurrectionists is what they are. Caught them dealing with Enosh, and you know what trouble that brings. The collar is too light a punishment, if you ask me."

The collar. They were going to be sold as slaves. It was a good thing Simon didn't have a sword on his hip, or he would have been gripping it so hard Erastes couldn't miss it.

Just to have something to do with his hands, Simon reached into the back of his belt, where he had tucked the doll. Having her there was uncomfortable and obvious—anybody who saw him from behind couldn't help but notice that he had something hidden between his pants and shirt—but he had to put her somewhere. Besides, he almost heard her indignant squawk when he put her back there. Eventually she would slip up and speak to him directly.

But once again, Simon was distracting himself from the matter at hand, trying to ignore his rising anger.

With a sigh, Erastes motioned for Caius to move on. "I wasn't going to tell you, boy, but Caius has the truth of it," he said. "We had captured some criminals up there a few months ago, and the Overlord was concerned that the rest of the village might unjustly blame him and turn to rebellion. We were sent in to get the feel of the place, maintain order. Didn't expect to find anything."

Behind the captain, one of the soldiers had untied a few of the villagers, and was herding them at swordpoint into one of the empty wagons. A bruised and battered Chaim happened to stumble, catching a glimpse of Simon as he did. Their eyes locked. Chaim's widened, even as the soldier grabbed him and brought him to his feet.

Erastes noticed nothing. He shook his head as though saddened by his own tale, but his voice did not soften. "It only took us about two hours to find out that they've been making daily trips into enemy territory. Accepting food, supplies, workers. They had even provided shelter to one of those enemy Travelers, if you can believe it.

"Naturally, we settled the whole thing down. Except a few of them escaped, we suspect headed for the capital to try and rescue their criminal friends. Spent the last six weeks hunting them down from here to the Badari Desert. And that's as much as you need know and more."

Chaim strained desperately against his captors, shouting, "Simon! Run, Simon!" The Damascans ignored him, or else didn't connect 'Simon' with the strange maybe-Traveler who had saved the Agnos children. It didn't matter. For whatever reason, they had missed their only chance to stop him.

Almost against his will, Simon drew more deeply on the liquid steel. The chains stretched up his skin, twisting around his forearms. The icy cold, rushing through his veins in complement to his anger. Ice leaked out into his voice as he spoke.

"Why weren't you going to tell me?" he asked.

Erastes shrugged and pulled on his last boot, stomping it on the ground to get it settled. "I don't trust you, boy," he said. "I don't even know your name."

"My name is Simon. Son of Kalman." His tone put heavy significance on the last three words. Damascans with a long heritage or those living in the city had family names, like Agnos. Only those who lived on the fringes of the nation, in remote villages, took their father's name. Simon watched Erastes' face as all those thoughts flitted through his mind.

Behind him, Chaim shouted one more time before he was shoved roughly into a wagon: "Run! Don't let them get you too! Run, Simon, run!"

Then Simon added, almost casually, the last part of his name.

"From Myria village."

It took the Damascan captain only a second to register the significance of the name. Once he did, his eyes widened, and his sword flashed from its scabbard. "Traveler!" he bellowed, deeply enough to be heard across a distant field.

The effect on the soldiers was immediate. One of them, behind Erastes, dropped a sack of flour to the ground and pulled his bow out of a case on his back, trying to string it as fast as possible. Ansher, still mounted, was more prepared; he put an arrow in the air before his captain's shout died. The arrowhead gleamed as it sped toward Simon, almost too fast for thought.

But not quite.

The old man's blood matched the rest of the room.

Leah and Malachi stood on a low balcony, surrounded by an iron railing, looking down on a rough room of stone. She might have almost called it a dungeon, except that it was filled, floor to ceiling, with an enormous tangle of leaves, roots, vines, and living wood. Branches crawled along the stone walls, moving slowly even as she watched, and fully half the room was obscured by a steadily shifting mass of leaves and thorns.

The worst part was that none of it was the healthy, clean color of living plants. Not a speck of green or brown showed in the whole indoor jungle. Every bit of it, from the rough bark to the tips of the soft leaves, was a bright red. A shade of red, in fact, that Leah recognized.

The scholars of Old Damasca had called Ragnarus by another name: the Crimson Vault. These plants—no, this plant—this plant was the color of Ragnarus.

She supposed she had found Malachi's Tree.

The wall of red vegetation was not alone in the room. Besides the balcony on which Leah, Malachi, and two of Malachi's guards stood, there was one more person present. Boez.

He hung in the air, branches wrapped around his wrists and ankles pulling him in opposite directions as though the Tree meant to rip his limbs from their sockets. All over his body, his skin had been shredded, as though the Tree had raked its thorns over him. He was so shrouded in his mask of blood that if Leah hadn't known who hung there, she would never have recognized him.

Feigning boredom, she very carefully looked away.

"It's quiet now," Malachi said idly. "Perhaps he's dead." He didn't look at Boez either, merely toyed with the edge of one of his fingernails. Leah wondered if he, like she herself, was just taking the excuse to look away from the dying man. But that was ridiculous.

Leah did not respond; she was afraid to open her mouth. Suddenly she wished she hadn't eaten breakfast. She fiddled with the crystal on her bracelet, letting its cool presence calm her.

"Each of the Overlords has one of these Trees, you know," Malachi said. "Your father told me that they're connected through Ragnarus, though of course you would know more of that than I. Whenever one is fed, it nourishes all the others, though to a lesser degree."

"Of course," Leah said. Her voice came out as a croak. Where was he going with this? And could they not have this conversation in another room?

"You know each Ragnarus artifact has a price, and this one is no exception. It requires blood. Nine people a year, one a day, ending on midsummer. And as long as they're fed, the Trees maintain the seal on the Incarnations."

In spite of herself, Leah took a sharp breath and stepped slightly backwards. "Then this is...there's one..."

"Here, yes," Malachi said grimly. "Underneath my house. Safest place for it, all told, where I can respond to any issues immediately. But here's my question, Ragnarus Traveler."

Suddenly Malachi loomed over her, and she had to turn to meet him, her back pressed against the cold iron railing. He was the Overlord again, grim and dangerous, staring at her with righteous anger in his eyes.

"Why?" he demanded. He gestured behind her, to the man she knew was still hanging there covered in his own blood. She did not turn to look. "Why this? Is there no other way? And if there is not, then *why are you here*, where you do not belong? Do you not trust me to handle my own business? Why can't you just leave me alone!"

He was shouting by the end, leaning close, with a fist raised.

And, intimidating Overlord's rage or no, blood-sucking tree or no, Leah decided she had had enough.

She twisted her wrist so that the crystal on her bracelet caught the light and gleamed. It wouldn't be as effective without moonlight, not enough to open a proper Gate, but she could call on what she needed.

The crystal bracelet flared with a white light, and she pressed her palm against Malachi's chest.

"Overlord Malachi Daiasus," Leah said coldly, and as she did she was proud to hear all the authority of Damascan royalty in her voice. "Take a step back."

For a few seconds she thought Malachi was going to try and use force on her anyway. His guards obviously thought so too, because from the corner of her vision she saw them take a step away, closer to the balcony's sides. They were wise enough to want nothing to do with a battle between two powerful Travelers.

She would have to kill him, of course, if he did attack. But she hoped she wouldn't have to.

Finally Malachi relaxed and closed his right fist, the one with the Naraka brand. Then he stepped back. Something seemed to drain from him and he was only Malachi again, weary and vain and a tad lazy.

"I apologize, Highness," he said. "I was overwrought."

Leah lowered her hand, letting Lirial's power flood out of her bracelet. "You are forgiven."

"But please, if you will allow me to ask, why? Just...why? What is your father thinking?"

Leah's instinct was to put the Overlord off again, tell him something vague and unsatisfying. That was how she had trained herself to deal with these matters. But there was a look in Malachi's eyes that said he genuinely wondered, truly cared, and that honesty demanded the same from her.

Unfortunately, she still couldn't give him what he wanted.

"I don't know," she admitted. Malachi searched her eyes before he nodded, once.

And then one of the guards screamed.

A thorny red vine had snaked up the side of the balcony and wrapped around his wrist. The vine stretched as long as Leah's leg but no thicker than a finger, and it looked like the brawny guard should be able to snap it with main strength, but he kept screaming, clutching to the railing with his other hand as though it took everything he had to keep from being pulled over the edge.

Suddenly the entire Tree was awake, every root and branch and leaf shaking at once. The whole was a deafening sound like a hurricane's roar, and it scared Leah far more than she would have ever admitted. She pulled light into her bracelet again, calling out for Lirial, but she wasn't sure where to strike.

Boez—or his body, since Leah still wasn't sure whether or not the man was alive—was seized around the middle by a huge branch and pulled back into the leaves, until he vanished into the thicket. The action reminded Leah eerily of prey being pulled into the mouth of some giant beast.

More thorned vines crawled up the balcony, slithering toward the rest of them. The plants were slow enough that she would never be caught as long as she was alert, but paired with the guard's screams, and with what had happened to Boez...

Leah stepped back hurriedly enough, preparing to summon something sharp and deadly from Lirial the instant these plants got close enough to touch. No sense in taking chances.

Meanwhile, Malachi had pulled the guard's sword, and had it raised. Leah wondered if he would even be able to chop this Ragnarus plant with ordinary steel—and wondered at the same time what might happen to the seal if he did—but he didn't bring the sword down on the branch.

In one smooth motion, Malachi chopped off the guard's hand at the wrist.

The guard's scream was almost lost in the ensuing roar from the Tree, which snapped the severed hand back into itself like a frog taking a fly.

They lost no time leaving the room and sealing it tight. The second Malachi cleared the rooms, he shouted new assignments for his troops: fourteen soldiers at the entrance with orders to maintain a vigilant twenty-four hour watch.

"And a healer!" Malachi called to his servants, who had rushed down the halls to find some soldiers. He and the uninjured guard were trying to bind the fallen man's severed wrist with a torn strip of shirt. As Leah watched, blood splattered up and splashed on Malachi's face. He seemed not to notice.

So Malachi tended to his servants personally, and with no concern for his appearance. That was a level of compassion Leah had never expected from the man.

Still, as she rested in her rooms at the top of one of Malachi's towers, Leah could barely shut her eyes without visions of the bloody Tree intruding. The seal on the Incarnations kept them safe, and the blood of the sacrifices maintained the seal. But that Tree of Ragnarus had been...gruesome. Barbaric.

Leah had never questioned the necessity of the sacrifices before, but her Lirial training taught her to look at problems from every angle. This time, she did not like what she saw.

What power was this that kept them safe? Could it be trusted? And if this was what it took to get the Incarnations sealed, how much worse would it be if they ever escaped?

It was a long time before she fell asleep.

CHAPTER 14

PLAYING WITH DOLLS

Simon called Nye's breath into his lungs, a rush of cool power that hummed in counterpoint to the steel flowing through him. He leaned back, letting Ansher's arrow fly past his face. He felt the wind as it passed him, and the Nye essence slowed the scene so much that he could see the individual ripples in the arrow's brown-and-white fletching as it brushed by his nose. He thought he could reach out and pluck it from the air, but he just watched as it flew by and buried itself in the wood of the wagon behind him.

Erastes thrust his sword forward in a move so smooth it would have done Kai proud. Simon twisted to one side, pulling the doll from his belt in the same motion. Carefully he placed her on the bed of the wagon, right next to Ansher's arrow. He didn't want her digging into his back while he fought, but neither would he risk her getting hurt.

Broken. He had meant broken, of course, not hurt.

Out of sheer reaction he turned, evading a return slash from Erastes that turned into a three-part combination pushing him away from the wagon. Heat on his back told him the older man was trying to maneuver him into the bonfire.

He could have dodged Erastes' sword all night—or at least until the Nye essence ran out—but two soldiers joined him, moving to flank Simon on his right and left. On top of which, Ansher sent another arrow in his direction. Simon almost impaled himself on Erastes' sword trying to dodge the missile.

Simon thrust his hand out and summoned Azura.

It appeared almost instantly this time, a seven-foot length of steel shining along its slightly curving surface. One of the soldiers stumbled back at its appearance, inches from a fatal stabbing, and the other took the opportunity to swing a sword down at Simon's head. Simon swept Azura around in an arc so fast it looked like a solid sheet of shimmering steel. It sliced neatly through the soldier's sword, sending the weapon clattering to the ground in two red-hot pieces.

He almost ran the man through out of sheer reaction, but something in him stopped. He was still strangely reluctant to kill these men. This was too different from training in the House, where everything was inhuman or else indestructible. The thought of actually ending a life, now that he was face-to-face with it, seemed almost incomprehensible.

Then Erastes was thrusting his sword at Simon's ribs. He tried to get Azura in between them, but his blade was far too long, and he was forced to dodge and leap back to put some distance in between them. He brought Azura down, trying to force the captain back, but the man raised his sword to intercept. Simon waited for the Dragon's Fang to cleave through this sword as it had done to others, but Erastes' blade met his with a clang like two bells clashing.

And both swords stopped. The impact ran up the right side of Simon's entire body, threatening to make him drop his sword. If not for his daily training with Chaka, he might have actually done so, which would have been both embarrassing and fatal.

Only now, with his blade still locked against Erastes', did he notice something odd in the other man's weapon.

It shone with a smooth mirror-brightness that no natural steel could match. Most swords had dings, dents, places where use in combat had scraped them up. But the steel of Erastes' sword was flawless. Like Azura.

Simon stopped putting pressure on the older man and pulled his blade back. If he had pushed harder, he would have overpowered Erastes and split him down the middle, supernatural blade or no. But what was that sword? Was Erastes a Traveler as well? If so, why didn't he use any other powers?

A blaze of pain burst in his left shoulder, and Simon screamed, twisting to avoid whatever was hurting him. Another soldier had snuck up behind him, and this one had a spear. He had scored a hit along Simon's shoulder, probably aiming to skewer him through the heart.

Simon slashed Azura one-handed through the spear, slicing it neatly, but more soldiers rushed in to fill the gap, each carrying a long cavalry spear. Other foot soldiers poured in, threatening to drown him in sheer numbers.

Images filled his mind, of men reduced to meat, of blood flowing into the sand. He didn't want that. But he wanted to die even less.

Overwhelming numbers pushed him onto the defensive, forcing him to keep up a constant circle of defense just to avoid being crushed.

Okay, he thought. *Maybe I need some help.*

A smug female voice, distant as a whisper, answered. *All you had to do was ask.*

Despite his danger, Simon had to stare between the line of soldiers at the doll he had left sitting on the distant wagon. *You can* talk. *Why didn't you say anything before?*

Back, to the left.

What?

A spearpoint sliced his skin just over his left kidney, and he barely managed to sidestep before it gored him. As it was, the spear still drew a line of fire across his left side.

Told you, the voice continued. *Turn right.*

Simon followed the instructions this time and spun Azura to the right, slicing through another sword. And the top half of one soldier's head. He collapsed to the ground in a limp spray, blood spurting from his exposed brain.

No! Simon cried silently. *I'm trying* not *to kill them.*

The doll sounded baffled. *Why?*

I...I don't know.

A whispered sigh. Then, *Jump back. Over the fire.*

Simon pushed against the ground into a ten-foot-high jump that easily cleared the bonfire. A trio of arrows swept through the space where his chest had been a moment before.

He landed in a half-crouch on the hard-packed dirt, waving Azura in front of him to keep his enemies back.

How are you doing this? he asked the doll.

We hear the voice of the wind, she responded. *We speak to you the words of the air, to keep you alive. This is how we advise you.*

So...you tell me how to dodge? Simon asked.

We speak the words of the wind, she replied loftily. *How you interpret them is up to you. And my name is Caela.*

Caela, he thought to her. *Nice to meet you.*

Then he attacked.

He shattered another weapon, reversing his strike at the last second to take the spear's owner across the chest with Azura's dull side. The impact slammed into the man, sending him tumbling into the sand. It would probably injure him seriously, maybe kill him, but Simon felt better.

He knocked the next soldier off his feet with another reverse sweep of Azura, but that was the last chance he got. The rest of the soldiers with melee weapons backed off, and a line of archers stepped forward.

"Fire," Erastes shouted. Twelve archers loosed an arrow at the same instant, all centered on Simon.

You have to stop worrying about their safety, Caela sent. Simon drew as deeply as he could on the Nye essence, until it burned his lungs with ice, until it seemed as if he and the arrows both were all but frozen in midair. For some reason, it didn't seem to affect the speed of Caela's speech.

Not now, please, Simon thought. *Help me out of this first.*

If I do, you'll only die. Unless you're willing to kill them.

I don't want to, he said.

Admirable. But childish. They're enemy soldiers. This is a battlefield. If you hesitate, you will die. And then who will save your friends?

The arrows drifted closer. And though they appeared to float on a gentle breeze, Simon knew they would puncture him like a skewer through a roasting boar.

Please, just help me out of this.

Then I want your promise that you'll fight with everything you have, Caela said. Her distant voice sounded firm. *The innocent people depending on you deserve nothing less.*

I promise, Simon said. What choice did he have?

So Caela gave him his instructions. When the arrows got closer, he leaped, twisting his back and spinning at exactly the correct angle.

The fletching on one arrow brushed his arm, but that was all. He landed, and the Nye essence flooded out. He should have had a little while more, but he guessed he had used up the essence by drawing on it so deeply. For some reason, the steel remained as strong as always, giving no signs of running out. Maybe it would last longer now—he should ask Caela.

Simon heard some of the arrows clattering to the ground behind him as time resumed its normal course. The archers in front of him went pale in the face, like they saw their own deaths approaching, but their training held them and they brought arrows to strings for a second volley.

Simon didn't give them a chance to loose.

He lunged, and his first strike shattered three bows. Two of their bearers crashed to the ground as Azura's tip snagged their armor, but the third lost his hand at the wrist. His scream wrenched Simon's spirit, but this was neither the time nor the place for regret. He stepped to the side and struck at the archers on his right. Azura pierced through the belly of the first soldier, but the two behind him dived away to safety.

That was when the more heavily armed soldiers stepped in with their spears and swords, leaving the bowmen to retreat for safety. Without essence, Simon wasn't fast enough to dance with them as he had done before. But he was still as strong as all of them together.

He ruined them. He cut them down like a farmer harvesting wheat, and it tore him apart inside. Every time he sprayed blood in the air, Simon's stomach twisted, but he did not let up. He spared anyone too injured to fight or those few who retreated, but the rest he killed.

As he pulled his sword from men helpless to defend themselves, he realized that he had spent most of his life without seeing real violence. Only the day his father was killed. And the night his mother died.

How far he had come.

Finally Erastes stepped forward, stepping calmly over the bodies of his men. His face was set in stone, and his gleaming sword left a silver streak in the air as it rushed for Simon.

Without enhanced speed, Simon got a better taste of what a swordsman the Damascan captain really was. Simon had him by a good three feet of reach and ten times the older man's strength, but he was still the one to step back in front of Erastes' relentless advance.

Somehow the Damascan got close enough to take a tiny slice out of Simon's ear. How had he done that? Simon had barely seen him move. A sinking feeling grew in Simon's gut as he realized Erastes had capitalized on the weakness of Simon's seven-foot blade and stepped inside its range. Simon's steps were awkward at best, and only Caela's stream of advice and his experience sparring with Kai kept him from getting impaled in the first handful of seconds.

Simon tried to call on the Nye essence again, but it wouldn't come. Erastes was smarter, faster, and more experienced. Not to mention that Simon's own sword was getting in the way. What was he supposed to do?

Lose the dead weight, of course, Caela sent. *If it's not helping you, lose it. Obviously.*

Simon almost panicked when he realized what she meant, but then he took another cut from the old soldier's flashing blade. If he didn't try something else, then he was about to die.

He let Azura vanish.

As soon as it did, Erastes lunged forward, thrusting his blade toward Simon's head. Just in time, Simon grabbed the older man's wrist.

The point of the sword shone an inch from Simon's eyes. It was hard to look at anything else. It just looked so sharp there, a bare second from splitting his eye in two.

I told you it would work, Caela said, sounding quite pleased with herself.

Erastes strained with all his might to push the sword forward. With Benson's steel flowing through him, Simon barely noticed.

That almost killed me, he thought in Caela's direction. He still couldn't take his eyes from the sword, even as he stepped around it, keeping his grip on the captain's wrist.

Caela's laugh sounded like the rustle of trees.

At last Simon turned his attention to Erastes, who by this time was trying to pull back. Without success. Simon's chain-shrouded arms might as well have been made of iron; he could feel the power coursing through his muscles, and the chains that had encircled his limbs now snaked past his shoulders and on to his back. His steel was running out now, finally, but he guessed he had about a minute left. He should use that time wisely.

Simon planted a foot against Erastes' chest and pushed, kicking the older man backwards. Erastes' gray eyes went wide as he stumbled back almost ten feet and fell flat on his back, lying with the top of his head inches from the dying fire. His back arched as if he were in great pain.

The captain had lost his shining sword, which now rested in the dirt beside Simon's feet. He ducked down to pick it up, holding it in his left hand as he advanced on the fallen Damascan.

Without thought he reversed the sword in his grip, holding it so that the blade pointed down. Like a dagger. The soldiers should be willing to surrender once their captain was defeated. One more death, and he could take his people out of here.

Andra came flying out of the flickering shadows and threw herself on top of Erastes, who writhed and gasped for breath on the ground.

"Please stop!" she begged. "Don't do it. Don't, Simon, please."

Simon froze. Her skirt shone bright red in the dim light. She evidently hadn't had a chance to change since escaping from the cave; her clothes still bore the scratches and stains of their combat. When he had saved her life.

"I've known him all my life," Andra said, her voice thick with emotion. "Don't do this to him. He's our friend."

Simon pointed with his stolen sword, suddenly so angry he could scarcely contain it. He stabbed the weapon in the direction of the captives' wagon.

"Those are *my* friends," he said. "Look what he's done to them."

A small sound made him look over, and he saw Lycus holding a sword that was far too big for him. He held it pointed shakily in Simon's direction. Tears streamed down his face.

Caius pulled his son back before he could hurt himself. Or before Simon could hurt him. The thought speared him, and the realization of all he had done, all the people he had hurt, fell on Simon like a great weight. The sandy ground ran sticky and brown with the blood of dozens of people. He was surrounded by the groans of the dying and the stench of the dead. He had done that.

Then the steel flooded out of his body. His strength left him, replaced by an empty weakness that threatened to knock him flat on his back. Erastes' sword suddenly felt like it weighed a hundred pounds, and only a supreme effort of will kept him from dropping it in the sand.

Not now, Simon told himself. *Later. The others need your help now.* The thought got him moving, and he stepped past Andra without a word. He walked over to the captives' wagon in complete silence. Out of the corner of his eye he recognized Ansher's weathered body curled up around a seeping throat. He had tried and failed to stem his own bleeding wound with both hands. Simon refused to look at the body directly, instead focusing on putting one foot forward, then the other.

He passed a few uninjured soldiers, but they didn't try to stop him. Most of them either ran off into the shadows or curled up behind their weapons. That sight almost made him feel better.

When he reached the wagon, he swept the corner of the canvas aside. It was the stink that hit him first, the odor of dirt and waste and unwashed bodies. The captives hadn't been given a chance to wash themselves or their clothes, then. The second thing he noticed was the space. The Myrians were packed into the wagon, lashed to one another with chains and rope. They were crammed closer together than livestock, so that they barely had room to sit, much less lie down.

The sight stunned him. He had never seen animals so mistreated, much less humans. Men and women he had known all his life. Most of them were men, he noticed, but there were some women among them. He picked out Nurita, Leah's aunt, immediately. Alone out of all the others, she looked like this was a minor inconvenience. Seeing her expression, Simon was almost surprised she hadn't talked the Damascans into setting them all free.

For a moment the sight of all of them like that stunned Simon into silence. But the captives apparently felt no such restrictions. At sight of him they all burst into a flurry of questions, pleas, advice, and general noise.

"Who were they fighting?" one boy asked.

"What are you doing here?" asked another, old enough to be Simon's grandfather.

"Did you see what happened?"

"You should get out of here!"

"Do you have any food?"

Chaim elbowed his way to the front. He obviously didn't have much strength left, so he wasn't as intimidating as usual, but people made as much room as they could.

"Get out of here, boy," Chaim said hoarsely. "I don't know who they were fighting out there, but they'll be back, and you don't want them to come for you."

"The fight's over," Simon said. He wasn't sure how much to tell them. "They lost. Now show me your hands."

Chaim looked confused, but he pushed his hands forward. They were tied at the wrist by a double loop of thick hemp rope. His wrists were coated in enough dried blood that Simon suspected that his bonds rubbed constantly through his skin.

Simon pushed his borrowed sword against the rope, intending to saw through it. The effort wasn't necessary; at the touch of Erastes' blade, the rope parted like rotted cloth.

The ropes fell away, and Chaim gaped at him. The look on the older man's face might have been gratifying some other time, but Simon felt little other than numb. He stepped up into the wagon, moving between the prisoners, sword flashing. Ropes fell free. People rubbed their wrists in wonder. Some of them started crying.

None of them, apparently, had the guts to be the first out of the wagon.

When Simon finished freeing the captives, he felt a broad hand on his shoulder. He turned to see Chaim's face beside him, standing among the others of their people still stunned at their good fortune.

"Simon," Chaim said. "What happened to you?"

Simon shook his head, unable to speak, and walked out of the wagon.

The people of Myria followed.

When they saw their tormentors injured or helpless, lying all around the camp, the villagers lost their restraint. One woman set upon a one-armed Damascan soldier with nothing but her hands, screaming as she beat him. He had lost so much blood that he just curled up around his injury, shaking. A pair of boys drove one mostly-healthy soldier off with spears they scooped up from the sand, and one—little older than Simon—beat another soldier with a burlap sack of potatoes.

At first, Simon tried to hold them back, but it seemed he had at last reached the end of his endurance. He almost collapsed from exhaustion, and the world spun queasily around him. For a moment his vision blurred, and the only thing his numb body could feel was the cold sting of invisible chains dragging down his arms.

Panic gripped him. Was he going to fall over every time he used up his powers? He couldn't stop so much as a five-year-old girl from sticking a knife in him if the world kept spinning, and he didn't know what Damascan soldiers were still in the camp. He stumbled toward what he thought was a wagon, trying pathetically to hide until the ground finished rocking.

When he came back to himself, the fire had burned itself almost down to coals, and the only surviving Damascans had run, crawled, or stumbled into the night. He vaguely remembered seeing some of that, men in uniform running fast, casting fearful glances over their shoulders. Someone might have tried to shake him back to his senses a while ago, too. Or maybe not. His sense of time seemed to have deserted him.

Simon found himself sitting on the ground, with his back leaning against a wagon's enormous wooden wheel. Judging by the muffled sounds, someone was in the back of the same wagon, loading or unloading crates. Probably some of the villagers, going through them to take stock, he reasoned. A few people huddled around the fire, either clutching one another and staring at nothing or feeding the coals some pitiful handfuls of twigs in an attempt to ward off the cold.

If you're done napping, Caela's whispering voice cut in, *I suspect you might want to intervene.*

Blearily Simon looked around. Aside from the general bustle of everyone moving around a camp, things seemed quiet enough. *In what?* he sent.

Come and find out.

Simon heaved himself to his feet, paused a moment as an aftershock of dizziness hit him, and lurched forward. A few people called out to him, but he ignored them. He didn't think he was up to much real conversation right then. On Caela's teasing, whispered directions—*Warm...getting warmer now... oh, it's quite cold in that direction...there you go*—he finally found his way to a wagon on the far end of camp.

The men and women from Myria surrounded both of the wagon's open ends, as though preventing someone within from escaping. They held borrowed weapons awkwardly—one young man with a huge nose, Alin's second cousin, squeezed a one-handed Damascan infantry sword in both hands like he thought it would run off without him—and they kept up a stream of taunts and jeers in the wagon's direction.

A pair of oxen that had obviously been yoked to the wagon stood nearby, unhitched. The wagon wouldn't be going anywhere.

Leah's aunt Nurita shouted, "You'll learn what it's like!" and a chorus of agreement rose from the others.

Simon's stomach tightened. Though he hoped desperately that he was wrong, he knew who was in the wagon.

Caela lay a few strides away, resting on top of an opened crate filled with odds and ends: scraps of leather, a half-full pincushion, a matching trio of painted wooden balls. Apparently someone hadn't known where to put her, but she wasn't food, so she had been stuck with the junk deemed useless by starving villagers.

"How long has this been going on?" Simon asked her. He found it easier to just speak than to focus on sending mental messages.

They've been in there for almost ten minutes, Caela sent. *I've watched the whole thing. If I do say so, this spot is quite convenient.* She sounded as self-satisfied as if she had picked the spot herself.

"Why hasn't anyone gone in yet?"

Olissa found a spear, Caela replied.

He had hoped to be wrong. He didn't want to be the one to decide these things. No matter whose side he took, Simon couldn't imagine everyone walking away from this situation satisfied.

But there was no one else. Simon set Caela back down in the box and walked over to the wagon, heart pounding.

Slowly, a fraction of an inch at a time, chains slid down his wrists.

Simon pushed his way through the thin line of people gathered around the wagon's entrance. Nurita demanded to know what he was doing, but he ignored her, stepping up onto the wagon.

Immediately a steel point leaped at his face. He dodged to one side, narrowly missing the spear—a trap like that wasn't much worse than the Valinhall armory, really—and tried to call up Nye essence at the same time. Nothing happened; the power remained empty. Was it taking longer than usual for the essence to refill? How long had he been unconscious?

The spear withdrew quickly and then stabbed back out with the speed of panic. Simon had taken enough wounds tonight; none terribly serious, but practically every inch of his skin felt sliced or scraped. He couldn't allow any more.

Simon's hand snapped up almost without his conscious direction, grabbing the haft of the spear below the head. The person on the other end, maybe Olissa, tried to pull back, but he moved with the motion, stepping inside the darkened wagon.

Olissa crouched in front of him, clutching the Damascan spear in both hands. She was leaning back, putting her whole body into the effort of wrenching the weapon away from him. Andra faced the opposite entrance, just barely short enough to be able to stand without bending over. She held a small knife up, and had glanced over her shoulder to see who was coming in. Her eyes were wide and terrified; a dark smear of blood covered the blade.

Caius and Lycus sat in the center of the wagon. All the cargo had been removed and sorted, so they leaned against the edge of the wagonbed rather than against a crate. Caius breathed shallowly, and a great dark stain spread over his right side. Lycus kept a bundled-up rag, apparently an old shirt, pressed to his father's side.

Olissa gasped at the sight of Simon stepping in through the canvas flaps. Outside, a few of the Myrians cheered or called Simon's name.

Leaving the spear in Simon's grip, Olissa ran to cover Caius and Lycus with her body. Andra turned and held the knife in his direction, shaking. Such a change. Two hours ago, they had thought him a hero.

"Please don't," Simon said wearily. "I'm not here to hurt you."

Andra's voice shook, and she sounded even younger than her years. Like a lost child. "Then why did you kill them? You killed everybody."

"No! No, I..." How was he supposed to explain? Everything had moved too fast. "They attacked me. And the captives were from my village. Was I supposed to just let them stay in chains?"

Suddenly Simon noticed the night brightening around them. Not long until dawn. Kai had said there were nine days left before Leah and the others were sacrificed to Zakareth's Territory. But nine days from when? Did this rising sun mean he had nine days left, or eight? And did that mean the first sacrifices would begin today?

He wasn't sure, but either way, he had too much to do and not enough time.

"Not nearly enough time," he muttered.

Chaim's voice bellowed, "Simon? How's it going in there?" A big shadow approached the canvas.

"Talking with the prisoners," Simon said, improvising. "I need another minute alone."

No time left. He had to do something, even if it made the situation worse. Reaching out his hand, he called steel and summoned Azura. The Agnos family wailed almost as one, and shrunk down against the wagon bed.

Spectral chains pressed against the back of his hands again—when had they vanished the first time? As he had done once before, Simon pointed Azura's tip at the top of the wagon's cover and reached through the sword to Valinhall. Dragging the blade down through the air, Simon tore open a Gate. It took thirty, maybe forty heartbeats, and every second Simon was sure someone was just about to jump in the wagon and demand to know what he was doing.

This hole was wider than the one he had made for Kai, though he wasn't sure what he had done to make it so. Yet another thing he was going to have to learn at some point. So many things to learn, and never enough time. The far end of the wagon completely disappeared behind the familiar scenery of the entry hall.

Andra and Olissa goggled at the Gate, then at him. Olissa looked like she was contemplating running, Andra as if presented with a new hope. Lycus continued pressing the rag against his father's side, though he sent nervous glances toward Simon and the Gate equally. Caius made no reaction; his skin glistened through a sheen of sweat, and he muttered faintly to himself. Simon wasn't sure he was even fully conscious.

"What is that?" Andra asked.

"My Territory," Simon replied. Olissa drew in a sharp breath. "You can stay there for the time being," he continued. "Once I settle things with the other villagers, I'll come join you. And when things calm down, I can take you back to your home."

"This was our home," Olissa said softly. "Everything we owned was in these wagons. Once we finished this job, we were going to find a place to settle in Deborah's realm."

Simon winced. If he hadn't gotten involved, their home wouldn't have been taken from them. They would have concluded their business and moved on. Of course, if he hadn't gotten involved, Andra and Lycus would probably either be dead or trapped in Orgrith Cave. There were no good choices, and nothing easy to regret.

"Well, then, you can stay in here for the time being. We'll work something out. But you should get going."

They're about to come in, Caela's voice whispered, just as the canvas behind Simon peeled open. Chaim poked his face in, his eyes growing huge as he took in the Gate. "What is that?" he asked. At his words, a few people behind him pressed their faces forward, trying to see for themselves.

Thanks for the warning, Simon sent to Caela. She loftily ignored his sarcasm.

"Hurry," he told Olissa, pushing her toward the Gate. She and Lycus grabbed Caius, half-carrying and half-shoving him into Valinhall. Andra stood, hesitating before stepping through. The Gate shrunk steadily as it sealed itself.

"The bedrooms are on either side of the hallway," Simon said hurriedly.

"It's past that door right there. You can't open any of the bedrooms, so just head on through. If you see the guys in the dark hoods, tell them I sent you, and they probably won't strangle you. Walk through the white-and-gold door, and you'll see a pool of water. You need to get Caius into it as soon as possible. It will heal him. Watch out for the water demons, they'll try to eat you."

Olissa, Andra, and Lycus stared at him from the other side of the Gate; judging from their expressions, they were trying to decide if they were better off coming back through. Simon released both his sword and his strength, and the portal shrank even more quickly.

Andra stepped forward before the Gate could close completely. "Simon!" she called. "Where's Erastes?"

Last time Simon had seen him, the captain had been struggling for breath on the ground. He was almost certainly dead by now. "I'm not sure," he hedged.

"Please save him," Andra said. Her pale eyes were practically the only things that showed through the narrowing portal. "I know you can do it."

The Gate closed.

Great. How was he supposed to refuse a request like that?

The wagon shook as Chaim stepped up. "Sweet Maker. How did they disappear like that? And what was that you were telling them?"

"I'll explain it to you later," Simon muttered. He walked out the far end of the wagon. The people gathered there gasped as he walked out and they got a clear glimpse of the empty wagon. At another time Simon might have worried about what they thought; not now. He had bigger things to worry about. Like the fact that he may have sent the Agnos family into even worse danger by trying to save them; they had no one to show them around the House. Simon would go there himself as soon as he could, but first he had to deal with the villagers. Villagers who would probably try and lynch him when they found out he had helped a family of Damascans escape.

He wanted to sleep for a year.

Circling around the wagon and ignoring a barrage of questions, Simon scooped up Caela and began walking to the other side of camp. When he reached the glowing embers that were all that remained of the night's fire, he stopped.

Erastes lay much as Simon had left him, though someone had stripped away his armor and his hands and feet were bound with rough ropes. Bruises marred his face and every inch of exposed flesh Simon could see, some already starting to swell. A gang of boys ranging in age from about fourteen to a few years older than Simon surrounded the Damascan captain. One used a stick to flick coals over Erastes' body. When he shouted, it came out muffled, so Simon gathered he had been gagged. If he wriggled away from the pain, another boy would use the flat of a short sword to smack him back into place.

The blade gleamed strangely in the predawn light, and Simon recognized it. They were beating Erastes with his own sword. Where had they gotten it? The last time he remembered having the weapon in his own hands was shortly before he passed out, so they must have either taken it from Simon's unconscious body or picked it up from the ground afterwards.

A dim memory told Simon which of the boys was in charge; he was one of the oldest, no bigger than the others, but harder of face. He had spent more of his childhood being punished for one reason or another than anyone else Simon knew; the kid had bragged about it, sometimes. Simon walked up to him.

"Simon," the young man said. He made it sound like a challenge.

"I don't remember your name," Simon replied. "Sorry." The boy's face hardened even further, and Simon couldn't find it in himself to care. "I need the soldier and the sword."

"What for?"

Simon reached out and grabbed the other boy's wrist, twisting a way that Kai had done to him a hundred times. The boy gasped, dropping the sword, and Simon plucked it out of the air before it hit the ground. Without a word, he turned his back on the other boy and walked away.

Even as tired as he was, some part of him enjoyed that.

When he reached Erastes, Simon knelt and examined the soldier's injuries. Some of the gang shouted at him, and he suspected they were beginning to find their spines again. So he called steel and held it. Icy power flowed through him, and he ignored their threats, returning his attention to the Damascan on the ground.

Erastes was fully conscious, steely gray eyes bright with pain. His gaze showed no fear, only hatred and anger. Simon pulled the gag out of his mouth. One of the boys, behind Simon, kicked him in the back. That boy screamed as though he had slammed his foot into a stone, and Simon heard him hopping around in the sand.

Simon smiled. With the steel running through him, he had barely felt a thing.

Erastes tried to swallow, found his mouth too dry, and tried again. He spoke as though he had a mouthful of sand.

"Coward," he rasped.

"If you can talk like that, you'll be fine," Simon said. "Probably. I'm no healer." He drew Erastes' own sword across the man's bonds, slicing them as easily he could have with a Dragon's Fang.

Then, standing, he summoned Azura into his other hand. The boys yelled and scrambled away, undoubtedly going to fetch someone else. That was fine; there was nothing they could do to stop him, anyway.

He drew Azura down the air, opening another Gate.

Erastes' raspy voice grated on his ears: "There's nothing more you can do to me," the gray-haired man said, as if Simon was about to take him into some new torment.

None too gently, Simon scooped him up in both arms. With steel flowing through him, it took about as much effort as picking up a newborn kitten.

Simon walked through the Gate, holding it open with his will. He laid Erastes down on a couch, saying, "Caius and Olissa are here somewhere. Tell them I said to get you into the water as soon as possible."

"Don't need a bath," Erastes said. "Need a miracle."

Simon thought about explaining, then decided it would take too much effort. He tossed the old soldier's bare sword down beside him. "Let me know if you find one," Simon said, and walked back into the world.

CHAPTER 15

THE ROAD TO BEL CALEM

None of the Myrians were happy about losing their few remaining Damascan prisoners, Chaim and Nurita least of all. They appeared to have taken charge of the surviving villagers, since no one of any greater influence had accompanied the group south.

"They're *gone?*" Chaim had demanded. "Where did they go?"

"Who gave you the right to send them anywhere?" Nurita had asked. "You're just a child."

Even more than that, as he had expected, they wanted to know about his newfound powers. Was he a Traveler now? How had that happened? Was he working with Alin?

He tried to dodge those, ashamed for some reason that he could not quite pinpoint. He had been proud of his abilities; if anything, he should brag about them to anyone who would listen. But he didn't feel like it. Maybe once he rescued Leah and the other captives from Malachi's grasp, then he would show his pride. Until then, he was almost afraid that he would look like a pretender, a child dressing up as a warrior of legend.

Still, the other villagers would not be put off by half-truths and misleading answers. Even if none of them had directly seen him draw on his Territory, they had already seen too much.

At last, when he could take Chaim and Nurita's incessant questions no longer, he told them. "I'm a Traveler now," he said. They looked at him warily, but didn't gasp in horror or gape in wonder as he had half-expected. They seemed almost...doubtful.

"What do you mean by that?" Chaim asked, as though testing Simon's words, trying to find something hidden.

"You don't have to compete with Alin, just because—" Nurita began, but she was cut off by the tip of Azura pointing at her throat. Simon stood the better part of ten feet away, holding the blade steady in his steel-infused right hand. With his left, he rolled up his right sleeve, exposing the shadowy chain marks that crawled steadily up his arm.

A few people did gasp then, at the enormous sword, at Simon's apparent strength, or at the fact that Simon had called the sword out of midair.

"You led the ones who attacked the Damascans," Chaim said. He sounded almost in awe.

"I didn't lead anybody," Simon replied. "It was just me."

Most of the bodies around the camp hadn't been removed or buried yet, simply piled where they were least inconvenient. Chaim looked from one stack of Damascan bodies to another, and he appeared to be doing sums in his head.

Nurita's eyes narrowed, and she spoke sharply. "Are you like Alin, boy?" She didn't sound impressed, but then again, he couldn't imagine anything grand enough to bend her self-importance.

"Not exactly," he said. "I think Alin was born to it. I had to learn."

"In six weeks?"

"It's been a long six weeks."

Chaim's face had frozen into a kind of snarl, and when he spoke he sounded rabid. "Then that Damascan family. *You* have them. In your Territory."

Wary of a trap, Simon nodded slowly. "Yes."

Smacking his hand into his fist, Chaim laughed. It went along with the new, cruel cast to his face. "Good. Then we have them trapped. They can't escape us now."

"That family is under my protection," Simon said. "No one's doing anything to them."

He knew before the words left his mouth that he should never have said it like he did. Simon had never prided himself on skill with words; he tended to think of the right thing to say only minutes or hours after the fact. This would do nothing but provoke the other villagers. Indeed, angry oaths and mutters rippled through the crowd. Chaim looked both shocked and disgusted.

Simon levered Azura down, driving her point-first into the ground. At an angle, like Kai had always done, because he couldn't reach high enough to drive it straight down. He hoped this would demonstrate that he was trying to talk, not fight, though it had the side benefit of reminding his fellow villagers that he was in possession of superhuman strength and a seven-foot unbreakable blade. If they brought it to a physical confrontation, there was only one way it could end.

Chaim, apparently, wasn't overly worried about his own safety. He stepped forward and grabbed the front of Simon's shirt in both his fists.

"You have no *idea* what they did to us," Chaim growled. His voice was pitched so that everyone could hear, though Simon suspected that had more to do with the man's temper than with any desire to perform for a crowd. "Do you know how many we buried when they first caught us? Do you? Do you know how long they've had us, what they made us eat, what they made us do?" Chaim shook him, hard. "Watch them kill *your* daughter, son of Kalman, and tell me how much protection they deserve."

Simon had intended to let Chaim vent his bile, but that was enough of that. Not only was the conversation headed nowhere productive, Chaim's shaking was piling on top of stress and injury, making Simon feel like he was about to pass out again. If the man didn't stop, Simon might well puke on his shoes.

Gently, Simon pulled the older man's hands away. Chaim weighed twice again what Simon did, but Simon's only concern was that he not grip too hard and crush the man's wrists.

"I saw Orlina die," Simon said. He kept his voice even, but made sure everyone could hear him. "It was right before the same Traveler killed my mother."

Dead silence. No one dared to say anything, because many of them had been in the same cave. They had seen what happened.

"This family didn't do it," Simon continued. "No one here did. I killed the soldiers who captured you." He regretted that, but he couldn't let them see it. "Some of them ran off, I guess, but we'll never catch them. And you're angry, I know that; I am too. But we don't need to get revenge—revenge doesn't help anybody. We need to get our people back."

A few people nodded. Nurita even muttered something approving.

Chaim visibly gathered himself, scraped tears from his cheeks, and nodded. He didn't apologize, nor did he even admit that the Agnos family might not be the correct target for his anger, but he did refocus. "That's what we were doing when these Damascan dogs found us. We're headed for Bel Calem."

"What do you expect to do?" Simon asked.

"We won't know until we get there. Whatever we can. Die trying, if we have to."

Simon thought about what to say for a long moment. "Myria can't afford to lose you," he said at last. "There aren't enough of us left as it is."

Chaim leaned forward, his hard face intense. "There are ten men and women from our village in Bel Calem as we speak, waiting on His Majesty Zakareth. We can't afford to lose them either."

"All the more reason that I should leave now," Simon responded. He was losing his edge, getting nervous, debating with Chaim. It wasn't long since he had obeyed Chaim as he would have an uncle. Chaim had the advantage of age and experience; what gave Simon the right to argue? Especially out here in front of everybody. And Simon was still so tired.

"By yourself?" Nurita demanded, stepping forward. She even put her hands on her hips, for that added bit of motherly authority.

I don't need your help. I'll be better off on my own, Simon thought. He tried to say so, but his earlier confidence was evaporating quickly. What he said instead was, "I just thought it would be better that way."

Chaim shook his head. "No, boy. We'll follow your lead, but we won't be left behind."

Simon considered just running off—no one would be able to catch him—but the adults seemed to take his agreement as a matter of course. Before he could say anything else, all the villagers were working like ants to shove crates, bags, and boxes into the wagons, clearing away bodies and stripping bloody corpses of armor and weapons.

Nurita, in her shrill voice, herded and bullied everyone into moving. Not that they needed much encouragement. Their captivity had made everyone eager to get away, it seemed, at least a little farther from where they could be found. The villagers stuck to the wagons as if they contained food, gold, and salvation all at once, and they tossed packages into the back with almost religious fervor.

He could still get away, leave them behind. But what if there were more soldiers in the area? What if the ones who had fled came back, in the night? He had to escort them, at least, past the forest and a little closer to Bel Calem. After that he could leave them. Or could he? He would have abandoned them in Damascan lands, after all, where every hand might turn against them. Just a little farther, then.

Simon's fists clenched, and he wasn't sure why he felt trapped.

Minutes later, when the oxen were hitched and Nurita called for everyone to fall in by the wagons, Simon followed.

"Sunset tomorrow?" Alin said. He raked fingers through his hair, trying to calm himself, trying to see the whole picture. "Then we must act now. If we Travel through Naraka, surely we can make it."

Miram shook her head sadly. "Forgive me, Eliadel. The Grandmasters have forbidden it."

Ezera, one of the Avernus Travelers that Alin had met once or twice, swept a feathered hat off his head and dipped into a perfect bow. "Do not fear. The Overlord has received our requests for parley, and our informants indicate that he may be willing to spare the remaining sacrifices from your village."

Alin was unable to keep the anger from his voice. "There have been *seven* sacrifices so far. Today makes eight. What are the odds that none of them have been people I knew?"

"We've tried," Miram said, "I assure you that we have, but we haven't been able to confirm the identity of the seven sacrifices so far. Even if they were from Myria, there's nothing more we can do for them."

"Malachi is caring for at least one of the Myrian captives at his own personal expense," Ezera responded, "and we should take that as a very good sign."

The Avernus Traveler sounded like he found the whole situation amusing, but that was no surprise. From what little Alin knew about the man, Ezera would sound that way five feet from his own noose.

"If I am to oppose Zakareth, then let me oppose him while there is still time," Alin responded. "At least me alone; there is no need to risk the rest of you."

Miram and Ezera exchanged a glance. "You are the last we should risk," Miram said finally. "It is hard to say, but even if Overlord Malachi were to sacrifice all the captives from your village, it would be better than losing you."

"The people love you," Ezera picked up. The two of them sounded almost rehearsed. "You are a symbol of our inevitable triumph and Zakareth's un-avoidable defeat."

The light of Elysia called to him, just out of sight, warm at the back of his mind. They wouldn't be able to stop him if he decided to force his way through; Ezera rarely saw combat, and Miram would hold herself back to avoid injuring her Rising Sun. He could do it.

But then what? They had done nothing but treat him kindly, and he would repay them by attacking them. Not to mention the fact that he couldn't get to Bel Calem in time without the aid of another Traveler; Elysia was not the best Territory for Traveling long distances.

He almost managed to persuade himself that he had no choice. His reasons were good, his excuses solid. Even Leah wouldn't blame him.

But the Grandmasters were always telling him what a hero he was going to be. Well, so be it. If they wanted him to be a hero, they would have to live with him acting heroic.

Alin sighed as though beaten and put on his most tragic face. "Just promise me," he said heavily, "that you will do everything you can to persuade Overlord Malachi. We don't have much time left."

Ezera relaxed visibly, but Miram looked sad. "Everything we can, Eliadel. And I am sorry." She squeezed his arm gently; her grip was rough and callused.

Alin nodded, blinking rapidly, and looked away. He had never been the most convincing liar, but he would have to pull it off today. He sank into one of the richly stuffed chairs scattered around his room and stared out the window, hopefully signaling to his guests that he wished to be left alone.

They got the message almost immediately; he heard them bow and murmur their respects before escorting themselves out.

As soon as the doors closed, Alin jumped up and reached out to the blazing star in his mind.

Golden light gathered in the air, swirled, formed into the misty outline of a distant shining city. Alin stayed focused, drawing in that distant light and pouring it into the doorway. It took less time and concentration than it had when he first began, back when he could barely open a Gate in an empty room with half an hour, but he still chafed at the delay. Someone could wander in at any second, asking after Eliadel's needs. He wanted to be long gone before that started.

At last he felt a warm summer-scented breeze blowing from the open Gate. Elysia's gleaming rooftops and soaring towers loomed in the distance as he stepped through.

His rooms were in the Grandmasters' palace, at the exact center of Enosh. So how far did he need to Travel to find someone who would listen?

Alin found Gilad exactly where he had expected: sitting on the flat roof of the Naraka Quarters, alone, hunched over a book. Alin felt a small spark of satisfaction; he had nailed his destination in one shot. If only Leah could see him now.

Gilad stumbled to his feet as soon as Alin stepped out of his golden Gate, his book clattering to the ground.

"Alin, uh, sir. How can I be of service?"

"I need to Travel, Gilad," Alin said, mustering up every crumb of authority he could. "Can you have me in Bel Calem tonight?"

Gilad's eyes darted from side to side as if looking for somewhere to hide. He paled. "Eliadel, sir, I don't think I'm supposed to do that."

"So you can, then?"

"Well, I *can*. But they said they didn't want you leaving the city." Gilad shuffled a little in place, not meeting Alin's eyes. "If you want to leave, um, I think I'll have to stop you."

Alin briefly pictured himself being hauled back to his room by a blushing, stammering Gilad. He didn't think he could stand the shame. Gilad was one of the few Travelers in existence with bonds to two different Territories, and everyone treated him with the respect he deserved as a powerful Traveler. Even so, to be beaten and dragged off by someone too scared to look you in the eye...

Leaning down, Alin looked straight at Gilad, like a big brother confronting a younger. Never mind that Gilad was probably three years the elder, and had been learning to Travel since he could walk.

"Gilad," Alin said, "what does this prophecy say that Eliadel will do?"

"Confront the Evening Star, and stem the tide of blood so the Gate of the Heavens may open once again," Gilad responded. He didn't hesitate, and he sounded as if he were quoting.

"Exactly." Alin had very little idea of what the prophecy actually said, but Gilad sounded sure. "Now, how am I going to do all that if the Grandmasters keep me here?" Gilad's eyes darted away again, and Alin pressed his advantage.

"Listen to me, Gilad. Some people I care about are going to die. They may already be dead. But if they're not, I owe it to them to do everything I can to save them. You understand that, don't you?"

Gilad nodded.

"Now, I can't do this alone. I need someone by my side. Someone who will stand with me against Damasca, even when no one else does. Can you do that for me, Gilad?"

Gilad's back straightened, and he nodded again, more firmly. He even glanced up at Alin's face, once. Briefly.

Alin didn't let his surge of elation show. He just nodded back, as though he had never expected any other response.

"I'm glad to hear it," Alin said. "Now, we need to leave as soon as possible."

"Grandmaster Naraka has sentries posted on the other side," Gilad replied. "They'll let her know if anybody tries to sneak past."

"Can you get past them anyway?"

Gilad issued a weak smile. "They don't call me a genius for nothing, I guess."

Alin grinned back.

"Then let's go."

Alin tried to keep the sleeve of his rich blue jacket away from the walls of the cavern, but it was an almost impossible task. The red stone of Naraka had a gritty, sandy outer coating, like a layer of fine ash—come to think of it, that was probably what it was. Regardless, as he followed Gilad through a twisting oven-hot tunnel of stone and ash, Alin found himself trying to keep his clothes away from the walls. The shirt alone was worth more than anything he had ever owned, and he didn't want it stained. Though he feared he was far too late for that.

A rattling screech, like the cry of an angry hawk, echoed painfully through the tunnel. Gilad twisted around to look, though he knew he couldn't see anything around the bend.

"Guardians from Bel Calem," Gilad whispered. "They've caught our scent."

Almost instinctively Alin breathed deeply through his nose, but all he smelled was singed meat and rotten eggs.

"On the bright side," Alin said, "that means we're getting close."

"Hurry," Gilad responded. "We have to hurry." He took off running down the tight corridor.

Alin ran after him, trying not to think about what a new set of clothes like these would cost. In a matter of seconds the tunnel opened up onto one of the huge caverns that seemed to make up most of Naraka. The heat, even compared to the stifling sauna of the tunnel, felt like a slap in the face.

The stalactites, hanging from the ceiling far overhead, glowed apple-red against the surrounding shadows, giving an eerie impression of bloody stars in a black sky. Wide streams of molten rock—Gilad had called it "lava"—poured in endless rivers from rents in the walls. A lake of lava below rippled and roiled as things stirred underneath the surface. Alin caught a glimpse of black scales and one gleaming ruby eye before he shuddered and looked away.

Their tunnel led onto a bridge of stone, wide enough for two to walk side-by-side. Technically. Alin was sure that he'd rather try it single-file. At the far end of the bridge, an obsidian pillar stood sentry at the center of its own circular island of stone.

The pillar, a jagged spike of gleaming black, stabbed towards the ceiling, fiery golden symbols gleaming on one side.

Gilad pointed straight at the obsidian pillar. "That's the way out, but it should be..."

Two brawny men walked out from behind the pillar, readying black wooden shields and long black spears. They were accompanied by a pair of ember-colored insects the size of wolves. They looked like huge ants painted in colors of flame.

"...guarded, yeah, I was going to say guarded."

Alin touched the golden light in the back of his mind, and everything seemed to brighten. He knew he was probably glowing, but didn't bother glancing at his own skin to check.

"Gilad, what are those things?"

The Naraka Traveler didn't look at him. He kept flexing his right hand as though working out sore muscles; Alin knew that palm carried his Naraka brand. Was it paining him, or was he preparing to use it?

"Itasas tribesmen," Gilad said. "Oh, wait, you mean the bugs? The natives call them *kush'na*, but that roughly translates to 'flame-walkers.' They can walk on the lava, you see."

The tribesmen stopped at the end of the stone bridge, shields forward and spears pointed at the ceiling. One of them called out, in a thick, awkward accent, "Stop. Turn back. Go away."

"Can you open a Gate right here?" Alin asked.

"No. You can only open a Naraka Gate at certain points. Trying here could kill us both."

"Then can we turn back? Go around?"

The shrieking cry came again, echoing from the tunnel behind them.

"No time," Gilad responded, and began to run forward onto the stone bridge.

Filling his palm with the deadly gold light of Elysia, Alin followed.

As one, the two flame-walkers let out a burbling hiss and skittered forward. Gilad pulled a red stone from his pocket and tossed it into the lava far below.

What was that supposed to do? The ant-monsters were still coming. Gilad hadn't done anything!

He hurled the gold light in his palm. It felt oddly heavy, and instead of blasting the flame-walker apart, it just knocked it back a few steps. He felt awkward and strained, though an attack like that should have taken barely more effort than throwing a brick.

"What's going on?" Alin asked, panicked. "I should be stronger than this!"

Gilad studied the lava below, ignoring the approaching flame-walkers, but he answered the question. "The Territories are far apart. You can never call up your full power in somebody else's Territory."

They only told him that *now?* He had counted on the power of Elysia to protect him in other Territories, but now he might not even have that!

The flame-walkers were only a few paces away, rippling with heat and ember-colored light. They hissed again, and Alin felt his skin crawl.

"Do something!" he yelled. Gilad, watching the lava, smiled and stretched out a hand.

"Okay," he said.

Something ripped from Gilad's outstretched hand, an almost-invisible ripple that expanded from his hand in a blast of silent thunder. An invisible wall passed through Alin, and he flinched back, but he felt nothing. When the wave of Gilad's power met the flame-walkers, they staggered back—startled, not injured—and hesitated for a moment, but then continued forward. The ripple shook dust from the walls, and the nearby lava threw up waves as though a strong wind had passed overhead.

Alin waited a handful of seconds for something to happen. If Gilad said he had done something then Alin trusted him, but as far as he could tell, the Naraka Traveler might as well have spit from the bridge.

Then something burst from the ocean of lava far below. It looked like a hawk, but a hawk built entirely out of campfire flames. Its eyes were bright coals, its beak white-hot, and sparks drifted from its spread wings. It let out a searing cry as it shot from the lava, and it snatched one of the flame-walkers in its blazing claws.

Only then did Alin realize that this hawk was the size of a horse.

It snatched up the flame-walker and kept flying, releasing the creature to splatter on the ash-covered rocks that surrounded the lava ocean. Then it banked away for another pass.

The flame-walker had stopped facing Alin, turning to hiss at the hawk instead, but Alin had no desire to play fair with a hellish creature from another world. He blasted it in the stinger with a pulse of golden light, knocking it from the bridge.

One of the tribesmen had turned toward the hawk, shield raised and spear held at the ready. The other charged across the bridge, heading for Alin, spear lowered.

"Gilad!" Alin yelled, but Gilad had practically collapsed, holding his head between his hands.

"Took...too much...sorry," Gilad said through gritted teeth. Blood leaked from one of his nostrils.

So it was up to Alin to deal with this man, was it? If he could have called on Elysia's full power, he wouldn't even be worried. As it was, though...

It took far too much effort to pull gold light from Elysia, like ripping out a stubborn weed. Each time he tried, he felt as though he had dragged a bag of rocks uphill with one hand. And when he did finally get a ball of golden light, it splashed harmlessly on the charging man's shield.

In sheer desperation, Alin reached deeply into Elysia, straining himself to the limits, for something that he had once called without thought: a golden sword of pure, translucent light.

It formed, finally, just half a second before the tribesman reached him with his spear. Alin stabbed the sword forward.

Then there was a rush of flame and heat, and the tribesman vanished. Alin blinked for a moment, clearing his eyes, before he saw the man tumbling through the air toward the lava below. The hawk, soaring overhead, screamed its triumph, and flew off deeper into the caverns. It vanished behind a falling stream of lava.

The bird must have flown by and snatched the man up just before he could attack. Alin shuddered. The bird could just as easily have taken him, and he would have never had time to react.

Sword in hand, Alin turned to meet the next tribesman, but he was gone too. He couldn't have left, since this bridge was the only passage between the obsidian pillar and the rest of Naraka, so that left two options: either he had opened his own Gate to the real world, or the hawk had gotten him too.

Either way, the bridge was clear.

Alin pulled Gilad to his feet, and together they hobbled over to the gold-marked black rock that stretched over Alin's head.

"Can you get us out of here now?"

Gilad didn't answer, just began whirling his right hand in a complex pattern. Alin took that as a yes.

Just as the Gate opened, sending cool air flooding out from the other side, Alin heard the sound of a hunting horn.

Reluctantly, fearing what he would find, Alin turned away from the Gate to look back across the bridge.

More tribesmen, blackened shields and spears in their hands, emerged from the tunnel that Alin and Gilad had used. They had another crowd of flame-walkers with them.

Great.

Alin wrenched a bolt of light from Elysia, ignoring the strain he felt in his mind. He hurled it forward, striking one of the ant-creatures with enough force to toss it from the bridge. The wind from the open Gate behind him felt cool.

"Gilad, come on! Gate's closing!"

Gilad ducked behind the obsidian pillar, gasping for air. "If I do...they'll just open it again. They'll be after you...in seconds."

"Get that hawk to do it!" Alin said.

"I might be able to call it back without a second summoning stone," Gilad responded, "but it'll take time."

"Then we fight together," Alin said. He tried to sound determined. "At least until you can manage something."

The Naraka Traveler shook his head. "Too risky. Grandmaster would kill me."

"I won't—"

Alin was going to say, 'I won't leave you,' but Gilad apparently got tired of listening. He spun, faster than Alin would have suspected he could, and kicked Alin in the gut.

Breath whooshed from Alin's lungs, and he stumbled backwards into a cool so sudden that it felt freezing.

Through the Gate.

Even trying to suck in air through aching lungs, Alin could only focus on one thought: he had to get back. Back through the Gate, back to help Gilad. He lunged forward, but the vision of the smoldering red cavern faded like smoke in the wind.

Finally Alin's lungs filled, and he shouted in frustration, passing a futile hand through empty air.

"Um...sir?" A voice said, behind him. "May I see your pass?"

Only then did it occur to Alin to wonder where he was.

Now that he took the time to notice his surroundings, Alin realized he stood in a room like some dark cathedral. He stood in the center of a circular room, roofed in a high vaulted ceiling, encircled by a dozen smooth pillars. Everything—floor, roof, pillars, walls—seemed made of the same red-streaked black stone. It had the effect of making the room look like it had survived in the aftermath of an enormous fire.

Alin turned to face the voice, trying to think of something to say. But the pale man in the purple-and-brown uniform barely seemed significant next to what stood behind him: a tall jagged pillar of obsidian etched with golden runes. An exact twin to the one in Naraka.

The pillar, and the lack of furniture in the room, told Alin what he needed to know: this room had been built for incoming Naraka Travelers.

"Sir?" The pale man asked again, a quiver in his voice. "Your pass?"

Well, that could be a problem. He wasn't going to be able to bluff his way past without a pass, so he might as well try playing it straight.

"I don't have a pass," Alin said. He shrugged. "Do I need to buy one, or..."

Malachi's officer cleared his throat and squared his shoulders, glancing from side to side. From the edges of the room, two more soldiers that Alin hadn't noticed stepped forward. Unlike the officer, these carried swords. And they loomed.

"Without a pass, I can't let you out of here," the pale officer said. "I am ordered to bring you straight to the Overlord's Master of Household. Come along peacefully, and everything will be sorted out soon."

The two guards already had hands on their swords, and they looked ready to charge him at any moment. Sweat glistened on their faces. The officer took one barely noticeable step back towards the obsidian pillar.

Abruptly Alin realized how he must look. He had stepped out of a Naraka Gate, smoking and covered in ash. His once-fine blue clothes had been charred and sliced until they looked more like battle-scarred rags than an actual suit.

To the guards, he probably seemed like he had walked through fire, fought a battle, and torn open a portal between worlds to escape unscathed. And he might be an enemy.

Of course, all of that was more or less true.

"Yeah, I'm not going to do that," Alin said. He turned and walked toward the door as if the armed guards didn't exist.

"Stop, in the name of the Overlord!" the officer said. "I've already sent for the other Travelers. Just stay where you are."

Once more, Alin tapped into the light of Elysia. To his relief, it remained as easy as ever on this side of the Gate. Part of him had worried that his difficulty in Naraka had been some failing of his, and not just because the Territories were distant.

Golden light rose from his skin like glowing smoke. The red-black walls gleamed as the room brightened. Malachi's soldiers flinched in unison.

"I don't have time for this," Alin said. "Keep quiet, or I'll have to come back."

He walked forward again. Nobody stood in his way.

Alin marveled at their reactions. Had it only been this spring when he would have reacted the same way, helpless in the face of a Traveler? He rarely thought about those days anymore. What had he ever done before that could compare with the things he could do now?

Storming the Overlord's stronghold with his powers, rescuing a maiden from the hands of a tyrannical Traveler. He should be afraid, he knew he should, but he wasn't; he was excited.

Who could stand up to him now?

An old balding man with a potbelly stumbled through the open front door, one hand marked with the glowing red rune of a Naraka Traveler. "Stop right there!" he wheezed, waving his palm to begin a pattern that would call upon his Territory.

Alin summoned golden light and blasted the man back through the door. He had to step over the old man's senseless body on his way out.

No one else tried to stop him.

Chapter 16

MIDSUMMER'S EVE

Simon lay in the rumbling wagon bed, head pillowed on a burlap sack of grain.

"How am I supposed to find them anyway?" he said. "It's not like I can just walk up to the Overlord and ask him."

Otoku's laugh was like chimes in the wind.

Poor child, she murmured in mock sympathy. *Maybe you should let Chaim tell you what to do. He can keep you in a box and take you out when he needs someone to swing a sword.*

"I can't leave them here, and I can't talk them out of going. So I might as well go with them. We'll all be safer that way." He wasn't sure he believed it, but he thought he sounded certain.

So you go forth to battle lying on the back of a wagon. The brave warrior, napping his way to battle!

Simon rolled onto his side and glared at the doll. She was a little smaller than Caela, with a red silk dress and long black hair. Her painted face looked similar, as though the same artist had designed them both, but where Caela's face showed an expression of peace, Otoku looked upon the world with a smirk.

"Did you make fun of Kai like this?" Simon asked.

Otoku's smirk suddenly looked like a grimace, and despite the shaking of the rickety wagon, Simon would have sworn she shuddered.

Kai never understood when he was being mocked. He just hugged us, and cradled us, and stroked our hair. It was awful.

"That doesn't sound too bad."

He stroked our hair. We need brushed occasionally, of course, but he's not a nine-year-old girl. There is no decency in his soul.

"Well, I always thought he was insane."

You don't know the half.

Over the creak of the wagons came the crack of a whip, the lowing of oxen, and the call of a man's voice. A few other Myrians scrambled onboard the wagon, crouching down next to Simon and the boxes.

"What's happening?" Simon asked, sitting up.

A girl of about eleven years answered in a whisper, "We're at Bel Calem, Master Simon. They're looking in the wagons."

"Looking for us?" Simon asked immediately. He reached out a hand, preparing to summon Azura.

The girl shook her head. "I don't think so. Master Chaim and Mistress Nurita are talking to them. I think they just want to see what we're up to."

"If we're not in danger," Simon whispered back, "then why are you hiding?"

The girl's face darkened. "I don't want them Damascans knowing what I look like. Not till it's too late." Her hand drifted down to her side, where a cheap dagger was tucked into the length of rope she used as a belt. She gripped the dagger hard.

Though he didn't quite understand why, Simon felt his heart clench.

A couple of Damascans in brown and purple uniforms glanced into the wagon, took in the suspicious Myrians, and let the canvas fall shut with bored faces. It seemed they really didn't care who came into the city.

If that was true, though, why check at all?

After a few more minutes of rumbling along, the wagon lurched to a halt. Chaim stuck his head in, motioning for Simon to come join him. Simon hurriedly snatched Otoku up and followed. The other villagers hiding in the wagon gave Simon odd looks.

Behold the conquering hero, Otoku murmured, *dashing off to war with his favorite doll.*

Don't flatter yourself, Simon sent back, careful to keep from speaking aloud. *You're not my favorite.*

Otoku made a sound that, even in her drifting, breezy voice, sounded like a 'hmph.'

Just give it time, she said.

The walls of Bel Calem were not as big as Simon had imagined: scarcely a dozen feet tall and not wide enough for sentries to walk atop them. That was something of a disappointment; he had always pictured grand walls big enough to block out half the sky. At least they were made of stone.

The group from Myria waited just outside the walls, though the gates stood open. Chaim had circled their three wagons as best he could, giving them some degree of privacy from the city. The oxen grazed on the sparse field outside Bel Calem, while industrious boys and girls removed their yokes and rubbed them down.

"They didn't want strange oxen inside the walls," Chaim told Simon, as soon as they were clear of the wagon. "Made us leave the animals outside. Don't care what we do, though."

The bulk of the group from Myria, maybe thirty or forty all told, milled around in the center of the circled wagons. Simon followed Chaim closer.

Chaim turned toward Simon and clapped his hands together. His smile was fatherly. "So, Simon," he said. "What now?"

Seemingly half the crowd turned to hear Simon's answer.

With all the wit Simon could muster, he said, "What?"

Nurita joined Chaim from the crowd, a stern look upon her face and voice pitched to carry. "We're on the Overlord's very doorstep," she declared, and the crowd murmured agreement. "You are our strongest sword. We have only to strike." Simon felt a twist of unease at hearing such words spoken openly a few feet from Bel Calem's walls.

"So...where do we go?" Simon asked. In his head, Otoku started laughing.

Chaim gestured vaguely. "Couldn't you just do something to find them? With your Traveling?"

"I don't think so. Once we find out where they are I can fight my way in, but until we do..." Simon shrugged self-consciously. "Any ideas?"

Nurita scowled at him, obviously disappointed. Chaim just looked baffled. But they recovered quickly, taking suggestions from the rest of the crowd. Soon they were discussing a plan that involved somehow finding where the captives were hidden, somehow forcing their way inside, and then somehow escaping without being torn to pieces by summoned beasts.

Simon shrunk into himself as they discussed such things without him. He could fight better than all of them put together, sure, but he had much less experience. And they had just as much of a reason to recover the captives as he did. Maybe more; some of those here had lost kin to the slavers' ropes, while Simon had not.

He had almost talked himself into giving up and waiting for Chaim to tell him what to do when a gold-armored dog bounded between the wagons. The gold plates of its armor shone even brighter than they should have in the direct sunlight, its bark somehow resounding like a great bell. Most of the villagers stumbled back en masse, crying at its sudden appearance. Some stabbed down at it with stolen Damascan swords, though their blades were turned by its armor.

The dog, a waist-high beast with white hair peeking out between the plates of its shining armor, ignored them all, circling inside the wagons and letting out more of those echoing barks. Oddly, Simon noticed that the oxen didn't seem alarmed by the beast's arrival, continuing to calmly chew on grass and brambles.

While the crowd was still milling and Simon was still trying to decide whether or not he should attack, Alin stepped in between two wagons.

His fine clothes—once a suit of blue, probably, and certainly more expensive than Alin had ever before owned—had gone through a forest of thorns and a house fire. Possibly at the same time. The ash streaked on his face looked like war paint, and he strode into their midst like a battle-scarred king among his subjects.

The Myrians cheered when they saw him. A few fell to their knees.

"Brothers and sisters!" Alin exclaimed, throwing out his arms. "Welcome! I can't tell you what good it does my heart, seeing you here today."

Simon almost gagged at the speech. Alin was speaking like he imagined a hero would in one of his stories. By all rights the other villagers should recognize it and laugh him away. Judging by their faces, though, they were eating out of his hand.

"Alin," Chaim called, "we're ready. They took us captive, but we escaped. We are armed and ready to stand against the Overlord."

Nurita shouldered her way to stand beside him. "And Simon's a Traveler now, apparently." She pointed a finger straight at him.

Now why had she said that? Simon hunched his shoulders and looked away from Alin's disbelieving glance.

"Really?" Alin asked politely. "Which Territory, Simon?"

"Valinhall," Simon responded. Why was he feeling defensive? He was a Traveler. He was! He had earned it! But for some reason he felt like a child propping up a disguise that the adults would soon see through. It made him angry.

"I've never heard of that one," Alin said.

And how would you? Simon thought. Alin was talking like he had had a fancy education in the ways of Travelers, but he had grown up a quarter mile away from the hut where Simon had been born. Alin didn't know anything more than Simon did.

But Simon kept his mouth shut. Otoku laughed again, scornfully.

"Will you be able to fight, when the time comes?" Alin asked.

"Yes," Simon responded. He offered nothing more. He didn't have to prove himself to Alin.

Alin looked doubtful, but he shrugged and wiped the doubt from his face, smiling instead. "Good enough for me," he said.

Alin knelt by Keanos, reaching between the plates of golden armor to ruffle the hound's ears. The beast leaned into Alin's hand, eyes half-closed, glowing with pleasure.

"Seek," Alin said softly, and Keanos let out one ringing bark before trotting off through the city gates.

The humans followed, walking together between the guards. The guards glanced at each other but let them pass, and Alin heaved a relieved sigh. He hadn't been sure they would be allowed to enter. Nurita had wisely insisted that the villagers limit themselves to whatever weapons they could hide, since a bunch of country folk marching into the city carrying weapons might well draw the wrong kind of attention. They should be safe, since there was nothing obviously dangerous about their group, but who knew what the guards would notice?

And then, of course, there was Keanos. Alin had never seen Bel Calem before, but he suspected glowing gold-armored dogs weren't common. As the hound leaped over the stone-paved streets of the city, weaving his way through the crowd with his nose pressed to the ground, people noticed. They gasped, shouted, or hurried out of the way. One woman with a woven basket in her hands turned, caught a glimpse of the glowing hound, and shrieked, tossing her basket into the air. Figs, olives, and tiny round loaves of bread rolled all over the street.

They had followed the dog for only ten minutes when two soldiers in purple-and-brown ducked in out of a side street, carrying long spears. Alin braced himself for a fight, reaching out to Elysia and stopping a hair's breadth from calling its power. If they attacked, he would be ready.

The helmeted soldiers surveyed the procession of Myrians and stepped back against the wall of a nearby shop to let them pass. As Keanos trotted past them, they kept their eyes fixed on the opposite side of the street.

Alin kept walking after the hound, his confidence growing. The guards clearly recognized the dog as Traveler work, and had apparently decided to keep their hands out of the matter.

Wise decision, Alin thought, and ignored the soldiers as he marched past. He didn't so much as turn to look in their direction.

Keanos finally stopped almost an hour later, plopping down on his haunches in front of an ordinary-looking house, the sort that Alin had seen a hundred times since passing through the Bel Calem gates. It was a simple cube, made of pale yellow bricks, with a door of plain wood and a single window covered by a red-patterned curtain.

"This is it?" Simon asked. He moved up to stand next to Alin, doubt showing in every line of his face.

Alin suppressed a twinge of annoyance. Who was Simon to doubt the hound's tracking? Simon certainly hadn't done anything to help. "Yes," he said. "Keanos found someone from our village inside that house. Isn't that right, boy?"

Keanos gave another ringing bark. A few women who had been chatting across the street stopped, startled, and turned to look.

"Then what are we waiting for?" Simon asked. He stepped forward and knocked on the door.

"Just a moment!" a woman called from inside the house. "Just...wait right there!"

Simon made as if to open the door anyway, but Alin gestured him back. They didn't need a hotheaded response, but a mature discussion. Besides, Alin was confident that he alone could handle any trouble that might be waiting inside. It wouldn't hurt to show this woman a little courtesy.

After a few more seconds, in which Alin heard the clatter of furniture and the sounds of someone muttering to herself, a woman tore open her door. Strands of white hair stuck out in all directions from underneath a red kerchief, and the wide-eyed expression of fear on her wrinkled face suggested she thought they were there to rob her.

"May I help you?" she asked. Her voice creaked and trembled.

Alin cleared his throat, embarrassed. This had to be the wrong house. But Keanos just sat there on his haunches, staring into the open doorway as though the woman didn't exist. How was he supposed to handle this?

You're the mighty Traveler now, he thought. *Act like it.*

But he had hesitated too long. The woman's eyes found the crowd behind him and widened even further. But that hardly touched her reaction when she noticed the bright gold-armored dog at her feet.

"Seven stones," she whispered. "What is that? Who are you? Did the Overlord send you?"

Behind Alin, Simon muttered something that sounded like "...getting really sick of that."

Alin put on what he hoped was a comforting smile. "Ma'am, is there anyone else at home? Anybody else in the house?"

She half-covered her mouth with one hand and glanced behind her, as though she thought his words might have summoned a thief into her home.

"No," she said. "I never had any children. What is this about?"

Alin cast about in his mind for an innocent reason that might bring a crowd of thirty country villagers to a city woman's door. He came up empty-handed. What he said instead was, "We're looking for some friends of ours."

The woman gasped, which told Alin what he needed to know. This woman was hiding something. But instead of admitting her guilt or trying to run, she shook her head vigorously.

"No one like that here. No one but me."

"You won't mind, then," Alin said gently, "if we come in and check?"

"Of course not," she replied, and stood to one side.

There was no way the entire group could squeeze into a house meant for one family. Alin followed Keanos, who sniffed around every corner of the floor with intense fascination. Simon came in afterwards, since there was nothing Alin could do short of rudeness to keep him out, and Chaim and Nurita followed. Stern words from Nurita served to keep everyone else in the street.

From the start, Alin could tell they had the wrong place. The house was all one room, stone floors covered in a layer of rugs, with a single reed mat in the back corner for sleeping. A second window, which he hadn't seen from the front, sat in the side wall and looked out on a dirty alley. A shaky table stood in one corner, covered in pots, pans, and half-chopped vegetables. What possessions she owned were meager, even by the standards of Myria.

Maybe the old woman hadn't been hiding anything after all. It wasn't like there was anywhere to stow prisoners in this hut.

Nonetheless, Alin didn't let that slow him down, glancing out of the side window and in each corner, just in case. Chaim lifted the few pieces of furniture, peering at the floor underneath. Nurita kept up a stream of questions directed at the woman, though she didn't seem to be getting any helpful answers.

Simon, on the other hand, just lounged against one wall. Sulking, probably, though his head was cocked as if he were listening. After a moment he raised one hand to look at—a doll? A little girl's doll? Where had Simon found that?

Well, it wasn't important now. He'd ask later.

It only took the three of them about five minutes to realize the woman wasn't hiding anything. Keanos just ran around the floor in apparent confusion, still following the scent.

The house's owner stood in the center of the room, patting her hair in a vain attempt to keep it in place. Her eyes bounced around like she was trying to find a place to run.

Alin walked up to her. "We're sorry for our poor manners, and we will leave as soon as we can. Have you heard of the group we're looking for? There would be about ten of them. Villagers, like us. Men and women both."

"Haven't seen anybody new around here," the woman responded. "Please, take your dog and go. My husband will be back soon."

"We will," Alin promised. Embarrassment flooded him, and he fought to keep it from showing on his face. The party from Myria had followed him, trusting in his abilities, and he had let them down. He would look useless.

"Hold on a minute," Simon said. He kept leaning against the wall by the door, arms folded, but his eyes stuck to the woman. "Ma'am, would you move?"

Alin was about to say something to shut Simon up—gently, of course, he didn't want this looking like a child's fight—but the woman's face went visibly pale. And she didn't move her feet from the rug.

"I can't," she said, and Alin realized that Simon had been right.

"What's under the rug?" Alin asked. She glanced from side to side, looking for a way out, and caught a glimpse out the window at the same time Alin did. Two uniformed soldiers in Malachi's colors were walking by, patrolling the streets for one reason or another.

Alin lunged forward to grab the woman, to stop her from shouting, but there was nothing he could do. He wouldn't make it in time. She filled her lungs, preparing to scream.

Then Simon was there, behind her, one hand clapped over the woman's mouth.

"Shush," he whispered into her ear. "Just relax." Her eyes strained so far to the side that almost nothing showed but the whites, and Alin got the impression she was trying to see behind her without turning her head. But she didn't even whimper against Simon's restraining hand.

Nurita walked over to the window and casually drew the curtain so that the soldiers wouldn't happen to see anything. Alin looked back out the doorway, hoping the rest of the Myrians had been smart enough to avoid standing around in a crowd. They had, lounging in much smaller groups on either side of the street, seemingly engaged in taking in the sights or haggling with a street peddler. The soldiers took a quick look around, since the street was still more crowded than they were probably used to seeing it, but in the end they walked away.

Alin turned his attention back to Simon. "How did you do that?" he asked.

He tried to make his voice demanding, but he was afraid he just sounded impressed.

"Do what?" Simon asked, though Alin could tell that he knew full well.

"How did you get there before me? You were way over there."

"We Travelers have to have our secrets," Simon said gravely. "You understand."

Alin glared, but let it drop. Simon could be so...irritating, sometimes. But the mature response was to leave it alone.

"In a moment," Alin said to the woman, "my friend is going to take his hand away. If you shout, or try to run, we'll have to hurt you. Stay quiet and we can all be friends. Understand?"

The woman nodded enthusiastically, kerchief-covered hair bobbing, and Simon removed his hand.

"You're Travelers?" the woman asked. Her voice was barely above a whisper.

Alin nodded, and she visibly relaxed.

"That explains the..." She gestured one-handed at the gold-armored hound sniffing around her house. "I thought to my self, 'who would have a great big glowing dog?' and I thought it had to be...but then you didn't say what you were supposed to, and I wasn't sure."

"Move the rug," Simon said. The woman stepped off and dragged the rug aside, one-handed, holding her other hand against her back as if it pained her.

Like the rest of the bare floor, this patch was made of stone blocks. But the block that had been covered by this particular rug didn't fit quite as closely with its fellows. There was just enough of a gap between one stone and another that one might be able to slip something between. Alin nudged it with his toe, and it didn't budge.

"I can't open it," the woman said quickly. "I can't. It takes—"

She was interrupted by Simon bending down and slipping his fingers into the crack, lifting the stone block out with one hand. It was a rectangular chunk of rock, two feet to a side and eight inches thick, that Alin would have wanted to lever out with two men and some tools. But Simon lifted it easily in one hand and set it to the side.

"Seven stones," the woman said again. "Can all you Travelers do that?"

Alin did his best not to look as awestruck as everyone else. "As well as many other things," he said. Simon snorted without looking up, but the woman began patting her hair again.

Underneath the block of stone was a hinged lid of wood. When Simon pulled it open, someone down below gave a weak scream. Only one voice. Where were the others? Or were they just too scared to scream?

Maker above. What had happened to them?

"They moved them here about three days ago," the old woman said, "when they thought somebody might come looking. I didn't have any choice. You have to believe me. I didn't have any choice."

She was shaking, now, as if she thought they would beat her. Alin gave her no sign whether or not he would hold her responsible, simply conjured a ball of golden light and held it above the trap door so it shone down into the darkness. She flinched away from that as if from a bloody knife, wrapping both arms around herself.

The light revealed a rickety ladder set into the side of the hole, and just a glimpse of a pair of grimy hands far below. Hands bound in thick, coarse rope.

Alin moved to head down the ladder himself, but he wasn't fast enough. Simon had already jumped.

They found only one person bound in that filthy basement: Leah's half-sister.

Simon knew her. Not well, true, but he had grown up around Nurita's family even before Leah had moved to the village. Seeing this girl cringing, broken, and dirty, hurt. But what hurt worse was the fact that there were nine captives missing.

Out of ten captives, one remained. And Leah wasn't here. Simon knew that shouldn't matter, that getting Leah back didn't matter any more than any of the others. But somehow he couldn't feel like he had succeeded until he saw Leah free.

And now she wasn't here. His stomach twisted in knots.

Once the girl—Simon couldn't remember her name, except that she was Nurita's niece and Leah's sister—had been freed, watered, and brought up the ladder, she still wouldn't speak for fear that the Damascan soldiers would return. Only once her aunt had convinced her that she was safe, that she would be taken out of the city and returned home, did she tell her story.

She spoke of being taken through a moon-lit wasteland, probably someone's Territory. She told about sacrifices chosen each day at noon, and how the soldiers said that some of them had a chance to live, but none of them had believed that. She spoke of being beaten, threatened, neglected.

Only after she had spoken for almost half an hour did she tell Simon what he wanted to know.

"They killed the others," she said, her voice shaking. "Every once in a while they'd come take somebody...they killed them. They told us they did, and nobody ever came back. Everybody else is dead, Simon. They're dead.

"But that's not what happened to Leah."

Simon heard Alin draw in a sharp breath. He stopped leaning against the wall, walking over to join Simon.

Simon cursed under his breath.

"What did happen to Leah?" Alin asked.

The girl shook her head. "She's different, somehow. They took her too, but they didn't kill her. I don't think they ever even beat her. Alin, they treated her like she was somebody important."

"What do you mean, important?" Simon asked.

Right on top of him, Alin asked her, "Rutha, where is she?"

Rutha, right, that was her name. Simon had always just thought of her as Leah's sister, or Nurita's niece.

Rutha glanced at Simon, but replied to Alin. Probably because he had remembered her name. "The Overlord took her himself. I think they brought her to the Overlord's house. That's what it sounded like they would do, anyway."

Simon clenched his fist, wishing for Azura's hilt in his hand. Summoning it in a house this small and crowded would kill somebody, but part of him still wanted the comfort of steel in his hand. The Overlord had taken a personal interest in Leah. Why?

Alin stood up and dusted himself off, visibly gathering himself for a speech. "Chaim, Nurita," he said, and they came. Simon couldn't believe it— Nurita should have slapped him for his tone alone—but they came.

"Take everyone back out of the city," Alin said. "I'm going in for Leah."

They protested, of course, but Alin wouldn't hear it. He held up a hand to stop their words. "I don't need your help. I may need to fight the Overlord himself, and in that fight you won't be able to help me anyway. Besides, someone needs to get Rutha back safely. Don't worry, Simon will protect you."

Simon rose to his feet. "I'll do what?"

"They need someone to keep them safe on their way out of Bel Calem," Alin said calmly. "I don't know much about this Hall Territory, but I'm sure it will be enough to get the job done. Besides, any Traveler is better than none."

There was so much to hate in that sentence that Simon felt anger choke his words off for a moment. When he finally got hold of himself again, he said, "I don't care what they need. I'm going for Leah. You want to protect them so bad, you do it."

Alin sighed, as if he were a parent facing down an unruly child. He locked gazes with Simon and spoke in a low, earnest voice. "Simon, you and I can do things that nobody else here can do. That means we're responsible for their safety. Do you understand? It's like we're soldiers, Simon, and we need to keep the ordinary people safe. But sometimes soldiers have to learn to take orders."

Alin put a hand on Simon's shoulder, in what he no doubt imagined to be a comforting gesture. "I'm ordering you to take them out of the city, Simon. I know you're brave enough to go face the Overlord with me, and I admire that. I really do. But I need somebody to take care of them, and you're the only one I've got."

For the next few seconds, Simon couldn't see anything past an image of his fist splitting Alin's lip. When his vision cleared, he twisted his mouth into a sheepish smile. "I guess you're right," he said. "Let her know I wanted to come along, will you?"

Alin nodded gravely. "I'll make sure she knows."

"Thanks."

After clasping hands with Chaim and enduring a few last-minute words of advice from Nurita, Alin walked out of the hut. That armored dog let out another of those piercing barks and followed.

"Okay then," Simon said, as soon as Alin and his hound had left. "You two can get everybody back to Myria on your own, can't you?"

Nurita and Chaim shared a glance.

"Alin told you to stay put, young man," Nurita said.

"Yeah, I'm not going to do that. What right does he have, giving me orders?"

Chaim shrugged. "In that case, yes, we can get everybody back just fine, assuming we don't run into any trouble. Tell you the truth, I'd be more comfortable if we had you along. Just in case."

Simon looked at the Damascan woman, huddled in the corner of her house, trying to avoid notice. He barely noticed her; his mind raced ahead, thinking of everything he still had left to do.

"Honestly, sir," Simon said, "you're probably safer without us. I get the feeling we're about to make a lot of noise."

CHAPTER 17
CONVERGENCE

Minutes after he left Chaim and Nurita, Simon stepped through a Gate into the entry room. He lifted Azura up, resting it on the wooden rack marked with the number seven.

A noise from the hallway grabbed his attention, and he nearly snatched Azura back.

So jumpy, Otoku murmured. He had almost forgotten her back at the house in Bel Calem, and she wasn't best pleased with him for that.

"I have good reason," Simon said. "Everything in this house wants to kill me."

Not everything. That sofa by the wall is calm enough, for now. But I've heard it can smell fear.

Simon gave up worrying and walked into the hall. If there had actually been any danger, Otoku would have warned him instead of joking around. Probably.

A gleaming silver sword-point lunged from further down the hallway as soon as he opened the door, stabbing toward his face. He barely managed to throw himself to one side in time to avoid losing an eye. He crashed heavily against the wall of the hallway.

"Otoku," Simon gasped.

The doll laughed.

The sword was clearly too long to swing in the narrow hallway, so the swordsman drew back for another thrust. Simon took that instant to flood his lungs with Nye essence.

His breath cooled, his body drifting up as though his feet were about to leave the floor. The world slowed down.

When the point of the sword came at him this time, he slapped it away with the palm of his hand and stepped in to confront the swordsman.

Only, it wasn't a swordsman. Andra Agnos stood in the hall, both feet firmly planted, gripping a sword that looked like a much-shorter version of Azura. Its blade was stained black in several places, in a pattern that made it look like it had been splattered with ink. Through the Nye essence, Simon watched her expression slide from determination to surprise. She pulled her sword back, though with the world slowed, it looked like she was pulling it out of thick mud. Her lips began to form a word, and Simon released his power.

The world lurched back to normal speed.

"Simon, you're back! Oh, I'm sorry, I didn't see it was you. Are you okay?"

Before responding, Simon lifted Otoku and stared her in the eyes. "I bet you thought that was funny, didn't you?"

Hilarious, yes, Otoku responded. *What did you want me to say? 'Oh, Simon, watch out! There's a little girl in there! You might be in danger!'*

Andra glanced in confusion from Simon to the doll. "What? No, I wasn't trying to be funny. I really didn't know it was you." Her eyes gained a mischievous sparkle. "But I wish my brother could have seen you crash into the wall. Like you were tripping over your own feet."

"I didn't mean you," Simon began, but gave it up. "Never mind. Is everybody still okay?"

She gave him a mocking smile. "Same as yesterday, Simon. I know it's dangerous here, but we're doing fine. You don't have to keep checking on us. And stop trying to dodge me: who were you talking to?"

"Oh, you know, no one. Who says I was talking to anyone? Is Erastes around?"

Andra, apparently, wasn't willing to let the subject go that easily. "Is that a doll? Were you talking to the doll?"

"Well, I...yes," Simon said. That sounded lame, so he tried again. "It's a talking doll."

Andra's eyes brightened. "Oh! She must be your advisor."

Simon was a little taken aback. She had learned quickly, if she knew about advisors already. "Yeah, actually, she is."

"Great!" Andra touched Otoku's face with a finger. "You can talk out loud. You don't have to pretend around me." She poked the doll again.

In Simon's head, Otoku let out a strangled noise. *Tell her to stop that! If she touches me again, I'm feeding her to the sofa.*

"She says to stop poking her," Simon translated. Andra's face grew confused. "But she didn't say anything," Andra said.

"That's how they talk. I just sort of hear them in my head."

Andra looked doubtful, but she shrugged. "Huh. That's strange. Mine will talk to anybody who stands still long enough to listen."

"Yours?"

A cloth bundle drifted out from the fourth bedroom, and for an instant Simon thought it was some sort of tiny, floating version of a Nye. On closer inspection, it seemed more like a ghost made of cloth. Its head looked like a ball of yarn wrapped in a gray rag; its eyes were made of silver buttons, its lips of black string. It was tied off underneath its head, and the rest of its body was just a skirt of hanging cloth that swung underneath it as it flew through the air.

As Simon stared, it opened its lips and spoke. "Well, Andra, hello. Aren't you going to introduce me to your, hmmm, friend?"

"Introduce you?" Andra asked.

"Yes," Simon said. "I haven't met very many other advisors."

"Oh, okay. Simon, this is—"

"Aaahhh," the advisor breathed, interrupting Andra. "You must be the new, ah, young one of Kai's. Irresponsible of him, hmmm, don't you think?"

"—Manyu," Andra finished. "Manyu, Simon."

Slowly, Simon put together some things in his head. He looked once again at Andra's sword, which she held loosely at her side. "If you've got an advisor..." he said aloud. "That's a Dragon's Fang? You got one that fast?"

"Oh yeah! Chaka says I got it much faster than you did." Simon winced. "Its name is..." She frowned and turned to Manyu. "Manyu, what's its name?"

The cloth ghost's lips made a perfectly round O. "Andra, hmmm, I'm surprised at you! Not knowing the name of your own sword! That would be like this, ahhh, boy not knowing the names of his dolls."

Otoku chuckled in Simon's head. *You do know all our names, don't you?* she said. *There are like fifty of you,* Simon sent back. *Give me time.*

Andra rolled her eyes at her own advisor. "Just tell me."

"You have the honor to possess, ahhh, Seijan, the tenth Fang forged by the founder of our House."

"Yeah, I'm not going to remember that," Andra said.

Manyu floated over to Simon's face, and Simon took a discreet step back. "You see, this is why the girl is not a full, hmmm, Traveler yet."

"Hey!" Andra said.

"Since she failed to tell you, ahhh, the whole truth, I will do so. She has the sword, but none of the other, hmmm, gifts. She has not yet proven herself worthy. As of now, she can only open her bedroom, the garden, and the bath."

Simon's pride recovered a little. At least she hadn't done in a week what had taken him months. "Andra, I'm actually here to talk to the Nye. Have you seen any around?"

She frowned. "Who?"

"The black robes that keep trying to strangle you."

Andra's hand rose to her throat and she half-turned, as though expecting someone to choke her immediately. "What? What are you talking about?"

Simon looked to Manyu, who cleared his throat apologetically. "The

Eldest was quite, hmmm, pleased to have new humans in the House. I believe he did not want to scare them off."

"You can't be serious. They tried to kill me before I was in here five minutes!"

"Is someone going to try and strangle us?" Andra asked.

Manyu bobbed in midair, a gesture that Simon couldn't quite interpret. "The Eldest was testing you, apprentice. He wanted to see if you had the, ahhh, correct potential."

Simon nodded. "I guess that makes sense." It didn't quite balance the scales, but the Eldest had been testing him. He could accept that.

"And of course, hmmm, Chaka doesn't like you. He may have influenced some of the more, hmmm, impressionable Nye to try and drive you out. So to speak."

A hunched shadow appeared behind Andra. A harsh voice whispered, "That is a fair way to say it."

Andra shrieked and whirled her blade around, but the Nye Eldest dodged it easily. The sword stuck in the doorframe of the tenth bedroom.

The Eldest let out a raspy chuckle. "I am sorry, child. That was cruel. We will fix the door tonight."

The faded Nye waved one long sleeve in Manyu's direction, and the advisor dipped respectfully in the air before floating back into the tenth bedroom. He even managed to shut the door somehow, though Simon would have expected it to be far too heavy for the little cloth puppet.

"Eldest," Simon said, bowing slightly. "Did Chaka really try to have me driven out?"

"We did not see that you had much potential, son of Kalman," the Eldest Nye replied. Andra glanced between his empty hood and Simon's face, plainly trying to decide whether to run.

"In truth," the Eldest continued, "Chaka still does not see your potential. But look!" One empty black sleeve gestured toward Andra. "Five healthy sons and daughters you bring to us, and one of them will carry Seijan into the world. I am very pleased with you. You have held our bargain well."

The Eldest was responding better than Simon had hoped, but he still decided to step carefully. "Thank you, sir. Your essence has kept me alive more times than I can count."

The worn, faded hood cocked to one side in a gesture reminiscent of Kai at his most curious. Then the Eldest flowed forward, around Andra, until he stood peering up into Simon's face. Simon resisted the urge to look away.

"You did not come here to listen to my compliments," the Nye rasped.

"Nor even to check upon the girl. You have a request?"

Simon nodded, suddenly less sure than he had been a moment before.

"Speak it," the Eldest said.

"I'm in a city—well, I mean, in the real world I am—and I need to save this girl. She's being held prisoner, but I don't know where. I thought you might know how to find out."

Andra grinned. "You're saving a maiden in peril? Real peril? How heroic."

She didn't have to mock him like that. Putting it that way, he sounded like a child, not a Traveler on a rescue mission. "I saved you, didn't I?" he said.

"That's true," she acknowledged. "Then again, I suppose I'll be saving people too, soon. Not maidens, though, I guess. Princes. Riding in and saving captive princes from...whatever it is that takes princes captive. This girl isn't a princess, is she?"

"Um, no," Simon said, having failed to follow Andra's half of the conversation.

"That's too bad," Andra said. "You should aim higher next time."

The Nye Eldest cackled. "It has been too long since I watched children playing."

Children? Simon glared into the black hood. "Can you help me or not?"

"One condition," the Eldest said. He flourished one sleeve like a juggler pulling a ball out of thin air, and suddenly he was holding a sheet of black cloth. It might have been a blanket, or some kind of curtain.

"What's that for?" Simon asked.

"For you," the Nye said. Simon took it hesitantly. He had chosen to trust the Eldest, but there was every chance this cloth might come to life and try to strangle him.

Simon held the cloth up gingerly, carefully spreading it out in front of him.

It was a cloak.

A hooded black cloak, long enough so that when it hung from Simon's shoulders it wouldn't quite brush the ground. Simon tried to picture himself wearing a cloak like that, but the thought was too ridiculous. In Myria, people only wore cloaks during cold or harsh weather, and never a cloak of solid black. He would look like a thief, sneaking around in an outfit like this. And how was he supposed to fight, with this thing flapping around and binding his arms?

"If you show up wearing that, this girl will think *you're* the kidnapper," Andra said.

Simon looked past the cloak, over to the Nye eldest, who somehow managed to look expectant. Simon would have to let him down easily. "I appreci-ate the thought," he began, "but I—"

"I have honored you," the Eldest rasped. "This is the cloak of the Nye. It is a mark of our bargain, and you will wear it. Unless, of course, you are ashamed of us."

Simon felt a cold chain at his throat.

For a moment he thought he was remembering the sensation, until he tried to look down and felt his chin pressing against links of iron. There was another Nye standing behind him, holding chains around his throat in a metal noose.

His first reaction was anger. *How dare they? If they want to make this a fight, I'll give them a fight.*

But that was childish. There was no reason to risk his life, and Andra's, when simple cooperation would get him what he wanted.

Andra, however, apparently didn't agree.

An instant after the chains appeared around Simon's neck, Andra's sword flashed at the Nye standing behind him.

It was hard to move without bruising his throat on the Nye's chain, but Simon managed to get one hand up and knock Andra's wrist back, throwing her strike wide.

"It's okay," Simon said. He looked back at the Eldest, who seemed to be silently chuckling. "I'll wear the thing."

The chain slid slowly away, over his shoulder, like an ice-cold snake re-treating.

The Eldest nodded. "Then my help is yours."

The Nye behind Simon stepped forward, bowing before his Eldest, who seemed to ignore him.

"Open a Gate back to your city," the Eldest said to Simon. "Then give this one just ten minutes." The younger Nye rose to his full height—almost a full head taller than Simon—and then both black-wrapped men began to glide down the hall toward the entry room.

Simon hurried to catch up. "Okay, well, her name is Leah. She's a little shorter than me, with dark hair—"

The Eldest slashed a sleeve through the air. "Not necessary."

"I was just telling him what she looks like."

"Not necessary. This one is very good."

Simon believed him. He walked over to the wall, where Azura rested on a wooden rack. Briefly he wondered if Azura just materialized there whenever he let it dissipate, or whether the Nye made sure that it was carefully racked as soon as it appeared. That didn't matter to him, he supposed, but it showed how little he knew about the real workings of Valinhall.

Simon took Azura down from the rack and began drawing it slowly down the air, stretching his mind through the rent to Bel Calem. A line of color followed the tip of the sword as it steadily descended, slicing the air in two.

"I don't understand," Simon said as he continued to work. "He doesn't know where she is or what she looks like. How is he supposed to find her? How will he even know which girl I'm looking for?"

"That is how good he is," the Eldest responded. Simon decided to just accept it. He had less than two feet of a Gate revealed, so that the whole of the Gate only stretched from slightly above his head to his chin, when the Eldest said "Go" and the other Nye flowed forward.

It was vaguely disgusting, actually, watching a man-sized robe deflate and flow through a Gate not much bigger than a melon. He had to implode in streams of cloth and shadow and squeeze himself through, like a snake slithering through a knothole.

"Wow," Andra breathed. She sounded in awe. "When do we learn how to do that?"

As Alin wandered deeper into the city, he became more and more certain that his well of good fortune was about to run dry.

Where the houses were mostly pale brick boxes, no one had questioned a man who was obviously a Traveler following his conjured golden hound. Farther in, where the houses were just as often wood or stone as brick, people began to call out to him, to ask him where he was headed, and if he was on some business of the Overlord's. Typically a display of gold light bursting in the air was enough to earn him some silence. Or at least applause. But here, closer to the center of Bel Calem, where everything was made of imported woods and rare stones and precious metals, no one would be intimidated by a nameless Traveler.

He actually saw a few native Travelers as he followed Keanos deeper into the heart of the city. One of the first things his tutors had taught him was how to identify the different stripes of Traveler, so he was able to identify the first two he passed as hailing from Avernus and Asphodel. The first glared at him, her face almost entirely covered in feathers, and looked as if she would march up and question him about his dog. He hid behind a display of confidence, nodding to her as if in greeting and never slowing. The Asphodel Traveler simply smiled at him and gave him a curtsy, never taking her eyes from the pavement. Not much trouble there, but then, according to the other Travelers from Enosh, Asphodels never made much trouble.

The third Traveler he passed was a pudgy older man in the burnt red robes of Naraka. He was panting and leaning against a wall for support, and looked like he had just come out the wrong end of a bar brawl. A fresh bruise marred one side of his face, and his scalp oozed a trickle of blood.

Then his eyes met Alin's, and widened. Alin drew in a breath; it was the old Traveler from the Naraka temple, the one he had blasted into the wall. Come to think of it, he probably should have handled that better.

On pure fear, he drew a globe of golden light into his palm. The gold-armored hound growled and crouched, ready to attack at Alin's word.

The old man raised one crimson-marked hand into the air, and Alin tensed, readying himself to meet the attack.

Then the man threw his other hand up beside it, screaming, "I surrender! Spare me! Help, Traveler! Enemy Traveler! Don't kill me!" He continued screaming as he hurried away.

Alin stood there in the street, frozen, holding a ball of deadly light in one hand, and feeling like a painted fool.

For a second, the city continued as if no one had heard. Silence flooded in, then the general bustle of the city, as if nothing out of the ordinary had happened. Alin relaxed. Maybe this wasn't that far from ordinary in Bel Calem, after all.

Then great bells began pealing from every corner of the city in a deafening voice that drowned out the sounds of the city. Keanos began to bark in competition.

A burning comet appeared in the skies over the city, flaring in red and orange as it plummeted down. Alin had only a moment to think *Here! It's headed here!* before the fireball smashed into the streets in an explosion that dwarfed even the bells. A cloud of dust and bricks shot out in every direction, and only a quick shield of golden light stopped some of them from crashing into Alin's face with bone-smashing force.

Out of the resulting dust cloud a night-black crocodile's face rose on a long, scaly neck. Its body was all but invisible in the cloud, but it stretched out two long, serpentine limbs that reached from one side of the street to another. Its ruby eyes locked on Alin, and it shrieked out a challenge. As it did, all of its scales burst simultaneously into searing flame, so that it was wearing a cloak of pure fire.

Wreathed in flame, the creature rushed forward, barreling toward Alin.

Maybe, Alin thought, in the last instants before he released his power, *I should have just tried sneaking in.*

In the end, it hadn't taken the Nye ten minutes. It had only taken him three. Simon counted.

When he returned, he led Simon directly to where Leah was being held captive. Of course, to the Nye, directly meant directly: Simon had to hold on to Nye essence and liquid steel almost constantly as he followed the shadow over rooftops and through locked fences as often as down the street.

The long black cloak billowed behind him as he ran along the tiled roofs of Bel Calem, flapping like a flag as he leaped over the gaps between houses. Once, as he leaped from one rooftop to another, his cloak snagged on a weathervane. It snapped tight, pulling him down to slam against the hard tiles of the roof.

Simon scrambled to his feet as soon as possible, freeing the cloak from the weathervane and feeling his face flush.

"This is why you don't wear cloaks," Simon muttered.

Nearby, a woman burst out laughing. A gray-haired grandmother in the building next door was peering out her window at him, a basket of laundry tucked under one arm. She laughed again, pointing with her free hand straight at him.

Simon ran after the Nye, who was rapidly vanishing into the distance. His face felt like a bonfire.

It didn't take long for him to realize that they were headed for the center of the city, where he had always heard the Overlord made his home. He didn't know which of those palaces belonged to Malachi, but of course it didn't really matter; if the Nye led him straight to Leah, he would never need to know the identity of the house's owner. They could just leave, hopefully without Malachi ever knowing Simon had been there.

Once, as he dashed along a roof of red clay tiles, every bell in the city seemed to start ringing at once. He was nearly startled off the roof, and had to grab onto a nearby chimney to regain his balance. Was that sound some kind of alarm? Had he been spotted? How had they known to look for him up here? Maybe there had been some kind of conjured guardian, some invisible sentry set by a Traveler to watch for invasion from the rooftops.

Then he saw the explosion a few streets over, watched dust rise like smoke followed by a shriek and a rising flame. Someone shouted, and he heard a sound like steel on steel. Was there someone fighting down there, right next to a burning building?

"Huh," he said to himself. "Sure glad that's not me."

He briefly considered going to check it out, but the shadow of his Nye guide had grown distant, and he would need to press himself to catch up. He hurried forward, following the black robe.

The Nye led him to a building that towered over its neighbors. It was built chiefly of some dark wood, and its huge windows were made of purple glass. Simon stared at that a moment. *Purple glass?* He thought. *Why does glass need to have a color? It's glass.* He stared for only a few seconds before following the Nye over its low stone wall and into a garden. The building didn't look like a palace to him, or anywhere that people would live; it looked more like a cathedral. But then, he had never seen a palace or a cathedral, and he decided it didn't matter in any case.

The Nye turned toward a tower, pointing a black-gloved hand toward the window at the top.

"The highest window of the tallest tower," Simon muttered. "Naturally. I'm never going to be able to tell this story to anyone; they'll laugh in my face."

Well, it does sound ridiculous, when you put it that way, Otoku put in from the back of his belt, where he had tied her.

"You're still here? I meant to leave you back in the House."

Oh, poor baby, Otoku said. *You can still bring me back, you know. But when you die because you didn't get my help, don't come crying to me.*

"So are you going to come with us," Simon said to the Nye, "or…" he let the rest of the sentence die. Where the Nye had stood, he now saw only the garden.

Don't feel too bad about that. The Nye can't stay out of the House for too long. They're bound to it.

Really? Simon sent.

Yes. Probably. That's what we've always assumed, anyway, and they've never said any different.

Simon began looking for the best handholds on the side of the tower. *So can they stay away from the House, or not?*

They never do leave, Otoku said. *That's good enough for me. Who knows anything about the Nye, really?*

Simon sighed, both in his head and out loud, and checked his wrists. The shadow-chains had not yet crept past his hands, so he should be able to draw on his powers for as long as possible. He wouldn't have to risk Incarnation, whatever that was, so long as he kept his power to a reasonable level.

Reaching out to Valinhall, he called the strength of steel and the speed of the Nye. Cold power flowed through him.

A heavyset woman in an apron opened a nearby door and saw him standing there, alone in the garden. "You, boy. What did we tell—"

Simon leaped at the tower, and the woman swallowed whatever she was going to say in a shriek.

There was some sort of wooden lattice covering one side of the house, ivy laced thickly through and around it. As Simon slammed against the side of the tower, he grabbed a double handful of the wood and ivy, hoping desperately that it would hold him.

Thanks to Benson's steel, he barely felt the impact against the wall, and he was sure that falling all the way to the ground wouldn't hurt much either. But if he fell after he had jumped up so dramatically, Otoku would torment him till his deathbed.

The grip under his left hand tore away, giving him a frantic moment to consider the distance to the ground, almost twenty feet down. But though the wood and vines in his right hand creaked and cracked dangerously, they held. He managed to find another handhold on his left and pulled himself up.

After only a few seconds of careful climbing, Simon managed to haul himself onto the sill of a purple window even taller than he was. He tried to look inside, but the dark glass was so thick he could barely make out vague shapes inside, none moving. Probably furniture. He put the room from his mind. The windowsill was wide enough that he could stand, but not so large that he wasn't just a little nervous. Besides, he was never quite sure how long the steel would last. The freezing torrent through his veins felt as strong as ever, but what if the power faded right before he hit the ground?

Just in case, Simon released the Nye essence. Outside of combat, the slowed time was more disconcerting than helpful, and holding on to two gifts at once would make the chains grow faster. He needed the steel, and this way the Nye essence would be fully recovered when he needed it.

As the world resumed its normal speed, Simon looked around, glancing up and to the side for a hold that might allow him to move higher. Most of the wall was smooth wood, but just outside the frame of the huge window were several gray rocks, circular, seemingly embedded in the wood. They seemed like an odd design choice to Simon, and more trouble than they were worth, but who was he to question rich people?

By standing on the tips of his toes and stretching his right hand out as far as he could, he was just able to wrap his fingers around the nearest rock. It felt like stone—hard and cold and covered in grit—and when he tugged experimentally, it remained solidly attached to the wall. Good enough. Simon pulled against the rock, heaving himself upwards.

Or he tried to. As soon as he applied real force to the rock it pulled free from the wall, as though he had tripped the balance on a hidden latch of some kind. It came completely off in his hand, dropping him back down onto the windowsill. For a moment he swayed dangerously back over the garden until he finally caught his balance and sunk forward against the glass, panting hard.

Get rid of it, now! Otoku demanded, and he had only a moment to wonder what she was talking about before a piercing shriek stabbed at his ears and nearly made him lose his balance.

Simon tried to cover his ears, but it did no good; the wail cut into his head as if he had his ear pressed against it.

That was when he noticed that what he had taken for a rock was not a rock at all. The side he gripped was still smooth and felt like stone, though it had grown uncomfortably warm in his hand, but the side that had been pressed against the wall looked like the underbelly of a roach. Except that it glowed bright orange, like new coals. Six glowing orange legs kicked frantically at the air, and the shriek went on and on.

Simon hurled it into the garden, more out of disgust than anything else. His steel-enhanced strength sent it flying much farther than he intended, and he heard the thing's wail steadily fade into the distance until it hit the ground. Then, at last, silence.

Otoku's voice bit into him: *You didn't expect something like this? Really? How else did you think a Traveler would protect his home?*

"This is exactly the sort of thing the Nye could have told me," Simon said testily. His heart was still pounding, and his ears ringing. "Can you find me another way up there? I don't want to be standing here when somebody hears—"

Otoku cried out a warning just as the window in front of him shattered, stabbing and slicing him in a thousand little pinpricks. Instinctively he squeezed his eyes shut and threw an arm across his face, protecting his eyes from the glass, but as a result he didn't see whatever it was that wrapped around his body and dragged him inside.

CHAPTER 18

OVERLORD MALACHI

Simon soon learned that he had been seized around the middle by a giant hand. A clawed, dark red, scaly hand, attached to an arm wider than his torso. It pulled him through the window and into a huge chamber with a vaulted ceiling that seemed miles above.

That was all he got the chance to see of the room, because he was far more concerned by the monster that held him. It looked like a tailless lizard standing on its hind legs, three times as tall as a man at least, all over scaly and the dark red of fresh blood. Its hand, wrapped around his body, was too warm for comfort, and growing hotter by the second.

The lizard looked at him with eyes like an alligator and let out a cry that sounded more like an angry bird than anything Simon would have expected from an angry monster. Its breath singed his skin and smelled like the worst parts of a slaughterhouse and an outhouse together.

Simon called as much steel as he could, until his bones felt like freezing, moving his arms outward with all his strength to break the creature's grip. As soon as he got a little space he could summon Azura, and then this fight would become much more fair. He strained against the creature's fist, resisting its strength for just a little room. The monstrous fingers started to pry apart, and the lizard lifted him high.

Just as he thought he might have enough space to summon the sword, the lizard smashed him to the ground.

Simon heard floor tiles crack with a report like thunder. Or maybe that was his skull; it was difficult to tell. Without the skeleton's steel power flowing through him he would have been killed instantly, he knew that, but he felt like someone had taken a pickaxe to the back of his head.

Still, his months in the House had not been wasted. Even in the midst of agonizing pain, he rolled away from the creature, though the motion set his stomach to rolling like a ship in storm. He staggered to his feet, keeping his eyes fixed on the red monster, and stuck out his hand to summon Azura.

Just then, through the fog in his brain, he heard someone clapping.

A solid-looking man in fancy purple clothes walked into the room, clapping. He had lines of silver at the edges of his dark hair and an easy smile on his face. The monster went completely still as soon as the newcomer entered the chamber, but Simon didn't trust it; he kept his attention divided between the huge red lizard and the man.

As Simon watched, the man reached back and shut the door through which he had walked, casually tugging his shirt straight with his other hand. For a moment he just stood there, adjusting his clothes and sweeping a hand through his hair. Simon wasn't sure what to do. He still hadn't summoned Azura, but the creature hadn't attacked, either. If it was just going to stand there, he sure didn't want to provoke it.

"You're sturdier than I expected," the man said, gesturing toward his ruined tiles. "Really, I am impressed. You must have access to some truly effective protection."

"Thank you?" Simon said, uncertain.

"From everything I had heard about Elysians, though," the man went on, "you would be the type to come running in through the front door. I posted my alarms on the window out of general paranoia; I didn't expect anyone to actually sneak up that way. I'm not sure if I should be intrigued or disappointed."

Simon edged slightly to his left, so he could keep man and lizard both in view. "Don't take this the wrong way," he said, "but who are you?"

The man looked startled for an instant, then he laughed and threw himself onto a throne to Simon's right. Until that moment, Simon hadn't even noticed the throne; he had been too preoccupied with the bits of charred meat between the monster's needle-sharp teeth. Now that he did notice, he wondered how he could have missed it: the chair was big enough for three people to sit in it side by side, and made entirely of expensive wood. It was carved with creatures that only existed in the depths of some insane Territory, if at all, and set with purple gems the size of Simon's fist.

"As ever," the man said, "my ego gets the better of me. Malachi Daiasus, Overlord in service to the Damascan Kingdom, faithful slave of His Majesty Zakareth the Sixth, our Morning and Evening Star. At your service." He gave a shallow, mocking bow from his lounging position on the throne. "And you are?"

"Simon."

Malachi waited for more, and when Simon said nothing else, it seemed to amuse him. He chuckled slightly anyway, and looked at Simon as though at a spirited child. At that moment, Simon realized that the Overlord actually meant to keep on talking. Was he stalling for time? Or maybe he was just so confident that he didn't see Simon as much of a threat.

On a gamble, Simon let the steel fade from his blood.

Immediately he sagged under his own body's weight, and the thousand little aches and cuts he had gained in the past few minutes flooded to the front of his mind. Malachi noticed.

"Ah, I see you're not well," he said. "A pity. I suppose you didn't count on being caught this early, did you? Not until you had slit my throat, I imagine." He drew a finger across his own neck, though by his tone you would think he had just made a joke.

"Slit your throat?" Simon asked. Either the Overlord knew something Simon didn't, which was actually pretty likely, or the man was making some strange assumptions.

Malachi waved a hand in the air. "Or blasted me apart, I suppose, or taken me away to your Territory. Whichever you prefer. If I hadn't been warned that you were coming, you might have even gotten me. I had it on good authority that you were in Enosh just this morning."

The chains were sliding down his wrists now, and the Nye essence was fully recovered. His steel felt shaky, like it wasn't quite at full strength, but it too would refill before long. If Malachi insisted on having a conversation before the fight, Simon could at least use the time to make sure he was at full strength.

"I'm not here for your life," Simon said honestly. He just needed to buy some time, but it would be interesting to find out who Malachi thought he was. "In truth, I wasn't even sure this was your house."

"You're dressed like an assassin," Malachi said, gesturing at him.

Simon glanced down at the black cloak, which settled in place around him. "Any assassin that would dress like this deserves to be caught," Simon said.

The Overlord smiled slightly, but then his face hardened. "Why are you here, Simon?"

"There's a girl in your tower. I'm here for her."

Malachi's face registered surprise, then something that might have been irritation. His gaze flicked to the red monster, which still stood frozen.

Dodge right, Otoku hissed, and Simon threw himself to the right just before the lizard's palm crashed down onto the tile. He barely called the Nye essence in time.

Back! Otoku said. *Left! Down!*

Simon followed her instructions instantly, dodging only as she directed, not even watching the monster. With Otoku's voice and the essence, he could have avoided its clumsy strikes forever.

Roll, Otoku said, and as he did, he felt the steel reach full strength.

The cold power of liquid steel flooded through him once again, taking from him pain and weakness. Instantly he summoned Azura and jumped forward.

The red creature roared and the temperature in the room rose to oven-hot in the space of a second, but none of that mattered. The power of the Nye made it seem as though the giant lizard was pushing his way through jelly, but Azura danced like a feather in his hand.

His blade passed through the monster's neck and hardly noticed the resistance. Simon landed in front of Malachi's throne, knees barely bent, facing the Overlord. The Nye cloak settled into place. He heard two thuds behind him as the head and body crashed separately into the ground, and heat flared at his back. He almost turned to look, but Otoku's voice told him what he needed to know.

It's down, she said, and he kept his gaze fixed on Malachi.

"That's not Elysia," the Overlord said. He sounded puzzled. "So you're not...wait. That sword. Valinhall."

It wasn't a question, but Simon nodded.

Malachi lowered his eyebrows thoughtfully, though he still seemed confused. "I know someone who would be very pleased to meet you, Simon. Very pleased. Where did you find that?"

Simon ignored him. "I'm just here for Leah. Let me go get her and leave, and we can go our separate ways."

Slowly, Malachi shook his head. "As much as I'd like to, I can't let you kill her. I'm sorry. And I very much doubt you'd be able to capture her."

Now it was Simon's turn to look confused. "Kill her? I'm trying to rescue her. From you." Why did Malachi sound as if he was the one protecting her?

Malachi looked as if Simon had slapped him. For a moment he just stared. Then he threw his head back and laughed a full, genuine laugh, as though he wasn't within easy reach of Simon's sword. He leaned back against the throne, relaxed, with an easy grin on his face, and Simon realized that his first show of amusement had been an act. This was the real thing. Overlord Malachi had actually let his guard down.

"You're trying to rescue the princess from the evil Traveler's tower?" Malachi said, still rolling with chuckles. "I mean no offense, but it sounds a bit ridiculous, when you put it like that."

I like this man, Otoku said.

"She's not a princess," Simon muttered.

"Oh really?" Malachi said, and suddenly he was leaning forward. His eyes were sharp again. "What is she, then?"

"One of us," Simon said, meeting the Overlord's eyes. "I can't leave her with you."

"And as much as I might want to, I can't let you take her." Malachi began drumming the fingers of his right hand on the arm of his throne. "So what now?"

It was going to come to a fight. Simon had been afraid of that from the first. Not only was he not sure that he could win, he wasn't sure he wanted to. Killing the Overlord would make him the most wanted criminal in the realm; even winning the fight would be like trying to get out of a pit by digging deeper. But what choice did he have?

A fat, balding man in red robes stuck his face in the room through a door Simon hadn't noticed before. One side of the robed man's face was covered in bruises. He shot a glance at Simon, and his eyes were hard. "We have engaged him in the streets, Overlord. No one has yet reached the house. Are you sure you don't need help up here?"

Malachi sounded thoughtful, and he kept drumming his fingers on the throne. "I don't think so, Petrus, but why don't you stand by in case you're needed? Over there, perhaps." He gestured to the side of the room, by the first door, the one through which Malachi himself had entered.

Petrus realized something then, Simon could tell—for an instant the man's eyes widened and his mouth opened—but he covered the expression quickly in a bow and walked over to stand in front of the door. What had he heard in Malachi's words? Had Simon missed some kind of code?

It didn't matter now. The problem remained.

"I don't want to fight you," Simon said, and was almost surprised at how much he meant it. The more he thought over his situation, the more he was sure there were no good outcomes.

"As you wish," Malachi said calmly. "We'll have plenty of time to talk later. Once you're safely restrained, of course."

And he raised the palm of the hand he had been tapping against the arm of the throne. It bore a shining red mark.

Simon cursed himself and launched toward the throne in the beginning of a lunge that would take the Overlord's head from his shoulders, but Otoku cried a warning, and he was able to twist himself aside just in time to avoid a screaming ball of orange flame that shot from Malachi's hand and blasted forward.

It was screaming in truth, he realized: there were faces inside that ball of fire, like burning ghosts, and just as the fireball was about to smash into the wall opposite Malachi they screamed again, and the fireball changed directions. Back at Simon.

Simon ignored the fire and swung his sword at Malachi with the full intention of chopping the Overlord, his throne, and the wall behind them in half. Simon put all his power and speed behind the blow, and even to his slowed vision, the sword seemed to split the air.

Malachi didn't even react. A blazing red rent in reality, like a huge red eye, appeared before him so fast it was as though it had really been there all along, and only now had the Overlord chosen to unveil its presence. The crimson Gate hung in the air before Malachi like a shield. Azura continued uninterrupted, but the Gate now stood between the sword and its target. Instead of slicing the Overlord in half, it swung through the empty air of another Territory and continued onward. The force of his own unopposed strike almost spun Simon like a top.

Only a moment after Azura swung clear, the Gate winked shut.

The Overlord had shielded himself with a Gate. Of course, the Gates of Valinhall opened far too slowly to be used in that way, but the thought had never even occurred to Simon. Yet another thing that he should have expected.

Turn around, half-wit! Otoku screamed, and Simon jerked himself around in time to see the wailing face of a fireball within kissing distance. He didn't duck so much as throw himself to the ground, and the ball of flame passed over his head. Malachi made a lazy gesture with one finger, and the fireball corrected its passage and hurtled toward Simon again.

"You don't have much experience fighting other Travelers, do you, Simon?" Malachi asked casually, as Simon ran around the room in an attempt to out-pace the fireball. "Don't worry. I'm not trying to kill you, I'm really not. You didn't do anything unjust, you were only in the wrong place at the wrong time. Once we've cleaned up this mess, we'll be glad to have you on the team."

Simon finally gave up running in circles. The fireball was apparently tireless, while he could already feel his gifts running out. He stopped and swung Azura at the flame.

The fireball exploded with a scream of agony, and the flare of light and heat was so intense that Simon threw up a hand to protect his face. The second he could see again, he ran as fast as he could. With the strength and speed of Valinhall in him, he should be able to out-pace any reaction of the Overlord's. He hoped.

But he didn't run at Malachi. On an instinct, he ran at Petrus.

The old, fat Traveler looked startled, but he had obviously prepared a defense. A swarm of glowing orange wasps, each the size of Simon's two fists together, raced from the air before Petrus' red-marked hand. Behind him, Simon heard the cries of another one of those spectral orange fireballs.

Simon drew on the Nye essence to its limits, so that the fiery wasps seemed to crawl toward him. Azura sliced one of the insects in half, but even that strike seemed slow to him.

"Si...mon..." the Overlord called from his throne. His voice sounded odd, not only slowed like everything else, but also for some reason slightly deeper.

Simon flicked another pair of wasps from the air and kept moving forward. Alarm spread across Petrus' face, but so slowly that it was almost comical.

"Face...me!" Malachi demanded. Was that just the strange effect on his voice, or did he actually sound afraid? "Come...here!"

Azura slashed again, taking the rest of the glowing wasps from the air. But Simon hadn't realized how close he had come, or else he wasn't quite used to Azura's length yet. The blade's tip drew a ragged slice diagonally down across Petrus' broad chest, then dug into the Traveler's left hand at the wrist. With the speed of the Nye, Simon was forced to watch every detail as Azura parted skin, flesh, and bone, as Petrus' face bunched up in horror. His left hand tumbled to the tiles.

Then the essence flooded out, his lungs warmed, and time resumed its normal flow. Petrus collapsed, staring at his bleeding stump, too shocked to even scream.

But he had left the door unguarded.

Malachi yelled something again, panic evident in his voice this time, and Simon knew he had been right. Malachi had had some special reason to guard this door instead of the other, though he had tried to distract attention from that fact. Was it Leah, perhaps? Did this door lead up to her tower?

He pulled open the door and jumped inside, ducking to avoid the fireball he was sure would be coming.

Nothing happened. No fire. Malachi wasn't even yelling, though Simon thought he heard running footsteps coming this direction. Simon looked up, intending to take a look around...

...and found himself almost nose-to-nose with a woman in a long purple dress. She was perhaps five years older than Simon, crouched on the floor, wearing a purple silk dress and dangling gold earrings. She held a dark-haired little girl in each hand, pressed against her shoulders. The woman was pretty, maybe beautiful, but her black eyes pressed against Simon like daggers.

"Do it, murderer," she spat. "If you are that low."

Simon wondered what she was talking about until he thought to glance down at Azura. The blade was so long that it took up most of the little room—a bedroom, now that he had the chance to look around—and he had barely paid attention when he threw himself in here. Azura's edge pressed against the woman's neck, hard enough that blood trickled down the front of her dress.

CHAPTER 19
BAD HABITS

Simon jerked himself back as though burned, letting his sword vanish. He almost stumbled as he stepped back, his foot catching the edge of his cloak. It was a miracle he had not killed the woman. Or one of the children, even. His hands trembled at the thought.

"I'm…I'm sorry," Simon said, because he could not think of anything else to say. The woman's glare faltered a little.

The footsteps caught up, and Simon turned to face the door. Malachi stood there, fear on his face, clothes rumpled. "Out here, Simon. Let's finish it out here." His voice held a strange, trembling mixture of fear, anger, and that tone people used to calm dangerous animals and madmen.

"Your wife and children?" Simon asked.

"No," the Overlord said, but his face said he was lying. "Servants. They are nothing to us. Just leave them be."

Simon didn't know much about life in Bel Calem, but he doubted the Overlord's servants wore silk dresses and gold jewelry.

"I won't hurt them," Simon said. "But I should." He wasn't sure what he felt, but it wasn't calm. The steel faded as well, leaving him aching inside and out. "The Traveler you sent killed my mother."

Fear flashed on Malachi's face again, and he held his empty palms out. Simon kept an eye on the one with the red brand. If Malachi so much as twitched it suspiciously, he would attack, never mind that the man's wife and children were watching. Then Malachi's face clouded over with confusion.

"Wait. Your village. What are you talking about?"

"Myria village," Simon said angrily. "Where I'm from. And Leah. Your men came into my home and killed my people."

"*That?* This is all over *that?*" Malachi passed his un-branded hand through his hair. "Seven stones, I have had more trouble over that village…Simon, believe me, I am sorry about your mother. I truly am. But this was just the sacrifice. Everybody pays the sacrifice! It's only nine people a year, out of the whole kingdom. Every village pays at least once. There won't be a sacrifice from that village again in your lifetime or mine."

"As if that makes it better," Simon said. He forced his hand to stop trembling.

Malachi licked his lips. "Please, Simon. Let them go."

Simon held the Overlord's gaze for a moment, but he was the one to look away first. "I'm not going to hurt them," he said again.

"Then come out of there. We'll talk, I promise. And I can get some help for Petrus before he bleeds to death."

Simon winced. "I just want Leah. Just tell me how to get to Leah, and you'll never see me again."

The Overlord kept one eye on Simon, but he had pulled off his belt and was cinching it tight around a semi-conscious Petrus' bleeding hand. A tourniquet, Simon guessed. "Simon...the door to the tower is behind my seat, just to the right of the window you broke. You passed within five feet of it when you came in."

Simon nodded and walked out the door of the bedroom, never taking his eyes from the Overlord. He did not trust Malachi's given word, not really, but he at least hoped to stall the man until his Nye essence had refilled.

"I never wanted this," Malachi said. He kept tightening the belt around Petrus' wrist. "This whole thing. It's a mess. I just wanted them to leave us alone—Enosh, the King, that girl, everyone."

"You mean Leah?" Simon asked. Shadowy chains slid, slow and icy, down toward his wrists. "She did leave you alone. You kidnapped her!"

"She's..." Malachi's mouth twisted. "I can't say anything else. Just take her. Take her out of my home, don't look back, and good riddance. But don't set your hopes too high on her, Simon. She will let you down."

"What are you talking about?" Simon demanded. But he didn't get an answer. Behind him, the door blew open on an explosion that rocked the entire house, and the room filled with golden light.

"Overlord Malachi!" Alin yelled, and his voice belonged to a king pronouncing judgment. He looked years older than he had only hours before. His blue suit, already torn, was now shredded as though he had rolled around on a bed of knives. A patch of black ash rested over his heart, and smoke billowed from him as though he had just stepped from an oven. And he glowed. He actually radiated angelic light, making his golden hair gleam like a crown.

In spite of himself, Simon was impressed.

Malachi rose to his feet at Alin's words, standing over Petrus. He opened his mouth to respond, but apparently his action was the only answer Alin needed.

"Simon, move!" Alin shouted, and thrust his hand forward.

The shadow-chains pressed like ice against Simon's arms, and the place in his mind where the Nye essence usually rested felt empty. So he did the only thing he could do: he staggered away from Malachi as fast as his wounded legs would carry him.

Not too soon. A stream of gold light, pure as lightning, blasted from Alin's palm toward the Overlord in an eruption of violent energy. There wasn't as much heat as Simon would have expected, but even standing five feet away from the actual strike, Simon felt the force of it catch him in the side and send him tumbling to the tiles.

A Gate to some red cavern hung in the air in front of Malachi; through it, Simon saw the gold light streak into the distance and blast a crimson stalactite from a far-distant ceiling. But the Gate hadn't stopped the strike entirely. Only half had passed through into Malachi's Territory, and the rest had struck the wall above and behind the Overlord's head.

A huge snapping sound echoed through the chamber, like an enormous tree breaking under its own weight, and the ceiling of the bedroom behind Malachi collapsed.

With his wife and children still inside.

Malachi screamed and took one half-step toward the bedroom, letting his Gate close. But with a pained look on his face, he visibly forced himself to stop and turn toward Alin, trembling with emotion.

"I won't let you get away with—" Alin began, but Malachi's voice cut him off.

"Shut up," Malachi said quietly. He began stalking toward Alin, reaching into his purple jacket with one hand as he did. "I've tried everything to settle this in a civilized manner. But you just won't let me go, will you? Fine, then." And he removed something from his jacket pocket.

Simon wasn't at the best position to see what Malachi held in his hand, but it looked like one half of a shallow red bowl that had been shattered down the middle. No, not a bowl. A mask?

Simon, Otoku warned. *That thing is dangerous.* No trace of her usual sarcasm remained, which did more to convince Simon of the danger than any whispered warning.

Malachi pressed the red half-mask against the right side of his face, where it stuck without anything visibly tying it on. The Overlord took a deep breath, and the wind whispered as though the entire room breathed with him.

"I'll deal with this as an Overlord should," Malachi said. His voice was granite.

Alin didn't respond, but hurled a blast of golden light. Malachi didn't shield himself this time; he reached up a hand and snatched the ball of golden light out of the air. Just grabbed it in one bare hand, as though catching a thrown apple. Then he squeezed, and the light popped like a pricked bubble.

There was a silent explosion of light when he did so, and Simon struggled to stay on his feet, but Malachi barely seemed to notice. "My turn," he said, and waved his hand in a small circle, palm down. That was all it took.

A thousand orbs of screaming orange flame, all as big as the one that had chased Simon earlier, rushed down from the ceiling and flowed toward Alin in a burning, howling gale. Even across the room, Simon felt the air slap at him like a hot desert wind.

And that settled it: it was past time for Simon to be gone.

Simon turned and glanced behind him. The door behind the throne was unguarded. He could slip away now, and maybe he and Leah could make it down into the city while the other two Travelers fought. But then again...

In the other direction, he could barely see into the broken bedroom through a half-collapsed doorway and a cloud of dust. The room was silent. Malachi's family could be dead, or they could be trapped under a thousand pounds of rubble, unable to cry out. Simon had a vision of one of the girls he had seen earlier trying to push a chunk of wood off of her, to move it just enough that she could get a full breath. She had looked only about seven years old.

I'm an idiot, he sent to his doll, and crept forward to the bedroom. Malachi, standing ten feet away, flicked his eyes toward Simon. For a moment Simon tensed, prepared to summon strength and Azura both. But the Overlord said nothing, turning back to face Alin. Either Malachi trusted Simon, which was a ridiculous thought, or he didn't consider Simon any threat. Either way, Simon was glad of it.

The doorway was partially collapsed and half-filled with wood and plaster. Simon knelt and shoved one beam aside; the whole pile creaked dangerously.

He stood back and considered his options, shooting glances from time to time back at the battle behind him. A gold-skinned man in armor stood over Alin, swatting fireballs out of the air with a spinning staff of pure gold. Malachi waved his hand, and ants the size of wolfhounds crawled out of nowhere and skittered towards Alin, blazing with all the colors of flame.

If Simon had needed another reason to hurry, he had one now. He pulled his hood up and tightened the cloak around him. The cloak would be no help against anything that either Traveler would summon, but somehow it made him feel more secure. He slipped underneath the cracked doorway.

Half of the bed had fallen in, leaving it standing on only two feet, but Simon had last seen Malachi's family huddling at the end of it. He decided to make his way toward the bed, as carefully as possible.

Can you help? he asked.

Of course I can, Otoku responded. *Run as fast as you can and never look back. You're welcome.*

A voice like a devil from the blackest pits of Naraka boomed out behind Simon: "YOUR DEATH WILL BE SWEET ON MY TONGUE." Simon refused to turn around.

The quicker I find them... Simon said.

Fine. They're under the bed.

Alive?

They're not moving. Perhaps they're simply asleep.

The wail of the orange fireballs sounded like a chorus of tormented souls. *Nobody in the city could sleep through that,* Simon said.

Then they must be dead. What a shame; we'll have to leave now.

Take me to them, Simon commanded. And, for once, the doll did as she was told.

A few seconds later, Simon knelt beside the bed. Otoku said the beam he rested on wouldn't make the rest of the pile collapse, but all the debris sounded like it would crack at any second.

He peered underneath the bed skirt and saw three pairs of eyes gleaming at him through the shadows and dust.

"Are you all right?" Simon whispered.

"Are you here to rescue us?" one of the girls asked, but her mother shushed her.

"Leave us now," the woman commanded. "We will be fine without your assistance." Even huddled in the dust under a half-broken bed, she glared thunderbolts at him.

"If you hadn't noticed, there's a battle out there," Simon said. "All it takes is one more hit, and this whole room's going to fall down on top of you."

A monstrous voice shouted something about demanding blood, and another explosion shook the whole room. Dust rained down, making the children sneeze.

"We cannot get out," the woman admitted, though her voice still sounded proud. "The bed is blocked on all sides."

"What's your name?" Simon asked gently. The chains slid down his hands like sap down a tree, reminding him to hurry, but if he just called steel and tore the bed off of them, they would be terrified. He might as well try to put them at ease.

"Without even giving me your name first? Do they have no manners where you come from?" she said, as though she couldn't hear the battle outside. The room shook again; one of the girls buried herself in her mother's sleeve.

"I am Simon, son of Kalman," Simon said impatiently. "And you are?"

"Adrienne Lamarkis Daiasus," the lady declared, and then she announced her daughters' names, but Simon didn't care enough to listen.

"Great, Mistress Adrienne—" she looked a little upset at the name, but Simon didn't know or care anything about the proper mode of address for a Damascan lady—"here's what's going to happen: in a few seconds, I will pick this beam up and hold it out of your way." He patted the beam he was kneeling on, which was as thick as his waist and stretched from one end of the room to the other.

"When I do," he continued, "you take your children and come on out. I can protect you until you can leave the house. All right?"

"What about my husband?" Adrienne asked.

"Your husband is doing fine on his own," Simon snapped, running out of patience. "And I don't know whether he wants to skin me alive or give me a job, so before I find out for sure, I'd like to take you out of here. All right?"

Adrienne glared at him one more time before nodding. Somehow, even crouched beneath a broken bed and covered in dust, she made that seem like a generous concession to an inferior.

Simon shook his head and called steel. What was he doing here, anyway? These three were alive, and he could get killed for this. Malachi's family was hardly his responsibility. He could just hear Chaka calling him an idiot.

Simon wasn't sure he disagreed.

As ever, Malachi found wearing the Ragnarus mask a disturbing experience. On the one side, it made him feel like a demigod, pulling enough power from Naraka to level Bel Calem itself. With this mask, he could call enough fire to blacken the sky with smoke and ash, and the strength and energy flowing through him made him feel as though he could bend steel in his bare hands. That feeling was a drug all its own.

On the other side, his body bore the strain. His skin stretched and thinned as he watched, and even without checking a mirror he knew that gray would soon start creeping over what remained of his black hair. The mask made him blaze with power to dwarf a dozen Travelers, but like everything from Ragnarus, it carried a price. His life burned away every second, like a wick under the flame. Only a few hours in the mask would age him to death.

But this boy, this arrogant child, may have killed Adrienne. Rage warred with terror at the thought, and Malachi hurled another ball of orange fire from the Furnace. It shrieked as it darted for the Elysian Traveler.

He had intended to overwhelm the boy immediately upon donning the mask and turn his attention to more important things, but he was proving a tough strand to snap. His gold-armored warrior batted away everything that came too close with its staff, and the boy himself wielded blasts of golden light that forced back everything Malachi could summon. Not enough to threaten him, of course; with the mask on, Malachi doubted anyone short of Zakareth himself could best him in a frontal contest.

The problem was that Malachi couldn't call anything too destructive inside his own home. The Elysian may have killed Adrienne in his carelessness, but if he hadn't, Malachi didn't want to bring the whole house down around her. Anything he summoned powerful enough to destroy the Elysian Traveler would blow his house in half, so he was forced to stick to lesser powers that he could control. He would win, eventually, but it would be a matter of wearing down the boy's defenses, waiting for him to make a mistake.

But the longer this fight took, the more of Malachi's life leaked away. He was already one, two, maybe even three years older than he had been when the fight started. What would Adrienne say, when she saw him as an old man?

The Valinhall Traveler would help her, if she could be helped. Malachi had great hopes for that boy, if he survived. Malachi had almost roasted him on pure reaction when he saw the child sneaking along in a black cloak, headed for his wife and children. Logic had restrained his power. Logic, and a feeling. Logically, if Simon had wanted Malachi's family harmed, he could have just left them there. And Malachi's instincts told him that a boy who would risk himself to save a captive—even a captive who wasn't really being held against her will—would only be trying to help.

He would be a great asset to the Kingdom, one day.

But that was in the future. For now, this standoff had taken long enough. It was time to be finished.

Malachi raised both hands and twisted them in unison, the screaming fireballs from the Furnace keeping his opponent too occupied to notice, much less do anything. The wall between Naraka and this world twisted, shrieking in protest. This was one of the few powers he had been warned never to call, except under the most dire circumstances.

Too bad. He was about to end the fight, even if he had to blast this prophesied savior all the way back to Enosh.

"Vordreith, Lady of the Just, I call upon thee," Malachi intoned. His whole body pulsed with agony, but that was a good sign. Attempting this summons without the mask might have killed him; he would accept a little pain. He did not usually have the voice to summon one of the Arbiters, but today the mask's power carried his request to every flickering flame and dark corner in Naraka. "In the name of my lawful authority, I beg the power to punish rebellion."

Vordreith's response was immediate, a somewhat amused and cultured female voice that echoed in his skull: *Putting down rebels, Malachi? You?*

"Please, my lady," Malachi said. Some of the boy's golden blasts were getting far too close to the bedroom door. He had to hope Simon had things well in hand there. "The Elysian Traveler is in my home. He may have killed my children."

Really, now? Vordreith murmured. Then all amusement vanished, leaving a voice as cold as a snowdrift in Helgard.

Then break him.

A swirling ball of fire appeared in his hands, boiling with all the natural shades of fire and beyond: the orange-gold of a blazing flame was streaked with red from a slaughterhouse, yellow from a thunderstorm, blue from an ocean's depths. The whole immense power of it, borrowed from Vordreith, whirled in a space he could just barely contain in his two hands together.

Every Naraka Traveler, upon first beginning his training, eats a fruit that protects him from heat to one degree or another. One of the measures of a Naraka initiate's potential power is how much protection they gain from the ritual. Malachi's protection was the strongest in generations; the fruit of the obsidian tree had granted Malachi a protection so great that he could wade barefoot through coals without a twinge, and it was a good thing. A hair less resistance, and the burning sphere he held would have scorched the flesh from his hands. Without the protection of the obsidian tree's fruit he would be dead. And without the power of the mask, he would never have been able to keep Vordreith's fireball contained; it already would have consumed the heart of Bel Calem in raging flames. His head throbbed with the pain of the effort.

The challenge now would not be killing the Elysian. It would be doing so without burning his entire mansion down, and maybe his wife and daughters with it.

Malachi glanced to the right, at the bedroom door. They should be spared the worst of it—enough that it wouldn't kill them, at least. If he controlled the energy correctly, if he could only do this right, then his family shouldn't even feel the heat.

Malachi held the ball of fire in front of him and, with a wordless shout, triggered its power. A stream of fire billowed forth like a dragon's breath, consuming all in front of it.

Flames swallowed the golden Traveler whole.

Fire gusted toward Alin, blasting apart the gold-skinned giant he had summoned. He barely had time to throw up an arm in a vain attempt to shield his face from the heat.

He had expected that, if this moment came, he would be able to die content knowing that he had done his best to oppose evil. What he felt instead was shame. He had told everyone that he would be the one to fight Damasca, even dared to think of himself as a hero.

The Overlord had proved him wrong. After all this, he was just a boy with a head full of pride.

Alin stood there, cringing and shielding his eyes, for almost thirty seconds before he realized that he wasn't dead.

He lowered his arm and flinched involuntarily, taking a step back. The stream of flame hung in the air as though frozen, the heat still enough that he felt as though his skin should have caught on fire. It filled the room with a blinding light, so Alin felt he could look at nothing else.

When he finally pried his eyes away from the fire, he realized someone was standing in front of him, where he had been standing a moment before. It was a young man with golden hair, standing frozen like the fire, with one arm held up in front of his face. He wore a slashed, burned, expensive suit that might once have been blue, and he cringed away from the flame.

From inches away, Alin stared into his own face.

Rhalia dashed in from the side, white dress blowing in a wind that didn't exist. Her golden eyes and hair shone bright with reflected firelight.

"Rhalia!" Alin said. "What is this? Am I dead?"

"Close," Rhalia said with a laugh. "You know, you weren't ready for this. I separated your mind from your body so that we could talk." She floated over the stream of fire and hopped up to Malachi. He stood still in his purple suit, one half of his face covered by a crimson mask, mouth still open in a scream. His hands were thrust in front of him, as though he had to push the column of flame forward. Rhalia waved a hand in front of the Overlord's face.

"You separated my mind?" Alin poked a finger at his own body, as it stood in front of him. It felt completely rigid, as though his flesh and clothes had turned to stone. "This is amazing! Could you do this anytime?"

"The longer I do it, the closer you come to frying your brain like an egg," Rhalia said, spinning around and hopping back toward him. "So let's make this quick, shall we?"

"That sounds fine to me," Alin said. He had never even heard of frying an egg, but it didn't sound like a pleasant process.

"You're in the frying pan now, so I guess I've got a choice. Do I let you die, or do I give you something you haven't yet earned?"

"That doesn't sound like a choice to me," Alin said, attempting a smile. Was she really still considering letting him die?

She wagged a finger at him. "Power unearned, in this case, could lead to worse than your death. Worse even for you." Rhalia shrugged. "It's hard to explain, really, but trust me. The more power I give you, the more likely it is to run out of control."

"I will earn it," Alin said. "I promise. I'll do whatever I have to." He tried to make himself sound as earnest as possible. He really would do whatever she asked, if it kept him from roasting like a chicken.

"Why did you attack the Overlord when you walked in?" Rhalia asked suddenly.

Truth to tell, he had been fighting his way through the Naraka creatures guarding the door first. There had been a few human guards as well, though they had mostly run when they realized Travelers were fighting. With his blood hot from the fight, he hadn't thought at all; he had simply attacked. "If I hadn't, he might have killed me," Alin responded.

Rhalia pulled her legs up underneath her, sitting cross-legged in midair. Her white dress hung down almost to the floor. "You don't even know for sure the girl Leah is here." She started to drift in a slow orbit around Alin's head.

"If she wasn't here, Simon wouldn't be either," Alin pointed out. "And Keanos led me to this house. Besides, Malachi is the one who sent his men to the village. Malachi is the one who ordered her taken in the first place. He deserves to die."

Rhalia floated back in front of Alin, smiling a little sadly. Her golden eyes shone with…tears? Was she about to cry? "That's what I mean, Alin. I don't see patience or temperance in you. You're not ready for this yet."

"I won't ever be," Alin said, "if I burn to death here."

"Well, that's true," Rhalia said. "And I don't want you to get incinerated, anyway. I kind of like you."

"Glad to hear it."

She stared into Alin's eyes until he gave her his full attention, looking more serious than Alin had ever seen her. "I'll give you the green, Alin, but I wanted to warn you first. Unearned power is a curse more often than a blessing."

Did she really think this was important now? "I'll be careful," Alin said. He extended out a hand. "Please."

Rhalia sighed and held her own hand out to Alin's. As she did, her palm was filled with a glowing green crystal. It spun in place, and Alin realized that the crystal was formed of dozens of tiny, whirling, ever-shifting plates of solid green light, like layers and layers of glass turtle shells, eternally spinning and dancing in mysterious patterns.

"The green light of protection," Rhalia announced. "It's a lot of fun. And it's usually earned through patience, but this time we'll make an exception." He could hear a smile in her voice, though she kept her face mostly serious. The tears were gone from her eyes, and she seemed almost cheerful again.

"Use it well," she said, and vanished.

Suddenly he was standing once again with his arm over his eyes, with heat washing over him, about to reduce him to something less than ash.

Then his world was filled with green light. He opened his eyes and saw a dome of interlocking crystal plates, like a honeycomb of green glass, covering him. It stretched around him in every direction, so that he could reach his arm out in any direction and touch solid green light. The fire washed over his shield and streamed on behind him, leaving him as unharmed as a rock in a river.

Well, almost. As he watched, cracks began to form in the green, glowing even more brightly than the plates around them. The cracks grew and spread as he watched, the bright light of the shield dimming, the heat growing.

The fire was too much. It was overwhelming even the protection of the emerald barrier. He had to try something else, or he was going to die in spite of Rhalia's gift.

Alin placed both hands against the wall and called on Elysia, picturing a star of green where he normally imagined a golden sun. He poured his own strength and the borrowed power of his Territory into the wall, as much as he could, holding nothing back.

The cracks held. They did not heal, but neither did they grow.

Sensation drained from his fingers and toes. He felt like someone had strapped a boulder to each of his arms, and it was all he could do to keep them in the air. He couldn't inflate his lungs, couldn't get a breath, and for a moment his vision fuzzed and almost went black. He kept pushing every-thing he had into the shield, kept calling power from the City of Light. He would not die. Not before he got back to the village. He would *not*.

After a handful of minutes, the great roar of the fire dwindled and faded away.

Alin let his shield fade with it, and his muscles shook. He sagged to his knees, vision dimming. Vaguely he was aware that everything on this side of the room was scorched and broken, except for a clean space immediately around him. Malachi stood on the opposite end of the room, the half of his face not covered by a mask looking shocked.

Shocked he may have been, but Malachi waved his branded hand in a pat-tern Alin recognized. He tried to struggle his way up from his knees, but his body wouldn't cooperate. Vaguely, Alin regretted that Rhalia had taken a risk to save his life, but it had all been in vain. Green light or not, he was about to die.

He needed one more attack. If he had just one more weapon, he could hit the Overlord before he finished summoning. He just needed one more weapon.

Just one.

CHAPTER 20

A VICTORY

Simon held steel and essence both, peering out of the broken doorway and into the hall. The fire had been almost blinding, blasting a ragged hole the size of a house all the way through the far wall. He could see a chunk of Bel Calem's rooftops in the afternoon sun through that hole; some of them smoldered with small fires. Unless Alin had gotten something really special from his Territory, he was nothing but a scorch mark on the tiles by now.

Simon wasn't sure how he felt about that. Alin had certainly asked for it, but Simon had never wanted to see Alin consumed in a fire.

Adrienne tried to push past Simon to reach her husband, who still stood in front of his broken throne. Simon held her back with one arm. Until he was sure the fight was over, he wouldn't even want to step out there himself. He certainly wasn't going to let Adrienne or the girls get themselves killed by walking out unprotected.

Simon squinted at something that knelt on the floor where the fire had been. Alin's body? Or had he somehow managed to survive?

Malachi began moving his hand again, calling on his Territory. Alin's hand raised, wavered with exhaustion, and then steadied.

And a thousand golden arrows burst from the air in front of him, spraying across the entire room.

Including a wave that rushed straight for Simon. Without the Nye essence in him, Simon would never have been prepared, but he was able to summon Azura before the arrows reached him. He was ready.

Malachi apparently didn't know that, or else fear for his family had overwhelmed his reason. The Overlord saw where the arrows were headed and threw himself to the side, putting his body between Alin and the bedroom door. His Gate went up, shielding him and the bedroom behind him, but it was too late: a wave of gold arrows streaked past him.

Azura's blade was too long to work well in the relatively small doorway, so Simon moved his wrist as little as possible, snapping the arrows from the air with the last few inches of the sword. Their speed was nothing compared to the dart traps from the Valinhall armory.

Not a single arrow made it past him.

The arrows stopped, and Malachi's red Gate shuddered in the air, then vanished. Only then did Simon notice the Overlord was wounded; one gold arrowhead stuck out from the back of his chest, one from just below his ribs.

Malachi fell to his knees. Adrienne noticed at the same time Simon did, screaming something and trying to push her way past again.

Simon held her back effortlessly. Alin was still out there, and Malachi still wasn't down. Not yet.

"Wait," Simon said to her without turning around. "It's not safe."

Alin walked unsteadily up to Malachi, who sat on his knees, blood trickling onto the tiles. His half-mask had fallen to the floor. Somehow he seemed older than he had before the fight, a few more wrinkles, more gray in his hair. Maybe he just looked tired.

Alin stretched out a hand in the same gesture Simon used to summon Azura. He grimaced, as if in pain, and the gold light that gathered in his hand seemed reluctant somehow, hazy, as if Alin's power was on the edge of running out. But the light formed at last, pooling in his hand into a solid outline. The outline of a broad-bladed sword.

"Alin, wait," Simon said. He started to move forward.

That was when he felt the knife slide into his back.

The liquid strength running through him numbed the pain, but he still felt like he had been impaled with a burning spear. He cried out and had to release Azura to catch himself on the half-solid doorframe. Adrienne ran past him, holding her purple skirts up with one hand, bloody knife clutched in the other as though she meant to use it on Alin.

"Alin!" Simon called hoarsely. "Hold on!"

Malachi turned and saw his wife running toward him. He smiled a little.

Then a golden blade swept through his neck, and the Overlord's head tumbled to the ground.

Behind Simon, two little girls screamed. He closed his eyes. No one should have to watch their parent die.

The wound in his back burned.

"Simon," Alin called. Simon looked up. Adrienne tried to reach Alin with her dagger, screaming, but he casually pushed her away. "Where is Leah?"

Simon tried to talk around the pain in his back. "You didn't have to do that, Alin."

"Yes, I did." Alin's voice was grim. Adrienne tried to stab him in the heart, and he shoved her to the ground.

"His family saw. His kids are right behind me."

Regret flashed across Alin's face, but he shook his head. "Please, Simon. Where's Leah?"

"I'll..." Weakness and pain surged through Simon. He had been going to say that he would get Leah himself, but he needed to go back to the House. Soon, before he lost too much blood. The imps would have a holiday with him as it was.

"Door behind the throne," Simon said finally. "Top of the tower."

Alin nodded and started jogging away. The bells were ringing again, and Simon thought he could hear raised voices in the house below. He didn't have much time.

He raised Azura, dragging it slowly down the air. As the portal opened, he noticed a bright spot of color at its base: a red half-mask. It had slid across the floor with Malachi's death. Hardly thinking, Simon scooped it up with his free hand tucked the crimson mask into his belt. Who knew? He might find a use for it someday.

His last sight before he entered the Gate was of Adrienne Lamarkis Daiasus cradling her husband's severed head and weeping as her two daughters ran to join her.

Success at last, Simon thought.

The only thing worse than a victory in battle, Otoku said, *is defeat.*

He couldn't tell if she was mocking him or not.

Leah winced, staring at the crystal disc in her lap. She sat on her bed, which sat in the center of her room in Malachi's tower. The disc, an artifact of Lirial, showed her Malachi's severed head rolling across the tiles several floors below. Malachi was vain, disrespectful, and he shirked his duties. But he hadn't deserved this. Certainly not in front of his children.

The whole street still shook from the fight, and the air had filled with screams and otherworldly howls, so even a blind woman would have been able to tell Travelers were fighting. But with the disc, she had seen everything since Alin strode through the door. Apparently Simon was there as well, but she had only caught glimpses of him.

Even Simon was some kind of Traveler now, judging by the way he had summoned that enormous sword. Tartarus, maybe, despite the black cloak. How had he learned that?

She had first intended to go down and intervene in the battle herself, but her orders had been not to reveal herself except in the face of personal danger.

Besides, she realized she didn't even know which side she would support. Malachi had served the Kingdom well, and she had no quarrel with him personally. Logically, she should find herself on his side. But Alin was her friend, and he was only fighting because she was here. What kind of person would she be if she let him die when he was only trying to save her? Then again, that was what her father would want her to do.

Even after more than two years, this spy business never got any less confusing.

Alin turned, letting his sword of light evaporate and walking away from the Overlord's bleeding body. Was he walking toward the throne? No, not the throne. The stairs. He was coming for her.

Two Travelers overthrowing an Overlord on her behalf. Her mother would tell her that she should be flattered, but all she felt was sad and a little sick. They really were naïve. If they learned who she really was, the truth would hit them like a knife to the gut.

Alin seized the iron ring of the door at the bottom of the stairs, pulling it open and stepping inside. Very well, then, she would wait for him here and pretend to be surprised. She would have to hide the disc, of course; a kidnapper would never leave his captive with a rare and expensive seeing crystal.

The disc was fading away, sliding back to the shelf of her sanctum in Lirial, when Leah noticed what she was wearing. Malachi had given her court clothes: a silver dress and shoes, with pearls at her throat and rings on her fingers.

Leah cursed, a habit she had picked up in Myria, and stripped out of her dress faster than she would have dreamed possible. A kidnapper would never let his captive wear expensive dresses, except in a few bizarre and complicated situations she didn't feel up to inventing for Alin's benefit. She tossed her dress into a corner, followed by her shoes. A few frantic seconds of searching turned up her old, brown village clothes. It had always been brown, in Myria, never any spot of real color.

Halfway through pulling on a stocking, she hesitated. Maybe she should let Alin catch her changing. He was young, and innocent in his way; the sight of her might distract him enough to let her dodge any awkward questions. No, perhaps not. That tactic could easily create more problems than it solved. She shrugged into her clothes and danced around, looking for the simple leather shoes that she had worn when she was playing a captive.

A knock at the door. That was somewhat adorable; if he really thought she was being held against her will, he should have charged in without knocking. Still, she welcomed the delay.

"A moment," she called, finally spotting her shoes. As she pulled them on, she noticed her fingers, gleaming silver in the light from her window. She had almost forgotten her rings! With hurried, jerky motions, she pulled them off and tossed them into a corner on top of her dress and shoes.

"Who is it?" Leah said at last, trying to adopt fear into her voice, as though she thought the man at the door might hurt her.

"Leah, it's Alin." His voice glowed with pride, even muffled by the wooden door. "I've come to rescue you."

Leah pulled the door open and faked a look of shock. "Alin! How did you...I mean, how did you get here?" Perhaps her shock wasn't entirely feigned; seeing him from a distance, through the Lirial lens, did not prepare her for the sight of him in person. Smoke rose from his clothes, he was covered in a layer of ash, and he smelled like a campfire. His dark gold hair shone through a veil of blood and dust. When she met his eyes, she almost didn't recognize the man behind them.

Leah cleared her throat and started again. "Were you the one making all that noise?"

Alin stared at her seriously. "Leah, are you hurt? Can you travel?"

For a moment she thought he was asking her to open a Gate for Traveling, and her thoughts grew panicked. *Does he know?* she thought. *How much has he realized? How did he find out?*

Then she caught the real meaning behind his question and relaxed. "Oh, no, I'm fine. Hurry, let's get out of here before the Overlord comes back."

He gave her a small, self-satisfied smile. "Don't worry about that. Malachi's dead. I killed him."

Leah made her eyes well up with tears, a trick with a thousand uses that she had perfected as a child. For some reason, men always expected women to be crying. "Oh, thank the Maker. Are we safe, then?"

"No, we need to run." As if to illustrate his point, shouts came from below, and running feet on the stairs. Alin immediately put his back to Leah, standing between her and danger, facing the stairs. He brought his hand up as if to call on his Territory, but nothing happened, and his fingers wavered in midair.

Exhausted, then, or so it seemed. Not surprising. That half-mask Malachi had used clearly came from Ragnarus, and nothing from her father's Territory gave anything but incredible power. The fact that Alin had survived at all was miraculous, but his exhaustion might come in handy in the immediate future. Maybe she should capture him and bring him to the capital?

That was probably the best option, but she found herself strangely reluctant to reveal herself. Alin would call it a great betrayal. She would save that option, then, for when she had no other choice.

The pounding footsteps reached the top and Simon stepped forward, looking years older instead of scarcely two months. He was thin and dark as always, but he had filled his scrawny frame in with a bit of muscle since the last time Leah had seen him in the flesh. Fresh stubble darkened his face, as though he had missed shaving this morning, and a black cloak flowed out into the hallway behind him. He wore a cloak, even in this heat. He must have been stifling.

Then she caught sight of his arms, with black chains that slid down his forearms like living tattoos. The sight of them triggered something in her memory, something she should have known immediately, but she couldn't quite call it up. Where had she seen those marks before?

To her surprise, the whole of Simon made him look...competent. Even dangerous. Though his hair was wet, for some reason, and he fiddled with the clasp of his cloak as though he had thrown it on in a hurry. Was it raining outside?

"Simon," Alin said, but Simon looked past him. He looked past Leah, too, though that wasn't entirely a surprise. Simon usually had difficulty looking her in the eyes.

"That's a nice room," Simon said. Leah blinked. She had thought herself beyond this particular danger when Alin ignored it.

"Simon, we have to get going," Alin said urgently. The shouts from below grew louder.

"A nice room," Simon repeated. "And are you wearing a necklace?" Curse those pearls, she had forgotten to take them off. Simon glanced at her neck, and then, just as much of a surprise, met her gaze. His eyes were steady and not accusing, but searching.

"He gave me gifts, sometimes," Leah said, as if this were admitting something terrible. "And he came to see me. I think he meant to...I mean, I think he was going to make me one of his..." She broke off, as if she wasn't sure how to finish the sentence or didn't want to.

A woman's voice called from below: "The tower! They went into the tower!"

"It's okay, Leah," Alin said soothingly. He shot a hard look at Simon. "We've got to go, now. Questions later." He put out both hands and focused on the air in front of him.

Leah had never seen a Gate to Elysia open—no one had, for the past three centuries—but clearly this was not going well. Gold light swirled, then stopped, then broke apart, then gathered again into a vague oval. Sweat gathered on Alin's brow, and he barely managed to keep from collapsing. Simon moved as if to catch him, but Alin stayed on his feet.

More footsteps pounded up the stairs, carrying with them a glow like a portable bonfire just around the corner. Naraka, then. Reinforcements.

Alin grunted at himself and heaved as though pushing a boulder uphill. Then, finally, the golden Gate snapped into clarity. Leah stood staring at a city of gold and rainbows under a golden sun, silver-and-diamond parapets sparkling with a thousand different colors. Very few of the Territories were plain or ugly, but this...

Leah had heard some of the older, more superstitious legends call Elysia a paradise for the virtuous. Seeing this beautiful city of gold and shining jewels, she could almost believe it.

"Move, now!" Simon said, and pushed Alin into the Gate. Leah followed, just as a pair of men in the rust-colored robes of Naraka crested the stairs. One of them began to wave his brand in a pattern that would call on the Furnace, but then they were on the other side of the Gate, and the opening slid shut.

All three of them stood on the lush grass of the field outside the city of Elysia, Alin panting as though he had just run up a hill. Simon stood in his black cloak, alert, scanning the tops of the city walls and flexing his right hand as if wishing he held a sword. Leah almost relaxed. They were safe, for now. No one but an Elysian Traveler could open a Gate here. Unless...

A horizontal slash in midair, where the gate had just closed, began to glow cherry-red. One of them had a gatecrawler, or whatever they called the Naraka equivalent. Not good at all. They would be able to force the Gate open in seconds. Gatecrawlers could only pry open a Gate seconds after it closed, but they were also by far the best way of following a Traveler into a foreign Territory. It looked like there would be a fight after all.

Inside Elysia, Leah could barely sense her Territories. It would take time to summon even a meager defense, and by that time she could be burning to death. Of course, she could reveal her identity to the Naraka Travelers, but she was hesitant to take that step until she had to. For one thing, if she revealed herself and the Damascans still lost, she would have some unfortunate questions to answer for Simon and Alin.

Which meant that her fate was now, more or less, in the hands of two half-trained boys.

Clearly, she was doomed.

Alin knelt on his hands and knees in the soft grass of Elysia, trying to gather his strength, trying to force his head to stop swimming. Leah grabbed him by the shoulders, trying to get him to focus, but all he could do was think about her blue eyes, and how strange it was that a person could have *blue* eyes, and how they reminded him of the sky back in their world, and how the blue sky was much better than the boring yellow one here…

Leah shook him again, harder. "They're forcing the Gate open!" she shouted.

"Can they do that?" Alin asked. His voice sounded hazy to his own ears.

"Apparently! We need to move!"

"Which way, Alin?" Simon asked. He spun around, looking for a way out, and the movement sent his cloak billowing behind him. Alin wondered if he had moved like that on purpose, to look dramatic.

Alin kicked his brain, forcing it to focus on important matters. If the Travelers were trying to re-open his Gate, then they would show up in the same spot he had. Which meant that they had to get away. But it also meant…

"Help!" he yelled, as loud as he could manage. He touched the golden sun in his mind, sending a bit of Elysia's power into the call. "I need some help!"

The crimson slash in the air widened a little, and Alin thought he could hear men's voices from the other side.

A golden giant, nearly a twin to the one that had given his life defending Alin earlier, strode into the meadow, using his golden staff as a walking stick.

"Initiate," the giant boomed, nodding to Alin. "Where is my brother?"

"Killed," Alin said, because he wasn't sure what else to say.

The giant howled, an enormous and mournful sound. "Where is his slayer?"

"Also dead. I killed him." Maybe that would prevent the giant from blaming him. Then again, maybe not.

"But his men are coming after us now," Alin hurriedly added. "They're trying to break open the Gate."

The giant planted his feet and held his staff in front of him. "Go, initiate," he said. "I will hold them."

Alin didn't recall ever hearing either giant's name, but he resolved to find out. "Thank you," Alin said.

The bright red slice widened like a broad mouth, and Alin caught a glimpse of familiar blood-colored robes before the giant speared his staff through the opening. Then Simon was grabbing him by the arm and hauling him forward.

"Come on," Simon said. "We've got to move. Can you take us somewhere? By Traveling or whatever?"

Alin panted as he staggered along, but he thought he could manage a single Gate back to the real world. Of course, there were still the other limitations.

"Yes," he said, "but it won't get us far out of Bel Calem. Maybe just past the walls. We're going to need a ride."

They emerged from the golden Gate riding three shaggy white bears. Simon wasn't sure if it was the best thing to ever happen to him, or the worst.

Each of the bears wore a suit of armor and a saddle made of gold, and they ran along at a smooth ground-eating pace that put the walls of Bel Calem far behind them only minutes after they appeared. Unfortunately, the gold saddles were even less comfortable than they looked.

"Why can't you take us back through another Gate?" Simon called. "We could go farther in your Territory."

"Can't," Alin yelled, from the back of his own bear. He still slumped over his mount as if he were exhausted, though he sounded lively enough. "I can only open one Gate each day. And the city only stretches so far, so we can only Travel from one end to the other."

"That's a lot of rules," Simon said.

"Why can't we use yours, then?" Alin asked.

Simon cleared his throat, though Alin was too far away to hear. "You can't exactly Travel through Valinhall. Every Gate takes you back to where you started."

"How can you call yourself a Traveler at all, then," Alin called. He sounded like he was teasing, but it still put Simon's back up.

"Let's try a straight fight," Simon said, "and we'll see who—"

"Boys!" Leah interrupted. "Eyes forward!" When she took the lead like that she sounded uncomfortably like her aunt.

Simon looked ahead to see a formation of men on horseback, in the purple-and-brown uniforms of Malachi's troops, form up in ranks. They were still distant, but he could see spearheads gleaming in the sun as they were leveled toward the three riders.

"What now?" Leah called.

Alin started to say something, but Simon called his gifts and hopped down. Thanks to Valinhall's strength and speed, he kept up easily with the galloping bear. His cloak streamed behind him, and he had to admit that he liked the way it looked, billowing along behind him like a black banner.

And, of course, he didn't bask in the look of astonishment on Alin's face, and the impressed look on Leah's. Not at all.

"I'll deal with this," Simon said. "Just keep riding straight." He put his hand out and summoned Azura, making completely sure to keep it pointed into the air. The last thing he needed was to drive his sword into the ground and trip while he was trying to look impressive.

Can you help me out? Simon asked Caela, who had replaced Otoku during his last trip to the House.

Of course, Caela replied. *You know, some of your other advisors are going to be upset with you, choosing me again. There are many more of us.*

I'll stick with the ones I know for now, thanks, Simon said. *Now, can you keep me from looking like a fool?*

I'll keep you alive, Caela said. *But as for the other? No promises.*

Simon smiled and would have laughed, except for what lay ahead. He was going to have to kill some men who were just doing their jobs, and he had had his fill of that for one day.

Still, he had no choice. Not really. Drawing on steel and essence both, he pushed his speed to the limit, leaving Alin and Leah far behind.

Chapter 21
The Hope of Escape

They had abandoned the road almost immediately after breaking through the cavalry line, intending to lose their pursuers in the countryside and circle around to the northwest, toward Enosh and Myria. They didn't get the chance.

The scattered trees and scraggly brush of the landscape gave very little cover, especially to those riding great white bears and being tracked by those who could search from the air. Simon's first plan had been to ride until they lost their hunters, then to open a Gate into Valinhall and shelter there until they felt the pursuit had passed. Maker only knew where he was supposed to put three huge armored bears in the House, but he would skin that cat once he'd caught it. The trick was to find a place where the Damascan Travelers wouldn't see him open the Gate. If they never knew where the Gate had opened, he reasoned, they couldn't force their way through.

It had been a good plan, but it seemed that every time he tried to stop and open a Gate, a Traveler would step out of nowhere, or a bird with steel talons would dive and try to rake out his eyes. He tried three times, each where he was sure they were unobserved, but something always interrupted at the last second.

"We'll just have to outrun them," Leah had said after the third attempt, when a creature like a steel porcupine had burst from the cliffside and leaped at Simon ten seconds before he finished tearing open the Gate.

He had to kill the thing, but by the time he did, the rocks around him tore themselves out of the ground and formed into a giant hand, which groped around blindly on the ground, trying to crush him. Simon was forced to flee.

Back on his bear and running, Simon called back, "Can we?"

Simon had no idea how a normal bear would fare carrying a human on its back and running at top speed for hours, but he suspected these creatures took a little something extra from their Territory. They never stumbled, even over rocky terrain, and kept up a far faster pace than a horse could maintain for any length of time. Still, they were beginning to show signs of weariness: Simon's mount panted loudly enough to be heard over the sound of their passage, and its gait wasn't as smooth as it had been earlier. Which, unfortunately, made the ride even more painful. He doubted he would ever be able to sit up straight again.

Alin shook his head, and it seemed to also have the effect of waking him up; he looked to be dozing off in the saddle. "They've run most of the day already," he said. "They can't keep this up much longer. I don't know how long, but..."

Not long enough, Simon was sure. Every couple of miles something would fly overhead or pop out of a Gate. If the mounts didn't at least last until nightfall, when they had a chance of hiding, they would all die.

Which meant that Simon was down to two options, the first of which was to keep running and hope they weren't killed. Since he was betting Alin and Leah's lives as well as his own, that was no choice at all.

Which left his second plan.

"Slow up," he called to the other two, motioning for them to draw their mounts alongside his. "I have an idea."

He told them. And, as expected, they didn't like it. Leah protested especially, which was gratifying.

"You'll be killed," she said. "Almost certainly. Even in the best case, you'll still have to get away, which leaves you in the same place you are now."

"Still better that one of us stays in danger than three of us," Simon pointed out. "And I'm the only one who can open a Gate to escape, if I get a chance. Just find a hole and stay there until tomorrow, and Alin can Travel you most of the way back to Enosh. Alin, can these bears get back to your Territory on their own?"

Alin shook his head. "I have to bring them through a Gate."

"Well then," Simon said. "I guess I'll be borrowing them for a while." He was trying to act more confident than he felt, which was surprisingly easy. He felt such little confidence that faking any was more than he really had.

"I guess so," Alin agreed. "We'll come back for you, Simon. If we can."

They wouldn't be able to, and Simon knew it, whether or not Alin did. He still appreciated the gesture, and he nodded his thanks.

Leah looked like she was trying to say something as well, so Simon saved her the trouble. "Leah, thank you," he began. He had planned all along to say this, but now that he came to it, actually speaking was more embarrassing than he had expected. He cleared his throat, adjusting the clasp of his cloak to give him something to look at besides her. "Thank you for...under the wagon. Running out. I wouldn't have escaped if not for that, and you wouldn't have been caught. So thank you."

Leah's face flashed in an odd mixture of emotions, but after a moment she just shot him a shaky smile. "I'm sorry about your mother," was all she said.

They were approaching a cliff that would, for a few moments at least, hide them from any watchers in the air. "Up there!" Simon called, and shifted his weight. The bear followed, heading in that direction.

"We'll have to be quick," Simon said. The other two yelled something, probably agreement.

When they rode between a cliff and another outcropping of rock, hidden as best they could from the sky, they slowed their mounts for just an instant. Just enough for Alin and Leah to hop off and go scurrying for cover.

Simon sped up again, one bear underneath him and one on either side, running together. Hopefully from a distance, it would look like nothing had changed.

Please don't die out here, Caela said from his belt. *It would take me ages to get back to the House.*

"I'll do my best," Simon said out loud. And he rode on, putting the steadily sinking sun behind him. South was death, and Alin and Leah would be heading northwest, so the least he could do was head east. Draw them off.

A cry sounded from far above, and a dry bush to his right burst into flame.

Well, at least some of them were still following him. If nothing else, that would give the other two a little more breathing room.

Steadily tiring, panting more heavily with every step, the white bears lumbered on. Simon wondered how long they would be able to keep it up.

Not long, as it turned out, but not from any fault of the bears.

Only an hour after Simon had left Alin and Leah, before the sun had even set behind him, a cliff rose up in the distance. It looked like a wall of rock stretching almost horizon to horizon, with only one broad crack in the center providing a way through.

A canyon. Perfect. The best way to get himself caught, especially in unfamiliar lands.

Worse, he could see his hunters to either side: far to the north and south, giant lumbering creatures of steel, or short beasts—maybe the size of a dog—that wore fire on their backs, and at this distance were little more than streaks of flame running through the scrub brush. All headed for the same cavern entrance he was.

"Maybe I can get there first and open a Gate," he said.

Not likely, Caela responded.

"Well, here's hoping." He booted the bear in the side. Simon wasn't sure that made the beast go any faster, but it made him feel like he was doing something, so he did it again. The bear growled a little, deep in its chest, and rolled one icy blue eye up to look at him. Simon stopped kicking the bear.

The canyon wasn't as wide as it had appeared at a distance, barely broad enough to contain all three bears side-by-side. That was an advantage, as Simon saw it: his pursuers wouldn't be able to see him as easily, and if they did catch up, he would be able to fight them better in a place where numbers wouldn't count so heavily against him.

Then again, he would have to be careful swinging around a sword the size of Azura in these confines. And a Traveler from a different Territory might even be able to bring the canyon walls down around him. Maybe it was best if it didn't come to a fight, after all.

As soon as he thought he was hidden well enough, Simon called steel and summoned Azura, not even dismounting before stabbing his sword in the air and concentrating on the Valinhall entry room, cutting slowly through the invisible curtain between worlds.

He drew steadily down, keeping his focus, even as shouts and unspeakable noises came closer and closer behind him. It had to be all the way to the ground, or it wouldn't be big enough, and a partial Gate would never hold for long enough to get the mounts through. In less than a minute he was almost there; the bottom of the Gate was down to the bear's chest. It was already wide enough for him to ride through, and the smell the wood and dust of the House cut through the hot desert air. Just a few more seconds.

A sharp-edged steel disc came spinning into the canyon, narrowly missing giving Simon his first haircut in months. It slammed against the canyon wall, rebounded without regard for the laws of the natural world, and came spinning back at Simon's face.

Simon jerked Azura up and slapped the spinning steel disc out of the air with his blade. It flew over his head, wavered, and vanished into the wind before it was entirely out of sight.

But the Gate hadn't been completed. It shimmered like heat haze and blew apart.

Simon's heart blew apart with it. Escape to Valinhall had been his best hope for survival. Now...

Things crowded into the canyon entrance: tall bird-like creatures made of sharp-edged metal, something like a man made entirely out of boulders, a small swarm of flaming ants the size of dogs. Above him, on the top of one canyon wall, a dark Gate opened, filled with a swarm of swirling rocks. A silver Gate leading into what seemed to be a forest of swords opened on the other.

"In the name of Overlord Deborah, put down your arms," a man shouted from the dark chaos of the rocky Gate. He wore all brown leather, though Simon had difficulty seeing more at that height, and more leather-clad figures were following him through the Gate. Many more.

"By the authority of Malachi, who is lord over these lands, surrender for judgment!" a woman called from the Gate of steel. She was wearing what looked like chainmail, and had several others following her.

"Catch me first!" Simon shouted, which was about as much insolence as he dared; he felt like he might throw up. Then, before he could think much about it, he hopped off the white bear and drew Nye essence to match the steel already rushing through him. As fast as he could, he ran farther down the canyon.

A crack like thunder rang in his ears, and Simon looked up to see that a huge chunk of rock had broken off from one side of the canyon and was falling—slowly, or so it seemed through the veil of Nye essence—falling to block the canyon in front of him. Maybe on top of him, if he was unlucky.

He started to slow, but Caela practically shouted at him. *No!* she screamed. *Forward! Go faster!*

So Simon ran faster, not daring to look up, afraid to see a hundred tons of stone crashing down on his head. The canyon was filled with a noise like giants knocking down a stone wall with hammers the size of horses, but Simon kept his eyes fixed on the end of the canyon. Even as a shadow grew wider overhead.

Finally the great chunk of rock slammed into the ground. Behind him. He was nearly knocked off his feet by the impact, saved only by the grace of the Nye. At last, he turned to look.

That end of the canyon was blocked off by a massive slice of rock wedged in between the canyon walls. No one would be following from that direction.

Of course, Simon reminded himself, *that still leaves the ones on top.*

The men and women on each side of the canyon—one group in shining mail, the other in dull leather—had simply walked forward to see if he survived. When they saw that he had, they began shouting. Creatures made of stone crawled out of the canyon sides, or else formed themselves from fallen rock.

His ears were still ringing from the noise—in fact, he wondered if they were not bleeding—but he still heard a short roar from one of the bears. He turned and, to his surprise, saw that all three bears had survived. One shoved his nose into Simon's back as if anxious for him to move on.

That sounded like a good notion to Simon, who turned back forward to continue running.

Only to stop almost immediately. The canyon opened mere feet in front of him, spreading out into a broad bowl. The bowl was huge, big enough to hold all of Myria, with walls even higher than the ones through which he had just passed.

The bowl held no shelter. No place to hide. And, to his frantic eyes, no other way out.

Simon trotted toward the center of the bowl, leading the bears, releasing Azura and both his gifts as he did so. Best to give himself as much time to recover as possible.

"Should I surrender, do you think?" Simon asked.

As far as they're concerned, you just killed an Overlord, Caela said. She didn't sound smug now, though she didn't sound as grave as Simon thought the situation deserved. *The only thing waiting for you is a long questioning followed by a swift death.*

"Yeah, I was afraid of that." Simon swallowed hard. "A fight, then?"

Only as much as it takes for you to get away.

"I could escape into the House." The walls were crawling with summoned beasts now, some made of rocks like the ones he had fought in Orgrith Cave, others made entirely of shining steel, still others blazing with flame.

They're not going to give you time to open a Gate, Caela warned him. *As soon as they see you try, they'll attack.*

Simon's breathing quickened, and he jogged a little faster for the center. Maybe he could make it to the far side, and then...there was no 'and then.' Then he would either have enough time to open the Gate—in which case they would pry it open and come after him—or he wouldn't, in which case he would die immediately.

They won't give you any time, Caela repeated. *So you'll have to earn it. Stop here.*

Simon stopped, not quite in the center of the canyon. The three armored bears faced away from him, ringing him as best they could. Trying to protect him, even now.

You are a member of the Dragon Army, Caela said. *A Traveler of Valinhall. Kai never told you what that means.*

It wasn't a question, but Simon responded anyway. "No."

What Valinhall Travelers are best at—where they excel—is in combat with other Territories. No other Territory better equips its Travelers for battle than yours. No one is more ready for this fight than you are.

"That's not saying a lot," Simon muttered, but Caela ignored him.

You have only one chance. You have to get to the Travelers on the top of the canyon before they realize what you're doing. You have to hit them so fast, so hard, that they either die, run away, or hesitate long enough for you to retreat into the House. That is your battle plan.

A silver javelin launched through the air, aimed straight at Simon's chest, but one of the bears reared up and knocked it down before it could reach him. The gold-armored beast roared its defiance.

The summoned creatures were closing in now. The silver-bladed bird shrieked, and when it did, dozens of other monsters made horrible sounds in concert.

"Can I do it?" Simon asked. His hands shook.

You're about to, Caela said, with enough confidence in her voice that Simon almost believed her. *Head straight for those Travelers, and carve through anything standing in your way. Wait for my signal.*

The shadow-chains twisted down his arms, hard and cold. Simon raised the hood of his cloak, cutting the glare from the sun.

Five seconds from now, Caela told him.

Four. One of the bears leaped to meet a rock golem, and the two went down in a whirlwind of dust and claws. Simon crouched on the balls of his feet, holding out one hand, ready to summon Azura.

Three. A fiery ant the size of a wolfhound scampered in to try and bite Simon's ankle, but before he could react, the insect was crushed by one of the steel bird's talons.

Two. The bird put its metallic beak inches from Simon's face and let out another earsplitting shriek, trying to intimidate him.

One. The beak drew back, preparing to strike like an uncoiling viper.

Now.

His power filled him, Azura flashed into his hands, and he leaped.

Not much chance that he would escape this canyon alive, but Leah and Alin would get to safety. That was what mattered. The surviving captives had made it out, and the one who captured them in the first place was dead.

Everyone was going home.

CHAPTER 22

AFTERMATH

358TH YEAR OF THE DAMASCAN CALENDAR
24TH YEAR IN THE REIGN OF KING ZAKARETH VI
THE DAY AFTER MIDSUMMER

Alin hobbled toward his rooms, covered in a frankly ridiculous number of bandages. If he took off his clothes, leaving only the bandages, he would still be decent for company. He looked like a body prepared for burial.

None of his wounds were that serious, anyway. Sure, when he had first returned to Enosh he had been covered in such a collection of burns, scrapes, and bruises that the Asphodel healer had called him 'seared and nicely tenderized.' But the people of the city—the Travelers, at least—had treated him as if he were suffering from half a dozen life-threatening injuries.

Not that he had any right to complain. The Enosh Grandmasters had been torn between relief at his safe return, fury that he had risked himself in such a way, and delight that he had managed to kill an Overlord in the bargain. It made meetings with them very confusing, such that at times he didn't know if he was being scolded, praised, or condemned.

The real problem, to them, was that he showed no signs of repentance. In his mind, the situation was very simple: he had taken a risk and it had paid off. Spectacularly, in his opinion. The man ultimately responsible for the deaths of at least a dozen Myrian villagers had paid with his life. Alin had heard that Malachi's wife Adrienne was managing the realm, though the Kingdom would soon appoint another Traveler as a replacement Overlord. Even so, the world was undoubtedly better off without Malachi Daiasus.

So no, Alin did not regret what he had done.

Except for one thing.

At Alin's repeated insistence, Grandmaster Avernus had sent out fliers scouting the wilderness between Bel Calem and Enosh. Within a day, the fliers had found the canyon where they suspected Simon had died.

With every speck of his remaining authority, Alin had demanded to ride out and see the site himself. The canyon itself was filled in with rubble, but the bowl-like depression at the end was even worse. It was packed with corpses and worse. The sandy ground was littered with empty armor, shattered rocks, torn and charred bits of flesh.

Alin had walked among them, surrounded by a half a dozen Avernus Travelers on huge white eagles, each prepared to fly him away at the first sign that one of these apparently lifeless bodies wasn't. He had seen Narakan flame-walkers torn up in grisly piles next to nameless beasts of razor-sharp steel from Tartarus and mounds of bleeding stone from Ornheim. The canyon walls had been cracked and pitted, ravaged with black burn scars, and the piles of alien corpses were dotted with something worse: human bodies. Travelers, maybe a dozen all told, lying up on the canyon walls or smashed and crumpled among their summoned beasts.

They were all dead, most decapitated or impaled. On top of that, no one had seen a body matching Simon's description, nor any of the gold-armored Elysian bears. The canyon bowl was a layered chaos of grisly parts, so that it would take weeks to sort everything out, but some of the Avernus fliers had very sharp eyes.

Alin had felt a great surge of hope when they failed to find a body, but the Grandmasters spoke more realistically. Even the most careful search could fail to find a body on a battlefield like this, they said, and when Travelers were involved the situation got much more complicated. They could easily have been taken into Ornheim or Tartarus and died there. Or worse, they could have been taken back to Cana alive.

He had refused to listen to them at first, but as the days stretched on with no word, he grew less and less convinced. What if Simon really was dead?

If so, he had died in Alin's place. If Alin was really full of valor and patience and whatever the other Elysian virtues were, he should have been the one to stay and die for the other two. But he hadn't done it. Simon had.

Simon had sacrificed himself for Alin, but Alin hadn't been willing to do the reverse. In truth, he hadn't even thought of it; he was too focused on getting back to Enosh. That was the thought that gnawed at him, waking and sleeping: that Simon had died, while he had not.

Until he pulled open the door to his bedroom and saw that it was filled with bears. Three white bears, each covered in golden armor.

They had shredded his bed, pulled his curtains down, and one of them gnawed on his most comfortable chair.

The closest bear made a sympathetic sort of whining sound when he saw Alin, and they all three padded over toward him.

Alin laughed.

273

Leah strode into the interior of Ragnarus still wearing the simple brown peasant costume that had been her uniform for the past two years. She liked to be better prepared for these meetings, but her father's orders had been explicit: as soon as possible, he had said, which meant as soon as she could be alone.

She stood in front of a stone wall, with heavy wooden torches burning an unnatural crimson at the far right and the far left. Taking up most of the wall was a pair of silver doors, closed now, and carved with the face of a one-eyed bearded man who scowled in disapproval. Only those descended from the first King of Damasca, those of his blood, could open the Gate to get to the Territory, but that wasn't enough of a restriction for this place. It demanded a higher price.

Leah scowled to see the doors closed. He should have left the doors open for her. But then, her father probably thought it would be good for her to pay the forfeit herself. It would strengthen her, he'd say, or some such nonsense thing.

With one motion, Leah pulled a knife from her belt and slashed it across the pad of her thumb. The cut burned, but she had endured worse already today, and likely would tomorrow. She pressed the blood to the center of the door, into the old man's beard.

In truth it didn't matter where on the door she put her thumb, so long as her blood made contact with the silver. But she liked to imagine she was messing up the man's beard. As a child, she had pretended that was why he was scowling.

The doors swung soundlessly open, revealing a long hall lit only by those oppressive crimson torches. This hallway was made almost entirely of marble—walls, columns, and shelving alike—and it stretched over a hundred paces to the back, where another portrait of the one-eyed man glared out from the far wall. The marble was probably white, though in this light it could have been red and no one would ever have been able to tell the difference.

Between the columns on either side of the hall stretched marble shelves, each labeled in gold. And sitting on these shelves were weapons.

Racks and racks of weapons the color of blood, each hungering for use. Crying out for life.

Leah hated this place.

Two men stood in the middle of the hallway, not facing one another. The first was Indirial, her father's oldest confidant and most trusted servant, who leaned with his arms crossed against one of the marble shelves. Indirial was supposedly in his fifties, but he seemed at least ten years younger, and fit for that. He wore a medallion openly on his chest—a gold coin with a nearly black amethyst embedded in the center—and tattooed chains snaked up his arms to above his elbows. He always cut the sleeves off his shirts, to keep those on display.

Today, he wore a black cloak tied loosely around his neck. He kept the hood thrown back, and the cloak fell open enough to keep his bare arms in full view.

That combination, the black cloak and the chained arms, struck something in her memory.

When Indirial saw her, he flashed a grin, though he did not relax his stance. Indirial was always cheerful, and always vigilant.

"Your Highness," Indirial said, bowing very slightly at the waist. Overlord of Cana, and second only to the King himself, Indirial needed bow to no one. That he did so anyway did not lessen his authority.

"Indirial," Leah said, bowing back. She didn't need to bow either, but she liked to match his manners. "You're looking well. How is your daughter?"

"Won't put the sword down," Indirial said with a laugh, "despite everything I tell her. In spite of my best intentions, I think we'll make a swordswoman of her yet."

Leah smiled; it was easy to do, with Indirial. One tended to forget that he would kill anyone his King commanded him to without hesitation. Even, should it come to that, the King's daughter. "My condolences," Leah said, "and congratulations."

Indirial laughed again, but the sound died out quickly, and neither of them picked the conversation back up. Which left Leah no choice but to turn to the second man in the room.

A muscular man of sixty-two, he held a spear in both his hands, holding it up to the light and inspecting it as though all of Ragnarus' weapons were not flawless. He appeared not to notice that anyone else was in the room, though Leah knew that in this case appearance deceived. His hair was entirely gray, his clothes worn casually, though they were expensive enough to buy a herd of horses. A thick scar ran from the top of his left eye socket to the bottom. The injury that had given him that scar had taken his left eye as well, and left something in its place: a smooth, round stone that gleamed bright red even in

275

this ruddy light.

Zakareth the Sixth, King of Damasca and Cana, Lord of the Morning and Evening Star, turned to stare at his daughter. One eye was sharp and blue—the same blue as Leah's own—but the other eye burned with scarlet flame.

She wanted to shiver, but self-control and long training kept the impulse in check.

"Father," Leah said, bowing much more deeply than she had for Indirial.

"Report," Zakareth said, his voice deep as a thunderstorm. He returned his gaze to the spear in his hands.

"I spent two nights in the wilderness with the Elysian boy," Leah responded. "We returned to Enosh this morning with the news of Malachi's death. Some treated him like a hero, while others seemed to think of him as an irresponsible child."

Zakareth ran a hand down the wooden shaft of his spear. "Did you sleep with him?"

Leah hesitated, sensing danger. "No, sire."

"A pity. He would have trusted you, then." He closed his real eye, studying the length of the weapon with his ruby replacement. "And why didn't you kill him?"

She tried very hard not to let the smallest drop of sweat onto her face. Sometimes he took sweating as an admission of guilt. Not always, but often enough. "I was afraid it wouldn't be wise. And your orders said only to keep an eye on him."

Zakareth nodded slowly, not looking at her. He gave no sign of what he thought about her answers. Suddenly he reversed the spear, grinding its point into the marble floor.

"Yesterday was midsummer," Zakareth announced. "Malachi died midsummer's eve. In the chaos, no one thought to water his tree on the ninth day. I Traveled to Bel Calem this morning and performed the sacrifice myself, but it was late. You know what that means."

Leah shuddered and nodded.

"This year, of all years," Zakareth continued. "When the Incarnations shake their cage and all the Territories tremble. The sacrifice is late. And now we are missing an Overlord, while all Enosh gathers for war behind their Rising Sun. Tell me, since you know him, is he as dangerous as they think he is?"

"I don't think so," she responded. "But he is growing. I hesitate to think what he will be like in a year. And in five years, I think he might really become a threat."

Zakareth spoke softly, but his gaze pinned Leah to the floor. "If he's not dangerous, then how did Malachi die? He was childish sometimes, but not weak. And you were there, in the same house when he was killed."

"There was another one," Leah put in quickly. "A second one." She shot a glance at Indirial, gauging his reaction. "A Valinhall Traveler. He summoned a sword that looked like most of ten feet long, and had chains of shadow on his arms. Just like yours."

Indirial leaned forward, a smile creeping onto his face. "Really? Did he find one of the lost swords, or did someone hang up their steel at last?"

Leah shook her head. "I can't be sure. But I've seen myself that he is both strong and extremely quick. Malachi had to face him before the Elysian arrived."

"And he's still alive?" Indirial mused. "Exciting. New blood after all this time. I look forward to meeting him. Maybe I can talk him out of siding with those maniacs in Enosh."

Leah shot a glance at her father. "I don't think Simon cares about Enosh," she said. She hoped Zakareth didn't read too much into that. If he started thinking Leah could be used as leverage against both the Elysian Traveler *and* a new Valinhall Traveler, well, she would never get her life back.

"Simon?" Indirial said. "Is that his name?"

"Yeah. Simon, son of Kalman."

Indirial swallowed his smile. A strange expression passed over his face: shock, pity, maybe regret. "He lived in Myria, didn't he? Before he became a Traveler."

Leah stared at Indirial before answering. How in the world would Indirial know *Simon*, of all people? Sure, maybe if they had met in their Territory, but Indirial had seemed surprised to hear that there was another Valinhall Traveler around. Which meant that he must have met Simon somewhere else. And how had *that* happened?

"Yes," she said finally. "His mother was killed by Cormac during the collection of the sacrifice. How do you know him?"

Indirial's eyes hardened. "I was there when his father died. He was killed at the edge of the Latari Forest by a pair of Travelers. Travelers from Enosh. They killed him and tortured his wife into insanity, just for being in the wrong place at the wrong time. Simon has more reason to hate Enosh than anyone."

Leah's mind reeled. Everyone knew Simon's father had been killed, but by

Travelers? Travelers from Enosh, no less? Did Simon even know the truth?

Her father raised the blood-red spear, pointing it at Leah to get her attention. "Is this young dragon in Enosh as well?" Zakareth asked.

"No. He stayed behind after Bel Calem. To..." she hesitated, but she couldn't stop now. "To give us time to escape." Leah glanced at Indirial, to see how he took the news that Simon was missing and probably dead. He stared off into space, saying nothing, clearly lost in thought. Maybe he hadn't heard her.

Zakareth stared at her again, and she wondered—not for the first time—if his red eye let him see into her mind.

"Here is your task," her father said at last. "Stay in Enosh. Keep track of the Elysian Traveler. Report to me everything he does, everyone of significance in his life. At the same time, watch the city. Judge their strength. As of this moment, whether they realize it or not, we are at war."

Zakareth lifted his eyes, staring above Leah, beyond her.

"They have gone too far. This time we will bring everything against the walls of Enosh. We will gather the Overlords, throw wide the Vaults of Ragnarus. We must use every weapon in our possession to grind that city to dust.

"For if we fail," the King said, "the world will burn."

THE END OF BOOK ONE

THE CRIMSON VAULT

BOOK TWO OF THE TRAVELER'S GATE TRILOGY

coming in **August 2013**

Also, check out **WillWight.com** for book updates, news, original fiction, and dark secrets long forgotten by mankind.*

*Not actually true

WILL WIGHT is the author of the Traveler's Gate trilogy, and he has dominion over all sea creatures. He has lived for 23 years, and plans on living for at least two hundred more. Under the light of a full moon, he is revealed as a sentient penguin.

Will graduated from the University of Central Florida with his Master's of Fine Arts in Creative Writing. He still lives in Orlando, and he can smell fear.

Visit his website at **www.WillWight.com** for dark secrets the world was not meant to know.

If you'd like to contact him, send him an email at *will@willwight.com*, or else just turn around. He's behind you.

(All books guaranteed 100% asbestos-free!)